Lake Mountain

by

Steve Gerlach

Probable Cause Publishing

Published in Australia by Probable Cause Publishing
steve@stevegerlach.com
stevegerlach.com
Copyright © Steve Gerlach 2016
The moral right of this author has been asserted
Art copyright © Vince Natale
Design copyright © Matthew Revert

All Rights Reserved. No part of this book may be reproduced or transmitted in any form or by any electronic or mechanical means, including photocopying, recording, or by any information storage and retrieval system, without the express written permission of the publisher and author, except where permitted by law.

Typeset in Dustismo Roman Copyright © 2002 Dustin Norlander
http://www.cheapskatefonts.com

All characters in the publication are fictitious. Any resemblance to real persons, living or dead, is purely coincidental.

ISBN: 978-0-9578641-2-2

To Blanket Girl.

The girl who came along for the ride and took me places I've never been.

Steve Gerlach novels coming soon to Probable Cause Publishing

Hunting Zoe and other Tales

The Nocturne

Rage

Autopsy I: Flesh of the Dead

Autopsy II: Darkness Burning

Autopsy III: All That Remains

Tuesday, July 9.

One

"I've killed Duke Morgan."

I'll never forget where I was or what I was doing when I was first told.

Sure, people say that all the time about tragic events and horrific news items and such. Like when JFK was shot. Or when Diana was killed. But, hell, I wasn't even born when Kennedy flew to Dallas, and I was too young to care when Diana was driven into that concrete pylon in Paris. Although I remember my mother cried a lot when she watched the funeral on TV, I was at an age when things like that just didn't bother me.

But I remember this.

I remember exactly where I was.

I was in the trailer. Raven's trailer. I'd just walked in and it was 5:37pm Tuesday evening, July 9. That's almost six months ago now, but I remember it as if it only just happened. That's how clear it is to me in my mind's eye. I'll never forget it.

Raven had that look in her eyes. That powerful, hypnotic stare she got sometimes when she knew she was in control. All powerful. I'd seen her like this before, but only rarely.

As soon as I walked in I knew something was wrong, something was different.

She usually asked me how my visit went. She always wanted to know what my father had said and if he was alright. But, more importantly, she would ask how I felt and whether I was coping okay. And it wasn't that fake concern you sometimes get from some friends, when they ask only because they know it's their duty to do so. No, Raven always asked because Raven cared. She was a true friend, no matter what.

But she didn't ask this time. I walked up the two steps from outside and let the door swing shut behind me. She was standing over by the sink, just staring at the door, as if she was waiting for me to arrive.

"Sit down," she said.

I didn't ask any questions, I just stood by the table and stared back at her.

That was when she told me.

And really, when I think about it now, I should've turned right around and walked straight out of that place and never returned.

But I couldn't. I didn't. In fact, I don't know if that option ever entered my mind. It was not something I could do. And while I now think I should've packed my stuff and said *adios*, I know deep inside I would never have done that anyway.

She was a true friend to me and I was a true friend to her. Friends don't turn their back on each other. True friends are friends for life. That's how it should work, anyway. That's why I stayed.

And I guess the rest really *is* history.

But this tale isn't about me, in case you're wondering. It's about Raven and what she did. And this is probably the best way I can tell my side of the story, just in case it's ever needed. I've got to get this written down, so people will know my side, and know what really happened. I've been debating with myself as to whether I should leave some hard evidence behind, by writing this journal, but I guess first and foremost I'm writing this for me. So I can remember the events in the order they happened, exactly as they happened, so my mind doesn't play tricks on me in the future.

If others find this and read it, well, I guess they'll have to make up their own minds about Raven and what she did. I'll enter everything exactly as it happened, from what I knew then and what I know now. I won't lie about anything. I mean, what's the point writing it all down if I'm going to make things up and lie about things, you know? Hell, all this writing may be even therapeutic for me. You never know.

I found this notebook down by the campgrounds. Don't know whose it is. Doesn't really matter anyway, I guess. The first few pages had sketch after sketch of trees and mountains and different plants and streams. All small and thumbnail size. Whoever did them has some talent, they were all mighty fine sketches, incredibly detailed and lifelike, but they're no use to me. So I tore out those pages and threw them away. That way, my journal can start on page one, line one. I just hope I don't run out of pages before I finish the complete story. If I do, I'll have to find another notebook somewhere.

But first, I guess, I should tell you about me. After all, I'm the one who'll be leading you through all the events of those couple of weeks.

I'm Amber. Amber Hamilton. Nice to meet you. Come here often? You're kinda sexy, you know. Wanta come back to my place?

Okay, sorry about that. Just trying to lighten the mood. You know, make you feel at home and comfortable and everything. Hmm, maybe I should just stick to the facts...

Stick to the facts, ma'am. Didn't some old cop on some old cop show used to say that? Damned if I can remember who it was now. It was a long time ago and I'm sure it was filmed in black and white.

Anyway, I'm Amber Hamilton.

I know, I know, with a name like that you probably think I'm some sexy young girl about to tell you my wild and amazing adventure. Well, first off, I'm not sexy. I'm pretty plain actually. "No, no, don't think that," you're thinking. Very polite of you, but trust me, I know these things and I'm not fooling myself anyway. Guys really don't show much interest in me, so I know I'm pretty plain. Hey, but don't get the wrong idea or anything, I'm no dog. I just don't have a face that could launch a thousand ships, if you get my meaning. I could probably launch a couple of tugboats, but that's about it.

Really, it's my name that trips me up every time. I think I need a nice, boring name like Alice Jenkins or Sue Johnson or something like that. Then I'd suit my name much better. You get a mental picture of what an Alice Jenkins should look like, and it's vastly different to the picture you get when you hear the name Amber Hamilton. It's the kinda name you'd expect for a famous P.I. in those trashy novels that sell so well.

"Amber Hamilton, P.I."

I knew the gig was up the moment I entered the trailer. She was standing there, see, and she had a look about her. The dame was trouble from the get-go and I knew it the first time I laid eyes on her. She was a dame with death on her mind, and I was just the raw kinda bait she was lookin' for.

Hey, it's pretty easy to write those P.I. novels. Maybe I'll do that when I finish telling my story. Maybe it could be a bestseller and I'd get a stack of money and the cash could help me move on out of here. Maybe. You never know your luck.

I don't really know what more I should tell you about me. I guess it's important to know something about my past, just in case it's ever needed. So you know it's me and not some other unfortunate sap whose name is the same as mine and who got caught up with all this. In the end, you may not believe what's written here anyway, but that's your problem, not mine. I'm not writing this for you, I'm writing it for me. Already I feel a whole lot better about everything. Looks like this writing will help me get all this stuff that's been building up inside me off my chest and out in the open. That's gotta be a good thing. Has to be.

Anyway, I'm 20 years of age now (but I was 19 when all this happened) and I have short-cropped, black hair. You'd know the style if you saw it. It's all the rage with those actresses in Hollywood and I bet they pay an absolute fortune to get it done. Me, I just do it myself. Cheaper that way. I used to have longer hair, but it always took me way too long to get it right, so one day about a year ago I just decided to cut it all back so that when I wake up in the morning all I have to do is run my fingers through my hair and it's ready to go. I did a fine job with it too. Maybe I should've been a hair stylist as well as a P.I.

Sometimes if it gets wet it starts to go curly, but I fix that by borrowing Raven's hair straightening iron. A few minutes under that baby and my hair doesn't stand a chance.

Isn't modern technology wonderful? I don't like curly hair and it sure doesn't look good on me, so I keep mine nice and straight at all times.

I'm five foot eight inches tall and I'm average weight for my height. I'm not fat, don't be thinking that. But I'm not about to appear on the cover of Vogue anytime soon. I don't have a problem with my weight, never have. Well, that's not true, but I haven't really worried about it for years. With a face like mine, the guys aren't interested anyway, so I'm damned if I'm going to starve myself to look all Kate Moss-ish when they're not interested in me anyway. Not worth worrying about. I learned that the hard way a long time ago.

That's me. Amber Hamilton. See? I told you the name was wrong and you agree now, don't you?

Just think plain and boring. I do.

But enough about me. I sound like I'm on some dating video or something. Not that I've ever done anything like that. I'd die of embarrassment if I ever had to do one of those things. But I know how those things work. I've seen movies and stuff.

"Hi, I'm Amber, I'm 19, single and downright plain. I live in a trailer with my best friend and she's just killed Duke Morgan. My hobbies are reading, writing my life story in notebooks, cooking, washing, and accessorising after the fact. I'd like a guy who could see past my plain face and boring looks and find my inner beauty, because pearls really are made out of oysters. If you're interested, please call me at 555-DESPERATE."

Yeah, drek. I wouldn't date me either.

As you know by now, I live with Raven. Before all this started we both lived in her trailer at the Pine Hills Trailer Park, about 25 miles west of Lake Mountain.

It was a nice, peaceful place to live. The trailer park was close to where Raven worked, so it suited her perfectly. It suited me too because no one knew I was living there. No one who mattered at least, so I was more than happy to stay there with her.

That's where it all started. And I remember it like it was yesterday...

Raven's been my best friend since I can't remember when. We grew up together. My mother went to school with her mother and they were always close. Our families lived just two blocks apart and I remember going over to Raven's parent's house on weekends when I was small. While my mother talked and laughed with Raven's mum, I would play with Raven.

Raven was five years older than me, but she was always nice and we got on really well. She would let me play with her toys and she would chase me and push me on the swing. We'd play hide and seek together and we'd talk about stupid kids stuff and we never argued. I always liked her, almost as if she were an older sister I never had. No, scratch that, she *was* my older sister. We just weren't related. If that makes sense.

She didn't seem to get along with normal kids either, just like me, so I guess that kinda brought us together. Of course, she always dressed in black and listened to death metal bands no one had ever heard of, so that kept some other kids away. But I think Raven liked it that way. Some of the kids in the neighbourhood were scared of her. They said she did weird things to herself, and that her parents weren't her *real* parents, because they'd died mysteriously in a fire Raven had started when she was younger. But that was just rubbish, the product of too many late-night horror repeats on cable. You know how kids are. They didn't understand her, so they tried to destroy her.

Didn't work.

I've always wondered, though, if our mums weren't best friends, would we have been? Who knows. You can't change the past either way. I know that now. We *were* friends, and we were happy to spend time with each other. In the end, that's all that mattered.

So, the upshot of it all was that we were always together and she always looked after me. That's why she was my best friend in the whole world.

Now, I don't know if I'm painting the right picture of Raven here. She's totally different from me in almost every way. Make no mistake about that. She's just a touch over six feet tall and she's nice and thin, without looking like those models who starve themselves down to just bone.

In fact, in her profession she needs a little bit of flesh, the guys like it that way. She was 24 when all this started and she has long, flowing richly-dark brown hair that stretches all the way down her back. I don't know what her secrets were for keeping her hair looking so luscious and so beautiful. She never seemed to do much to it, but it was always perfect. I'd love to have hair just like hers, but it was never going to work on me.

Raven had a strand of hair on each side of her head which she dyed purple to help her "stand out from the crowd." I mean, like she needed it! These dyed strands fell all the way down her back. If you looked real quick you might think she had a purple scarf wrapped around her head, but it was no scarf, it was her hair. And, damn it, if it didn't look really good on her.

Would look stupid on me, though.

When all this went down, she was working nights at Rawhide Gentlemen's Club down on Harrington Street. "Gentlemen's Club" is just a fancy name for a strip club, you know, and it doesn't fool anybody. Everyone knows exactly what goes on down there, but it seems it's okay as long as it's referred to as a "Gentlemen's Club." Don't ask me why.

Raven was a performer at Rawhide (that means she was a stripper) and provided exotic dancing (that means lap dances...you getting the hang of this?) for any patron (half-drunk guy) willing to pay for services (throw twenty bucks down her g-string.)

And believe me, guys went for her. They went for her in a big way. And it's not just because she's a stripper. It's because of who she is.

She's Raven.

She's one of a kind.

I've known her for so long, I know there's something about her. It's just so hard to describe on paper. But I'll do my best as we go along. You'll get the idea real quick, I'm sure.

But I'll tell you more about us both when I think of it. I know there'll be more to tell you, stuff I can't think of now.

Stuff I don't *want* to think about now. But I'll get around to it. That's the whole point of writing this story down, so I can capture it all before it slips from my memory. So the true facts will be written down and be testament to what happened and how.

So, that's who we were and where we came from.

And this is how it all started…

Anyway, I remember where I was. I can even still picture it in my mind. That whole scene. Life was so easy, so simple before that night.

Before she told me.

It was one of those ideal summer evenings. Not too hot, as the sun was setting, but the sky was clear and there was a soft breeze blowing in from the north. Even though walks home after visiting my father were always depressing, sad times, there was no arguing that this evening was beautiful, simply perfect. The day had been a hot one, just like the days before it, but tonight's breeze brought a drop in temperature and a muted aroma of rich earth and sun-drenched trees, the kind of smell that makes you glad to be alive. Even my dad couldn't ruin this for me tonight. It was simply too perfect an evening.

"I killed him," she whispered again.

I didn't know what to say, so I just stared.

"Strangled him, right here in the trailer," she continued.

At first I didn't really know what she was talking about. I couldn't put it all together fast. Sometimes my brain doesn't work like it should. It had been a hard couple of hours for me and I was looking forward to coming home and just relaxing before going to bed. I really didn't have my thinking cap on and my brain was a bit sluggish as it got into gear.

But then it clicked into place.

Duke Morgan.

It made sense.

And I had to grab for the table and sit on the couch. No wonder she told me to sit down. News like this just turns your knees to jelly.

She'd killed him.

Really killed him.

Just like she'd threatened.

"And there's more," she added, as she slipped behind the table and onto the couch next to me, moving right next to me.

She was dressed in her red bathrobe. One of our towels was wrapped around her hair and tied tightly on the top of her head. A small snake of purple hair had escaped, curling across her brow and over her left eye. The robe was tied with the little cloth belt, but it hung loose on her. I could see the soft skin of her neck line and the tops of her breasts.

From where I sat, I had a good view of her left breast and nipple, a glint of metal shining back at me. It was the barbell. Both nipples were pierced with those little metal barbell things. Personally, I don't know how she could stand all the pain of getting a needle plunged through two of the most sensitive parts on her body, but she said the guys go ape when they see she's pierced and that it has helped her get more and more tips every night. So, I guess if it helps the money roll in, it was worth it.

I'd never do it though. No one would look at my breasts anyway. They're much smaller and less attractive than Raven's. She has these perfect breasts. Perfect for what she has to do every night anyway. Mine just sort of sit there like they don't fit well on my body, like someone slapped them on as an afterthought. I'm pretty sure one's smaller than the other and a bit lower too, whereas Raven's are perfectly round and level, perfect in every way. While I was down at the five-and-dime picking out my breasts before I was born, Raven was shopping in Nieman Marcus for hers.

Raven pushed the table out of the way to give us more room, and as she did, her robe dropped away slightly and I could see her long, smooth, legs. They're those classic, beautiful legs that you see on billboards and ads and magazine covers all over the place. I'm sure she could've been a model if she'd tried, but she always said the money was better as an exotic dancer.

I never believed that though.

And, now I come to think of it, I don't think Raven did either.

Her leg touched mine and she reached out with her manicured hands, her fingernails all painted in red with the very tips painted in white, and she whispered, "He's still here."

I looked around the trailer, as I let Raven's words sink into my head.

I've killed Duke Morgan.
He's still here.

They swirled around my head as I turned from her and let my eyes sweep from left to right.

The trailer was small and cramped, but somehow we made do. It didn't worry us then and now, when I look back, I'm surprised at how small it really must have been.

Honestly, you could see everything and everywhere in the trailer by just turning your head around. That's how small it was.

But I couldn't see Duke Morgan anywhere. He just wasn't there.

But Raven said he was.

So he must have been.

Under the bed, maybe? It's true I didn't check there. Or maybe she meant he was in her car outside, or under the trailer?

He wasn't on the bed or on the floor; I could see every part of the place, but I couldn't see him.

My eyes jumped back to Raven, and the look on my face must've given me away. She smirked as she knew the question I was thinking.

She *always* knew what I was thinking.

"He's in the wardrobe," she said. Her head tilted, pointing across to it.

My eyes slowly swung to the wardrobe next to the kitchen.

The wardrobe.

Our wardrobe.

The door was shut. The little latch that all the cupboard doors had (a press-clip device to make sure the doors didn't

swing open when the trailer was on the move) was shut firm and holding tight.
He was in *there*.
In the wardrobe.
I turned back to look at Raven.
She was looking at me. She nodded.
And I knew.
I felt my world drop away.
Nothing would be the same again.

<u>Two</u>

I think I must've sat there for quite a while, just staring at Raven and not saying anything.

She sat back on the couch and drew her robe closed across her chest and tightened the belt.

I wanted to say something, but I didn't know *what* to say.

"I think I need a drink." Raven finally broke the silence. "You want one?"

It wasn't like Raven to drink. She saw what alcohol did to people. She saw it every night at Rawhide, and she knew about it from what I told her too. But I guess once you've killed a man, a drink isn't out of the question.

I didn't answer as she stood and turned and grabbed a bottle from the cupboard above us.

Jack Daniels.

Just like my dad drinks.

She poured us both a glass and was back by my side before I was ready to talk. I looked at the glass and the way the alcohol swirled around inside. Swirling like my mind and my life. Endlessly.

She lifted her glass and waited for me. Following her lead, I lifted mine and she reached out with hers. Our glasses clanked loudly in the silence.

"Cheers," she said, as she swallowed the whole drink in one gulp. For someone who had just murdered a man, she was incredibly calm and in control. But that wasn't unusual for Raven. She was always like that. Some might say she was too cool, even cold, but I knew better. I watched her hand on the glass. It wasn't even trembling.

Not like mine.

I sipped the JD, trying to keep my hand steady, trying to show I was cool too. But I think I failed miserably. The liquid was strong and sharp and I guess it was what I needed to jar myself out of the shock I was in, to slam me back to reality.

Maybe that's why dad drinks it.

"How did it happen?" I heard myself ask.

Raven nodded, as if she was pleased that I'd finally caught up with her and asked the question she was waiting for.

"Remember the troubles I had at the club?"

"Last night? Yeah." I nodded.

"I didn't tell you who *caused* the problems, right?"

I nodded again.

"Well, it was Duke."

I took another sip and slowly shifted the pieces around in my mind.

The troubles Raven was talking about happened the night before, on Monday.

Usually, Raven would sneak into the trailer very quietly and get undressed and go to bed. Because she comes home so late, like at four or five in the morning, I'm almost always asleep, and she never likes waking me if I'm asleep.

"Never wake sleeping beauty," she would say. But I'm guessing that was a joke of some kind.

Anyway, the night before, I was woken by the sound of the trailer door slamming. I sat up in bed and fumbled for the switch above my head, turning the light on just in time to see Raven throw her stilettos across the room.

"You okay?" I'd asked, wiping the sleep from my eyes.

"Yeah, fine."

"You don't look it."

"Don't worry about it," Raven replied as she turned and smiled at me. "Sorry to wake you."

"It's okay, I wasn't sleeping too well anyway," I lied.

Although it wasn't much of a lie. I *had* been sleeping badly lately. My father played on my mind more than ever. Even though I swore not to let him get to me, he was getting worse and worse, and that made me worried, and when I worry I can't sleep.

"Rough night at work?"

"You could say that, yeah."

The money at Rawhide might be good, but along with it came problems and danger. Sure, they've got security people and cameras and whatever, but Raven had told me many times about guys who were too drunk and went a little too far. Stories of girls being groped and fingered, attempted rapes and assaults, all before the bouncers could get across the crowded room to stop it all. Luckily, so far, Raven had escaped all that. Guys were probably intimidated by her and wouldn't try to push her too far. She had a look about her that said, "Don't fuck with me." And no one ever had.

Until last night...

She didn't tell me what happened then, and probably I was too tired to really ask, but I wasn't going to let it go now. Raven was always there for me, and now it was my turn to be there for her.

I sipped again.

"Want to tell me all about it?"

Raven smiled sadly, leaned forward and refilled our glasses (even though mine wasn't empty).

"I guess I better, huh?"

"Yes."

She swallowed the JD in two gulps, sat back on the couch and removed the towel from around her head. Her hair fell down around her face, framing her features in a dark tangle of brown and purple. She ran her hand through it, shaking it all into place. She sighed deeply.

"Okay, here goes. Last night Duke was in the club."

I nodded, obviously missing the point.

"I've never seen him there before," Raven continued.

"Oh," I replied.

I don't know why that surprised me. I guess I just assumed every man visited those kind of places and that it wouldn't be a surprise to find Duke hanging out at a strip joint. After all, he wasn't the nicest guy on the planet by a long shot.

Duke lived in the trailer park. Well, more than that, he actually managed it for the owners. He took the job very seriously and always seemed to be cocky, as if running Pine Hills was the most important job there was. He'd come down hard on you if you were late with your monthly payments, if your music was playing too loud, if you put your garbage out too early, or left the trash can out too late.

Basically, "Duke" was a good name for him. He was like John Wayne, except without the plot.

He was an old guy and neither Raven nor I liked him very much. Actually, he probably *wasn't* that old. I mean, to *us* he was, but that's because we're so young. I'm guessing he was probably only in his late thirties or early forties, but we saw *anyone* that age as being old anyway. We had nothing in common with him and didn't like his arrogant attitude towards us. He was taller than Raven and worked out in a little make-shift gym just off to the side of the shower block. I think he thought he was well-built and that every woman should love him, but with his receding hair, crooked teeth and weird behaviour, he just came across as plain strange and a little bit scary. And, of course, he had to strut around in check shirts, tight jeans and cowboy boots.

He just looked like a jerk.

Which is good for him, because he *was* one.

"*Was*" being the important word in that sentence.

Oops, shouldn't joke about things like that.

Anyway, back to Raven's story…

"When I first saw him there, I didn't think much about it. He was with a group of friends and they were sitting up the back of the club and I kept well away from them."

Raven always had this rule that if people she knew entered the club, she wouldn't dance anywhere near them. She would swap tables with one of the other girls and keep right away. I guess that makes sense. Like imagine if your father turned up and you were dancing for him?

That's *gross*.

And that makes me wonder if *my* father ever went to Rawhide.

Don't wanna think about that!

"It was during my second set, though, that I think he recognised me for the first time."

Raven performed two "sets" a night. One around ten o'clock and another around midnight. I guess it involves all that pole dancing and stuff you see on TV, but I never really asked her because I never wanted to know. I just couldn't imagine her up there, thrusting herself on and around a slippery metal pole, let alone sitting in some stranger's lap, grinding her private parts against his for some money.

"I was dancing and I was trying to check if he was still there or whether he and his friends had left. The next thing I know, he's standing right by the edge of the stage and he's holding a hundred dollar note in his teeth."

"A hundred bucks?" I was amazed. I didn't think Duke would have that kind of money, let alone be ready to just give it away. I wouldn't have thought he'd *ever* have that much money to blow on *anything*.

"Yep, a whole hundred. I tried to ignore him and dance away from him, but he followed. He pushed through the others around the edge of the stage and kept trying to get my attention."

"Making a scene..."

"Exactly, hon. And you know the rules about having to accept all customers no matter who they are."

I didn't, but I guess that makes sense. Discrimination and all. You can't even turn down a paralytic brain-dead moron who wants to feel you up because he's got money and it'll be bad for business if you don't take it.

Ah, ain't the world a wonderful place?

"So, before he causes too much more trouble, I go over to him and take his hundred bucks. That calms him down for a few seconds, but he knows my set must almost be finishing and he wants me to make sure he's first in line."

"Well, he's paid a hundred for you. That's like, what, double?"

"More like triple! And if it was anyone else, they would get the royal treatment for sure, but I just didn't want anything to do with Duke. You know what he can be like."

I sure did. Duke made a habit of getting drunk, even while managing the trailer park. Some of the other residents said he'd made trouble in the past, knocking on doors late at night and demanding to be let in. Usually he'd have some story about how he needed to search for drugs or weapons or something, and as manager he had the right to search all property for anything that was "untoward."

As far as I could tell, the only thing "untoward" at Pine Hills was Duke himself.

He'd tried it with us only once. He'd hammered on the door in the middle of the night and Raven had answered. He mumbled something about having to check the gas connections to our oven, but Raven wouldn't let him in. He demanded access to the inside of our trailer and Raven told him to go get a warrant, which was pretty damn funny at the time.

Of course, Duke didn't think so, and he tried to force his way in.

Being drunk, though, meant that he didn't put up much of a fight, and Raven turned him around on the steps and he stumbled off them, falling flat on his face. He yelled at us pretty good from where he was, face-down in the mud, but Raven told him to fuck off and slammed the door on him.

We didn't hear from him or see him for a *long* time after that.

She was pretty sure he just wanted to go through our clothes and underwear. One of the other girls on the lot had let him in a few weeks earlier because he said he was checking for termites, but it seems all he found was her underwear drawer.

Guys like that make my skin crawl.

And as Raven got back into bed that night, she whispered to me, "If he *ever* tries anything like that again, on either of us, I'll kill him."

Of course, I thought it was an empty threat at the time. But maybe it really wasn't.

"So, after I finished my set," Raven continued, "the only way I could really see to keep both Duke and Andy happy – "

Andy is Raven's boss at the Rawhide, by the way.

"– was to swallow my pride and give Duke exactly what he paid for." Raven kept looking over at the wardrobe as she talked, like she was visualising him in there, almost talking to him as if to say, "See all the trouble you've caused?"

Meanwhile, I was trying to blot the wardrobe out from my line of sight completely. I sat turned, looking at Raven, so the wardrobe was just out of my sight and to my right.

"So you did it?" I asked.

"Yep." She nodded. "All one hundred bucks worth."

I didn't ask what that entailed, because I really didn't want to know. I'm a big girl and I can work it out. I'm guessing it's a pretty thorough lap dance to get the guy real horny. I know the rules are that the guys can't touch the girls and the girls can't go too far, but I'm sure a hundred big ones buys you extra time and extra opportunities to get all...ah... over-stimulated.

"He just went crazy," Raven continued. "I mean, I did it right, I didn't skimp on anything. I tried to imagine it wasn't Duke and that it was just some other drunk bastard male, but it didn't work. He was looking at me. He had something about his look, like it wasn't the lap dance he really wanted, it was the knowledge of who I was and what I did for a living. It was like he had even more power over me because he'd *paid* to have me do this. Like the prick was saying 'I know who you are, what you do. You're mine.'"

I could see Raven was getting angry. I could certainly understand why.

We tried very hard to keep the fact that she was a stripper from almost everyone. Especially those people at Pine Hill. It's none of their business anyway, and Raven felt better about people not knowing. I don't think she was embarrassed by the job or anything. Hell, it gave her enough money to buy whatever she needed, and also to look after me, but I guess she thought if everyone knew then people like Duke would take advantage of that knowledge and use it against her.

Which is exactly what happened.

But the small community at Pine Hills meant that most of the residents knew each other's business, even without trying. Now I think about it, Raven's job was probably pretty obvious to everyone who lived there.

Even Duke.

Of course, I always told Raven that she shouldn't wear the kind of clothes she wore when travelling to and from the club. Most girls who work there arrive in track suits or jeans, but Raven – ever practical – always got dressed in what she would wear on stage and travelled to work wearing it already.

"Sweets, I'm *not* about to wear a track suit for anything," she'd said at the time. "Why change clothes twice when you only need to once?"

But I guess the outfits gave her away. Maybe Duke even followed her one night and discovered her secret identity.

Maybe, maybe, maybe. In the end, it doesn't matter.

"So what happened?" I asked.

Raven sighed again and poured more Jack. "Drink up," she said.

I shook my head. "No thanks, I've had enough." I knew my limits. I didn't want to get drunk.

She smiled at me and tilted her head slightly. A curly long wisp of purple floated across her face.

"Maybe it's better you don't know," she said. "I don't want to draw you into this."

"Don't be like that."

"It's my problem and I have to sort it out, I can't have you getting into trouble as well."

I reached across the table and grabbed her hand. I squeezed it tight. It was cold. I've never felt Raven so cold. Ever.

"We're the best of friends," I said to her. "You've always been here for me, through all my shit and problems and stuff, don't for one minute think I'm not going to help you out of yours."

"You can't," she whispered, her voice sounding so small and weak. It scared me to hear her like this. My Raven, my strong, powerful, self-assured soul mate, sounded weak and defeated and so...well, so *girly*.

"Yes, I *can*. And I *will*."

She smiled at me then, and the light came back into her eyes. The fire was there.

My Raven was back.

***

So, dear reader, what do you think?

Think about it for a moment or two and you realise it's not so clear cut. Not so easy to make the decision.

What would you have done in the same situation? Should I have packed my bags that minute and *vamoosed* out of there? Or did I do the right thing, staying behind to take care of a friend in trouble? What would you do for your best friend in the world? A friend who looked after you when no one else cared. A friend who took you in and cared for you.

What would *you* do?

On nights when Raven wasn't working (she only worked four nights a week because that's all the money she needed to survive), before we went to sleep, we'd be lying there in the trailer, with the lights off and the darkness all around us, and we'd be silent for a long time and then one of us would ask the other, "Are my eyes open or shut?"

I don't know how it started or even why it started, but it was a fun game, and it was *our* game, a game we shared with each other that no one knew about. And there was something special about it being a game played at night, in the dark, when we're in bed, just before going to sleep, just Raven and me. It would be the last thing either of us would say to the other every night when we were alone together.

One of us would ask the question, and the other would guess whether their eyes were open or shut. We'd play it back and forth until someone guessed the wrong answer.

But it was so much fun, sometimes I'd tell Raven she guessed right, that my eyes really *were* open, even though they weren't. That way the game would continue for longer. And I kinda guessed she was doing the same thing.

So, now you know the situation I found myself in when I walked into the trailer on that warm summer's night six months ago. You know what's happened, and you know I'm going to help Raven out.

What do you think?

Were my eyes open or shut?

Open or shut?

I'll let you be the judge.

Three

We stared across the table for quite a while until Raven noticed the time.

"I better get ready for work," she said.

"Are you *serious?*"

She looked at me strangely, "Why?"

"You've just *killed* a man," I said to her, pointing towards the wardrobe. "You can't go to work now."

Raven slipped her hand from mine and stood. "My dear, that's *exactly* what I have to do. I have to go to work and make it look as if everything is normal."

"But everything *isn't* normal."

"I know that, and you know that, but no one else does. We have to go about everything like we usually do, so nothing looks suspicious."

She stood up and walked across to the storage area and started rummaging through the clothes. They usually hung in the wardrobe, but I guessed she must've thrown them there when she was making room for Duke.

"How can you?" I asked in a quiet voice.

"I have no other choice," she replied without looking around.

I turned to face the wardrobe and realised for the first time that I hadn't actually *seen* Duke's body. I had a weird thought all of a sudden that Raven was having me on, having a joke at my expense.

But Raven wasn't the type to pull practical jokes or stunts like this. It wasn't very funny anyway.

"He really *is* in there," I said, probably to myself, but Raven heard me.

"You want me to show you?" she asked as she turned around and undid her robe.

"No, no!" I replied. "I believe you."

She stood there and dropped the robe to the floor. She was naked in front of me, and I could understand why guys found her so powerful and so attractive. All oiled and sweaty on the stage, she would certainly have the guys begging for more. I know women spend too much time fixating on looking for the perfect body and trying to make their own perfect in every way, but Raven's body *was* the perfect body, there's no doubt about it. Basically, I sat there in awe, looking her over and wishing I had a body like hers.

First, the black PVC bra wrapped around her perfectly shaped breasts, cupping them and pushing them slightly against her chest, making them seem even fuller. Then she slipped the short red PVC mini-skirt (one of her favourites) up her long legs and thin thighs, her vagina disappearing under the material, the small elongated strip of her pubic hair the last to disappear.

And, yes, I'm well aware she was wearing no underwear.

Her thin and shapely stomach was covered by the red PVC buckle underbust corset, which wrapped around her like a second skin. The ripples of her ribs underneath her skin were the last thing I saw as she buckled up the shiny chrome buckles. She was dressed in under a minute, and even though she looked drop-dead gorgeous in her PVC outfit, I wished she was still naked in front of me. But then again, I'd only compare her to me again, and that was a total waste of time.

Like comparing diamonds to pears.

Now you understand why I thought she should always get dressed at the Rawhide and not here in the trailer, right? Clothes like that could give *anyone* the wrong idea.

Jeez, like, maybe *Duke* for example?

I'd never wear stuff like that. Ever.

It's just not my kinda scene.

Jeans and jerseys for me. Nice and plain, muted colours, nothing too outlandish. That's about all I have and all I need. They do me fine. I'm not complaining. I just like to be comfortable.

That hasn't stopped Raven trying to get me *into* those types of clothes in the past, though. She used to say I'd look great in them and I'd be surprised by the difference it could make, but I never believed her and I always refused to try them on.

You can't change me. Not that easily.

Dangerous and Amber Hamilton don't mix.

The most dangerous I get is my black bra. It's my favourite. It's the same style as the one Janet Leigh wears in *Psycho*. Every time I put it on, it makes me feel dirty and evil, on the edge, even though I'm not.

Raven sat on the other couch and started lacing up her knee-high boots.

"Like I said, he just went crazy," she said.

Even though I hadn't said anything, she obviously needed to get the story out, to tell me what happened. Maybe she had decided to let me in after all. I felt good about that.

"I finished the lap dance and went to climb off him, but that was when he grabbed me," she continued. "He held me down and I could feel his cock through his jeans, jutting into my thigh and wanting to work higher. I tried to get away, but then his mates surrounded us and helped hold me down on him. His cock was sliding further and further up my leg. It was then I realised that it *wasn't* jutting through his jeans. Somewhere along the line he'd pulled his zip down and his cock was there, erect and throbbing, pushing closer and closer, trying to get inside me."

Customers touching the girls was just not allowed. It was rule number one and Duke and his mates had broken it. Not to mention the fact he had his *thang* out there, trying to get inside Raven.

"Where was Andy?" I asked.

"Oh, he was coming. So were the bouncers. But it was a packed room and it took them what seemed like ages to reach us and struggle through his friends. They'd surrounded Duke and were acting as a buffer, keeping my boys out. Luckily, they were all so drunk that they didn't put up much of a fight."

"Were you hurt?"

She smiled. "No, sweets. I wasn't. It all just scared me, you know? I *knew* something was going to go wrong the moment

I saw Duke down there by the stage with the money in his mouth. He was going to cause trouble."

"So then what happened?"

"One of the bouncers managed to drag me off him. He wasn't too pleased about that and he tried to swing at Andy, but missed. He was too drunk to control anything, except his cock, of course. It was out there, swinging from side to side as the bouncers pounced on him. They put him in a headlock and carried his sorry arse out of there. They threw him and his friends out."

"Good. So they should!"

"And I thought that would be the end of the matter."

She finished tying her boots and sat staring back at me. The only sound was the soft stretching of the rubber of her corset and mini as she moved.

I wanted to say something, anything, to fill the void of silence, but I knew she would tell me the rest when she had her thoughts in order. If I gave her the space and the time, she would let me know.

I sat and smiled back at her. Her eyes shifted from me to the wardrobe and back again. She was thinking things through, working out the best way to tell me. Best friends know how to tell each other things. They know the right things to say, and the wrong ones.

Jeez, I'm sitting no more than *three feet* from a dead guy and I'm calmly having a conversation with my best friend!

That's how much of an influence Raven had on me. If she was there panicking and pulling her hair out and not knowing what to do, I'd be an emotional mess too.

But she was strong, calm, and all together.

Cool.

As always.

And because of her, so was I.

We sat and looked at each other, with Duke Morgan no more than an arm's length away. I hope he didn't mind that we were talking about him.

He sure didn't complain!

Okay, okay...sorry about that.

"It was about half an hour after you left to visit your dad," she began again.

See? I told you if I gave her some time, she'd tell me.

I nodded slowly.

"As usual, I decided to go and have a shower before getting ready for work. I didn't do anything different to what I've done every other day since I've been here, but obviously Duke had a bit of payback on his mind."

"I can't believe he'd take it that far," I said.

"Well, I guess I thought he'd be smart enough to leave the events of last night at the Rawhide, or at least that he'd been too drunk to remember what the hell happened. But that wasn't the case, sweets. I think he must've been sitting in that office since the moment he carried his sorry arse home, just *itching* for an opportunity to get back at me."

Raven was probably right there. Duke's office was at the front of the trailer park. It looked like a little command post that you see in all those World War II documentaries, the ones with all the guards who would stop people and check their passports. I have half a mind that Duke saw it the same way; he was like an angry little border guard most of the time. The office had large windows all around, so he could see who entered the lot and where they went. He would sit on a little swivel bar stool, so he could rotate 360 degrees at any time, just in case he had to. He had a perfect view of all the trailers, as well as the shower block.

Damn it, he could see *everything!*

And he would've seen me leaving to go visit my dad.

And he would've known Raven was alone.

And he would've seen her walk out of the trailer and over to the showers.

Bastard.

"I had my shower as usual, and didn't notice him there until I stepped out of the shower stall. He was standing right behind me, holding my towel."

"You're not *serious*?" I couldn't believe what I was hearing.

"Yep, I'm deadly serious. I didn't hear him come in, and with all the steam, I didn't see him either. He gave me one hell of a shock, though. He was standing there and he had a smirk on his face and he said 'You look even better than you did last night.' I told him to fuck off, but he just laughed. I had nothing to cover myself with, so I lunged for the towel, but he took a step back and told me he was there to get his money's worth."

"I knew he was sleazy, but this is crazy."

"Exactly."

"Did you scream?"

Raven shook her head. "Nope. What good would that do? It would just make him panic and he'd probably try to lay a knockout punch or something. And it's not like anyone else around here would come to help, now would they? You *know* what they're like."

Yeah, everyone minds their own business at Pine Hills, especially if there's any trouble. That's why we liked it so much in the first place. No one ever asked questions, they mostly just assumed. But if she screamed, they would know.

"So what did you do?"

"I just tried to talk him down. To calm him down. I told him I wasn't at work now and that he was invading my privacy. I told him if he'd like to come back to the Rawhide it'd be my pleasure to dance for him again, as long as he didn't get so drunk and didn't try to touch me."

"But that didn't stop him?"

"Nope, he said in a deep whisper, 'But I *want* to touch you.' What an asshole."

Raven looked across to the wardrobe as she said "Asshole."

"I shouldn't've gone to visit my dad," I said.

Raven shook her head. "You weren't to know. Neither of us knew what was to come. If you hadn't gone today, he probably would've waited for tomorrow. Don't blame yourself, dear. It's not your fault."

"How did you get out of there?"

"Well it wasn't easy. I took a step forward to get at my towel, but he took a step back again, holding it further out of my reach. He told me I had a gorgeous body and that he'd like to slide his cock right deep inside."

"He *said* that?"

"Sure did. He even pushed forward with his hips to give me an idea of what he meant. Like I didn't already know. I could see it pushing out of the front of his jeans, but luckily he'd kept it caged today. I told him to watch out, because he was probably going to cum just standing there looking at me, and that's when he got angry. He flew at me and pushed me backwards, slamming me back against the shower wall. My back and head rammed against the tiles and it stunned me for a moment or two. His arm pinned under my neck and his whole disgusting body pushed against mine. I could feel his cock poking at my hip as well, like it was trying to find a way to burrow inside. He told me he was going to do me right there and that if I made so much as a whimper he'd knock me cold and make sure I'd wake up with not just a sore pussy, but a sore arse as well."

"You don't mean...?"

"Yep, his *exact* words were, 'I'll cum in your arse too. And every time you take a shit, you'll remember I fucked you there.'"

I'd like to say I was disgusted by what Raven was telling me, but I was more than disgusted, I was *way past* disgusted. I was just cold and despairing that creatures like Duke existed.

Well, I guess he doesn't anymore!

"How did you get free?" I asked. "Did you yell for help?"

"Nope, I couldn't. His arm was crushing my throat. I couldn't breathe, let alone scream. So I did the next best thing. I kneed him in the balls."

I laughed then. I don't know why, but it just served the bastard right and I had to laugh. He was so horny and so determined, that he forgot all about his crown jewels and left himself wide open. It was funny. So funny. So I laughed.

And then, so did Raven.

We both had a real good chuckle over that.

Sorry, Duke, not laughing *with* you, just *at* you.

"He cried out in pain, let go of me and fell straight to the floor. I stepped over him and jumped out of his reach and grabbed my things," she continued once the laughing subsided. "I'm sure he wanted to call me every name under the sun, but he couldn't stand and all he was doing was moaning while he rocked back and forth on the floor of the shower, holding his nuts. I couldn't see *any* sign of his cock by now! I went to leave, but then stopped myself. I told him he needed to cool off, and I reached over and turned the cold water on full and let him have it."

"You *serious?*"

"Sure am." Raven was beaming now, her wonderful smile spreading across her face. "I left him there, holding his cock and having a nice cold shower."

"Perfect."

"Yes, my dear. I thought so too."

"So you came back here?"

"Yep." Raven's smile vanished. "And that's when the trouble really began."

Four

"I walked straight back to the trailer and came inside, locking the door behind me," Raven continued. "I really thought that was the end of it. I thought he'd calm down, pick himself up and drag himself back to the office and say nothing more."

"But he couldn't just leave you alone," I said, nodding.

Some men just don't know when they've gone too far. They don't know when to stop. When enough is enough...

"He didn't like to lose the first round, I guess," Raven replied.

She stood up once more and walked the length of the trailer, down to the bed. Her boots sounded loud on the linoleum, and the trailer rocked gently with each footstep. She walked directly past the wardrobe, but didn't so much as even glance at it. Reaching up into one of the cupboards above the bed, she grabbed her make-up kit and hair brushes, along with her red handbag.

"I didn't even think it through. I thought it was over so I walked to the bed and began to get ready for work, just like I'm doing now, trying to push what he did from my mind. I don't know what it was that made me turn around, but all of a sudden I knew he was there with me. I think the trailer rocked slightly, just enough to make me want to check. So I turned and faced the doorway, and he was inside the trailer with me."

"*What?* Inside?" I couldn't believe it. "But you said you locked the door!"

Raven nodded. "I did. He was standing there, his hand stretched out towards me, a key dangling on a small piece of string between his fingers. He'd let himself in."

"How?"

"That's what I asked. I demanded to know where he got the key, and why he'd come inside. But he answered with,

'I'm the manager, I can go anywhere, anytime I like. You can't stop me. I can access any areas I want, beautiful.' Somehow he'd got a spare key cut and used it to get inside."

I felt dirty then. Soiled and yucky in my own home, knowing he could have been here anytime we weren't, going through our things, poking and looking and sniffing...

"And then what?" I asked.

"I asked him for the key, told him it was an invasion of privacy to be in here, that he was breaking the law, but he wouldn't hand it over. He pulled open the front of his jeans and slipped the key down inside and said, 'Come and get it, darlin'.'"

"Asshole."

"My feelings exactly."

"Then what?"

"Then nothing. We both just stood there facing off."

"Is that *all* you did?"

"What else could I do?" Raven shrugged her shoulders. "He was between me and the kitchen, any knives or pans or whatever I could use for protection were well out of my reach. There was nothing I could do."

Well, call the police, I hear you think? Well, yes, that *would* be an option. And those of you who live nice and comfy in your normal homes with normal lives probably could do just that. Pick up the nearest handset and dial 911 and the cops would be on their way. Simple. Easy.

Or you could run to the closet under the stairs and pull out your revolver and tell the bastard to take a flying fuck because if he doesn't you'll fill his sorry arse full of lead. Yep, that'd work too.

But those options weren't open to us. We had no weapons, and we certainly didn't have any phones. The only payphone on the entire Pine Hills lot was inside the office (so Duke could hear every word) and the last time I tried to use it to call my father, it swallowed my coins, but wouldn't connect the call.

Duke had his own phone, of course, but it had one of those locks on it with a sign saying "FOR MANAGERIAL USE ONLY."

I'm not even sure if "managerial" is a proper word. But I'm sure Duke didn't write it. He wouldn't know how to spell it.

Anyway, the only *other* payphone is about a mile and a half away, down near the local McDonalds.

So, as you can see, that was out of the question too. A tad hard to run for that phone when the guy you want to escape from has you cornered in your own trailer. All of a sudden, the idea of having a mobile phone wasn't sounding so stupid.

"So what happened next?"

"He was angry, I could see that. So very angry at me, and I knew it was going to be hard to try and turn the situation to my advantage. I told him we could discuss the whole thing like rational adults, if he calmed down and got his temper under control."

"And he did?"

Raven stifled a laugh as she reached into the cupboard and pulled down her bottle of perfume. She uses *Black Widow*. You know the one? It's in a cute little black bottle, with only two small triangles printed on it. I bought it for her birthday about two years ago. It was only meant to be a sort of joke gift, but she loved it, the name, the bottle, the smell, and she's been using it ever since. It's got a nice, dark fragrance, a bit like roses and a bit like a winter's storm. It's really hard to describe, but it suits Raven nonetheless.

"No way, honey," she said as she sprayed the Black Widow onto her neck and wrists. "He was swearing under his breath and dripping water and he wasn't making a lot of sense, but that wasn't going to stop him. I guess he knew to keep his anger in check, nice and quiet, so none of the other tenants could hear us. I stepped forward, closer to him, my hand reaching out, and I asked him for the key once more. 'Fuck you, you whore,' was his reply. Then he pushed me aside and started pacing up and down the trailer, pointing his finger at me, spit flying from his mouth as he said stuff like, 'You women are all the same, leading guys on and then not putting out. You frigid lesbian bitches who think you can dance and strut around on stage for us and then go home without giving us what we deserve. I'll make sure you get *exactly* what you deserve! I'll fuck your brains out and show you that you can't fuck with me and my friends.'"

Ah, Duke. The Pine Hills answer to Shakespeare.

"He sounds crazy."

"Not crazy, hon, just still drunk. I think he probably continued his little binge when he got back to the office. I don't think he stopped drinking until he decided he'd come after me."

Drunks. The world's full of them. And I know too many.

Raven sat on the edge of the bed and twisted a few strands of purple hair around her fingers. Her eyes shifted to the wardrobe as she continued telling me what happened.

"I told him to back off, to calm down, that he wasn't going to get anything from me here, but he wouldn't take no for an answer. 'I'm going to screw you right here, right now, on this bed,' he said as he kicked at it hard. 'I'm going to make you bleed and make you scream, and if you so much as complain or cry out, I'll make sure each of my mates gets a turn at filling you so full you'll choke.'"

I felt sick. I couldn't believe Duke would go that far. Or I didn't want to believe. Raven had been in grave danger, and I hadn't been here to help protect her. Not that there would've been much I could do anyway. But it still made me fearful for what might have been.

I could've come home to find her dead in the trailer, or raped and bleeding on the bed. Anything could've happened.

"He slammed his fist into the wall, he threatened me some more, and then he punched the wardrobe door. The force of the punch triggered the latch and the wardrobe door swung wide open."

Oh oh!

"And that was when he saw all my outfits."

Raven had a...well...*interesting* assortment of costumes and outfits for work, and she stored them all in the wardrobe. The amount of PVC and black leather in that wardrobe alone would make even the most open-minded person look twice and blush, so I guess it wasn't surprising that Duke reacted the way he did.

"When Duke saw what was in there, when he saw the whips and the ropes and the handcuffs and the dildos, I think he must've thought he hit the jackpot. 'So, *this* is what you lesbians get up to in here!' he smiled. 'You *kinky* fucking whores.'"

"Why does he call us lesbians all the time?" I asked.

"My dear, we *live* together. That's all a man needs to start thinking that two girls are on together. That's *all* a man needs to *hope* two girls are on together. And then, if you just happen to look into one of their wardrobes and see this kind of stuff, they're going to assume we *are* on together."

Men. What can I say? You should all be ashamed of yourselves.

"'No wonder you'd never let me search this place,' he said. 'What *other* secrets are you two bitches hiding?' He started rifling through the wardrobe, pulling out my outfits and rubbing his hands all over them, licking the PVC and rubbing his crotch into the corsets and bras. 'You'd look fucking hot in this one and this one,' he was saying. 'Take off your bathrobe, I want to see you in this one. I want to fuck you in this one. Fuck you from behind in this one. Cum all over you while you're wearing this one.' I just didn't know what to do."

Raven shook her head and rested her face in her hands. Retelling the story was obviously harder on her than either of us expected.

"Couldn't you stop him?"

"I thought about it, but with what? I didn't want to risk reaching for a knife or bottle or anything. Then I wondered if I let him go through the wardrobe, if he looked at everything and embarrassed me as much as possible, maybe then he'd leave us in peace. But that wasn't going to happen. I *knew* it wasn't, but I hoped maybe it would. Maybe that was all he wanted, to embarrass me. But I was wrong."

"So what happened next?"

"I asked him to be careful with all the stuff, but he didn't listen. He was fingering the gags and the handcuffs and the whips, but he had his eye on the rope. He was saving it til last, I could tell."

Raven performed a host of different "acts" at the Rawhide. On one night, she might be playing a cop in her latex cop uniform, complete with handcuffs and fake walkie-talkie. Another night she might be a dungeon mistress, with whip and eight-inch stilettos. And another night, she might be a bound slave girl, covered in mud and with her hands and feet tied.

That was what the rope was for.

And *that* was what Duke wanted.

"'You girls are so *fucking kinky!* I had no idea,' he continued, as he reached deeper into the wardrobe. 'You must get so wet and so horny, dressing up like this in your trailer at night, playing out your little fetish fuckfest roles. So fucking *wet* you'd be dripping as you eat each other out.' He was totally gone by now. His cock was pushing against his pants again and he turned to face me. He held the rope tightly in both hands. I thought about running, just getting the hell out of there, but there was no telling what he might do to the place. He could destroy my livelihood by ruining all the clothes or, worse still, destroy the trailer someway. I wouldn't put it past him to set the place on fire or blow it up, you know."

And neither did I.

"And if I left him here and you came home..." She left that thought unfinished, like she didn't want to think about it.

Neither did I.

"So he came at me with the rope. I tried to calm him down, to talk sense into him, but he held the rope tighter and tighter in both hands, stretching it and testing it to make sure it wouldn't break."

It wouldn't break. I've seen the rope myself. It's coarse white nylon rope, about an inch thick, made up of three separate strands of smaller rope, all woven in together. You know the kind I mean. You see them on ships and boats. They use it to put up the sails or tie the boats to the wharf or something. It's thick and heavy and large, so even the guys in the back seats at the Rawhide could see it easily. At both ends, the rope was tied off, creating two large knots that would hurt like hell if you were beaten with them.

"'I'm going to tie you up,' he said. 'And I'm going to fuck you in the ass, just like you did to me last night when you got me thrown out of Rawhide in front of my friends. You'll pay, bitch.' I told him he wasn't getting anywhere near me, not with the rope or his cock, or anything, but he just laughed. He lunged at me then, when I didn't expect it, and grabbed me by the hair, swung me around and bent me over the table."

My arm was resting on the table, and I quickly moved it off the surface. I have no idea why. It was an instinctual thing, I guess. I looked at the table too, trying to imagine Raven bent over it, Duke behind her, a smile on his face.

Bastard.

"He was strong, Amber. *So strong.* I could feel his cock pushing against my ass. Even through his jeans and my robe, I could feel it there, forcing itself against me. I didn't want to cry out either, because I had no idea whether he would go further. He could knock me out and really hurt me, I mean, try to kill me or something."

Raven stopped, buried her head deeper in her hands, and shook her head.

"I was so scared, hon. More scared than I've ever been in my whole life."

I stood up and quickly walked around the table – *the* table – and sat down next to her on the bed. I put my arm around her and patted her bare shoulder. The plastic PVC mini-skirt and corset creaked as I leaned her against me and held her tight. Her curls brushed against my forehead and chin. Her Black Widow perfume wafted over me. I didn't mind.

"It's over now," I said.

"No, no it isn't," was her muffled reply. "Because of what I've done, it's only the beginning."

I could tell she was trying not to cry. It wouldn't look good if she went to work with red eyes. Andy would know something was wrong and probably wouldn't let her perform looking like that. It'd be a night with no pay, and I knew Raven wouldn't like that. So I tried to keep her mind focused and not to let her get too emotional.

"Come on," I said. "You have to go to work soon."

"I know."

"Can't have you crying and looking all blotchy."

"I know."

"Finish the story. Tell me."

Raven looked up at me, her gorgeous dark brown eyes burrowing deep into my soul.

"Thank you," she whispered.

"For what?"

"For being here. For being you. For being my friend."

I smiled. And didn't have to say anything. Raven was always one for hiding her emotions. For as long as I'd known her, she was like that. Remember, people thought she was cold? Well, I knew she wasn't, but I knew she didn't like showing her inner thoughts or emotions either. It's almost like she turns them off from life, from people on the outside. I guess it's the same way she turns off her real thoughts and emotions when she's out there on the stage, dancing and strip-teasing for humanity's prime seepage.

"Soul mates, remember?"

"Yep, soul mates," she agreed as she patted my knee.

There was silence for a while, but I needed to know what happened, and I thought maybe Raven didn't want to tell me. So I prompted her.

"He didn't hurt you, did he?"

She shook her head. "He didn't get the chance. He had me bent over the table, and he was trying to get both my hands behind my back. I was resisting him, trying to struggle, but he leaned against me, using his body weight to pin me down onto the table, using his legs to hold mine, stopping me from moving. I could feel his breath by my right ear. 'Stop struggling, slag,' he whispered. 'Play nice for daddy and if you're good, I won't arse fuck your friend Amber when she gets home.'"

We sat in silence for a moment, just staring at each other.

Poor Duke. He really couldn't've picked a worse threat.

"And that's when I *really* got mad," Raven replied, her eyes darting back to the wardrobe. "I struggled harder, I pushed back, I wouldn't let him get hold of my hands long enough to tie them with the rope. And I guess that's what did it."

"You overpowered him?"

"Well, no, not really. I mean, I ran back from the shower and didn't have a lot of time before Duke let himself in. I guess I was standing near the table when I first got back from the showers, and the water from the shower must've been dripping off my body as I stood there. I didn't notice it at the time, because it certainly wasn't something that seemed important right then. And Duke was wet too, from that little soaking I gave him in the shower. I was struggling and Duke was trying to keep me pinned down, but his feet must've been in a puddle of water and somewhere along the line, as I fought him and pushed back at him, they slipped out from under him and sent him flying backwards hitting his back and neck on the oven. He crashed down hard and loud, and he let out a massive cry as he did so."

The trailer isn't very wide, and someone falling backwards from the meals table would end up with a nasty welcome coming from the oven and stove in the kitchen.

Just like Duke did.

"And the fall killed him?" I asked. I just couldn't believe it. "But, Raven, that's *self defence!* You didn't kill him. It was an *accident.*"

She shook her head and her eyes came back to mine.

"No," she whispered. "*I* killed him. Not the fall."

"I know you feel that way now, but trust me, it's just the shock or something. You *can't* be held responsible for that. No one in their right mind is going to say you killed him when you tell them what really happened!"

I was talking way too fast and I knew it. She raised one finger to my lips and pressed it gently onto them, silencing me.

"The fall didn't kill him," she whispered. "It merely stunned him."

"Oh." That's the best I could come up with. I looked over to the floor between the oven and the table. I could almost picture Duke there, lying on his back, the bulge in his pants subsiding.

"As I straightened up and turned around, I could see him on the floor. He was rubbing the back of his head and moaning and calling me a fucking bitch. I just got so angry, so mad at him. How *dare* he think he can treat me that way, and threaten to treat us *both* that way. What gives him the right to think like that and to act like that? Who the *fuck* does he think he is?"

I understood completely. And I nodded in agreement.

"The rope was lying on the floor, right next to his left hand. He'd dropped it as he fell, I guess. So I bent down and picked it up. I stepped over him, placing a foot on either side of his hips. Slowly, I squatted down and sat on his stomach. I sat there and I just stared at him. I gave him one last chance, Amber, I truly did."

Her eyes pleaded with me to believe her.

She didn't have to worry. I *did* believe her.

"I sat there with the rope in front of his face, looking down at him. He had a chance, a moment or more to apologise, to realise he'd been wrong and to say sorry. But he didn't take it. Instead, he sneered at me as he said, 'Yeah, bitch, that's it. I knew I'd get your dyke cunt all wet. Do me. I'll treat you like no man's ever treated you before. I'll make you feel like a real woman, you fucking lesbian filth.'"

She shook her head and turned to stare at the wardrobe again.

"The stupid prick just didn't understand."

I could work out what was coming, but I needed to hear it from her. I wanted to make sure I had the story straight. So I asked what sounds like a pretty dumb question. "What happened then?"

"I wrapped the rope around his neck, wrapped it twice, and strangled him."

One simple sentence brought the reality home to both of us. I hugged her more, rubbing her bare shoulder. She felt so cold, so fragile, not like the Raven I knew. Maybe this was the first time ever that *I* had to be strong for *her*, for both of us.

"Strangled him..." she whispered again.

It sounded so foreign, so alien, to hear her say something like that. But I guess, given the situation, she really didn't have much choice other than to do what she did. When you think about it all and know all the facts, you realise she did the right thing.

Duke deserved what he got. It was that simple.

"He didn't even put up any resistance," she continued now, talking fast, as if she wanted to get to the end of the story and never have to repeat it again. "It didn't take long. Maybe he thought it was part of a kinky sex game or something. He smiled his stupid smile all the way and it was only towards the very end when he couldn't breathe and I pulled the rope tighter and his lungs were aching that his smile melted into concern and then into a look of terror.

"He tried to fight back right at the end, but I was on his chest and he was too drunk and his hands only grabbed at me for a few seconds before his eyes rolled back into his head and his mouth flopped open and he stopped breathing.

"I sat there on top of him for a long time, keeping the rope tight and making sure there was no way he could come back to hurt either of us. I guess I lost it there for a few minutes, my mind just went blank and I sat, staring at the rope, at how the cords twisted and combined with each other, how they pushed into the skin of his neck, making it bulge and forcing his adam's apple down at a weird angle. It was only when my wrists and arms started to ache that I let go of the rope, stood up and climbed off him. 'Fuck you, Duke,' I said, and then turned away."

"Jesus," I muttered.

"Nope," she replied. "Just Duke."

She smiled then, a sad, forlorn little smile. And so did I.

"So you put him in the wardrobe?" I asked.

"Yeah. Well, Duke had made a mess of all the clothes anyway. And I had no idea where I was going to put him. I sure didn't want him lying there on the floor. So I dragged him across to the wardrobe, picked him up – not easy either, he's damn heavy – and shoved him inside. Then I cleaned up all the clothes and put them in the storage area. I'd only just finished it all when you came home."

I nodded. I was up to date. I knew all that had happened. I guess now was the opportunity for me to evaluate everything, pack my bags and get the hell out of there. But, I wouldn't do that, not to Raven. We were friends, she needed me, and I was going to stand by her side no matter what. I mean, you know the story now too, you can understand it from my point of view, right? I'm guessing the only people who would have trouble with what we did would be Duke's family (let's hope he doesn't have one) and some prosecuting attorney who's taken on the case for the publicity and the esteem, to try to make his career by bringing to justice the cold-hearted murderer (and her assistant) of Duke Morgan.

Anyway, like I said, that's probably why I'm writing this. So you get *our* version of events before the media and police and lawyers twist it all around against us – if they ever *do*, of course.

Let's just make this whole thing our little secret for now, okay?

Deal?

Good!

"I better get going to work," Raven said as she stood up and grabbed for her handbag.

"Are you sure?" I asked.

"What choice do I have? We have to make it look like everything is normal. If I don't go to work after what happened last night, and then Duke is found missing and the guys at the club remember him and then remember I wasn't at work the next day, they're going to think something happened. And they'd be right. They might have *no idea* exactly what happened, but the suspicion could be there. We have to go on as if it's just another day and that everything is normal. If I go to work and act as if nothing's happened, then last night's little incident with Duke will be forgotten."

"But everything *isn't* normal, Raven. We've got a *dead guy* in the wardrobe!"

She nodded. "I know, I know."

"What are we going to *do* with him?"

"We could have a party," Raven suggested. "Invite all the other tenants on the lot. I'm sure they'd all be thrilled! We could call it Duke's Deathday Party!"

"I don't think so," I replied.

"I know, I'm only joking. I'm still thinking about what we're going to do. I've got to work something out."

"He can't stay there."

"I'm more than aware of that, hon. I just need time to think. And while I'm thinking we have to make sure everything looks normal. I'll try to work something out tonight while I'm doing my sets. I'll figure something out, I promise."

She smiled.

The real Raven was back.

In control. In command.

"You just try to get some sleep and I'll be back at the usual time, okay?"

"Huh? You're not *serious?*"

Puzzled, she looked at me. "What do you mean?"

"I'm not staying here with *him*." I pointed to the cupboard.

"Yes, you are. Where else will you go?" Raven asked.

"I'm coming with you!"

There was no way I was spending a night alone in the trailer with Duke Morgan dead in the cupboard.

"No," Raven shook her head. "You've never come to the club before. If you show up with me now, they're going to remember you and wonder why you're there. If the cops drop by and ask questions about Duke's final few hours before he went missing, and they ask if anything was different or unusual about me, the girl he tried to rape, they're going to remember I brought a friend along to the club for the first time the night after."

"So?"

"*So?*"

"Bringing a friend to Rawhide doesn't make you a murderer."

"It may not make me one, but I *am* one. Amber, honey, please, trust me on this. *Everything* needs to be exactly the same as usual if we're to have *any* hope of getting away with this. You have to stay here. You *have* to act as if Duke isn't in the wardrobe."

I wanted to say so much. I needed to tell her that being within three feet of a corpse at night – hell, at *any* time – was not something I could do. But I was just dumbfounded and couldn't get the words together in time.

She smiled at me one last time, leaned towards me and kissed me lightly on the forehead. Then she turned around and headed for the door.

"I'll be back before you know it. You'll do fine."

Oh yeah, *real fine*.

And then she was gone.

She'd left me alone.

Well, technically *not* alone, I guess.

She'd left me with Duke.

Five

Okay, I've had some time to read over what I've already written and I guess I should take a timeout here to fill in some of the blanks.

There are a few issues I haven't touched on and I want to make sure they're clear for you before we go any further, okay?

This trailer of ours, well, of Raven's, it was a 1973 Viscount Royal, just in case you have the impression that we were living in the lap of luxury in some huge RV or something. Wrong!

It really was just one of those dingy old crappy trailers you see on TV. I don't know where Raven bought it from. In fact, there probably should be laws against selling trailers that small and that old. She told me once that an ex-boyfriend gave it to her, but I didn't believe that. I would've known about it. Raven never seemed to date anyone, so I'd be sure to remember any boyfriend who came along, let alone one who would say, "Hey, I'm breaking up with you but, here, have my trailer. No hard feelings, ok?"

So, it was small and old and dingy. But, really, there were many other trailers on the Pine Hill lot that were just as bad – or worse – than Raven's, so I guess I might be wrong about how bad it was.

I'll let you decide.

First of all, the colour scheme. Straight out of the 70s for sure. The curtains and fabrics were browns, oranges, whites and yellows. The linoleum pattern on the floor was browny-orange fake tiles with brown fake grout.

When you walked in the door, to your left was a browny-orange couch that could fold down to a bed. It was just long enough for an average-sized person, so if you were a bit taller, you'd be sleeping scrunched up all night. So, we used that as a couch most of the time. It wasn't really wide enough for anyone to sleep on really, so we never did.

Above that couch was a fold-away storage area where we kept most of our belongings: cases, handbags, books and cds. When you live in a trailer this small, storage space is at a premium. This was where Raven had moved all our clothes after wardrobing Duke, by the way.

This storage area had two little mustard-coloured curtains that you pull across to hide the mess if anyone dropped by, although they wouldn't hide the mess of clothes there right now. There was a window between the couch and storage area, but considering it looked straight into the back of Raven's car, we usually kept the curtains shut.

Directly across from the door as you walked in was the kitchen. Well, kitchenette. Okay, okay, meals preparation space. That's about all it was, a space with a sink, four hotplates, small stove and small refrigerator. But we called it the kitchen.

Oh, and there was a microwave as well. Doesn't get much more modern than that! The laminex was white and orange and the fake wood on the cupboard doors was grey and orange.

Maybe Raven *did* get the trailer from an ex-boyfriend. No one in their right mind would want a trailer like this... and I'm sure Raven could've bought a better one if she'd wanted to. I mean, the money she was getting from Rawhide *was* good. Good enough to keep us both fed and clothed, after all.

There was a (small) window over the sink, and two (smaller) cupboards for crockery and stuff over the window. Under the sink was a small cutlery drawer, and between the small fridge and small oven in this small food area was a long but not very wide cupboard that stored the broom. It was a special broom that had a handle that could fold in half, making it easy to store in the small, long, thin cupboard.

My, those trailer designers think of everything, don't they?

Anyway, next to the "kitchen" was the wardrobe both Raven and I shared. It was big and roomy and held more than you would expect. It went from the roof down to about your knees, and then there were three drawers underneath for underwear and socks and whatever.

Although, what was in there was mostly Raven's stuff. I mean, she was the one who worked and she was the one with the money to buy all this stuff. She was never short on cash and could always buy whatever she wanted. Especially in clothes. Raven loved splashing money on clothes. That was her *second* most fun thing to do.

So, with the kitchen directly across from the door, the wardrobe was actually to the right of the door, as was the bed. It was a double bed at the other end of the trailer. It was surrounded on three sides by walls, each with a couple of (you guessed it...small) windows in them, and the fourth side, of course, gave you access to the kitchen and the rest of the trailer.

The "bedroom", such as it was, could be separated from the rest of the trailer by pulling a mustard-coloured curtain along a little track that ran across the ceiling. The curtain was virtually see-through, so we never bothered. I mean, we both knew what each other had anyway, so we never felt the need for privacy like that. Raven was used to walking around practically naked anyway and I, well, I just got used to seeing her that way.

There were some more cupboards above the windows on the three walls, and this was where we stored bed linen and bath towels and other miscellaneous items that I can't remember right now. All I know is that we didn't have a lot of storage space and what space we had, was mostly all filled. What didn't fit in the trailer was stored in Raven's car.

The final area of the trailer, directly across from the wardrobe, and immediately to your right when you walked in, was the L-shaped couch and meals table. The couch wasn't that comfortable, but was wider than the other one that could be converted to a bed.

The fabric on the couch was orange and brown and black, with long stripes of yellow running through it.

"Ugly" is a safe term to use.

Above the couch were more small cupboards, but these cupboards had smoky brown plastic sliding doors on them (obviously more funky and at home in your "entertaining area") and this was where we kept our bottles of alcohol, wine and spirits, just in case we ever felt the need to wallow in self-pity.

I did that a lot, although Raven hardly touched the stuff. So I guess it was my alcohol. I shouldn't drink the stuff, I know. Not a person in my position, and I tried not to. I only did it when I was feeling really low. It never made me feel better though. I drank to forget. Now, *that's* really funny. I sound like my old man all of a sudden.

This white laminex table – the only surface in the whole trailer without an orange colour running through it – was where we always ate our meals together and generally where we sat to pass the time and read or talk or whatever. You know, do what it is that girls do. When you weren't in bed or cooking a meal you were at this table. That's about the size of it, really.

So, basically, that's what the trailer looked like. Think brown and orange, and cramped. See? Not too hard to get the picture across on that one.

"Hi, I'm Amber. I live with my best friend in a cramped trailer decorated in early 70s Americano-White-trash modern Belch. Wanna date? Call me on 555-NO TASTE."

Still, I miss the times we spent around that table. I miss the chats and the laughs. Most of the memories are good.

Most of them…

And yes, it was a small trailer and, *yes*, in case you've been thinking there *was* only one bed and *yes* we both slept in it together. It's just how it was… One trailer, two people, not much space. Girls room together all the time, nothing new there.

Capice?

When friends help other friends out, they don't usually think about incidentals like where they're going to sleep or if there's enough room. When Raven offered to let me stay, it was at a time when I was very close to killing myself, to finishing my sorry fucked up life. But she saved me.

Ironic, isn't it? She saved one life, but now she'd taken another. I guess that made her even.

Anyway, let's not go there right now...

I've mentioned my dad a whole lot too, even though I haven't really said too much specifically about him. And, now that I've read over what's here, I'm thinking I need to fill you in just a little bit more.

My dad's an alcoholic.

I know that, the world knows that, but he refuses to admit it.

In a way, I guess I can understand the way he feels. He never used to be an alcoholic. In fact, I can remember times as a kid when I was laughing, my father piggy-backing me around the lounge-room, my mother sitting on the sofa smiling and waving and laughing too. We'd always sing stupid songs together and make up words that didn't exist and fall around laughing all the time.

They're the memories you want to keep, to savour for the rest of your life. They're the ones you wish would blot out the dark, horrible memories that seem like nightmares but are worse, because they're real.

Dad owned a successful hardware store. It kept us all in food and clothing and allowed us to have vacations and buy the things we wanted. It was a family store and dad knew all his customers by their first names and where they lived and who their kids were and what their wives did. Everything. My father had a terrific memory for things like that back then.

The store was a success, of course, until one of those huge conglomerates opened an airport-sized hardware store just two blocks away. They turned hardware into supermarket shopping and while dad tried to retain his customers, he just didn't have the range or the price reductions like the juggernaut down the road. Slowly, the business died.

And that was when dad started drinking.

I don't know why he did it. He'd always liked a beer or two, but suddenly once the money wasn't coming in, he and mum would argue more, and he'd go for a drink down at the nearby bar for hours on end. He'd drink and drink. And when he came home, he'd be loud, and sometimes violent.

I guess what happened next isn't really that surprising.

When the writing was on the wall that his hardware store was going to fail, he had a big sale and sold as much as he could. Then he put the store itself up for sale and after quite a while, a buyer came along and suddenly we were flush with cash again. Happiness returned for a while. Maybe things would work out okay, after all.

But, hey, "happily ever after" is just a fairy tale, right?

One of the last days I can remember my father being happy was the day he took the phone call from the manager at the huge hardware store down the road.

I'd just got out of bed and was having breakfast in the kitchen when the phone rang. Dad was already out and in the garden, pottering around as he always did, trimming his bushes and hedges. I picked up the phone and a man on the other end asked to speak with Keith. (That's my father's name, by the way. My mother's name was Rose, just in case you're wondering.)

Anyway, I called dad in from outside and handed him the phone.

"Hello....yes, this is Keith Hamilton....Oh....hello......Well, a bit of a surprise, yes.... Really?..... Are you serious?... Well, of course....no, no, I'd love to.... Wednesday at 2pm is fine.... okay, yes, I'll see you then. Bye."

So, you see, the manager from the big hardware store was looking for new staff, and a whole lot of customers had talked about dad and his knowledge of hardware and stuff. They'd highly recommended him and so the manager called to set up an interview with dad to see if he'd like a job.

I remember dad smiling, dancing around the kitchen, calling out to mom.

"Rosie! Rosie! Get down here, I've got some great news!"

Sure, it was only an interview, but dad was confident he would get the job. Wednesday came and dad left for the interview in a nice blue suit and apparently they offered him the job on the spot. He accepted and was to start the next Monday.

Things were working out just fine.

Just fine...

To celebrate, dad told mum he was going to take her out on the town. She quickly agreed and he booked a classy, upscale restaurant for that night.

It was right in the middle of school exams for me, and seeing mum and dad so happy together, I told them to go out and have a good time.

"Aaaah, a romantic evening, Rosie!" dad had said, hugging mum around the waist, lifting her and swinging her around in a circle in the air. "Just you and me!"

I didn't even think twice when they weren't home by 2am. That's when I turned out the lights and went to bed. I mean, I just assumed they were out having a good time.

The police didn't arrive until 5am.

It took them a while to find any form of identification, they told me.

Plus, they had to cut mum and dad from the vehicle, so that held things up as well.

Mum was in a coma for three weeks; severe head injuries the doctors said. Eventually the doctors concluded there was nothing much else they could do for her. The machines were keeping her alive and the moment they turned them off, she would die.

Dad was in no fit state to make the decisions he was then forced to make. He was still in hospital himself, recovering from two broken hips, fractured ribs and a shattered collarbone.

He was lucky to survive too, according to the doctors. The airbag in the driver's seat was the most important contributing factor.

If only there'd been one on the passenger's side...

He blamed himself for the crash. Veering off the side of the road at that speed and down an embankment and into a tree head on.

And the police blamed him too.

Judging by the blood sample they took, he was three times over the legal limit.

He'd killed mom. And he knew it.

Nothing I could say would change his mind. Nothing would bring her back.

He blamed himself.

I blamed him too...

I couldn't help it. He'd taken my mother away from me because he was drunk and he got behind the wheel of a vehicle and he knew he shouldn't've but he did so nonetheless.

She wasn't coming back.

It *was* his fault.

He was really depressed about it all (as you'd expect, of course) and he couldn't even get out of hospital to go to the funeral. The doctors seemed to think he would improve once he got home and was "among familiar things."

I thought he would improve too. But he didn't.

Being home with those familiar things just made him worse. Wherever he looked, memories of mum remained. Photos, her jewellery, her clothes, the books she read, the music she listened to. Even right down to the brand of cereal she loved.

Everywhere he turned and everything he looked at just served as a reminder of his wife. The wife he'd killed.

Sure, when I was around, dad put on a brave face, telling me everything would be okay and that the hurt would heal. But I always got the feeling he was saying that more for his benefit than for mine. Like he was repeating it over and over again, like a religious mantra, to convince himself that soon, one day maybe, the hurt would suddenly disappear.

But you could see it in his eyes. The pain would never leave.

He would wait until I went to bed before he'd start drinking. But he couldn't hide it very well. After a few beers or bottles of bourbon, he'd be stumbling around in the kitchen, clanking glasses together too loudly or trying to do the dishes that just continued to stack up higher and higher.

One morning I woke up to find the glass window next to the front door smashed. I still have no idea what happened that night, and dad never explained it either. There was a large hole in the middle of the glass, with splinters of cracked and shattered glass radiating out from it, like some mad spider's web.

I kinda figured he'd gone out drinking and when he came home he realised he'd left his keys inside and so he smashed the window to get his arm inside to unlock the door.

I could be right, but we'll never know for sure.

Sometimes, late at night, I could hear him crying too…

I guess I didn't help much. I blamed him for killing mum (well, he *did*!) and I probably wasn't as supportive as I should've been. I felt that it was his fault she was gone (and it *was*!), so it was his job to do the things she used to do. I expected him to do the housework and the food shopping and the cooking and to clean the dishes, and when he didn't do any of that, I got angry.

But I'm not the kind of person who would explode and have a huge fight with my dad. I'd just keep it all inside, let all that darkness and hate mount higher and higher, resenting my father for what he had done, cursing him for what he wouldn't do, hating him for what he had become.

Wishing my mother would come back to save me.

I didn't think anyone noticed. I thought I was covering my feelings pretty well.

But Raven noticed. She knew.

"There's an aura of sorrow around you, hon," she said to me one day when I went over to visit her. By then, she was already living at Pine Hills in the trailer. She'd left home a long time before that, "escaped" she called it, and had bummed around from one cheap boarding house to the next, until she had somehow wound up at Pine Hills, in the trailer. I tried to get out there to see her once every week or so, just to catch up and spend some time with her.

It also served as an escape for me. Somewhere I could hide from my father, his problems and the world.

She'd been there for me the whole time, through all the shit that went down. She stood beside me at the funeral, holding my hand, giving me the emotional support I needed – and that my father couldn't provide – as my mother's coffin was lowered into the grave on that rainy winter's day. I knew I could talk to her about my thoughts and feelings, my hurt, and she wouldn't judge me or think I was crazy.

In fact, most of the things she said about death made a hell of a lot of sense, and she helped me through those dark days when I truly did think about taking a blade and ending it all.

We'd been having coffee as we sat outside the trailer and, I guess, I wasn't being much of a conversationalist. So Raven had switched the conversation to me.

"All that inner hurt and turmoil will eat away at you," she'd said.

She sat in one of those brightly-coloured deck chairs you usually see on expensive cruise liners, and I sat opposite her on an upturned milk crate. She had dark sunglasses on, even though the day was overcast, and she was wearing a black vinyl fitted bodice top with lace trim across the top. The top started just above her breasts and ended just below her ribs, giving you a good view of her midriff and her belly button. To finish off the outfit, she wore a satin panelled purple skirt that came down to just above her knees. She had webbed stockings on her legs and black ankle-high boots. She called the outfit her "Lolita" costume, and she wore it about once every month for all those guys at Rawhide who dreamed of having sex with kids. When she wore it and danced for them, she took home nearly double in tips. So it was a *very* successful outfit indeed. (Not as successful as her schoolgirl one, though. But she didn't wear that very often anymore – only when she really needed the money for something.)

Not exactly what you'd expect to find in a trailer park, I know, but she hadn't bothered to get changed after coming home from work the night before.

I was wearing blue jeans, sneakers and a brown jersey, so I'm sure the contrast was extreme.

"That anger will sit in your guts and grow like some cancer until it takes over your whole body," she continued. "Don't let it. You're better than that. Don't let it beat you. Your mother wouldn't want that."

And she was right.

"Feelings are there for a reason. They *hurt* for a reason. You gotta let them out. It's not healthy if you keep them inside. I can see they're killing you already."

I guess Raven really knew what she was talking about. She'd had more experience with family problems than I had. So she really was the right person to talk to.

Remember when Duke was holding Raven over the table, trying to rape her? Remember how he'd said, "Play nice for daddy and if you're good, I won't arse fuck your friend Amber when she gets home"?

Play nice for daddy.

He'd really said the *worst* four words he could possibly have picked to say to Raven.

Because of the problems she'd had with her father, I respected Raven's advice and ideas about my father.

"You should tell your father what you think and how you feel. He needs to know. Then invite him to tell you how *he* feels too. Don't let the gulf between you both get any wider."

She leaned forward and took my hands in hers. She must've been staring deep into my eyes, but with her sunglasses on, all I could see was my own reflection staring back at me.

"Promise me you'll do that. And soon."

I promised her I would, as soon as possible.

On the walk home, I realised everything she'd said made sense. I was excited about the possibility of starting again with my father, of making things up to him, us both trying to make things right.

I guess my timing was just lousy.

Or I pushed it too far too fast.

I *really* wanted to make it work.

But it all went terribly wrong.

When I got home, dad had obviously been on a drinking binge all night. He was asleep in the lounge room, half on the couch and half on the floor. The beer cans were scattered around the floor like aluminium petals on a dying flower.

The signs were all there that this wasn't the best time. But I ignored them and went ahead anyway.

Sometimes I guess I don't use the right words or I don't get the message across like I should. I'm the one who usually keeps all these emotions locked away inside anyway, so I really had no idea what to say or how to say it. And I think that's where it went wrong.

It took a couple of minutes to wake dad up, and by the time he came to, I could see that he still really wasn't with it.

"Rosie? Rosie, is that you?" were the first words he muttered.

It almost broke my heart, hearing him say that.

"No, dad, it's me. It's Amber."

"Oh, Amber," he slurred. "Go get your mother."

"I can't," I replied as I helped him sit straight on the couch. He smelled of beer and sweat and maybe even of vomit, although I couldn't see any.

"You heard me, girl, go get your mother. This place is a mess."

"No, dad," I said in a soft voice.

"Damn it, just DO IT!" he yelled, his stale breath hitting me full in the face.

I took a step away. It was so sad to see him this way.

"I can't, dad, mom's dead."

He sat there in silence and stared at the floor.

"She's not here, and she's not coming back."

He didn't say anything. He didn't even move.

"And it hurts me to see you this way. Right now I need a strong father, someone who can help me heal and talk about how I feel. Someone *I* can help as well. Someone who understands all these feelings and sorrow I have inside me. I need you."

The tears were starting to roll down my cheeks, but I really tried to keep my voice level and to be strong. I needed to be there for him now, in the hope he would be there for me in the future.

"I need my old daddy back," I whispered.

But there was no reply, no movement. He let out a small sigh. That was all.

"*Please,* daddy?" I asked.

Nothing.

My father died the night he drove the car into that tree. His body was still functioning, but his soul had already joined mom. I realised that when he wouldn't reply to my pleas.

The manager of the hardware store had been very nice, way more cooperative than I would've expected. He told dad that he would hold the job at the store open for him, for whenever dad thought he was able to go back to work. But dad was old and the wounds took so long to heal, even now he still has to use a walking stick because of his broken hips. They never really healed properly.

He still had enough money left over from the sale of the store to pay the bills and buy the necessities, but it soon became clear that the only necessities he needed were bottles of alcohol and cans of beer.

So, in the end, instead of pouring out my feelings and soul to my father, I poured them out to Raven. She understood. She knew how I felt. And, for some strange reason, she was scared for me.

That's why she made the offer. That's why she said I could move in with her.

I guess I was pretty upset the day she asked me to move in. Dad had been on a three day binge that culminated with the police picking him up out of the gutter and locking him in a cell to sober up. They brought him home and told me I should be more responsible in knowing where members of my family were at all times.

Like it was *my fault* dad was turning into an alcoholic!

I sat him down and tried to talk with him. I really was beginning to come to the end of my patience on this. My studies had gone right out the window and my grades were suffering, but he just didn't care anymore.

I told him it was time to grow up and act like a real man, a *real* father who looks after his daughter.

"What would mum think if she could see you now?"

Probably not the wisest comment I've ever made.

He took one look at me and I could see the sadness in his eyes turn to anger. He bolted up straight, the kitchen chair flying to the floor behind him. He leaned forward and slapped me right across the face.

"Don't you *ever* say that again, you hear me?" he spat.

My hand came up to touch my stinging cheek, the mental pain worse than the physical pain. I just stared at him, my eyes trying to blink back the tears.

"You say that again and I'll hurt you, you understand? I'll beat you within an inch of your life."

See what I mean about bad memories always being the ones you remember, instead of the good ones? Well, this is a prime example.

I turned and ran from the room. From the house.

I went straight to Raven and cried in her arms for what seemed like hours.

And that's why she said I could move in with her. She was worried that the anger in my father could escalate even further, that he would take that anger out on me. She didn't want that to happen. She didn't want to see me go through something like that.

And, really, I didn't want to either. I wanted to remember the good times, and happy times. But I can still see my father standing before me, as plain as if it were happening again right now.

"You say that again and I'll hurt you. I'll beat you within an inch of your life."

Mum would've been so sad and disappointed... so unbelievably hurt.

So, you can see why there was no planning about "Oh, who will sleep where and where will I put all my things?" because it really wasn't an issue. When I left the house that day, I took all that was important to me. Everything that I could fit into a backpack. My school books, my letters, a few favourite books.

And a picture of my mother.

I didn't care about anything else.

I still went to school and, living with Raven, my grades improved and I graduated high in my class last year.

Maybe this part of the story *does* have a happy ending.

Well, actually, it probably doesn't. I've been meaning to look for a job, but I haven't been very successful so far and, luckily, there's still a bit of money left from the sale of the store that I can use.

Raven doesn't make me pay any rent. She's happy to let me stay rent-free, as long as I do the washing and the cleaning, which I'm more than happy to do. After all, she *has* let me stay with her. So if cleaning and washing needs to be done (and it's only a small trailer anyway) then I'll do it. Seems only fair to me.

She earns enough to pay the bills and buy the food we need (we don't eat much anyway) although I help pay for the gas in the car if she has to drive me somewhere. Not that I ever go anywhere much by myself anyway. Usually it's only back and forth from dad's place once or twice a week, and I use the bus for that. I don't have a licence yet, but I've been meaning to fix that situation so Raven doesn't have to be my chauffeur. Although I'm not too sure if she'd let me drive her car anyway! She loves that car.

Oh yeah, and I should say that my relationship with Dad has improved. I mean, when he's sober we can actually have a good old chat. I think he's sorry for what he did and said to me (if he remembers it) and he is genuinely interested in my well-being. But he never apologises or even says what's really on his mind. I try to visit him usually on a Monday or Tuesday because it seems the further the week progresses, the drunker he becomes.

So, that's where I'd been when all this happened. I'd gone to visit my father, as usual, on Tuesday afternoon.

Upon my return, Raven would always ask how the visit went. I never really wanted to talk about it straight away, so we instituted a sliding scale to give her a quick idea of how I was feeling. "Light" meant that the meeting was pretty good, and that dad wasn't drunk. "Heavy" meant the total opposite.

Which is why, when all this started, I was surprised she didn't ask me how the visit went.

But we *both* know why she didn't, now don't we?

In fact, if she *had* asked, I would've said "Medium" because it wasn't one of the best visits I'd ever had.

I think dad had run out of alcohol and he was being nice, too nice, obviously fake nice, in the hope I'd go and buy him some more. I'd told him before I would *never* buy him alcohol, and he knew it.

And it hurt him. Got him angry.

The first time I'd said that to him, he'd thrown an empty Jim Beam bottle at my head. It missed by only inches and shattered on the door frame.

Raven said the violence could escalate…

So now, instead, we just danced around the topic, both of us knowing what the other wanted, and neither of us willing to discuss it.

Hell, he's a grown man! He can walk to the store and buy the stuff himself, he does every other damn day of the week. I didn't have to do that for him. I *wouldn't* do that for him.

Somewhere along the way, he got me one of those ATM cards that was linked directly to his (was once *mum* and dad's) bank accounts. I could withdraw money whenever I needed it.

That was really nice of him, I thought. I was surprised when he did that.

"It might be his way of saying sorry," Raven had told me. And I think she's right.

But then when he asks me to run errands for him, buying him food and alcohol, I think that maybe I got the ATM card for another reason. To be a surrogate mother, a second mom, a second wife. A replacement.

And that gets me very *very* angry indeed.

I'll never go back to live with him because it's not worth the risk. I know what can happen. Raven's told me what can happen. And I don't want any of that.

And I don't want to be mom.

It's not possible anyway. No one can replace her.

It's his fault she's no longer here. He has to deal with it. I won't make it easy for him. It's not right to.

And that's why I've never told Dad where I live (and he's never asked either). I wouldn't tell him anyway. I don't want him turning up on our doorstep half drunk, banging on the walls and doors, yelling at us, ordering me to buy him more food and more beer. I don't want to be a part of that, and I have no right to get Raven tangled up in that either. It's better this way, I'm sure of it.

Instead, I'll try to remember the good times and the happy memories.

I just wish I could erase the bad ones.

Bad memories always haunt you for longer, and there's nothing you can do about them.

Fights, arguments, accidents, deaths.

Murders.

<u>Six</u>

So, it's Tuesday, July 9, at around 8:30pm.

Raven says her goodbyes to me and leaves the trailer. I stare at the door as it shuts behind her and part of me is thinking, "This has *got* to be some kind of joke! She can't possibly leave me here with Duke."

But I hear the car door open and then slam a few seconds later. I hear the engine start up and the tires on the gravel outside. And the car drives off, taking Raven to work and leaving me alone.

With Duke.

He was never much of a conversationalist, and tonight was no exception.

Sorry, just trying to lighten the mood a bit.

Jeez, even now, as I write this, I'm getting gooseflesh just remembering sitting there on the side of the bed, staring at that wardrobe and thinking about Duke being inside it.

I have no idea how long I sat there, but I can remember feeling very cold and very scared. My eyes never once moved from the latch-handle that kept the wardrobe door closed.

What if he leaps out at me?

He's dead, Amber.

But what if he does?

The door's locked from the outside.

What if the latch breaks?

It won't.

What if he falls out?

He *won't*, Amber.

But what if he DOES?

He WON'T!

The Pine Hills trailer park is on the main highway to Lake Mountain. And even though it's a highway, there's really only major traffic on the weekends; mostly tourists going skiing in winter or sight-seeing in summer.

The Pine Hills lot holds about forty trailers and, depending on the time of year, it can be full or almost empty – only us "permanents" staying all year round (and there's only about seven or eight of us anyway). Raven's trailer is towards the back of the lot, so we can't see the highway from where we are (but we can see Duke's office), and we can usually hear the traffic as it speeds past, especially at night.

Well, this particular night, I couldn't hear anything. That might not be true, but it sure felt as if the world outside the trailer had simply stopped. It was holding its breath, waiting for me (or Duke) to do something.

I stared at the wardrobe.

I concentrated.

My ears listened for any sound. *Any* sound at all.

I leaned forward, trying to hear anything.

I haven't the faintest notion exactly *what* I was listening for. A *pop*, a *wheeze*, a *gurgle*. No idea at all.

But everything was quiet.

Deadly quiet.

And, to be perfectly honest, I had absolutely *no idea* what to do next.

Raven had gone to work, so she wouldn't be back until about 4 or 5am. Usually, I'd make some dinner and sit down and read a good book. This was the time of night I really enjoyed, when I could truly be on my own and do whatever it was that I wanted to do. Which was usually nothing more than reading or relaxing but, still, it was *my* time. We didn't have a TV in the trailer, in fact, not even a radio. Raven liked it that way.

"They never report anything other than bad news," she'd told me when I moved in and asked about it. "It's always fire storms, love triangles or mass shootings. There's enough bad news in everyone's life without the media having to give us more."

At first it felt strange, like I was cut off from the outside world and didn't know what was happening, but in the end I got used to it and very quickly learned to live without either the TV or radio.

In fact, it's nice and peaceful without them!

Occasionally I'd pick up a newspaper or magazine, just to keep in touch a bit, but otherwise I didn't miss any of it at all.

Without the media to tell you what you *should* think or care about, you have time to focus on your life and the people that matter to you.

I like it this way now.

But on this particular night, I didn't know what to do.

I knew there was a wardrobe door between Duke and me, but that didn't stop me feeling as if he was watching me. Watching and waiting, with that stupid smirk on his face. Just waiting for me to let my guard down.

What was it he told Raven?

"Play nice for daddy and if you're good, I won't arse fuck your friend Amber when she gets home."

Ass fuck.

Very romantic.

Well, now he's got his chance.

No, he doesn't. He's dead!

I don't know that for sure, do I?

Raven said he was.

But what if Raven's wrong?

Well, check for yourself!

And don't worry, I thought long and hard about doing *exactly* that!

It was simple enough, really. Walk over to the wardrobe, reach out for the handle, press down on the latch, open the door, inspect Duke, make sure he's dead, close the door and get on with life.

Yeah, *real* simple.

And I almost did it.

I actually stood up from the bed slowly and took the first two steps to the wardrobe. I held my hand out and *almost* reached for the latch.

But I couldn't do it.

I *wouldn't*.

I didn't want to see him. I didn't want to see a dead body.

They asked me if I wanted to view my mother for one last time, just before the funeral. Even though it was a closed casket funeral because of all her injuries, the guy from the funeral home told me the mortician had done an excellent job.

An excellent job, like she was a piece of furniture of something.

I'd said no.

If I wasn't willing to view my mother, I sure as hell wasn't about to view Neanderthal Of The Year, who just happened to be on display in the wardrobe.

Thank you very much, but no.

I dropped my hand back to my side and looked around the trailer. There simply was *nothing* to do.

I could put Raven's clothes away.

No, you can't, Duke's in the wardrobe.

I could fix myself dinner.

Suddenly don't feel so hungry.

I could read.

It was worth a try. So I walked over to the table and sat down on the couch. I grabbed my book – I like thrillers and romance, but not horror – I don't like being scared – and tried to take my mind off things.

I think I probably read the same sentence over and over a dozen times, trying to commit it to memory, but it just wouldn't work. My mind was a jumble of worries about my father, Raven, and Duke. Mostly about Duke.

What the hell are we going to do with him?

He can't stay here.

We'll have to get rid of him somewhere.

But where?

And what if people start asking questions?

Someone's going to know sooner or later he's missing!

What if another tenant goes into the office for something and he's not there?

What if the owners call him to ask him a question and he doesn't answer?

What if one of his mates drops by to help him teach Raven a lesson or two?

Shit.

So many possibilities, and none of them good.

I just hoped that Raven was thinking about the exact same things. We couldn't keep Duke around for too long.

Even scum is missed eventually.

Our chances of him simply ending up on a milk carton, his sneering face looking out to the world under the words "missing person", were slim.

> *"Duke Morgan, last seen trying to rape a stripper at the Rawhide Men's Gallery. Gruff features to match his disposition. Ugly, rude, arrogant and full of himself. Believes he's God's Gift To Women, but really isn't. If seen, please keep away. Contact authorities with whereabouts at 555-I DON'T GIVE A DAMN."*

And that's what I really hoped for. That no one really gave a damn. That they'd just assume he packed up his stuff and left after losing face in a bar-room brawl. Grabbed a bus and headed to another state, or back home, wherever the hell that was.

But to do that, it would have to *look* as if he really *did* leave. And that would mean packing up his stuff and getting rid of it. And I certainly wasn't about to do that.

I made a mental note to discuss all this with Raven.

Jeez, I'm already sounding like a murderer, aren't I? Cleaning up the crime scene, making sure there's no evidence, planting a false trail to fool the police.

Makes it sound like I was cool, calm and in control.

But, in truth, with Raven gone and Duke in the wardrobe, I was starting to feel the pressure and stress. I was starting to panic.

I tried to continue reading, but there was just no way I could get past that first sentence.

If only dad were sober enough to help. He'd know what to do.

But then again, he'd probably tell me to get the hell out of there and report Duke's death to the authorities. But I wasn't about to do that, I wasn't about to turn Raven in. Anyway, I'd probably go down for accessory after the fact or something like that.

Nope. No way was I going to end up as some footnote in legal history.

I'd wait to see what Raven came back with. She'd have a plan. She'd know what to do.

So you know what I did next?

I can't believe it myself, but there really was *no* other option.

I got out of my clothes and climbed into bed. Turned off the light and I went to sleep.

Well, of course, I didn't go *straight* to sleep.

No, Sir.

It wasn't that simple.

I lay there in the darkness, the sheets and blankets pulled up tight around my neck, and I stared at the wardrobe (once my eyes got used to the dark) and I waited and watched and listened for anything. Any sound or any movement. I really did expect to hear the click of the latch and see the door of the wardrobe swing slowly open.

But it didn't happen.

Nothing did.

But I still couldn't get to sleep.

I don't know how long it took me, but at some stage I reached out for the curtain and pulled it across the gulf between the bed and the wardrobe. The sound of it scooting across the little metal track was loud in the darkness.

Shhh, don't wake him.

I actually *thought* that!

Seems hilarious now, but it wasn't at the time!

The curtain was see-through, I know, but for some reason it helped. It put another layer, another barrier between Duke and me. It wouldn't stop him attacking me, but he was dead and I really didn't expect him to do that.

But it's weird how your mind plays tricks on you at night.

And that was a long night.

Just me and Duke.

At some stage I rolled over, my back towards the wardrobe, and I reached out for Raven. But, of course, she wasn't there.

"Are my eyes open or shut, Raven?" I whispered.

There was no answer.

Wednesday, July 10.

Seven

It was the blowfly I noticed first.

Buzzing around my ears, it finally landed on my nose, its sticky little feet and wet tongue searching for something tasty to feast on.

I wiggled my nose, but it stayed there and walked closer towards my nostrils. Only a quick swipe from my hand forced it to fly off. But within a few seconds it was back, landing on my forehead and searching feverishly for food.

Little bastard.

I was having such a nice sleep too.

You know what it feels like when you first wake up, those first few seconds where you're truly relaxed and at peace, just before your brain kicks in to remind you of all the terrible things: that your mother is dead, that your father's an alcoholic. Other things too. Like there's bills to pay, or you have to get the kids to school, or that today's the day you have to fire someone or it's time to call it quits and walk out on the person you vowed to love forever. Serious stuff like that.

But just before that, in those few precious moments, I love that morning twilight. Those few seconds of true peace.

And then I remembered Duke.

I wished it had been a dream, but I knew it wasn't. I opened my eyes. I was lying on my side, staring out into the trailer. The curtain was still pulled across the space between the bed and the rest of the trailer, but the sunlight was streaming through the window over the kitchen sink. I could see the rest of the trailer anyway, that's how thin the curtain was. Mornings always seemed so bright in here.

Raven's clothes were still in a heaped pile, and the clothes she wore last night were folded neatly on the table.

I smiled. She'd managed to arrive home again without waking me. She was very good at that.

I could feel her warmth at my back, and I leaned slowly towards the middle of the bed. My back touched her side, her skin against mine. She was so warm and so soft. I felt safer knowing she was there next to me, protecting me as she'd always done. Slowly, as not to wake her, I rolled over so I could look at her.

She lay on her stomach, her arms crossed under her head and on the pillow. She was turned to face me, her eyes shut and her mouth turned up at the corners in a little smile. I always liked seeing her like this. She told me once that lying on her stomach was her favourite position for sleeping. She said it was a great position for something else as well, but I didn't ask what. She'd laughed and she knew she'd embarrassed me, but I knew exactly what she was getting at.

I looked at her face. Even early in the morning and without make-up, she was a beauty. Her hair, while all messed from sleep, still framed her features perfectly, the long strands of purple darting here and there, falling over her face, across the bed sheets, slipping down her back and down even further.

Her well-defined cheeks were rosy, her eyebrows immaculately plucked, and even the small scar on the left side of her nose where her nose stud used to be looked perfectly suited on her face.

She was so lucky she didn't have to do anything to look so beautiful.

I hate when I wake up and looking in the mirror makes me want to cry. I feel so ugly and self-conscious that I dread going out some days.

Raven has everything I don't, and that is *really* hard on me some times.

I try not to show it. I try not to let it get to me. But it's hard, you know? Really hard. I hate waking up on those days.

But not today.

She looked so peaceful and so relaxed. I smiled, just happy to know I was there with her. Her shoulder poked out from the sheets and I could see, further down, the side of her left breast, squashed between the rest of her and the bed, trapped there all round and perfect.

No wonder the guys go ape for her.

I thought about waking her so we could discuss what we were going to do about Duke (see, my brain had kicked in by then, ruining such a wonderful moment) but I also knew she hadn't been asleep for long. Getting in at 3 or 4am meant she'd probably only had four or five hours sleep. So I decided to let her sleep a bit longer.

Not that it mattered, because that blowfly returned and landed right on Raven's shoulder.

I tried to shoo it, but it held fast, skittering around, searching for food. It had beady little red eyes and a big ugly body. It almost looked as if it were striped, rows of metallic blues and greens and blacks stretching down its length, and its hairy legs and face were enough to make me feel sick. The sun made its large wings shine and it used its tongue (or whatever it's called) to prod and poke the pores on Raven's shoulder, looking for God-only-knows what.

Its head moved from side to side, searching, maybe wondering if I was the next course.

Raven's hand darted from underneath her head and swatted at the blowfly. She missed and it flew off with a loud buzz, high above the bed and back and fourth above our heads.

She stretched her whole body, her feet and legs reaching out and rubbing against mine, and then she rolled over onto her back. Her smile remained, though, and her eyes were still closed. Her hair curled around her arm and her face, so she had to swipe it aside with one of her hands. She blew a strand or two away from her mouth while she was at it.

"Open," she whispered, her smile growing wider.

And she was right. My eyes *were* open.

"Correct," I replied.

She nodded. "I thought so."

She finished our game from last night. She'd known I would ask the question before going to sleep, and she'd answered it hours later.

That's the kind of thing Raven does, always thoughtful, always thinking of others. She knew me *so* well. That's why she's my soul mate.

"How was last night?" I asked.

"Much less eventful than the night before," she replied, reaching her hands up above her head and stretching once again.

The sheets slipped away from her and I could see both her breasts and, as she stretched, her ribcage moved under her skin. Like I said, she was perfect; there wasn't any fat on her anywhere.

Her nipples were erect, and the small silver barbells that pierced them reflected the sunlight. One barbell was correctly aligned, the nipple sitting right in the middle between the metal balls on both ends, while the other was off centre, one ball pushing hard against the nipple.

I wanted to reach out and fix it. But I didn't.

I wondered if it was painful, pushing against her nipple like that. It didn't seem to be, though, otherwise Raven would surely have fixed it.

"No problems?"

"Nope," she yawned. "Andy didn't say anything to me about it. And the bouncers were too busy so they didn't get a chance to say anything either. I think all's cool from that end at least."

"Good."

"Well, no one's probably noticed he's missing yet."

Raven opened her eyes for the first time that morning and smiled at me. I was sitting propped up against her, my left elbow on my pillow and my hand holding my head on the side.

I smiled back. She felt good right there next to me; we felt perfect together. Warm and soft and just right. But the worries were starting to crash down on me again. This wasn't the end, it was only the beginning.

"How do you feel?" she asked me.

"Okay, I guess."

"Last night?"

I shook my head. "I survived. Nothing happened."

"I thought you might freak out a bit."

"I did at first, but I just went to bed and everything was fine. I even fell asleep pretty quickly."

"Good."

"I did a lot of thinking though," I continued.

"I know what you mean," she nodded.

"About what we have to do next."

"Yeah."

"He can't stay here, you know."

"I know."

"Not in the wardrobe. He just can't."

Raven nodded.

"We have to make it look like he just upped and left on his own."

"I know."

"Like he just took off without telling anyone where he was going."

"Yep."

"I don't think anyone would be surprised if a guy like Duke did that."

"I sure as hell wouldn't."

"And neither would I."

Raven put her hands behind her head and stared up at the ceiling, her eyes darting back and forth, watching the blowfly as it cart-wheeled around the space above the bed.

There was silence between us for a little while. I watched her as she stared; I could tell she was thinking. I swatted at that damn blowfly a couple more times before she spoke again.

"I've asked for some time off," she said.

"Huh?"

"I asked Andy if I could take a couple of weeks off. I have it owing to me and I told him I needed a break."

I was surprised. "And he said *yes*?"

She nodded. "I think he thought it had to do with the night before, and that the experience had shaken me up a bit. We didn't discuss it specifically and he certainly didn't say anything, but I think we both knew what I was getting at."

I guess Andy didn't need a dancer whose heart wasn't in it right now, or who was scared to approach the customers just in case they pulled something like Duke had tried to do.

Much better to give the girl a couple of weeks vacation until she's ready to come back and give it her all.

That's what I was thinking, anyway.

"So what are we going to do?" I asked.

"Well, I was thinking about that." Raven turned to face me. As she did so, she rolled onto her side. We were mirror images of each other now, our bodies touching from our stomachs all the way down to our toes. "We can't stay here. I don't think either of us could take that."

I didn't quite understand what she was getting at, and it must've showed on my face.

"We need to *leave*," she continued. "I don't think either of us would do too well if the police suddenly knocked on our door and started asking questions about what we thought of Duke and when we last saw him."

She was right about that. I didn't have a Poker face. I knew it and so did Raven. I'd probably cave right in, and they'd know I was hiding something right away.

"So, I suggest we pack everything and head up the mountain."

"But won't it look like we're fleeing or something?" I asked "Like the criminal always flees the scene of the crime?"

"Hon, I don't think we have much choice!" She reached out with her hand and rubbed it along my bare shoulder. "It's the lesser of two evils. We either stay here and jump at every sight and sound, wondering when the police will arrive, the owners, Duke's family or God-knows who else, or we can get the hell out of here. Andy already knows I'm taking a couple of weeks off, he understands why, and I told him I was going to go for a drive somewhere, just to relax and let my hair down, and he was fine with that. I think it's the better option."

"And what about Duke?"

"We take him with us."

Huh?

I know, you're thinking the same thing, right?

But that's what she said.

I must've sat there with my chin on the floor (or, in this case, on the bed.)

She smiled at me.

"Don't worry. We're not taking him on an around the world trip. I thought it would make sense to drive further up Lake Mountain, check out the sights and look for a suitable place to get rid of him. There must be plenty of ravines, crevasses or cliffs, holes and caves up there. A perfect spot for getting rid of our uninvited guest. And no one will ever know. Even if they do *finally* find him, it'll be too late to try and work out how he got there. They might even conclude he took a hike and never returned. Stupid bushwalkers are doing that all the time."

Well, of course, that made sense. We couldn't leave him here in the trailer, and we sure as hell couldn't leave him buried somewhere on the lot. First of all, someone would probably see us digging a hole, and second, the police were bound to search the area and find him anyway. Especially if his mates had dropped him back home after being thrown out of Rawhide.

"And we can't just dump him in his trailer and leave him, can we?" I asked, already knowing the answer.

"Nope, someone might find him too soon. And there's bound to be some forensic test they can do on him to link us to the body. It's just too risky."

Raven was right. It *was* too risky. So we had to go with her plan.

Okay, so we're not talking about a plan designed and recommended by Mensa, I'm well aware of that. But it was the only plan we had.

Our only chance, really.

I couldn't think of a better one, so I agreed with Raven.

"At least if we're away for a couple of weeks, we won't be here worrying about what's happening."

"But if we leave this morning, won't it look suspicious?"

"Well, no one *really* knows when Duke left, or when he died, do they? So there's nothing to say he's not still here on the lot, still alive and still being the bastard-manager-from-hell. We could even tell the police we saw him this very morning, told him we were heading off on a road-trip and to keep our lot open, because we'd be back in a few weeks. After that, we never saw him again, so we have nothing more to add! Our story ends there. Plain and simple."

It made a good deal of sense to me.

"We have to make it look like he's left, though," I added.

"Agreed. That's something we *do* have to take care of, unfortunately."

Raven sat upright, the sheet falling from her chest, revealing her bellybutton, stomach and hips to the morning sunlight.

"And we have to do it soon, before everyone wakes up and gets going. Things need to look right. Duke's never up this early anyway, he's always sleeping off his latest binge, so that should buy us some time. No one will be expecting to see him. But we'll need to pack some of his stuff and make it look like he left in a hurry."

"But why did he?" I asked.

"Why did he what?"

"Leave in such a rush?"

"I don't know," Raven shrugged.

"Shouldn't we come up with something? Like a family crisis or a debt collector or something?"

Raven shook her head. "No, why?"

"What if the police ask?"

"But that's just it, sweets. We don't know *anything*. We haven't the faintest idea. If you start feeding the cops a story that he had a sick uncle or that he owed the local heavies money, they'll go and check it out, and when they find the story isn't true, they'll start to wonder why you lied and they'll come back to find out what you're hiding. No, no, we have *no idea* about where Duke is or where he went. He's a creep and we tried to stay away from him as much as possible. He didn't talk to us and we didn't talk to him."

I nodded. She was right.

Raven threw back the sheets, moved further down the bed and then climbed over my legs (she can't get out on her side of the bed, remember, because of the walls). She stood by the bed, reached for the curtain and pulled it open, sending it flying back to the side wall near my face. The sun

LAKE MOUNTAIN

shone through the windows, highlighting her back and buttocks. I could see her spine, the ripples of it cascading down her back, past her ribs and down to her behind. Perfect in every way.

I still got jealous sometimes.

It was stupid, I know. This was my best friend in the world, but I still got angry sometimes when I saw her this way or thought about how she gets paid for dancing and showing off her body.

I could never do that. No one would *ever* shove a hundred bucks down my g-string.

Yeah, like I'd wear a g-string anyway!

Hang on, I want to point out here that I *am* experienced with sex, just in case it's coming across that I'm not.

Well, I am. *Very* experienced, actually.

Okay, okay, maybe not *very* experienced. But I'm certainly not a virgin or anything. Been there, done that!

In fact, it may surprise you to learn that I lost my virginity when I was only fifteen.

Yeah, exactly! I know what you're thinking. Just as long as you don't think I'm a whore or anything. And that you don't think I'm Little Miss Frigid either. Just stick me in the middle of that scale somewhere, okay?

Of course, when I did lose my virginity, I kept it to myself. I didn't want anyone to know.

In fact, I'm pretty sure my dad still thinks I'm a virgin. He'd be in for a shock if he found out I'm not, and haven't been for quite a while. But that's not something you can tell mum and dad. I wouldn't want them to know anyway...none of their business. And the fact that my ex *raped* me that first time, well, that doesn't help either. I say "ex", but we weren't really even dating.

Just one of those things a girl learns about, I guess.

You learn from your mistakes.

And it probably didn't even feel like rape at the time. We went out, we got flirty, he went a bit too far, I let him, but then he wouldn't stop, even when I asked him to. Even when I hit out at him and yelled at him. He hurt me, but he was too strong for me and there was nothing I could do about it. He left me on that park bench in the middle of the night and I never saw him again.

I think that's a good thing.

But it wasn't until much later that I realised I was as good as raped that night. For a long time I thought that was what sex was all about. A guy has his way, the girl lies back and takes it. End of story. But there's a lot more to it, I know that now.

I hope I never see his sorry arse again.

He was an asshole for treating me like that. And I have a sneaking suspicion that he knew exactly the right buttons to push, when to drop compliments, how to look deep into your eyes and tell you the things a fifteen year old girl wants to hear. He'd played me, and played me well. I'm sure I wasn't the first virgin he'd nailed, and I probably wasn't the last either.

Asshole.

The blowfly landed on my shoulder. I swatted it away.

"Damn fly. How did it get in here?" I asked.

Raven turned to look at me. "No idea."

"So, what's the plan?" I asked.

"Hmmm?" Raven was thinking, her head turned back to the wardrobe.

"Where do we start?" I prompted.

"We act as normal," she muttered, almost to herself.

"Good luck," I replied as I lifted the sheet and swung my legs over the side of the bed. The sunlight shone on them, highlighting all the little fair hairs I had on my legs, shining across my vagina and mingling with the coarse crop of dark pubic hair that resided there.

Maybe I should shave down there like Raven does, I thought to myself.

Raven reached out towards the wardrobe door.

I looked up and watched her.

Her hand clasped on the latch.

"What are you *doing?*" I asked.

"Just checking… something," she replied.

The latch clicked.

She pulled open the door an inch or two.

I heard the sound before I saw anything, an intense buzzing that sounded like a hundred busy crop dusters.

But they weren't planes.

They were blowflies.

Dozens of them, maybe hundreds.

Swarming in and out and around the wardrobe.

Raven quickly shut the wardrobe door. The sound was cut off, and so were the majority of flies, but quite a few had escaped, flying around the trailer now, searching for something juicy to feed on.

Like the fly that had landed on my nose earlier.

Had it been in there with Duke?

Did it touch him before it touched me?

I didn't want to think about that.

And I'd been lucky. From where I was sitting on the bed, I couldn't see inside the wardrobe. I could see Raven and the wardrobe door, but I couldn't see inside, the angle wasn't right for that. So, I'd been spared the actual sight of Duke and what was going on in there.

I'm sorta glad about that.

"Oh dear," Raven said.

"How did *they* get in there?"

"Probably from underneath," Raven replied. "Through the wheel arch or something. They can be pretty damn intelligent creatures when they want to get at something."

Yeah, pretty damn intelligent.

Unlike Duke.

So now we had a dozen or so blowflies flitting and bouncing around the walls of the trailer, while inside the wardrobe we had *corpse a la carte* for every blowfly within a 200 mile radius.

And if they were swarming inside the trailer, there must have been at least as many swarming outside, trying to get in.

Isn't nature wonderful?

We had a plan, we knew what we were doing, but one of the biggest obstacles was now a mass of blowflies that could probably give us away in seconds.

Perfect.

"Go and have a shower," Raven said.

For a moment, I wondered why she wanted me to do that. Did she think I was dirty because a fly had touched me? Did she want me to be clean for a particular reason? Did I smell?

"We've got to keep up our usual routine," she continued, as if reading my mind. "You have a shower in the mornings, so go and have one now."

It made sense.

"And you?"

"I'm usually asleep."

"I know, but –"

She nodded. "I'll head over to Duke's and pack some of his stuff."

Duke lived in the very first trailer on the lot, the one directly behind the office. It was risky to go snooping around there, because anyone entering or leaving the lot would see you. But I guess we really didn't have any choice.

"Can I help?" I asked.

Raven shook her head. She was still staring at the wardrobe door, her hand clenched firmly around the latch, and it was as if she was looking right through it at Duke.

Even with the door shut, I was sure I could still hear the buzzing of those flies, even though I couldn't hear them before.

I can *still* hear them, all these months later. Sometimes, late at night, that very sound invades my dreams and wakes me up, leaving me shivering and sweating at the same time.

Sometimes I dream a great mass of darkness is following me, bearing down on me, wanting to swallow me whole. Other times I dream about being locked in a small, dark, enclosed place. I'm fumbling for a door knob, a light switch, anything, but I can't find one and I'm yelling and screaming for help, but no one comes to save me. In both dreams, that loud buzzing drone is heard in the seconds before I wake.

Thankfully, those dreams are visiting me less and less these days.

"No, no. I can do this myself. Probably better that way," Raven whispered, without taking her eyes from the wardrobe door. "You go to the showers as usual. I'll slip around to Duke's place and pack him a bag or two."

Almost as if he *was* coming on vacation with us.

I nodded and quickly stood, slipping into my robe and getting my toiletries.

"You need anything?" I asked as I turned to leave. It was a stupid question (I was going to the shower block, after all) but I couldn't leave without asking it.

Raven shook her head. "No. Just get back here as fast as you can."

I nodded and opened the trailer door, stepping out into the warm sunlight and away from all our troubles.

At least, for a little while.

Eight

Everything looked normal as I walked back from the showers and towards the trailer.

I walked in a direct line, and tried to do so at my usual pace, even though I knew I was walking faster, hurrying to get back, to hide inside so no one would see me.

The trip to the shower block and the act of showering itself was uneventful. It was just after 8 in the morning and no one was around. Most of the people who lived there didn't have anywhere to go anyway. Most didn't have jobs, and those who did were shift workers who could be coming and going at any time during the day or night.

Nice and easy, Amber, I'd told myself as I walked across to the showers.

I checked each of the stalls and luckily I was the only one there. I don't know what I would've done if one of the other tenants was there also. I took a steaming hot shower and tried not to think about what happened last night, or what we had to do today.

All I *could* think about was leaving Raven in the trailer, her hand still holding shut the wardrobe door, her eyes burrowing inside through the laminex, as if cursing Duke for everything he'd ever done.

And I was worried about her trek to Duke's trailer. What if someone saw her? What if someone noticed that something was wrong?

What if they *already knew*?

So, even though the shower was wonderful and I didn't want it to stop, I quickly turned off the taps and left the stall, climbed into my robe and walked back towards the trailer.

The day was wonderful.

The sun was already high in the sky and its rays were golden and warm. I could feel the gooseflesh on my back as the sun warmed me. The air was still cool from the night before, and I could feel it mostly through my wet hair as I walked, its touch cooling me down after the shower.

It felt good. Everything felt good.

I glanced up and down the trailer park, being careful not to move my head from side to side. I just used my eyes, trying to find anyone or anything that looked unusual or different, out of place.

Like a cop car at the park's entrance.

Nope, not one of them.

Or worried relatives of Duke's, combing his trailer for answers.

Nope, nothing like that either.

Or Raven dragging Duke's body across the driveway to his trailer.

Nope. Nada. *Zilch.*

Which was good. Everything looked as per usual.

Maybe this wouldn't be so hard to pull off after all!

Yeah, right!

I guess Pine Hills is best described like a car park, that's really all that it was. A large car park for trailers. The office was at the top, nearest to the highway, and one gravel driveway ran straight down the middle of the lot. There were trailers on each side, every lot numbered out the front with a badly written black scrawl on an old ice-cream bucket nailed to a pole.

At that time of year the lot was only ever half full (if that), and the permanents were always placed down towards the back, for some strange reason. Anyway, Raven's lot was number 36, and we were right down the back. There was probably only space for about forty trailers in total.

The shower block was halfway down the lot exactly, on the left, and it was an old concrete building with a metal roof that was supposed to keep the rain out, but really didn't. It was rusty and full of holes and should've been replaced, but hey, we were just tenants who didn't have any say, right?

Next to that was Duke's makeshift gym. But only he had the key, so I'd never seen inside. Not that I'd want to, anyway.

On the other side of the drive, halfway down and on the right, was where we did all our laundry in those industrial-type washers and driers that cost two bucks for ten minutes. If they didn't rip your clothes, you were lucky. If they ever worked for longer than five minutes, you were also lucky.

So I hurried across the lot, eager to get back to the trailer, but at the same time not so eager. I looked around for Raven, but I couldn't see her anywhere. If she was out here, no one would see her.

Our trailer wasn't the oldest on the lot, but it was damn near close. Duke's was certainly the oldest, and the least cared for. It was rusting from both ends and one of the tires had been flat for months now. It looked more like a wreck than a place to live.

Raven's trailer was small and old, but she looked after it and kept it clean. Well, come to think of it, I guess *I* looked after it and kept it clean. And that extended to making sure there was no trash or weeds out the front as well. Not that anything would grow in the gravel and dirt that surrounded the place.

Still, she was proud of it, and so was I. It was our place. Our home.

If you saw it, you'd have no idea that there was currently a dead body stored inside it.

Quaint. That's the term to use.

You'd never believe Raven owned it. And maybe that was the whole point. It hid us from the world. No one expected us to live there, in someplace like that.

In fact, you probably wouldn't notice it at all.

That was the great thing about Pine Hills, no one noticed anything. And we liked it that way.

Parked on an angle at the front of the trailer, and partly on the driveway, was Raven's pride and joy, her 1972 Chevy 3 Door Suburban. It was long and sleek and very shiny. I had to squint as I looked at it, the sun's rays reflecting brilliantly in its polished paintwork. I never knew what Raven did with all her money, but I could guess a whole stack of it went into keeping this baby looking like new. It was two-tone, midnight blue on top and white on the bottom. I'm not sure the best way to describe it, other than the fact it only had three doors, two on the passenger side and only one on the driver's side. It was weird but Raven preferred it that way, because she never liked people climbing into the car behind her. I have no idea why. Plus, it also looked kinda like a hearse.

She loved that car.

"It looks like a hearse, but it's built like a tank," she told me once.

She treated that car like it was her only child.

She would wash and buff it once a week, on one of her days off, no matter if it needed it or not. I offered countless times to clean it for her, but she always said no. It was one thing she did by herself. She didn't want me to help.

I thought that was strange at first, but I grew to understand. We all need a little private time to be on our own, and that was Raven's.

The Suburban never broke down or got into trouble pulling the trailer, even though it was, like, over thirty years old. It never leaked oil, and it never overheated. Those Chevys are built to last! And, like Raven, it was cool, sleek and very *very* stylish.

I bent forward slightly as I passed the Suburban and looked through the windows. No sign of Raven there either, so she must've still been over at Duke's trailer.

"I hope this works," I said to myself as I reached the trailer door and opened it.

Walking up the two steps that led inside, I looked around for Raven, but she wasn't there. My eyes darted directly to the wardrobe, but the door was still shut and there was no sign of Duke anywhere. A few blowflies were still doing laps around the ceiling though.

I turned back and looked outside again, my eyes searching up the driveway to the office at the front of the lot. I couldn't see her. I checked out Duke's trailer too, but from where I was standing, I couldn't see anything different over there either.

She must still be in there.

Hurry up, girl, don't get caught!

I closed the door behind me and sat on the couch across from the wardrobe. I could hear the sounds of the blowflies inside, and they really unnerved me. I couldn't sit there for long. I looked around, trying to figure out something to do, but there wasn't anything that came readily to mind.

I could start making breakfast, but I didn't feel like eating right then.

I could tidy up or read my book (didn't work last night) or *something!*

So I stood, made sure my robe was still tied tight around my waist, and opened the trailer door again.

I glanced up the driveway.

Still no sign.

What the hell is she doing?

I climbed down the steps and slowly walked around the side of the trailer, trying to look calm and nonchalant, trying not to look panicked or worried, but probably failing dismally.

I slipped around the back of the trailer to check out the other side, the side where the wardrobe was located. Where Duke was located.

There were a hell of a lot of blowflies back there.

They were flying around the wheel and the wheel arch, a miasma of movement and sound. Thankfully, this side of the trailer faced directly into the forest that surrounded the park, so that bought us some time at least.

Not much time, but *some* time.

No one from the lot would see the flies unless, for some reason, they walked behind Raven's trailer and into the forest. And I didn't think that was too likely. But if the sound of the flies got louder, or the numbers grew, someone might decide to have a bit of a sticky-nose. We couldn't risk it.

We've got to get out of here, I remember thinking.

Quickly, I marched back around to the front of the trailer and, as I did so, Raven stepped out of the bushes to my side.

"Hi." She smiled, her eyes hidden behind her sunglasses.

She was wearing a customised black tank top, ripped down the middle to produce a plunging neckline. The words

I'VE BEEN A BAD GIRL were written across the front in row after row of small white print. The tear down the middle was held together loosely by three safety pins, so there was enough cleavage to distract anyone from trying to work out exactly what she was *really* up to. She also wore a short dark blue plaid skirt that covered only the bare essentials, and she wore no shoes on her feet. In her hands she held an old battered and bulging leather sports bag, filled to the brim with clothes and other items.

"Duke's?" I asked, which was a pretty damn obvious thing to say.

She nodded. "No trouble?" she asked.

"No. I was just checking the flies," I replied.

She looked over my shoulder and back along the side of the trailer. Worry crossed her brow. "We'll have to do something about that," she said.

"No one can see them."

"Not yet anyway."

"Did anyone see you?"

"I don't think so. I circled around through the forest and came out at Duke's trailer. He'd left the door unlocked, so I slipped in pretty easily. Locked it on the way out though," she smiled.

"Did you get enough?"

"I think so. He didn't have a lot of useful stuff anyway. So I took what I thought he would take with him."

Raven had a weird look on her face. A look I didn't really understand. But I would later.

"What's next?" I asked her.

Raven moved to my side and put her arm around my shoulder as we walked back towards the trailer door.

"Next, it's our turn," she replied.

"Huh?"

"To disappear."

Nine

It took us until about 10:30am to get ourselves ready to leave.

Of course, I wanted to leave *pronto*, but it's never that simple, is it?

We had to make sure everything was secure inside the trailer, so that nothing would fall out while we were on the road (Duke included), and we had to latch the trailer onto the back of the Suburban as well.

Sure, we're two strong girls, but a pair of male hands would've been of help to us right about then, to position the trailer in the precise location, to lift the cap onto the tow ball on the back of the car and lock it in tight.

Where's a man when you need one?

Well, there was one in the wardrobe, but he wasn't much use now... or ever, for that matter.

Eventually, we decided to back the car into the right spot and managed, together, to lock the trailer on. It took longer than expected, and in the warm sunlight, we were both sweating.

Raven wiped her hand across her forehead, her hair streaking across with it, sticking to the sweat that remained there.

"Let's hope nothing else takes us so long," she whispered to me.

It's hard to concentrate on what you are doing when your mind is on two things at once. We had to make sure we had everything we needed, tied down safe and ready to go, but we were also conscious of the rest of the world around us. More conscious and aware than we'd ever been before, I'm sure. We'd worked hard packing up the deck chair and milk crates, transferring the clothes into the back of the Suburban, unhooking the electricity and water from the trailer, but all the time, we still had half a mind and one eye on the other trailers around us.

Who's watching us?
What if they come over and ask questions?
What if they think we're acting suspiciously?

We tried to act calm and collected, like it was just another day, but who knows if we succeeded or not? It all seems like a feverish dream to me now. I'm not sure if we didn't look anything other than panicked.

It didn't help that I was a bit upset too.

When Raven had returned from Duke's trailer, she'd placed his sports bag on the bed. While we were cleaning up, I was the one who moved the sports bag into the back of the car.

But before I did that, I put it on the table and looked inside.

I mean, I didn't *plan* to, it just happened, you know? When I lifted the bag off the bed, it was heavier than I thought, and I didn't have a proper grip on it anyway, so I simply rested it on the table so I could grab the handle a different way.

What the hell did he have in here that was so heavy anyway?

I decided I'd have a look.

I felt a bit dirty about going through someone else's things, especially when that "someone" was dead. Especially when they were Duke's. But he'd wanted to do much *much* worse to Raven and me, so I think I deserved to have a little look-see.

I wish I hadn't.

The bag was filled with an assortment of odd and mismatched clothes. Some checked shirts, board shorts, white and not-so-white socks and underwear, a windbreaker, jeans and a couple of pairs of shoes. But further down, towards the bottom of the bag, is where I found the stuff that really made me feel ill.

Raven had packed five or six porn films, their covers graced with lurid pictures of naked women bending over or spreading their legs, showing everything they had for the world to see. There were titles like BOMBAY BABES, SLUT QUEENS and FUCK ME BLUE; they're the three I can remember right now. And next to them was a pile of *Cheri* and

Hustler magazines. I didn't want to pick them up, or even touch them, because I knew Duke had. And I knew what Duke had *done* with them.

I pushed his clothes back over the top of the porn and quickly closed the zip.

I know, I know, I'm not a prude and I'm more than aware that guys (and some girls) watch and read this stuff all the time, but I just didn't want to know it about the guy who was currently dead in our wardrobe.

I mean, what if he'd got his way with Raven? What if he'd managed to tie that rope tight around her arms and she was left spread-eagled on the table, so he could do whatever he wanted?

Remember what he said?

"Play nice for daddy and if you're good, I won't arse fuck your friend Amber when she gets home."

So, it was pretty clear what he had in mind for *me*, right?

The trailer door swung open and Raven popped her head through the opening.

"You almost ready?" she'd asked.

I nodded.

Her eyes dropped to my hands on the sports bag.

"Not a very wholesome collection, is it?" she asked, her face taking on that weird look I mentioned earlier. Seems like Duke's favourite films and reading material made her feel ill as well.

"No. I feel sick."

"Don't worry. I think that would be the perfectly normal reaction."

"Why do we have to take all this stuff with us?" I asked.

"So it looks like Duke has left in a hurry."

"No, no, I understand that. I mean the *porn*."

"Because that's all I could find in his trailer," Raven replied, turning around and sitting on the top step. Her back was towards me and she pushed her sunglasses further up her nose. She stared out into the lot, looking from side to side, checking to see if anyone was watching us.

"You'd think he'd have family pictures or sporting trophies from school or letters from a girlfriend... anything. But all I could find was a huge pile of dirty laundry and more porn than you could ever imagine. Plus a couple of empty bags that looked like they had once held cocaine."

"Cocaine?"

Raven nodded. "I think so. It was white powder, for sure. At least we now know where he got his money for the Rawhide on Monday night."

"Cocaine..." I said again. I just couldn't believe Duke would be into that.

"So, I stood there and tried to think like a male," Raven continued. "No, scratch that. I stood there and tried to think like *Duke*. And I decided that if he was going to leave in a hurry, he'd take enough clothes to get by, and his favourite porn."

"Did you go into the office and see if he had anything there?"

"No." Raven shook her head. "I didn't want to risk it. Someone might've driven in or seen me or something. But I don't think Duke had any personal items in the office."

She was right. I couldn't remember seeing anything in the office that might've belonged to Duke.

"Especially not any porn," I said, half to myself, as I looked down at the sports bag again.

"Exactly. He wouldn't risk having any of that stuff out in the open where others could see it."

"It's disgusting."

Raven nodded.

"All those stupid women just selling their naked bodies for the cheap thrills of some fucked up men. It's sick. They're all sick."

You know when you hear yourself say something, and even when you're saying it you know you're saying the wrong thing, but you can't stop yourself? That's what I was feeling right then.

It was a dumb thing to say.

Raven didn't reply.

She sat in silence and nodded her head slowly as she stared down at the ground.

I just stared at her back, at the strands of dark brown curly hair escaping the make-shift ponytail she'd put them in.

Shit. That was stupid.

"Raven, I didn't mean –"

I tried to make amends, but Raven stood quickly, turned and offered me a sad smile.

"We better get going, hon," she said.

And then she was gone from the doorway, the door slowly swinging shut.

And I felt like the village idiot.

Well done, girl. Go to the top of the class for lack of tact.

So, on top of worrying about leaving Pine Hills with a corpse in the trailer and making sure we were calm and collected and not acting suspicious, I was now feeling a bit sick, having seen those magazines and videos, and I was also feeling like a heel for hurting Raven with my Ill-Conceived Comment Of The Year award.

It wasn't one of my finest hours, that's for sure.

Anyway, we packed the final things, hooked up the trailer and were ready to leave. We didn't say much to each other during that time, we both kept to ourselves and kept busy. But I'm sure we were both thinking about the same things: what to do with Duke, and how to stop me from putting my foot in it again.

I really wanted to apologise to Raven. But I knew bringing it up again would just raise the matter to the surface once more. Raven wouldn't want that. She'd just want us both to forget it. Hell, *I* wanted us both to forget it. But I didn't like our chances.

So, we prepared in silence.

And then, we were ready.

We were so close to getting away from there – clear away – without anyone noticing. Everything had worked just so perfectly.

Too perfectly.

Because that's when I saw them.

Raven had gone back to lock the trailer door, and I walked around to the passenger side of the Suburban. I opened the heavy blue and white door and was about to climb in, but something stopped me. I looked up the lot towards the office. There was a big, black Ford sitting to the left of the driveway, pulled up alongside the office. Both its doors stood open and its emergency lights were flashing.

At first, I thought it was a cop car, but it had no writing on it and there were no lights on the roof.

I hadn't noticed it there before.

How long had it been there?

"Get in the car, Amber."

I heard Raven's voice from behind me. It sounded cautious, steady and low.

My eyes skipped from the car to the office. I was straining to focus, to see if I could spot anyone in the building. But I couldn't. I couldn't see anyone in the car either.

Where are they?

Who are they?

But the office was too far away to make out anything or anyone properly.

"In the car," she whispered again.

Slowly, I climbed into the car and shut my door, trying hard not to let it slam or click too loudly (not that anyone from the office would hear it this far away anyway.)

Next thing I knew, Raven was in the car too. She was still wearing her *I'VE BEEN A BAD GIRL* tank top and the blue skirt, the only difference being she was now wearing sneakers. She didn't wear them very often, so I thought it was kinda ironic she was wearing them when we were "sneaking" away from the scene of a crime.

The day was already nice and warm, so I was wearing an old white business shirt of my father's. It had long sleeves and a big collar and I'd left the top three buttons undone to let the cool breeze in, as these business shirts could get pretty stuffy if you buttoned them all the way up to the neck. I had no idea how dad could stand to wear them day in and day out for years in the hardware store. I was also wearing some faded old jeans and a pair of sneakers.

I won't even start to describe how I felt having to get dressed in that trailer after I got back from my shower. I was sure Duke was watching me (even though I knew he couldn't), and the sound of those flies drove me crazy. So I grabbed whatever was handy and climbed into them quick smart. Which is why I probably wouldn't win any fashion contests with what I was wearing right now.

Still, with my short hair and business shirt, maybe I looked like a guy. Maybe anyone who would happen to see us would think that this was a normal couple out for a relaxing holiday. Raven being the girl and me being the guy. We can only hope. Ever since I cut my hair short, I have been asked countless times:

"Are you a guy?"

and/or,

"Are you a lesbian?"

Well, let's tackle both those, shall we? What about a nice "None of your damn business!" kinda answer?

But I never used that one. I was always too scared. I mean, if I *did* say that, they'd probably think I was gay anyway. So I always answered no to both. It's *my* hair and I'll wear it however I damn well want. It's none of their business. It's short because it's easy to manage.

Simple. End of story.

And, yes, I sleep with Raven. I know that, and you know that (now). But that's because it's only a one bed trailer and I'm telling you nothing ever happens between us. I'm not like that. It's just the way it is.

And, it just so happened that on this occasion my short hair, along with what I was wearing, might just help us out of a tight squeeze.

"Two girls, officer?" the witnesses would ask. "No, sir. I only saw a happy couple, a guy and a girl."

Perfect.

Raven started the engine, never once taking her eyes off the car at the top of the driveway. The engine roared into life, sounding loud and powerful and angry, but maybe that was just how it sounded to us.

"What's going on up there?" I asked.

"No idea."

"Do you think -?"

"I don't know. Let's just play it nice and easy."

She let out the brake and put the Suburban in gear. Slowly, she pressed on the accelerator and the car inched along, taking up the weight of the trailer behind it.

I turned to look out the back windows, making sure the tow bar was holding and the trailer was moving along with us. It was. I even wound down my window (Raven's was already down) and stuck my head out to check.

Everything was working nicely.

There was still no one around; we hadn't seen anyone all morning. Although we did hear one of the washing machines chugging and moaning in the laundry. So, someone was up and about, but we had no idea who.

I'd asked Raven if we should investigate, but she said it would seem unusual if we did that. Suspicious. So we just ignored it. It stopped after five minutes anyway. So, someone had done their two bucks worth.

Raven angled the car up the driveway, moving forward painfully slow. She had her sunglasses on, but I knew her eyes were still focussed on the office in front of us.

Mine were too.

The closer we got, the more we could see.

There was no one sitting in the black Ford. Luckily, even with the Ford's front doors standing open, there was just enough room for us to drive past the office. The last thing we needed was to create a scene.

We drove on ever slower, the powerful engine almost idling, just waiting to be given its head to charge down the highway at top speed. The Suburban didn't like being driven at anything under thirty miles an hour.

We got closer.

There were two men in the office. We could see them through the windows.

They were standing at the welcome desk, talking to each other. So, the good news was maybe they were too caught up in what they were saying to notice us.

The bad news was they were both facing our way, and we were driving right into their line of sight.

Cops?

They didn't look like cops. But you really can't tell these days.

Friends of Duke's?

Well, as we got closer, I could see they were dressed pretty well. Duke wouldn't have friends like these.

Would he?

One was tall and thin, wearing dark sunglasses (yes, even inside), and the other was balding, had a moustache and was of average height. They were both wearing dark suits and ties.

"Here goes everything," Raven said as she pushed her foot down on the accelerator and the car sped up, the tires biting into the gravel and spinning faster. We drove closer and closer to the office.

As we drew level with it, Mr Moustache pointed in our direction and said something to his friend. Mr Sunglasses turned his head and nodded.

Suddenly, they were both dashing to the office door.

"*Fuck!*" Raven said as she floored the accelerator. The Suburban shot forward, but strained under the weight of the trailer. It didn't take off nearly as quickly as we had hoped. All the extra speed did was bring us level with the office doorway in time for the guys to run out and meet us.

"Hey!" one yelled as we drove past, the side of the trailer narrowly missing his waving hand and shoulder.

I looked over at Raven. She was looking out the side rear-view mirror.

I heard one of them call, "Wait up!"

"Shit." Raven pumped on the brakes, slowing the car down to a stop.

"Are you *crazy?*" I whispered.

"They've seen us now. There's no point," she replied. "Just act normal."

You may notice how acting "normal" was getting harder and harder by the minute. And it really wasn't getting us anywhere either.

We could hear their running footsteps on the gravel; within seconds they'd caught up with us. Mr Moustache leaned forward and placed his hands on Raven's open window.

"In a bit of a hurry, aren't you?" he asked in a gruff voice.

None of your damn business, I thought. I think these things, but I never say them.

"We're just running late," Raven replied, smiling her best smile and moving closer to him. I was sure he was getting an ample view of the top of her breasts through the tank top. She really *was* right, those babies could divert attention from us completely.

"Ah, you must be going somewhere pretty exciting," he replied, bending down closer to them. His chin, mouth and nose slipped into view. That's all I could see of him from my side of the car, but I didn't need to see his eyes to know where they were looking. His moustache curled with a smile.

"Nowhere you'd be interested in," Raven replied with her nicest voice, but I could tell there was tension in it too.

"Do you know the manager of this place?" It was a different voice, Mr Sunglasses now.

Damn it, I remember thinking. We're fucked.

"Know him?" Raven asked.

"Well, know where he is?"

"Isn't he in the office?"

"No."

"He usually is by this time. But then again, he's a heavy drinker, so some days he doesn't get home until he wakes up in a gutter somewhere and remembers where he lives."

"I see." Mr Moustache nodded. "You don't think he might be somewhere else?"

"Huh?"

"Perhaps he's taken a drive down to the store or something?"

Raven shrugged. "Doubt it. He doesn't own a car."
"Oh."
"Well, he *did*. But he had it impounded months ago. DUI or something."
"I see."
"Anything else I can help you with?" Raven asked.

I couldn't believe she'd asked that.

Mr Moustache was still looking at her breasts, I was sure of it.

"No, no," he replied. "Don't want to hold you up any longer."

"Okay," Raven smiled. "Well, good luck finding him!"

"Have a nice day," Mr Moustache said as he straightened up out of sight.

"You too," Raven replied.

They stepped back from the car and Raven accelerated away.

It wasn't until we were on the highway and away from the place that she finally let out a big sigh, almost as if she'd been holding her breath all that time.

"That was close," she whispered.

"You're telling me!" I said, watching the road ahead. "Are they following us?"

Raven checked both side rear-view mirrors. "Nope. I don't think so."

"Who *were* they?"
"Who do you think?"
"I'm not sure," I replied.
"Neither am I."
"And you offered to *help* them!" I turned to face her.

She nodded, strands of purple and brown hair dancing around her head in the breeze. "Well, I was only trying to find out what they wanted. I thought they might tell us."

"Didn't work."
"I'm aware of that, hon."
"Do you think they're suspicious of us?"

Raven let out a short laugh. "What do *you* think? We almost ran them down trying to get out of there."

Not a good start to our Grand Plan, now was it?

"Well, at least we're on our way now," I replied, sitting back in the seat and trying to relax. I was glad to be out of the trailer park, glad to be away from the memories of what happened there. And I'm sure Raven was too. It was just unfortunate that Duke was following right behind us, in the wardrobe still.

I wondered whether I'd ever be able to truly relax in the trailer again, even after we got rid of his body. I'd *always* know that he'd been stored in there. I'd *always* know what he tried to do to Raven on the table.

On the *meals* table.

I think Raven did the community a service, getting rid of scum like Duke. He deserved what he got, in the end.

Except all we got was trouble. Duke's trouble.

"Where are we headed?" I asked a few minutes later to break the silence.

Raven was biting her bottom lip. She shrugged. "Lake Mountain."

"Yeah, but *where* on Lake Mountain?"

"No idea, sweets. We'll find out when we get there. Just sit back and try to relax, we've had a stressful morning."

She was right about that.

I leaned my head back on the headrest and closed my eyes. Raven turned on the car radio and inserted a cassette of classical music.

I didn't know what the music was called, or who composed it or anything, but I had to smile to myself.

Here's Raven, this goth-chick stripper, dressed in dark clothes and driving a Suburban, the closest thing to a hearse on the road, pulling behind it a trailer with a dead body in the wardrobe, and she's listening to classical music.

She always said it helped her relax, and I'm sure she got enough of that heavy-bass techno rubbish to dance to every night at Rawhide. So she always played classical in the car.

Strange but true.

Plus, the radio didn't work. So we had to listen to *something*.

"Well, at least we're out of trouble," I said, my eyes still closed.

"Yep," Raven said. "In the end, we got out of there pretty well. Should be smooth sailing from here."

I nodded.

How *totally* wrong could we both be?

Ten

I guess I must've fallen asleep for a while. I'm not sure for how long, but with the sun shining through the windows and the breeze wrapping around me, I probably nodded off for a few minutes, anyway.

It was the rough bumps of the gravel road that first woke me. Gone was the smooth ride of the highway and suddenly we were bouncing around pot-holes and wheel ruts.

I opened my eyes and squinted outside.

"Where are we?" I whispered.

"Sorry, didn't mean to wake you." Raven smiled and leaned over, patting my thigh with her hand. "You must've been tired."

"Sure looks that way," I agreed, rubbing at my eyes with the back of my hands.

We were pulling into an old gas station.

I thought we'd be at Lake Mountain by now, but we weren't. Sure, we were close, but we weren't there yet.

"Running low on gas," Raven explained.

I nodded my head and looked out at the gas station.

It looked derelict and half falling down. The Texaco sign out the front had three large holes in it, like someone had thrown rocks through it and no one had bothered to get them fixed. The sign was dirty too, and its pole was stained with blotches of deep red rust.

The gas station itself had four old pumps out the front and the driveway up to the pumps (if you could call it that) was just plain dirt, dotted with potholes and crevices everywhere.

The Suburban bounced along, jarring us inside as it did so. Raven kept an eye in the rear view mirrors and I held tightly onto my door and looked over my shoulder. The trailer was still there, wobbling back and forth too.

I just hoped Duke was still locked in the wardrobe. I didn't want to be opening the trailer to find him stretched out on the floor, like he was lunging for the door, trying to escape. But I was sure I checked the latch. Double checked it, in fact. He wouldn't be getting out. At least, I hoped not.

The gas station looked abandoned. It had old signs out the front for Coke, Pepsi and Dr Pepper that could probably have been hung in an antique store. They were so old and windblown and dirty, I was sure they wouldn't help sell anything.

Just in front of the glass sliding door in the entranceway to the office was a small metal sign. It was hanging from a frame that had overturned, lying on its side, the words WE ARE OPEN flapping sideways, back and forth in the breeze.

To the left of the sliding door were two large windows that were covered with boxes. You couldn't see in, and I'm sure whoever was in there couldn't see out. The boxes looked old and sun bleached, the words printed on their sides having faded with age. They were stacked from floor to ceiling and crammed up against the windows.

Ten or twelve large rocks were half-buried in the ground on both sides of the doorway, creating a rocky guide up to the door. It looked like maybe, at some stage in the past, there'd been a small group of plants or bushes of some type on either side of the doorway. Now, there was only dirt, gravel and rocks.

The fluorescent lights above the doorway swung in the breeze, and I noticed one of the lights was broken anyway, only half its tube hanging from the socket.

You're getting the picture, right?

Not a nice place.

Not your usual gas station.

Not this far out, anyway.

I turned around and looked out my window. I could see the highway in the distance, and I watched as other cars zoomed past, heading up and down the mountain. We were the only ones at the gas station though.

The whole place gave me an uneasy feeling.

"You sure?" I asked.

Raven nodded. "Only take a minute. We *are* pretty low. I hadn't planned on taking this little trip, otherwise I would've bought some earlier."

She climbed from the car, opened the fuel latch and started pumping gas.

"Come on, come on," I whispered under my breath, hoping and wishing for the gas tank to fill quickly.

My eyes danced from Raven to the highway to the boxes in the window of the gas station.

No one drove in. No one came out from the office.

Just her and me in the middle of nowhere, stopped at a gas station with the trailer. Anyone could see us. The longer we stood still, the more chance anyone could notice us, whether it be from the gas station or from the highway.

What if Mr Moustache and Mr Sunglasses drove by and saw us?

They'd have an excellent view from the highway.

I didn't want to sit still, I didn't want to be trapped. I wanted to be moving, fast.

"Come on, *come on!*"

The bowser shut off with a clank after what seemed like an eternity. I heard Raven jiggle the nozzle to get the last few drops of gas from the hose, and then I saw her return it to its home on the side of the bowser.

She walked back to the driver's window, leaned inside and grabbed her purse.

"Do you want anything?" she asked.

I shook my head.

"We haven't had breakfast yet."

"I know, but I'm not very hungry right now."

I was too nervous to eat. I didn't want to create a scene by throwing it all up somewhere along the way.

"Not a drink or anything?"

I shook my head.

"Okay, I'll get some water anyway."

That was a good idea. I could handle some nice cool water.

"Okay."

She smirked. "That is if this place *sells* anything like that!"

I watched her as she walked towards the sliding door; her sleek figure, held tight by the black tank top, the way she pushed her hips from side to side in that little skirt. I also noticed she looked back and forth, as if she were checking if anyone was watching us as well.

I was glad we were both being as careful as possible.

She stepped up to the sliding door and grabbed the handle. There was a handwritten sign above the handle that said "SLIDE." Another sign above that said "CLOSE THE DOOR BEHIND YOU!"

Hadn't anyone told these people about automatic doors? Might be worth the investment.

Raven slid the door open, walked inside and then turned to slide it shut.

I waved to her, but she didn't wave back. I'm guessing she wasn't looking at me. I couldn't tell what she was looking at through those dark glasses of hers.

And so, I sat back in the seat and continued my surveillance.

The highway.
The gas station.
The trailer.
Nothing.
No one.
Maybe we'd be fine after all.

I felt uneasy sitting there by myself. I was alone and I felt vulnerable and I wanted to get out of the car and make a dash for the office. But that could be seen as suspicious and I wanted to play cool. Just like Raven.

Take it easy, girl, I thought to myself. Don't panic.

Raven was in there an awful long time. At first, I didn't think it was too long, but then the more I got to thinking, the more worried I became.

How long does it take to walk into a store, grab some bottled water, pay and leave?

Should be no more than a minute or so, right?

Not like the place was busy or anything...

Okay, add to that the fact that the owner probably didn't hear us approach and he was out the back somewhere and Raven had to call him and he had to walk all the way to the cash register. But still, that's only a couple of minutes, right?

"Come on, come *on!* What's going on in there?"

I stopped looking at the trailer and the highway. All of a sudden I didn't care who saw us.

I studied the windows.

So full of boxes.

I tried to peer through, looking for a gap anywhere, trying to spot some kind of movement from inside to let me know everything was okay.

Nothing.

All was quiet.

The sun shone. The breeze blew.

So quiet and peaceful.

So nice and relaxing.

So damn *unnatural.*

After I don't know how long (but it seemed like ages) I'd had enough. I reached for the handle on my door and pulled it. The door popped open.

And then I heard the scream.

Eleven

My eyes darted back to the office. I couldn't see anything out of the ordinary and I wasn't a hundred percent sure the scream came from that direction.

But there was no one else around, so it had to come from there.

I climbed out of the car. I had no plan, no idea of what I was going to do next.

But it *was* a scream.

Wasn't it?

Or was my mind playing tricks on me?

Frozen on the spot, I stood by the car on tip-toes and stared across its roof to the sliding door of the office. The sun reflected off the roof of the Suburban and I had to squint to see properly. I wanted to call out Raven's name, to ask if she was alright, but I didn't dare.

Then I heard the sound of breaking glass.

Then another scream, louder and more frantic this time.

And Raven came rushing into sight, grabbing for the handle on the sliding door, a look of fear on her face.

Her sunglasses had been knocked sideways, and I could see her left eye clearly. She looked straight at me as she pulled open the door. Her tank top was ripped in two, straight down the middle, her breasts swinging in tandem as she used all her weight to push the door open.

"Amber, get in –!" was all she had time to yell at me.

The old guy suddenly appeared from behind her. He was wearing dirty blue overalls and a grease-smeared smirk. His hair was grey, and combed to one side, but the stubble on his face was still dark. He was probably in his early 50s, but I didn't take much notice at the time. He reached out for her, just as Raven stepped through the doorway and outside the office. He grabbed her by the hair and yanked hard.

Before I could warn her, before she had a chance to know, her feet flew out in front of her and she was falling backwards, her arms cart-wheeling in the air, and she hit the ground hard, flat on her back. I heard the air rush out of her and she let out a small yelp of pain.

I watched on, not knowing what to do. I wanted to help her, but the guy would be too strong for me. I wanted to call the police but I didn't have a phone. Raven wanted me to get back in the car, but I couldn't do that either. I needed to do *something*, and soon.

She lay motionless for a few seconds, her body flat across the entranceway, half in and half out of the office.

The guy sniggered as he reached out and grabbed both her hands, dragging her back inside. They both disappeared behind the boxes.

I don't even know if he saw me. I don't think he did. He was too caught up in what he was doing.

Honestly, what could I do?

I opened the back door of the Suburban and climbed inside. I looked around the back of the car, trying to find anything I could use as a weapon. All our clothes were there, as was Duke's sports bag. There were a couple of boxes that held personal possessions of mine (mostly old schoolbooks and assignments and stuff), but there was nothing in there that could help. And the only other thing was Raven's big canvass elephant sack, which was where she stored all her fishing gear (not that she'd been fishing anytime recently.) Unless I was going to bait and hook this guy, I didn't see how anything in the sack could help us either.

I climbed from the car and heard Raven scream again.

"*Don't!*" she yelled.

I admit I was panicking by now. I had no idea what to do. I looked all around for help, for anyone. The cars sped by on the highway, but there was no one closer, no one rushing to our aid.

I had only one option. And I didn't like it.

I ran around to the driver's side of the car, opened the door and climbed in.

I sat staring at the steering wheel. The keys were still in the ignition and I was sure I could remember what Raven did to drive it.

It couldn't be that hard to work out. Everyone else does it.

I reached out for the key and turned it in the ignition. The engine kicked in and I placed my foot on the accelerator, revving the motor loudly. My eyes moved to the brake and the gear lever.

This bit could get tricky.

But I decided as long as I got the car in gear and could point it in the direction of the office, I'd be able to charge in and ram the doorway or something.

That would get the bastard's attention.

I revved the engine some more, and turned to look at the office.

Raven was crawling towards me, out the doorway and down onto the dirty path. Her sunglasses were missing, and she was bleeding from the temple. Her tank top was still around her shoulders, more like an open vest now, and her breasts hung low between her arms as she continued to crawl. I couldn't see her skirt anywhere. She sure as hell wasn't wearing it.

She was yelling to me, but I couldn't hear what she was saying over the noise of the revving engine.

And then the guy was on her again. He appeared from nowhere and moved so fast. His overalls were around his ankles and I could see the bobbing head of his erect penis as he grabbed Raven by the thighs and started to pull her backwards.

She lashed out, kicking backwards at him, but the guy was too quick. He ducked out of the way and grabbed her legs, pinning them between his left arm and side. Then he stood to his full height and made a fist with his right hand. He slammed it into the base of her back, punching her right in the kidney, and Raven fell flat, her face showing the pain.

She must've screamed, but I didn't hear it.

He turned her over, right there in the doorway, right where I could see, and spread her legs apart.

His cock bounced from side to side, as if it were looking her over, ready to plunge deep inside her.

He kneeled between her legs and pulled her closer to him. Raven reached out behind her and tried to grab one of the rocks near the door. But her hands couldn't grip. He pulled her closer, her legs sliding up his thighs, opening further, her vagina inching closer and closer to his throbbing cock.

He had a wide smirk on his face. He was loving every minute.

And all I did was push down harder and longer on the accelerator, revving the engine over and over again. But the guy didn't notice, or didn't care.

He was on top of her then. He pushed forward, hard and fast, his teeth heading straight for the barbells on Raven's nipples. She tried to resist, but he was too powerful for her.

"No!" I yelled, but I'm sure no one heard me either.

He was still on top of her, his white arse rising and falling quickly. Raven was trying to get away, to scratch at him, but it didn't seem to help. Her hands pulled at his hair, hit at his back, but to no effect. He just swatted them away as he continued thrusting.

The revving wasn't working. I glanced back at the gears.

I could run him down.

But not with Raven in the way. I couldn't risk that.

I glanced back at them both.

The guy had stopped pumping. He was staring at Raven's face. She was telling him something. I could see her mouth moving quickly, but I couldn't hear the words. I took my foot off the accelerator so I could hear, but I was too late. Whatever Raven had said must've touched a nerve.

But in the wrong way.

Because he rose up and slapped her clear across the face. Her head darted to the right, her whole body shaking with the blow. Her breasts jiggled with the force and her hair (all dirty and messed now) flew sideways. Her hands stopped fighting then. They just fell down by her side.

Then he was down on her again, pumping away faster and faster.

Raven had stopped struggling completely.

For a moment or two, I thought she was unconscious. But she wasn't. I could tell because very slowly, her right hand was reaching out for the rocks nearby. She grabbed each one in a slow and deliberate fashion, testing them, trying to see if they moved. They'd obviously been dug in a long time ago to border the now non-existent garden. They'd been placed there to stay.

The first two rocks didn't move. But the third did, ever-so slightly.

Raven's long fingers wrapped around it and rocked it back and forth, just like the guy was doing to her. She matched his thrusting movements perfectly, using the same timing, the same movements, probably so he wouldn't notice what she was trying to do.

Not that he would notice anything anyway.

He had more than his hands full right now.

His left hand was on her right breast, squeezing and pulling on her nipple and barbell. The other hand was pulling hard on her hair, making sure her face was out of the way so she couldn't bite or spit at him. Meanwhile, he was concentrating on biting and sucking her left breast.

Fucking animal.

How could he get away with this in broad daylight? He was so damn confident and self-assured. Had he done this countless times before?

That thought made me go cold.

This bastard was just like Duke. Exactly the same.

Maybe all men *are* the same.

I could see the rock was loosening. With each and every thrust, the rock tilted and tipped more and more, and after what seemed like an eternity, it popped out of the ground surrounding it.

Raven left it there for a few seconds. I couldn't work out why, but she seemed to be watching the guy, waiting for the right time. I even saw her hips start to work with the thrusts, like she was helping him now, co-operating, wanting him to finish what it was that he started.

That didn't make sense to me, but that's what I saw.

His arse moved quicker and quicker, he pumped faster and faster.

I watched. I didn't even rev the engine anymore. I just sat there, dumbly and uselessly.

Raven picked up the rock, held it for a few seconds in her right hand. Then, slowly, as he thrust harder and harder, she brought the rock up above her head where she grasped it with her left hand as well.

He was still too caught up in what he was doing to notice. His face was buried in Raven's left breast. His teeth were pulling at the barbell and his tongue kept slobbering his spit all over her.

She held the rock over her head for a few seconds longer.

The thrusts were faster, deeper, harder. He arched his back suddenly, his head leaving her breast and rising above hers. His eyes were closed and there was a look of ecstasy on his face, his smile wide. He was missing two teeth.

He was about to be missing some more.

He didn't see it coming.

Raven used all her force to bring the rock smashing down on his nose and forehead.

He kinda spasmed for a moment, and the smile was wiped clean off his face. Blood started to pour out of his nose and the deep gashes across his forehead and he flopped straight down onto Raven. She rolled out of the way quickly, so his chin came down heavily on her left shoulder before he slid off her and to the ground. He hit the dirt hard and didn't move. He just lay there on his side.

Raven crawled back from him, watching him closely, making sure that he was out and not faking or anything.

Quickly, I turned off the engine and climbed from the car. I didn't walk any closer though; I didn't really know what to do. With the engine off, the silence was heavy all of a sudden, eerie.

All I could hear was the heavy panting from Raven. She wiped a hand across her brow, but that only succeeded in smearing more blood and dust and dirt across her face.

Slowly, she knelt up and reached towards the guy.

"Don't!" I called.

Her face swung towards me, a look of fear etched across it. But then she realised it was me and she smiled a sad smile.

She turned back to face the guy and prodded his shoulder with an outstretched finger. He didn't move.

Out cold.

I sighed deeply. It was over.

Now we could get out of there...

Raven picked up the rock again.

...before anyone could find out...

Raised it high about her head.

...before any more damage was done...

And brought it down hard on the side of the guy's head.

There was a muffled *thunk* and I could see where the rock had torn open the skin just below his ear. The hole was deep. It started to bleed too.

He deserved that.

Raven raised the rock again.

Once was enough.

"Raven!" I called.

She brought the rock down again, harder this time. It bounced off the guy's head, tearing the skin on his scalp. I could see white shiny bone reflecting in the sunlight before blood pooled in and covered it up.

"Let's get out of here," I said.

She raised the rock again, slowly and purposefully.

"*Raven!*"

She didn't look at me. She continued staring right down at the guy.

"*RAVEN!*"

She brought it down again, harder, more precise, the rock hitting just above the ear this time. I'm sure I heard a loud crack, but by that time I was running towards her so I can't be certain *what* I heard.

"Stop it!" I called as I reached her.

She lifted the rock over her head once again. I looked all around us, making sure no one was watching or driving up for gas.

It's crazy. Before I was hoping, *praying*, that someone would drive by to help us. Now, I was hoping for the exact opposite. There would be *no way* we'd be able to explain what was going on here now.

Luckily, it was still just Raven, myself and Mr Rapist. But the cars on the highway worried me. Even though the Suburban probably hid a lot of what was going on from those driving past, I didn't want to risk it. Someone might stop, or look back, or come this way for gas. Too damn risky.

"Come on," I said. "We *have* to go."

Raven readied herself for another attack.

She was still kneeling, so the rock was at a perfect height for me to grab. Which is what I did, just before she struck again. I grabbed it from her and threw it away from us. It was heavy, and very jagged. I'd hate to think what damage she'd caused.

With the rock gone from her hands, Raven collapsed in a heap in front of me.

Her tank top was smeared with blood and dust and dirt. I still couldn't see her skirt anywhere, all I could see was the dust caked on her ass, and the long thick streams of milky-white cum running down her thighs.

Asshole. What gave him the right to do that to her? Who the fuck did he think he was?

I wanted to kick him, to strike out at him myself. Maybe Raven had every damn right to pummel the guy's head to mash with the rock.

But we already had way too much to handle with Duke, and I didn't want – or *need* – another dead body in the trailer with us.

One dead freak I was getting used to. Two would be way too much.

This guy *had* to survive. I knew that if he did, he wouldn't call the cops or anything like that. I mean, what's he going to say? That Raven attacked him while he was raping her?

Somehow, I thought (I *knew*) he'd want to keep this whole episode very quiet indeed. At least, I hoped so.

I knelt down next to Raven and ran my hand through her hair and along her arm. She was turned away from me, but I could tell she was crying softly to herself.

"Come on," I whispered. "Let's get you back into the car."

She didn't say anything. She just nodded and slowly let me help her to her feet.

I wanted to ask her if she was okay, but I knew that was a stupid question. I just put her arm around me and helped her walk back to the car. She was limping a little and seemed to favour her left leg, but thankfully we didn't have far to walk.

I carried her around to my side of the car and sat her down on the back seat.

"Just sit here and try to relax. Don't go anywhere," I said to her. I didn't want her going back to attack the guy while I was gone.

She didn't reply, but I'm guessing she heard me.

She sat for a moment, but then slipped backwards, lying down across the back seats, her breathing still fast and her legs dangling outside the car.

This I had to do quickly. No telling who would see her lying like that, especially as that side of the Suburban faced the highway.

I just hoped our luck would hold out.

I took one look around before marching back towards the office. I kept my eye on the guy as I walked closer and closer. I wanted to make sure he wasn't faking us out or maybe even coming to. But he was lying there on his side, perfectly still. The only thing moving was the ever-growing puddle of blood seeping out around him on all sides.

Oh, that and his rapidly deflating cock.

He wasn't half the man he thought he was...

I stepped past him quickly and entered the office.

It was a dark and dingy cramped space that smelled of body odour. There were no lights switched on inside and the only illumination came from the sunlight seeping in through the cracks between the boxes piled against the window. The light arched through the darkness here and there, reflecting the dust in the air and throwing shadows just about everywhere. Different angles and different shapes. Very unnerving indeed.

There was a small selection of food and drink, mostly potato chip packets and candy bars, with one grubby old refrigerator housing the limited selection of drinks. On the far wall were piles of different sized sacks, stacked one on top of the other, each pile a different product. One pile was garden mulch, another was chicken feed, another manure, another cat litter, another lime and so on.

Maybe that's why it smelled so bad...

I didn't mess around taking it all in. I checked to make sure no one else was in the office.

"Hello?" I whispered.

No reply. So that was good.

I couldn't see anyone, although the shadows made it hard to tell. Sometimes it looked like people were hiding, but when I went to investigate, it turned out to be a chair or a newspaper rack or something. Sometimes I thought I heard footsteps or breathing, but I put that down to my state of mind right then. Every movement, every sound was amplified and exaggerated. So, I blocked it all out and concentrated on what I had to do.

Raven's purse was still on the counter right near the old cash register. The purse was open, money spilled out to one side. Next to it were two bottles of water. Quickly, I walked over, put the money back in the purse and slipped it into the pocket of my jeans. I picked up the two bottles of water too.

The place was an absolute mess. There was dust everywhere, plenty of cobwebs too, along with half-eaten sandwiches and messy old oil-stained rags. Broken glass was spread across the counter and on the floor. The shards crackled, split and broke loudly under my sneakers.

As I turned back around to leave, I spotted Raven's skirt lying on the ground and pushed into a corner by the doorway. It was covered in dust and dirt and it was ripped down the side. It was useless to her now, she wouldn't be able to wear it again, but I didn't want to leave it here as evidence, so I bent down and picked it up too.

I tried to find her sunglasses while I was there, but it was too dark inside to really see anything. I just couldn't see them anywhere. I didn't have the time, or the inclination, to go hunting for them.

I marched quickly out of the doorway and back into the sunlight and cool breeze.

Stepping around the guy once more, I made sure he wasn't going to try anything with me. But he just lay there in his own blood, his overalls wrapped around his ankles.

Served him right.

I kept my eye on him anyway. Watching for the slightest movement.

He didn't move.

I kept walking.

I felt better being outside and away from the office. It felt wrong somehow. Way too eerie for me. And I wondered exactly what *did* go on in there when no one was around.

I sure as hell didn't want to find out. I had a pretty good idea as it was, thank you very much.

I opened the driver's door and leaned across the seat into the back.

Raven was still lying there, her eyes closed, one arm across her forehead.

"Here," I said as I reached over and handed her one of the bottles of water. "This'll help."

Raven opened her eyes and looked at me. She didn't say anything. She just stared.

I held the water closer to her. "You thirsty?"

She shook her head.

"You should drink something."

She closed her eyes.

I put the bottles of water and her purse on the front passenger seat, and I threw the tattered skirt into the back of the cabin.

"I'll be right back," I said.

She didn't reply.

Grabbing the keys from the ignition, I hurried over to the trailer and unlocked the door.

I looked around again.

No people. No cars.

Just a half-dead guy bleeding in the driveway.

I opened the door and quickly climbed inside the trailer. In fact, I don't even think I looked over towards the wardrobe as I entered, to see if everything was okay. I really didn't have the time and my mind was on other things.

I rummaged through the storage area above the couch and found what I was looking for.

The first aid kit.

It was a small metal box that had been bashed around over the years, but I just hoped it would have what I needed. I walked down to the bed and opened the cupboards above it, pulling out two bath towels which I flung over my shoulder. Turning, I reached out for the wardrobe so I could get Raven's bathrobe.

My hand grabbed the latch.

And then I remembered.

I took in a sharp breath, let go of the latch and stepped backwards.

In my panic, I'd almost forgotten!

"Careful," I muttered to myself.

We'd moved all the clothes into the back of the Suburban.

"Easy girl. You almost blew it!"

So, I had everything I needed.

Trying to shake off the gooseflesh that had sprung up along my spine, I climbed from the trailer, shut and locked the door, and looked across to the Suburban.

I could see Raven peeking out of the passenger window, her eyes wide and fearful. She was looking across to the office and then, in a flash, her head disappeared from view.

I looked back across at the office too, fearful the guy had regained consciousness and was coming after us, but he was still just lying there, unmoved. Maybe Raven had been worried about him too, and had to check just to make sure.

So far, everything was still okay.

I raced back to her and found her lying across the back seats again.

"Are you hurt anywhere?" I asked.

Stupid question.

She didn't say anything.

"I've brought some towels and the first aid kit. To help you clean up."

Only her chest moved up and down, her breathing was shallow.

"Are you okay?" Probably, now I think about it, another stupid question.

She didn't move. So I guessed it was up to me. I bent forward over her, using the towel to dab at her wounds. The gash to her temple didn't look too deep, more like just a flesh wound, and the blood seemed to have stopped flowing. I emptied some of the bottled water on the towel, making it nice and wet, and I dabbed at the wound, wiping away the blood. Raven didn't stop me.

Her left cheek was a fiery red colour. That was where he'd slapped her. I pressed the towel against her cheek for a few seconds, hoping the coolness would help some of the colour fade.

Further down, blood was oozing from her right nipple. The barbell had been pulled way too hard. Part of the side of her nipple had torn away, the barbell leaving a small jagged gash. There were teeth marks around her left breast, and it looked a little bruised as well, but it had escaped anything more serious.

I opened the first aid kit. Thankfully, it was well stocked with antiseptic creams, bandages, cotton balls and bandaids. I grabbed the antiseptic cream and dabbed some of it on a cotton ball. I reached forward and placed it lightly on Raven's right nipple.

She arched her back and sucked in a deep lungful of air when I did so. Her hand shot out and she grabbed my wrist hard.

"Hey!" I yelped; her grip was tight and it was hurting me. "Raven, let *go*!"

She lifted her head and opened her eyes. She stared at me for a second and then her grip loosened on my wrist.

"I'm only trying to help," I whispered.

I pressed the cotton ball back on her nipple. Her breathing was still deep and fast.

Grabbing one of the larger bandaids, I carefully placed it across the nipple. It'd hurt like hell to remove, but I thought it was important to stop the bleeding right then.

I moved further down her body. She was bruised and dust-covered all over, small scratches and cuts here and there. There was grit in the thin line of her pubic hair, but I really didn't want to touch down there. I didn't spend more than a couple of seconds looking anyway.

I grabbed the second towel and quickly wiped down her thighs, removing the pools of drying cum that streaked there. It stuck to her skin, so I had to use more of the bottled water to peel off some of the more stubborn stuff.

It was gross.

I feel sick just thinking about it.

"Where is he?" Raven whispered.

I looked up at her, but she was still lying flat. Her eyes remained closed.

"Huh?"

"Where is he?" she spat.

"You knocked him out. He's lying in the doorway of the office."

"Can you see him?" she asked.

I lifted my head and stared through the windows of the Suburban. The guy was still floating in his puddle of blood.

I nodded.

"Can you?"

"Yes," I said, realising Raven hadn't seen me nod. "He's out cold."

"Is he dead?"

"I don't think so."

I certainly hoped he wasn't.

Raven didn't say anything more for a few seconds. I continued removing the cum from inside her thighs. I also wanted to make sure we got rid of this towel the first moment we could. I didn't want his juices anywhere near us, or for the towel to remind Raven of what had just happened.

Like cum on a towel is going to bother Raven when the guy's already cum inside her…

"Can he be seen?" she asked.

"Huh?"

"From the road. The highway. Can he be seen?"

I turned and looked out at the highway. I already knew the answer, but I double checked anyway.

"Yes, I guess," I answered. "The car is probably hiding him for the most part right now, but when we leave, he'll be seen."

"Gotta hide him," she said.

"You can't, you need your rest. You're in no fit state –"

She shook her head. "Not me. You. *You* have to hide him."

"Me?"

She nodded.

"Hide him?"

"Yes."

"Where?"

Raven sighed. She raised her hands up to cover her face and she started to cry once more.

I didn't want that. I didn't want her crying again. I had to do something.

Think for yourself, girl. Do it for Raven. You can do it! Just THINK!

"I'll be back, ok?" I said. "Don't worry, I'll hide him. You just lay there and try to relax."

I left the towel across her stomach and legs, hiding her private areas, and hurried back towards the office.

Hide him? Hide him where?

Part of me was panicking, but the other part was worried about Raven. I didn't spend a lot of time thinking about what I was doing, I was sort of operating on auto-pilot, I guess.

Raven said to hide him, and that was what I was going to do.

All I needed to do was get him inside where he wouldn't be seen from the highway. He'd regain consciousness eventually, so the main purpose was to try and get him out of sight to buy us the most amount of time.

I crept up beside him and leaned forward, looking at his smashed and bloody face. He wasn't going to be showing his face in public for quite a while. The wounds looked deep and were still bleeding. Part of his ear seemed to be hanging off, and I wasn't sure if the flat, matted down hair on the side of his head meant he was bleeding quite a lot, or that part of his skull had been caved in by one of Raven's blows. Either way, I didn't care.

He was still breathing, I could see that, and I guess that's all that mattered.

Looking around, I checked the coast was clear. Which it was. My eyes searched the Suburban too, but there was no sign of Raven. She was still lying down and resting.

I walked over to his feet. He was wearing dirty old boots and no socks. I bent down, grabbing his ankles and crumpled overalls at the same time.

I pulled. He was heavy and he hardly moved an inch.

I pulled again.

Almost nothing.

This was going to take longer than I expected.

But I knew I had to do this. Not only because Raven had asked me to, but also for myself. For *both* of us.

I grabbed him tighter, got myself ready, and pulled again. He moved further this time, maybe six or so inches. I pulled again. He moved more.

Slowly but surely, I was able to drag him through the doorway and into the office. Once I got the hang of it, I managed to move him pretty quickly. I don't know how long it took, but I soon dragged him down by the cash register. I was sweating by the time I got him there, the drops rolling down my forehead and into my eyes, but I didn't mind the stinging. At least it wasn't blood.

His wounds had left a long, slimy trail of blood and dirt from the front of the office all the way down to the counter.

Anyone stopping for gas was going to see it and call for help. But there wasn't much I could do about that.

I dragged him around behind the counter and propped him up against the wall.

I checked his breathing. It was still shallow, but it was constant. It smelled of rotting fish. Old people's smell. Some of the wounds to his face had stopped bleeding, but I was more worried about the ones to the side of his head, caused by Raven's well-placed blows.

Slowly, I stood up and looked over the counter. There was a phone by the cash register. One of those slim-line, cheap plastic ones. I thought about calling for an ambulance, ringing for help. He could probably use some medical attention, and the sooner the better. But I didn't do it.

I couldn't.

Not in this situation.

We needed all the time we could get.

The more distance between us and Mr Rapist here, the better.

So the guy would just have to sit there. After all, he only had himself to blame for it anyway.

I looked down at the blood trail again. No one would see it from the highway, but once they got to the office, they would. Not that it really mattered, because if they got this far and walked to the counter, they'd see the guy sitting there all bloody and beaten to a pulp anyway.

I was more worried about the pool of blood outside the doorway.

That was what you could probably see from the highway. *That* could call attention to his plight sooner rather than later. So *that* was my next problem to solve.

I walked back to the doorway and looked outside.

No sign of anyone.

No sign of Raven in the car.

The cars on the highway sped past soundlessly in the distance.

I really wanted to get back to Raven as quickly as possible, to make sure she was okay so we could both get out of this situation ASAP.

LAKE MOUNTAIN

The pool of blood was large, but it was also starting to soak through the dirt. I was sure that, given some time, it would soon all seep away. But I knew a dark stain would remain.

Gotta have it fixed before we leave, I thought.

But how?

I turned back to stare into the office, my eyes searching for anything I could use to cover it all up. A blanket, a sheet, boxes, anything.

And then my eyes hit the sacks stacked against the far wall.

Mulch.

Perfect.

I raced over to the sacks and pulled down two from the top of the pile. They were dusty and darn heavy, but I managed somehow. I dragged them back over to the door and used the car keys to tear them open. Once I got a hole big enough, I poured the mulch out, the little chips hitting the ground with a pitter-patter that reminded me of the sound of rain.

"Come on," I told myself. "Quicker. *Quicker!*"

It actually took four sacks of the mulch before I was satisfied with the result. The first sack pretty well just soaked up the blood and the chips started to turn a dark coppery red themselves.

No good.

I began to worry that maybe this wasn't the answer I thought it was.

But by sack three and four, you couldn't see the blood anymore. It was gone, buried under a nice smooth layer of forest-smelling mulch.

Of course, I didn't just build a pile of mulch over the blood, that'd probably look just as weird as the blood I was trying to cover. No, I spread the mulch out, pushed the pile to the left and the right, smoothed it with my hands, and levelled it all nicely. I tried to make it look as if someone was hoping to revive the old garden bed that used to be alongside the office. It wasn't a very good job, but it might just hold off suspicions for a while longer.

Until they walk into the office.

But I couldn't worry about that now.

I threw the empty sacks inside the doorway and took one last look around. I thought about going to check on the guy again, but decided against it. What if he was coming to? What if he saw me? I even considered pouring more mulch inside the office, to hide the blood trail up to the counter, but there wasn't that much really, and the office was dark and maybe no one would see it.

Maybe. They would see the guy soon enough anyway.

I also wanted to check around the office one last time, to make sure I hadn't missed anything, and to try to find Raven's glasses. But I knew the longer we stayed there, the greater the chances were of being caught.

I was sweating heaps by this time, and my father's old white business shirt had become pretty mucky, but I couldn't see any blood on it, so that was good. I wiped the sweat from my forehead and walked quickly back to the car.

As I approached, Raven was starting to sit up in the back seat.

She looked at me and then turned her head, staring through the windows to the doorway of the office.

"Don't worry," I said as I stopped by the car door. "He's hidden."

"Good." She looked back at me and smiled. "Thanks."

"How do you feel?"

"I've had my better days, that's for sure." Raven's smile broke, filled with sadness.

"I can't believe he did that to you. What happened in there?"

She shook her head. "Later. We have to get away."

"Can you drive?" I asked.

She nodded. "I think so. I have to. We need to leave here."

Now that she was sitting up in the back seat, I had room to climb in next to her. I kneeled on the seat and bent forward into the back of the Suburban. I searched through the pile of clothes until I found Raven's red bathrobe.

"Will this do?" I asked as I pulled at it.

"Yes," she whispered. "Thank you."

I handed it to her and tried to smile my best smile, but I don't know if it worked. Her hair was all messed and dusty, her face bloody, blotchy and bruised. Her nipples must've been sore and numb from the assault. I felt so sorry for her.

Raven, *my* Raven, was usually so full of life. But right now she looked as if that life had been taken from her, beaten from her. I wanted my real Raven back. I needed her. I wasn't going to be able to cope with all this unless my Raven returned.

She was the strong one. Always had been. And I needed that strength. Without it, I was likely to go crazy.

I sat there and watched her struggle into her bathrobe. As she moved her arms and turned her back, I could see the pain registering across her face. I could see more bruises now, along her sides and back, as if, like a Polaroid photo, they were developing magically before my eyes.

The guy had done her over real good.

But she did the same to him.

Finally, the robe was on and she was tying up the belt at the front.

"You need rest," I said, my hand reaching out to hers.

We sat there for a few seconds, looking at each other.

She squeezed my hand.

"We can't afford it," she replied. "Not yet. We have to get away from here."

I knew she was right.

But I felt so tired all of a sudden. All the exertion of the last half an hour or so had drained me as well. I just wanted to crawl into bed, to feel her body next to mine, to hold her tight as we spooned and kept each other warm. Falling asleep in each other's arms.

I needed that comfort. And I guess so did Raven.

But first, we had to flee from the crime scene.

Again.

Twelve

We arrived at a little out-of-the-way bush track at the base of Lake Mountain. We wouldn't have picked there by choice, but it was more out of necessity. We had to hide.

Quickly.

The visit to the gas station had gone completely wrong and we didn't know how much time we'd have before someone found the guy and called the cops.

Five minutes? Twenty? Half an hour? Five hours? Three days?

I'd helped Raven walk back around to the driver's side of the Suburban, and after a few minutes of driving, she stopped wincing and moaning in pain. I guess she got used to it, or had worked through it somehow so she could drive.

We'd just passed the sign that said LAKE MOUNTAIN 5 MILES when I asked Raven if she had any particular place in mind where she wanted to stay.

"No," she replied. "I guess we'll just have a look around some places and pick the one with the least number of people."

"Won't it be busy up the top of the mountain? All those sightseers and everything?"

During summer the mountain was popular for those who like to *ooh* and *ahh* at great scenery and mountain views. I didn't see the sense in it myself. They'd stand there and take pictures, and even I knew that the photos they took would never look like the real thing. Still, everyone seemed to do it. They'd rather live through their cameras than through their own eyes.

Of course, there was the added attraction of Wentworth Dam, halfway up the mountain. But why anyone would want to go and visit a huge concrete wall built into the middle of a forest is beyond me completely.

Not for its stunning natural beauty, that's for sure.

"I don't know how many tourists would be out here on a Wednesday, but I wasn't thinking of heading up there anyway," Raven continued.

"Oh?"

"We've gotta find a place no one knows about, a disused camping ground or something like that."

Well, we lucked onto something better.

Actually, I didn't even see the track to begin with. I was looking out my window, watching the sunlight cascade through the trees all around us, shadows falling across us and then disappearing just as fast, replaced by the sun in a staccato effect.

Next thing I knew, we were braking fast and turning to the left. I reached out for the dash, thinking we were trying to avoid something, but it was just Raven, heading us off down a bumpy old overgrown track.

"Is this even a road?" I asked.

"Doesn't look like it."

"Should we be going down here?"

"Probably not."

The track hadn't been used in a long *long* time, and there were moments along the short journey that I worried about the trailer breaking away from the towbar lock. We bounced and jarred and jittered our way through the forest and along the unkempt track.

"I hope you know where you're going," I said as I hung on tight to the side of the door.

"Nope," Raven turned to me. I thought she'd smile, but she didn't. She had a look of grim determination on her face.

Sometimes it was hard to tell where the track ended and the forest started. A couple of times we had to stop and look around us, trying to guess where the track went next. Thankfully, a gap in the trees usually gave us an indication.

We guessed right. Every time.

Well, *almost* every time.

At one stage, I was sure the track turned sharply to the left. Raven agreed.

We followed it.

And if it wasn't for Raven's quick reflexes, we would've ended up nose down in one of the deep Lake Mountain streams like Wile E. Coyote falling off those cliffs in the old Road Runner cartoons. The road (well, it wasn't a road) just fell away from us suddenly and we were staring at a steep embankment, straight down onto rocks and chilly mountain water. I'm sure if we'd been travelling even a fraction faster, we wouldn't've had time to stop. But Raven slammed on the brakes and we shuddered to a halt.

Just in time.

No Acme parachutes needed for us!

I won't tell you how long it took us to reverse out of there with the trailer behind us. It took a damn long time. I had to get out of the car and direct Raven backwards, this way and that way, making sure the trailer didn't swing too much one way or another, or jack-knife all of a sudden. We took out a couple of trees and scratched up the trailer real good, but I made sure we didn't scratch the Suburban (otherwise Raven would've been real pissed at me.)

And so, we took the opposite way to the way I first picked. Driving this way, we discovered we were moving parallel to the stream we'd almost driven straight into.

"At least we'll have fresh water," Raven said, and we decided to stick as close to the stream as possible.

As long as we didn't end up *in* it!

Just when it seemed like we were going to be stuck on this non-track forever, the trees thinned, the track ended and we drove into a small clearing.

"Wow," I muttered as I looked around us.

The stream we had been following suddenly opened into a large lagoon in front of us. The ground leading to the lagoon had been cleared of all trees, of everything, actually, leaving only grass and a small wooden bench made of old railway sleepers off to the right. The lagoon itself was surrounded by a thick wall of forest, the trees coming down right to the very edge of the water on two sides, except for where we now sat and also to our right. There, the incline was steep and rose high above us.

We were obviously somewhere at the base of the mountain.

While the sheer wall of rock rose high, there were still trees and bushes growing out of it at acute angles, stretching right up the mountain, still giving it a lush green appearance.

To our left, on what I guess you'd call the low side, was a small hillock covered by lovely bright wildflowers. They were on the far side of the stream, just near where it met the mouth of the lagoon.

"What do you think?" Raven asked.

"I *love* it!"

"So do I."

We drove forward some more, out into the middle of the clearing. I looked all around us, trying to take it all in. The high wall of rock on the right protected us from being seen by anyone. And the thick tree-line in front and to the left served the same purpose. Our lagoon was literally cut off from the outside world on every side. It was safe. It was perfect. We had fresh water and privacy. All we needed.

It made me wonder why we'd ever stayed at Pine Hills in the first place. This natural wonder beat that shitty old trailer park hands down. Easily. And it was all ours.

We drove closer to the lagoon, Raven turning the Suburban to the right, over towards the rock wall.

The lagoon itself was pretty large, probably sixty feet across and maybe eighty feet wide. The water was so still it looked like glass, greeny-blue glass. It looked deep, and *very* inviting.

There were some old wooden stairs built into the rock wall. They were weathered and worn, and I wondered if they'd been used very often recently. I hoped they hadn't.

I followed the stairs as they stretched up along the rock wall. I lost sight of them because of the roof of the Suburban, but I guessed they went to the top of the rocks, high above the lagoon, and gave you access to the mountain above.

We were driving close to the wall now, and Raven was looking at the side rear-view mirrors. I turned my head and looked back at the trailer. She was aligning it straight along the rock wall, getting it into a position she was happy with.

The next thing I knew, we'd stopped driving and Raven had turned off the engine. We sat with the windows down, listening to everything around us.

Listening, in fact, to nothing.

It was *so quiet*.

After the sounds of the engine and the cars and trucks on the highway and everything else today, sitting here in peaceful tranquillity was just marvellous.

In fact, for a moment or two, I wondered if I'd actually gone deaf. But the more we sat in silence, the more our ears attuned themselves to the sounds that actually were all around us.

The sweet summer call of birds in the trees, the trickling of the water over the stones in the stream, the breeze gently pushing through the trees above us.

Raven let go of the steering wheel, her hands falling to her side. She closed her eyes and sighed deeply.

"This will do," she whispered.

We sat there a few minutes longer, before I realised it was getting cold. While it was still some hours before the sun would set, it moved behind the rock wall above us, so that meant the evening shadows would cover us pretty early in the day. And the dampness would hit early too.

I reached over and grabbed the keys from the ignition. Raven still hadn't moved. It was up to me to set up camp, unlock the trailer and get Raven inside to rest.

And that's exactly what I did. And soon, I received my reward.

Because with Raven wrapped up in bed, resting and recuperating, I was able to slip in next to her. I curled myself around her back, felt her warmth, her skin touching mine, and we both fell into a deep long sleep.

Thursday, July ll.

Thirteen

And on the third day, the Raven did rest.

Although, not without some convincing from me.

When I woke on that Thursday morning, she wasn't next to me in bed. The bed-sheets were cold and when I looked around the trailer, I couldn't see her anywhere.

It took a second or two for me work out what was going on. (Remember that "morning twilight" I was talking about earlier?) I thought we were still at Pine Hills, and that maybe she hadn't yet come home from work.

That was when I spotted the small stains of blood on her side of the bed.

Her wounds must've seeped a bit during the night and I was worried about her then. I wanted to know that she was okay and not in trouble.

Quickly, I jumped out of bed and threw on my robe. I walked to the door and opened it.

The view took my breath away. The lagoon looked even better in morning sunlight. The water sparkled, flowing quickly down the stream and out of sight. The forest was bathed in a warm glow, the trees golden browns and golds and yellows and greens.

It was a hidden paradise and I loved it.

I never wanted to leave.

My eyes dropped lower. In front of me, about ten feet from the trailer, was a small circle of rocks. Inside the circle was a stack of dried leaves and twigs. To one side of that was Raven's huge canvass elephant sack, empty and open. Laying at the mouth of the bag was Raven's old fishing line. On the other side of the rock circle was one of our saucepans, half filled with water, and inside the saucepan were two large fish.

I have no idea what they were called, but they looked fat and nice and I realised all of a sudden I was feeling very hungry.

Raven *had* been busy.

And, I guess it all made sense. With no access to electricity out here on the lagoon, we'd probably have to make do with a campfire for our meals. Sure, we had a small propane gas cylinder and backup generator but, if I was thinking like Raven would, we might want to save what little gas and power we had left for emergencies.

I stepped down out of the trailer and walked over to the campfire.

The morning was chilly, but it was bracing at the same time. I thought about going back inside and getting dressed, putting on some shoes too, but I really didn't think it was necessary. No one was around. Even still, I checked the belt around my robe was firmly tied in front of me.

Just in case.

It felt good to be alive and all the worries of yesterday seemed so far away.

Of course, they *weren't* that far away. One was still in the wardrobe no more than ten feet behind me, and the other was probably in some hospital bed by now.

"Good morning!" I heard Raven's voice behind me and to the right.

I turned around and saw her slowly making her way down the old wooden stairs. Each step she took, she winced. She was wearing her purple and black cotton twill vest and pants. They were hand-dyed with a cobweb design all over them. The vest had no sleeves, and one long zipper straight up the front. The pants had two zips on either side for the pockets, and zips down the legs as well to allow them to be worn flared. Raven had the leg zips open and I could see her calves and ankles. The vest and pants were a size too big for her, and I remember Raven saying she really couldn't wear them because they were too big. But they *were* nice and soft. I guessed she was wearing them now because they were loose and wouldn't rub on her wounds. She was also wearing her sneakers again.

"Where have you been?" I asked, probably sounding a bit surly.

"Scouting around."

"Do you really think you should?"

"I did at first," she said as she stepped from the last stair. "Now, I'm not so sure. Probably overdid it."

"You should've told me what you were doing. I got worried." I walked over to help her back to the trailer.

"It's okay, someone had to check it all out."

"I could've."

"But you were asleep."

"You could've woken me."

Raven shook her head. "No, you needed the rest."

"Oh, and *you* don't?"

Jeez, I could belabour a point, couldn't I? I don't want to sound all overbearing mother or anything, but I really *was* worried about her and I didn't think she should be walking around in her condition. She needed rest, and I told her so.

She nodded. "I know. Don't worry. I'll rest now. I just had to make sure."

"Good."

We stopped walking just before we reached the trailer.

"Isn't it marvellous?" Raven asked as she looked around us.

"Yes, it's beautiful."

"Makes you glad to be alive."

"Certainly does."

Two small birds darted out of the trees and flew across the lagoon, spiralling in and out, playing with each other.

"Did you find anything?" I asked.

Raven looked at me.

"On your little trek?"

"Oh," Raven smiled. "The stairs lead up to the top of the rock shelf. I think it was probably used as some walking track a long time ago. You can walk up the top of the rocks and further on up the mountain. I didn't go very far though. I think I'd overdone it by then."

"See?"

"Yeah, yeah, I get the picture. But there's lots of fish in that lagoon, that's for sure."

"So I noticed."

"Didn't take more than ten minutes to snare those two for breakfast."

"Good, I'm starving."

"Well, if I remember correctly, you didn't eat at all yesterday."

And she was right.

"Is the water deep?" I asked.

"Hard to say," Raven shrugged her shoulders. "I only walked along the edge. Oh, and in the middle of the rock-face there's like a big hole. A blowhole, I guess. It lets the water run down the mountain into here. At least that's what I think it does."

We walked over towards the water's edge, and as we did so, the blowhole came into view. It was right in the middle of the rock wall, just as Raven had said, and it was probably eight feet wide by five feet high. You could tell by the current of the water that the lagoon was being fed by the blowhole. Somewhere up the mountain the water was running down through the rock into the lagoon, and then on down the stream.

We stood there for quite a while, just looking at our surrounds, enjoying every second.

And then my stomach rumbled.

Raven laughed. "See? Hungry!"

"Apparently."

"Let's eat. I'll fix breakfast."

"Oh no," I said. "*I'll* fix breakfast."

We walked back to the trailer and I left Raven standing there as I went inside. I pulled out the deck chair and milk crate for us to sit on. I also grabbed the matches from the kitchen cupboard, knives and forks, and a couple of plates. As Raven settled down in the deck chair, I lit the pile of leaves and twigs, got the fire going nicely, and then prepared the fish for us to eat.

Once I cooked the fish, we let the fire die, not wanting the smoke to give us away. Thankfully, there wasn't much smoke anyway, and the cool breeze seemed to disperse it pretty quickly.

We sat for a long time without speaking. We just took in the view. It was so quiet and so peaceful. This was so totally different to what we were doing yesterday. To be honest, I didn't want to ruin such a wonderful time by talking about horrible things. But I guess it had to be discussed, and the sooner the better.

And so I began.

"Are you okay?" That's how I started. I was sitting on the milk crate by now, next to Raven. We were both looking over at the lagoon, eating our delicious fish.

I didn't know if Raven would necessarily know what I was asking about, but she did.

She nodded.

Conversation ends.

So, I tried again.

"Feeling sore still?"

She nodded.

Stop.

"Do you want me to check your bandages and wounds and stuff?"

"No, it's okay. I did that already."

"You *did?* When?"

"When I got up this morning."

"Oh."

Silence.

"So you're okay?"

"Yep."

Silence.

Time to stop dancing around the issue, Amber, my girl.

"What happened yesterday?"

"You don't want to know, sweets," Raven whispered.

"Of course I do! I want to know what went on in there."

She shook her head. "Can't we just leave it?"

"Leave it? You almost *killed* a guy."

Her head turned slowly towards me, her eyes cutting through me.

"And he *raped* you!" I added quickly.

She turned back to look at the lagoon.

"No, he didn't," she said quietly.

It took a second for that to filter through to me.

"He *didn't?* Are you crazy? I saw him!"

Raven sighed and ran her fingers through her hair. It fell around her face, her curls bouncing back and landing exactly where they had to. The purple strands looked so vibrant in the sunlight.

"No, he didn't."

"Are you sure?"

She turned to face me again. "Amber, I think I would *know*. He tried pretty hard to get inside, but when guys are all hot and flustered, what they think is your pussy ain't necessarily so. He thought he was humping me, but after a few attempts of missing badly, I managed to get my legs closed under him. He didn't *fuck* me, he was porking the space between my legs, my thighs, just under my pussy, okay?"

She put down her plate of fish. She obviously wasn't hungry anymore.

So that was why I'd seen so much of his cum. She'd closed her legs around his cock and he'd cum down her thighs.

On one hand, I was relieved. On the other, I still felt a little sick about it all.

"But why did he do it?" I asked, trying to push this to the limit. I wanted the answers, and I wanted them now. That way, we wouldn't have to talk about it any more and we could move on.

"Why do guys do half the things they do?" she asked, crossing her arms over her vest.

"He must've been sick, or insane or something. Why would he attack someone in broad daylight like that? At his own gas station?"

"I don't know." Raven shook her head.

"He was an animal," I replied. "It's just not natural."

"Oh, it was natural alright."

I didn't understand. And she knew it.

She turned the chair around, so she could face me without turning her neck. It was probably still sore from yesterday's attack.

"Hon, you have to remember that our early ancestors were more in tune with their environments and with their own roles in life than we are today. Life was survival - scrounging for food, fighting the environment - and they always had to be geared toward procreation; producing and raising offspring. And the more kids you raised, the better chance you had that some of them would survive the conditions and make it through and maybe live until they were at least thirty or something. It was all about continuing the species, continuing the line. By comparison, today we concern ourselves just as much with recreation and material wants and trying to control our natural sexual urges through social guilt and intimidation. You see what I'm saying?"

I didn't.

"The old natural instincts are still with us," she replied. "They're in you and me, and they're in every man. We've tried to tame them, and men have tried really hard to hide their primal urges and thoughts, but they're still there, buried deep inside. We can't take the animal out of the man, it's just not possible. And we should *never* think that we can. Those old instincts can rise to the surface at any time. They did with the guy yesterday, just as they did with Duke."

"But why couldn't he control himself?" I wanted to know. "Why lose it yesterday when you walked in? Why *then*?"

"He saw a young, good-looking girl enter his gas station, and he saw an opportunity to further his line. The instincts were there, and he tried it on. Oh, he didn't want to get me pregnant, he wasn't thinking like that, the *last* thing he'd want would be a kid around to get in the way. But those primal urges were still there, and he wasn't thinking straight. He probably hadn't had a chance like me for years, and in that situation, he'd risk everything for it. And he did."

I sat staring at her.

"He almost succeeded."

"So you say he's not responsible for what happened?" I asked, incredulously.

"Oh, he *is*! He's responsible for not being able to control the animal inside him. But we shouldn't sit here and naively think that it could or should never happen. We're all animals, in the end, no matter how civilised we become."

Her cold, clinical response to what happened the day before shocked me some. I didn't expect that she would say something like that, and I really didn't know how to respond. I just sat there and thought about what she'd said. She wasn't saying the guy *wasn't* to blame, but she was sort of saying it was to be expected. And that unsettled me.

Raven turned the chair back so she could stare at the lagoon. She looked away from me and across to the stream where the water trickled over the rocks.

"I don't think telling you what happened yesterday will help you in any way, but I can see you won't rest until you hear it. So, here goes."

I watched her closely as she began.

"I finished putting the gas in the car, picked up my purse from the front seat and walked into the office, where I grabbed our two bottles of water. I didn't see the guy to begin with. He was sitting over by the counter, but I guess in all that darkness, he was well hidden. I walked over to the register and put the bottles and my purse on the counter.

"He sat there and smiled at me, looking me up and down and nibbling on a tooth-pick half in his mouth. Then I noticed the bottle of beer by the register and I could tell – and smell – that he was half pissed already. I'm guessing my tank top and skirt didn't help much, but I was nice and civil and told him I wanted to pay for the gas and the drinks. And he asked me *how* I'd like to pay. I said by cash, and he said he could think of a better way. He laughed to himself and I already realised things could get out control if I wasn't careful.

"I smiled at him and told him I couldn't right now, because I was in a hurry and my friend was in the car waiting for me. But I don't think he believed the friend story because he laughed and said he had a friend too. He thought I was making it up. He accused me of lying, but I told him I wasn't. I said I'd go out and get you to prove it, even though I'd already decided I was coming out to get in the car and leave straight away. Fuck paying. I thought that would work, but instead he decided to call my bluff another way.

"As I turned to leave, he grabbed me by the hair and dragged me across the counter. My back hit the counter hard and I yelled out, and I think he thought I was going to scream the place down. So he smashed the beer bottle across my face."

I grimaced. Now she was telling the story, I was finding out way too much. She was right, I *didn't* want to know all the details. My fault for going all Angela Lansbury on her. But I couldn't stop her now. Maybe it was good for her to get it off her chest anyway.

"Next thing I knew, he had his arm around my neck, choking me, telling me, 'I haven't had a pretty young darlin' like you in so long.' Probably never, if you ask me. His arm was all hairy and sweaty, and his breath smelled foul. So I struggled and hit out at him, trying to break away. But he just kept slapping me with his free hand, telling me to be quiet and to keep my voice down. I grabbed his hand at some stage and bit down on it hard. That's when he let me go. I scrambled from the counter and he grabbed at my side, digging in deep and hurting hard. And I screamed again. I kicked out at him and I think I hit him in the chest. I hit him hard and I think I hurt him. He stopped for a second and looked at me. I looked at him too and I said, 'I wouldn't fuck you if you were the last man alive, cocksucker.' And I ran for the door."

There was silence between us.

"And you know the rest," she added.

I nodded.

I looked across at Raven. At the red, puffy wound on her temple. The other wounds were covered by her clothes, but I wished I could see them, to remember what that animal did to her. Right then, I felt sorry for making her relive it all.

"I'm sorry," I replied. "I just –"
"It's okay." She didn't turn to face me. "Now you know."
"Yes, I do."
But I wished I didn't.

We sat for a long time, lost in our thoughts. I felt unclean and sickly. I didn't want to bring this up now. But I knew I had to. I needed to, because it was playing on my mind as well.

"And what about Duke?" I asked.

"What about him?"

"We can't leave him in the wardrobe."

"Yes, we have to," Raven replied.

"*Have to?* Why?"

"Because I can't get him out."

"Huh?" That confused me. It wasn't the answer I expected.

"He's stuck in there."

"Stuck?"

Raven sighed and sat forward in the chair. "Yes, Amber, *stuck*. I tried pulling him out this morning. I wanted to get him out of there while you were asleep so that you didn't have to see him. But he's gone all stiff and hard and I can't get him out."

Oh, fuck.

"So he's *stuck* in there?"

"That's what I said, hon. At least for now."

"For now?"

"Yes, but don't worry. Rigor mortis leaves the body after a while. We just have to wait here until it does."

Perfect.

Just what we needed.

Wonderful.

I was stunned and speechless and really didn't know what to think or do. I put my plate on the ground and stood up, walked in a circle for a moment or two, shaking my head and then I just headed off to the water's edge.

This was unbelievable.

Even dead, Duke was causing us problems.

If we could just get rid of him, we'd be free of all these hassles. But now, he'd wedged himself all stiff in the wardrobe and he was causing even *more* problems.

And the bastard was *dead*!

It's true what they say, men *never* give up.

Fourteen

So that was pretty well how we spent the whole day. We relaxed and sat around, looking at the view.

Raven went inside to lie down and recuperate a couple of times, and I busied myself around the trailer, cleaning the plates and catching more fish for dinner. The water was calm and the day was wonderful. I crossed the stream and picked a few of the wildflowers, bringing them back to the trailer and putting them in a vase on the meals table. The water in the stream was cold, and it ran across the rocks quickly, but it wasn't very deep, so I managed to walk across and back without too much hassle.

It was late afternoon when Raven came back outside after a long nap. She smiled at me and she looked better than she did earlier. She was recovering fast.

I knew the events of yesterday wouldn't keep her down for long, and I was glad because I needed her strength and her guidance. Always did.

Especially in times of trouble.

She was the one I'd turned to when I was worried about my dad becoming more violent towards me, and she was the one who had all the answers. And, of course, that was only natural, because she'd been through it herself. But much worse than I ever had.

"How you feeling?" I asked her. I was sitting in her deck chair, reading my book when she stepped outside and walked across to me.

"Really good now." She smiled and stretched her arms and legs. She was back in her red bathrobe and wore nothing on her feet. The robe wasn't tied at the front, the belt hung by her side, so I could see the middle of her chest and stomach, and everything below it as well. But I didn't think it mattered too much, no one could see us.

"Damn flies," she said. "Woke me up."

"Huh?"

She nodded her head towards the trailer. "The blowflies, they're back."

Shit.

Our drive out to Lake Mountain seemed to have dispersed most of the raging pack of blowflies. But it sure didn't take them long to zero in on their target once more. Within a couple of hours of stopping, they'd found us again.

"We've gotta do something about that," I said, placing my book on the ground.

"I know. But we can't until we're able to pull Duke out of the wardrobe."

"Do you think that will be long?"

Raven shrugged, walking over to the milk crate and sitting on it, her legs apart (I could see everything.) "He's getting there."

"Excuse me?" I didn't know what she meant.

"I checked. He's softening up."

"*Terrific!*" I turned to face the lagoon.

Sometimes you just *don't* want to know all the details.

The sun was beginning to set. Well, of course, it wasn't really, but it was heading behind the rock wall, so the shadows were becoming longer. It was setting, at least, for us.

I didn't want to sleep another night in the trailer with Duke there, but I guess we really didn't have much choice. I was glad there was a wardrobe door between us and him. Not only did it keep the flies out, but I was pretty sure it was keeping the smell down as well. The trailer had taken on a very stuffy, sickly smell since we'd stopped there, and even though I opened the doors and windows, it remained. I was hoping the breeze would also keep down Duke's stink until we managed to get rid of him.

"What do you think is happening out there?" Raven asked me.

"You mean at the trailer park?"

She nodded. "The gas station too."

I could see it was playing on her mind. I had to make sure I reassured her, so I turned to face her. "I've been thinking about that too."

That wasn't a lie. I had been.

"I'm guessing no one's even noticed Duke's missing. I mean, no one at the park got along with him, so I'm sure if he's not around for a few days, they won't mind. It'd only be if something went wrong and they needed the manager and couldn't find him, then they'd start to worry."

"And the two guys in the Ford?"

I nodded. "Yeah, I have no idea about them. But if they *were* cops, all they're going to do is get a warrant and search his trailer and hopefully conclude the bastard has fled."

"They got a pretty good look at us."

"I know."

"The car, the trailer, you and me. Probably took our licence plate number as well."

I couldn't deny it. She was right.

"We should stay here for as long as possible." I wasn't sure if Raven was telling me, or talking to herself, making up her mind.

I agreed. I'd come to that same conclusion too.

Raven leaned forwards, knelt down by the circle of rocks and picked up the box of matches. She built a new pile of leaves and sticks (I'd scrounged them up earlier while she was asleep) and struck a match. Within seconds, the new fire was alight. It was small and weak, but I could feel its heat on my legs already. Raven must've been colder, sitting there only in her robe.

"You saw the guy at the gas station," she continued as she sat back on the milk crate, this time drawing the front of her robe across her, covering everything.

I nodded.

"How bad was he? I mean, you know, how serious were his injuries?"

"He was pretty banged up." I wasn't going to lie. "But I think he'll survive. He was certainly still breathing when I left him."

"Where did you hide him?"

"Just behind the counter. You know, near the cash register."

She nodded. "I went a bit too far," she whispered, almost to herself. "But I couldn't help it."

She was staring into the fire and she seemed a long way away. Events were starting to catch up with her, and maybe she was a little scared. I didn't know how much sleep she'd had in the trailer, but I was guessing not too much. She'd probably laid awake, going over everything in her mind, reliving each and every event, and worrying herself sick about it all.

I climbed from the deck chair and walked over to her. Kneeling in front of her, I put one hand on her shoulder and another on her knee.

"Don't worry about it, Raven. It'll do you no good. Don't think about it, okay?"

Her eyes met mine.

"You did what you had to do to get away from him. His injuries were bad, but nothing more than he deserved. He's probably in hospital now, or out the back of the gas station, hiding somewhere, feeling really sorry for himself and not wanting anyone to know what a complete asshole he's been."

"It's just like before," she said. "I had to act. Otherwise it would've been like it was with dad and the others."

I nodded. I understood.

But I didn't want her going there.

The last time she'd been this low, this down, was over a year ago. I'd found her sitting at the meals table in the trailer, carving knife in her hand, using it to dig out huge strips of flesh along the inside of her arms.

Don't get me wrong, she wasn't trying to slash her wrists, commit suicide or anything, she was just sitting there, cutting herself, hurting herself, feeling the pain.

Almost as if she thought she *deserved* to go through something like that.

Most of the time, Raven is incredibly positive and inspiring to be around, but every-so-often she crashes and burns harder than anyone I know. And it's usually because images or memories of her past come out of nowhere to haunt her.

I'd been shocked and scared when I saw her sitting there, carving into her own skin with a look of grim determination on her face. At first I didn't know what to do. I'd quickly taken the knife from her and tried to shake her back to reality. I couldn't do it though, she just stared right through me, and it wasn't until I'd bandaged up the bleeding cuts and given her some bourbon that she'd come slamming back home to me. In a second, she was out of the self-imposed exile inside her memories, and she looked at me as if she had no idea what had happened.

And I had a very real fear she was heading that way again.

"Raven," I said, staring straight at her. "*Stay with me.*"

I knew I had problems with my father, but really, they were nothing compared to Raven's problems. After that night when I found her cutting herself, once she came back into the real world, she'd finally broken down and cried and told me the whole story. It was only then that I understood the real Raven, the way she was and the way she thought about things.

Her earliest memories, those that she could remember, were of her father punching her mother in the stomach, or slapping her in the face. And I want to make it clear, it wasn't like Raven was hiding watching all this take place, her father made sure she was in the room and watching every second of it. Trying to teach *her* a lesson at the same time he was teaching her mother.

One clear memory was when her father arrived home late one night, later than expected, and his dinner was cold. Raven's mother was putting her to bed when her father stormed in and demanded to know why dinner was cold. It wasn't good enough that *he* was late or that *he* was the cause of the dinner being ruined. Her mother had tried to explain this all to him, but he'd dragged her kicking and screaming out of Raven's room, and Raven sat in bed, clutching at her covers, trying to hide, as her father punched and slapped and beat (and more) her mother in their bedroom next to hers.

After what seemed like an eternity, her father marched into her bedroom and pointed a bloody finger at her.

"You better not grow up to be as useless as your mother," he screamed, before slamming her door and leaving the house for days.

I remember Raven telling me that the best days of her childhood were when her father was away from the house. He was some sort of salesman and that meant he could be gone for days, and sometimes weeks, at a time. It was during those periods that she and her mother had a wonderful time.

Money was always tight, and Raven could never work out why. Her father worked long hours, was never home, but still her mother would have to find work to pay the bills and to put food on the table. It was never good employment, just odd, casual jobs that she struggled to keep. So, a lot of the time, Raven was left alone to play in the backyard or in her bedroom.

After a while, when her father's business trips became longer and longer, her mother would have other friends around. Male friends. But Raven wasn't allowed to tell her father about them. At first, Raven had been scared of them. They were men and that meant they could hurt her and her mother. But the sounds Raven heard coming from her parent's bedroom night after night on these occasions were totally different. Her mother didn't scream, she didn't yell. They were quiet, soft, loving sounds.

A couple of times, Raven snuck into the bedroom to see what was happening. Of course, back then she didn't understand. It looked violent, it looked like what her father did to her mother, but her mother wasn't screaming while her friends were on top of her. Sometimes, even her mother got on top, to ride, like she was riding a horse.

As she grew older, it just became the norm. Mom's friends would drop by and mum would go to play with them. Raven didn't mind, because mum was no longer crying and no longer bruised or bloody.

Then the news came that Raven was to have a little brother or sister. She couldn't understand why, because her father had always said she was enough trouble as it was. She remembered it being very weird, because her mother looked all nervous and worried and didn't want to tell her father. But when she did, her father was overjoyed, and Raven could remember him being happier than ever.

Nine months later, Raven's sister was born.

And family life improved.

But only for a while.

Now you and I both know *exactly* what's going on here, okay? No Mensa memberships needed for this one, right? Good. I think it took a long time, probably until Raven was in her teens, before she put it all together. But I guess that's to be expected. You don't question what's normal, and it's only once you go out into the big world and find out that the lives your parents are living *aren't* normal, that the light goes on and you realise something is very *very* wrong indeed.

Raven's sister, Paige, is a whole other story, and I don't think I want to write about her yet. So I'll skip her for now. I know I'll have to fill you in on her at some stage, but not right now, alright?

Anyway, family life soon deteriorated again, and Raven's father left on countless more trips. Her mother could no longer hold down even the smallest job, as she had to look after two young girls, and even with Raven in school, her mother didn't seem to be able to cope.

And then Mr Mac died. He was the only pet Raven ever had. He was a small, lovely little budgie whose trill would wake her up every morning. Until, of course, that morning when she found him dead. At first she thought he was sleeping, but birds don't sleep like that usually. She was devastated, and her mother helped place him in a little box and they buried him in the backyard. But the sight of the empty cage hanging in her room was too much for Raven, so two days later, she dug up the grave and retrieved Mr Mac, wiring him back onto his perch in the cage.

It didn't take too long for her mother to find him, yell at her for being so sick, and remove both the bird *and* cage from her room, this time for good. Raven never found out what happened to Mr Mac after that.

When Raven was twelve, one of her mother's friends was suddenly very interested in her. He bought her the best presents, played with her in the backyard, and gave her countless rides on his knee. For the first time, she was the centre of attention and she loved every second of it. He'd buy her ice creams, take her for walks, wrestle with her, even take her to the beach during summer.

And it was on one of those long drives back from the beach that, one day, he forced himself onto her. He said he was stopping to buy some drinks, but there was no shop nearby and the next thing she knew, he was pushing her down on the back seat and pulling down her bikini.

Raven didn't know what to do, but she knew what her mother would do. So she didn't fight back, she didn't yell or scream, because she didn't want him to hurt or beat her. And soon, they would play this little "game" (as he called it) on every trip back from the beach. And then, in the backyard, and even in her bedroom when her mother wasn't around.

He told Raven to keep their game a secret, and she did for a long time. It was a couple of years later before she finally broke down and told her mother. But her mother didn't seem surprised or to even care. She told her that was the hand life had dealt her, and that she should be grateful a man took such an interest in her.

Hello? Talk about time-warp to the dark ages! *Sheesh!*

Her *mother* said that!

"Feeling useless and need someone to bash some sense into you? Then call 555-MENRULE and we'll send a prime Missing Link right to your door!"

It was much *much* later, when Raven started to fight back, that she discovered the guy was paying her mother for the privilege of *raping* her.

You still there, dear reader? Read that sentence above again.

Yep, you got it. Her mother was *selling* her to this guy. Making money off her so she could live without having to work.

So, as you can imagine, Raven wanted *nothing* to do with her mother after that. And she certainly didn't want anything to do with her father. She left home, and never went back. She'd meet her sister every-so-often, trying to convince her to leave as well, to come and stay with her, but she was five years younger than Raven and was just too scared to leave.

"What would mum and dad do to me?" she'd ask.

That was *exactly* what Raven was worried about.

But in the end, it wasn't mum and dad Paige really needed to be worried about.

But, like I said, that's a whole other story.

And that's why I think it was easy for Raven to live the life she did, and to be a stripper. She didn't see sex as being linked to love. I think she saw it as a chore. A necessity. Something that has to be done to keep the species alive. And so while I sit here and *know* I'd never be a stripper, that I'd never show *my* most intimate places in public, I'd show them only to the one I loved and wanted to be with, I think Raven saw it as a means to an end, a way to make money (just like her mother, but I'd never tell her I said that!)

And I'm pretty sure that's why there weren't many boyfriends (if any). That's why sometimes she could seem so cold, so aloof. Sex and love. Total separation for her. Which is weird, because for me, they're entwined so deeply.

We sat, both looking at the fire for quite a while. I rested my head on Raven's shoulder, and she leaned her head to the side, resting the side of her face on the top of my head.

"Thank you," she whispered, eventually.

"What for?"

"Everything."

"Huh?" I turned to face her.

"The last couple of days." She smiled at me, but it broke halfway into sadness. "I'm glad you were here with me."

"It's okay." I ran my hand through her curls. "You know I'm *always* here for you."

She nodded.

"No matter what," I added. "Through the good times and the bad."

She smiled again then. "And these times are bad," she whispered.

"They'll get better."

"I hope so."

"I know they will."

She looked so deeply into my eyes. Her deep brown pools staring right into my very soul. She'd never looked at me that way before.

All around us, the world stopped. It disappeared. It was just Raven and me. I was still kneeling beside her. My hand rested on her shoulder, entwined in her hair. I could feel her breath on my face. She was breathing fast. The light from the fire danced across her features, throwing shadows and light across her, making her expression hard to read. There was no way I could work out what she was thinking.

All I knew was she and I were together in this, together against the world. We'd do anything for each other, no matter what, until the end.

I leaned forward, closer towards her.

She leaned in towards me.

Gunshots blasted the silence.

Fifteen

We hit the ground hard.

It was instinct.

Even though we were relaxed and enjoying each other's company, a little part of us was still switched on alert and primed for panic mode.

I remember Raven reaching out, taking me in her arms and pushing me backwards hard and fast.

The ground slammed into my back and my head hit hard, jarring me for a couple of seconds.

Raven was on top of me, her robe spread over us, her eyes darting all around the lagoon, taking in every corner.

"Did you hear where that came from?" she whispered.

"Not really," I said. "It sounded like from directly behind me."

She nodded. "That's what I thought too. But *where* exactly?"

The shots had been short, sharp and loud. Two of them. They broke the silence and echoed around the lagoon. Birds fluttered overhead, disturbed, singing a song of complaint. From where I was on the ground under Raven, I could stretch my neck and see the rock wall. I searched along it with my eyes, trying to see anyone up there, maybe holding a rifle and training its sights on us. But there was no movement, and the silence soon returned.

We stayed sprawled on the ground for a few minutes, Raven's body pressing against mine. I could feel her ribs digging into my stomach, and her hips resting on my thighs, but I didn't ask her to climb from me. She was protecting me and that made me feel safe, even though we were out in the middle of the clearing, easy targets for anyone who wanted us.

"What do you think?" She stopped looking around the lagoon after a while and looked down at me.

"A hunter?"

"Possibly, but hunting for what?"

"I don't know. Whatever it is hunters hunt."

"As long as it's not Raven." She smirked.

I smiled back.

I think we both realised that if there was a gunman aiming to take us down, he would've already done it by now. Plus, when I thought about it, I didn't remember hearing a bullet whiz past my ear or ricochet off the trailer or car or anything like that.

We were out in a forest, on the side of a mountain.

There was probably a hunting lodge nearby.

There was nothing to panic about.

Still, we took our time getting to our feet. Slowly, we turned a full three-sixty degrees and checked every point of the clearing and lagoon again.

No sign of anyone.

Nothing.

"I think we should eat inside tonight," Raven said.

I agreed.

So we doused the fire and took the fish inside.

The incessant sound of the blowflies drove us crazy, and the knowledge that Duke was in the wardrobe still, slowly smelling up the place, made me feel uneasy. But I think we both felt safer inside the trailer that night. Just in case.

We even used some of the propane to cook the fish. Sure, it probably wasn't an emergency situation, but we were both a little nervous and on edge. Better to be safe than sorry.

And in the end, it was a good idea.

We'd just finished eating the fish when we heard the second round of gunfire.

It didn't catch us as much by surprise this time. We both stopped what we were doing and stared at each other, listening.

Raven moved to the door and opened it. We both looked out.

Over past the lagoon, we could see some birds flying off in the distance. The rifle shots still echoed in the air.

It had been loud, but not that loud.

"Whoever it is," Raven said. "They're not very close to us."

And she was right. The shots had come from a long way away. We'd got used to the silence, probably, and that was what made them sound so loud.

"Well, at least we know he's not hunting us," I said.

Raven nodded. "Let's hope not."

She smiled, but I could tell it was fake.

And then I got to worrying too.

We knew people would be nearby. I mean, after all, this is a public forest on a very popular mountain and everything, but I guess we just got used to our own little piece of paradise and didn't really expect to be disturbed.

Or *want* to be disturbed.

Not that we had been, really. But I just hoped no one would come in to crash our little party, our new life.

Things were just so nice here.

So right.

I'm not religious, never really have been, but that didn't stop me sending up a little prayer right then and there. If there was a God out there somewhere, I was hoping he'd hear my plea.

Please, God, I remember thinking to myself. Don't let anything ruin this, or put an end to the time Raven and I are spending together!

God, it seems, was out of the office.

Friday, July 12.

Sixteen

On Friday, we heard the gunshots again.
I guess, slowly, we got used to it. We learned to live with the idea that there *were* other people out there, whether we liked it or not. But we also came to realise that they weren't gunning for us, either.

So that helped plenty.

The shots seemed to come from all around us. At different places and at different times. I started to think maybe there was more than one hunter. Maybe two? Three?

But we both knew that it wasn't the cops. They weren't in the habit of shooting up wildlife while they were closing in on wanted criminals.

If we *were* wanted criminals. We really had no idea right then if anyone was searching for us, or if Duke had even been reported missing.

For a change, I woke up that morning to find Raven still asleep next to me. That was good, as it gave me the opportunity to check her wounds, without her trying to stop me.

I carefully dragged the sheet from her shoulders and pushed it down around her thighs.

She was still bruised in some places, but many seemed to be a lighter colour now. The bandaid was still across her right nipple, and the wounds to her left breast and forehead were scabbing over and healing nicely. She healed quick, this girl. Her thighs looked pretty good now too. Everything down there looked just fine.

I smiled.

My Raven was coming back.

"I'm getting cold, you know," she said to me.

My eyes darted back to her face, and I saw she was squinting through one eye. She was smiling too.

"Sorry," I said.

"You trying to give me pneumonia as well?"

"No, no," I replied, grabbing the sheet and pulling it back over her body. "I was just checking you out."

"A-huh," she replied in a slow voice.

"Your *wounds*, I mean. I was checking out your *wounds*."

"Sure you were." She smirked.

"I *was*!"

"Oh, I believe you."

I didn't know whether she did or not.

She grabbed the sheet and let out a low chuckle before rolling over onto her side, her back facing me.

"Sorry," I muttered.

"Don't be sorry," she replied.

But she made me feel like I *should* be sorry.

I sat there staring at her back for a while. I counted the bumps in her skin, where her spine ran along and stuck out. I could clearly see the outline of her ribs too. She had a bruise low down on her back. I hadn't seen that before, and then I remember the guy at the gas station punching her hard there.

Bastard. He didn't have to do any of that.

We didn't speak.

I sat listening to the never-ending buzz of the flies. Although, they didn't seem as loud this morning. Maybe I was finally getting used to them, or they were getting sick of Duke too.

I really couldn't blame them, Duke was that kinda guy.

It was then that we heard the gunshots for the first time that day.

"They're out early," Raven said without rolling over.

"Yeah," I replied. The shots sounded a long way away though. "How many animals do they need to shoot anyway?"

"Probably as many as possible."

Which was weird, because we were staying at the lagoon, and I thought that if the forest was filled with animals, we would've spotted one or two drinking from the lagoon. The water seemed perfect, clean and drinkable, no industrial sludge or bubbles anywhere, just fresh mountain water. But we hadn't seen anything other than birds so far.

So, what *were* they hunting?

Raven stretched out in the bed. She rolled onto her back and moaned in pleasure. She stretched long and hard, her legs knocking mine, her right hip rubbing against my thigh. The sheet slipped down below her nipples.

"We probably should take that bandaid off and look at the damage," I said, pointing at her nipple.

"No hurry," she yawned.

"We really *should* check it."

"I know, I know. I was thinking about taking a swim in the lagoon this morning," she said. "I'll take it off then."

"Are you serious?" I sat up in the bed and stared at her.

"What?" she seemed surprised.

"Swimming in the lagoon?"

"Well, hon, I love your company, and I'm glad you're here, but we're both going to have to bathe sometime. The water out there is fresh and clean – if a little cold – so we might as well use it."

"But what about the hunters?"

"The hunters are probably one old guy and his teenage son shooting cans from a tree stump for a bit of fun. They're not here, they're not even close. And they're certainly not about to stop me taking a swim in that lagoon!"

I guess I over-reacted a bit. It certainly wasn't the most pleasant way for us both to wake up. The conversation had put us both on edge, and I didn't help matters by taking it further.

"And what about Duke?" I asked.

"Sweets, he's not going to see me swimming," she replied.

"I *know* that! I meant about getting him out of the wardrobe."

"Yes, yes. Later."

"How later?"

"Why, Amber?"

"*Why?* Because I want him out of here! I want him out of the trailer and gone from our lives. I want things to be as they were, like they were last week, and the week before that, and the month before that. I want things back to normal."

"I don't think we'll *ever* get back to normal," Raven sighed.

"You *know* what I mean."

"We'll get to it. We'll take care of him."

"I want him gone, Raven."

We stared at each other for a long time. The silence was heavy between us.

"Maybe," she smirked.

"Huh?"

"I said, maybe."

"What do you mean?"

She propped herself up on her right arm, her head resting on her hand. "I mean *maybe* we'll get rid of him, and *maybe* we won't."

"You're not serious!"

She nodded. "We should keep him around a while longer."

"Why?"

"He could be fun."

"*Fun?*"

"You don't get a lot of choice in life. You just have to take what comes along."

"Are you crazy?"

Raven lifted herself up into a kneeling position, the sheet falling from her, the small line of pubic hair disappearing down between her legs. She took my hands in hers and stared at me, an excited look on her face.

"Think about it, Amber," she said quickly. "He's no longer in control. He's dead. He can't do a damn thing to hurt us anymore. He can't use us or try to control us. *Now*, the tables are turned. *We* control *him*. We can *use* him."

"For what?"

"For anything we want!"

I sat and just stared at her. I was speechless. I wanted to run or scream or shout or something, but I just sat there.

"Think about it," she said. "Once you get used to the idea, it won't seem so strange."

And with that, she leaned forward and kissed my cheek. Then she let my hands go and climbed from the bed.

I sat where I was, staring at the sheet and trying to get my mind under control.

Use him.

We control him.

What the fuck did she mean?

I'm not the sharpest pencil in the drawer at the best of times, but even I knew that whatever it was she was suggesting was crazy talk.

"I want him around, Amber. We're going to keep him around for now," she added.

The slamming trailer door brought me back to reality and I turned to look for Raven.

The trailer was empty. I was alone.

Except for Duke.

I glanced quickly at the wardrobe door as I climbed from the bed and put on my robe. As I walked towards the door, I saw Raven's robe still folded nicely on the meals table.

She'd gone out there *naked!*

I opened the door and looked outside just in time to see her wading into the water. When it reached the top of her thighs, she lifted her arms above her head and dived straight down. She disappeared from sight in a flash, her back rising, then her arse and legs, and then she was gone, swallowed by the lagoon. But I could see where she was swimming due to the wake in the water. I could follow her without seeing her. After about twenty seconds her head and shoulders broke through the surface of the water. It cascaded down her back and I watched as she lifted her hands and ran them through her dark, wet curls.

She spun around, wiping the water from her eyes, the sunlight glistening off her face and breasts.

"Come on in, Amber!" she called to me.

I wanted her to keep quiet. Not to yell.

"It's lovely in here!"

I turned around quickly and shut the trailer door.

"*Chicken!*" I heard her call.

I sat down at the meals table and played with the belt of my robe. My eyes focussed on the wardrobe door.

It's all your fault, Duke. You fucking lowlife.

And it was then that I made up my mind.
If Raven wouldn't do it, I would.
I'd get rid of Duke.
Now.

Seventeen

It was the best chance I had. While Raven was swimming in the lagoon, I could pull Duke out of the wardrobe and get him out of the trailer for good.

Just one problem.

That meant I had to *open* the wardrobe door.

I actually had to *see* Duke.

And so I sat there a while longer, staring at the wardrobe door and thinking about what I had to do. I guess half of me hoped Raven would walk in the trailer, putting an end to the opportunity of getting him out. The other half just dearly wanted to be rid of him forever.

I didn't really give much thought to what I'd do with him once I got him out of the wardrobe, I just wanted him out of the trailer. Out of my home. I was pretty sure once Raven saw what I was doing, she'd take over and work out what to do. But it was obvious that I was the one who had to start it all.

Okay, I thought to myself. Here goes.

I stood and walked towards the wardrobe. Then, I stopped in my tracks, turned, and detoured to the bed to put on some clothes.

Yes, I was probably procrastinating big time. It's not every day you have to do something like this. So, I climbed into an old Sublime t-shirt, my oldest pair of jeans (the ones with the holes torn across the knees) and my sneakers. If things got messy, at least I wasn't wearing my good clothes.

I sat at the edge of the bed and put my hands on my knees. I fiddled with the frayed ends of the holes cut into my jeans, twisting them around my fingers over and over again. My eyes stared at the latch on the wardrobe door.

Walk over. Reach out. Open it.

Simple. Just do it.

And then I saw it fall.

Just out of the corner of my eye.

It was so quick, I wasn't sure I'd seen it. I had to lean forward and stare at the linoleum floor.

I spotted it in a few seconds, wriggling around down there. Its creamy white colour almost camouflaging it against the floor.

A maggot.

I breathed in quickly and gulped down a lungful of air.

I guess I shouldn't really have been shocked. But I was. I hadn't considered this. I just expected that Duke would be cold, still a bit stiff and probably quite smelly, but I really hadn't thought at any stage about exactly *what* the blowflies were doing in that wardrobe for all this time.

Laying their little maggoty eggs never entered my mind.

Somehow, the maggot had fallen out of the wardrobe, through a small gap between the wardrobe door and inside.

It spasmed around, both its ends reaching up high, trying to find something to cling onto.

I didn't feel so well all of a sudden.

And then another maggot fell to the floor, right next to the first one.

My eyes darted from the floor to the latch on the wardrobe door, and then across to the trailer door. I wished Raven would appear, that she would come inside and take charge. But the door stayed shut and Raven didn't come to help.

I could feel the sweat break out on my forehead.

You gotta do this. And do it now!

I can't!

You have to!

I swallowed a couple of times. My throat had suddenly gone real dry and kinda furry.

Standing slowly, I took the few steps to the wardrobe, my hand out, reaching for the latch.

My eyes stayed on the maggots on the floor. They were about two inches apart from each other, both no wider than a nickel and searching desperately for (probably) where they'd been. I could see little dark specs through their skin (if that's what it's called) and the specs were moving around quickly. I had no idea what they were (eyes? Couldn't be!) but I watched them nonetheless. I knew they couldn't jump up or attack me or anything, but just the sight of them made me feel very uneasy.

My hand clasped around the latch. It felt cold in the morning air. The metal sent a chill down my fingers and arm.

I stood there for a few seconds, my eyes darting from the maggots to the latch to the maggots and back again.

I had one last chance to leave him where he was. A couple of seconds remaining to let go of the latch and turn around and walk out of the trailer.

Turn my back on it all.

I could go and join Raven, climb out of my clothes and dive into the lagoon, into that nice cool, clean water, and be out there with her, in the water, just the two of us, close and wet and together.

I considered it.

I almost did it.

Instead, I pushed down on the latch and heard it click.

The wardrobe door was unlocked.

I took a deep breath.

And opened the door a fraction.

The sound of flies grew louder and a smell like rancid wet animal fur and putrid eggs hit me in the face, making me want to gag. But I didn't let go, I didn't stop. I opened the door a little bit further.

And a pile of maggots fell to the floor with a *splat*.

They hit the floor hard, some of them bouncing up and landing on my jeans and sneakers.

I took a step backwards, letting out a little yelp of fright. I stepped away from the writhing pile of them and tried not to step on many. But they were already crawling behind me and I heard a few pop and crunch underneath my sneakers as I did so.

I bent down, quickly brushing off the few that had attached themselves to me. They wriggled and crawled on my sneakers and jeans and some wouldn't come off without a real good flick. I didn't want to touch the horrible things, but

I didn't have much choice right now. I got them off me in a few seconds, but it felt like a lot longer.

That's when I straightened up again.

And saw the wardrobe door was wide open.

And saw Duke sitting in there.

I wanted to scream and be sick at the same time. But I didn't do either. I just stared.

First of all, I thought Duke was moving. But he wasn't. What *was* moving was the huge mass of maggots that covered his face. I couldn't really see a lot of Duke, but I could make out his hairline and the clothes he was wearing (a checkered shirt and tattered old jeans, Duke's favourites) clearly identified him as the guy who managed the Pine Hills Trailer Park.

Opening the door had disturbed the balanced little climate inside, that was for sure. The blowflies were in the trailer now, flying around my head and landing on me.

Landing on me!

They'd touched Duke, and now they were *touching me*!

Large masses of the maggots broiled and writhed around Duke's nose, mouth, eyes and ears, and every so often vast waves of them would fall backwards, spilling out of the holes and falling down onto his chest. Then, slowly, they'd make the arduous climb back up towards his face.

I was sure I could see movement underneath his clothes as well, and I wondered if there were maggots under there, eating him away from inside. But I didn't want to find out for sure.

I guess I stood there stunned for a while. A long while. But then it must've all hit home. There were too many maggots, too many flies, the smell of Duke was oppressive and sickening. I felt as if the air in the cabin was being sucked away. That soon I would choke on the stench of death and maggots and rotting corpse.

I didn't feel well, but I didn't want to walk over to the sink. I'd have to walk past (no, no, *through*) a sea of maggots to get there, and I didn't want to do that.

Another wriggling pile fell to the floor of the trailer with a loud wet *slap*.

This group had fallen from the side of his face, where they were eating through his cheek from inside, their sharp little mouths chewing ferociously away. A surge of maggots from within the mouth must've pushed this front group out over the edge, and they swirled down his face, pulling more maggots with them, as they fell down onto the floor. This left a gap on Duke's face and shoulder for a few seconds, totally maggot free, and that was the first time I saw the thick, white rope.

It was still there.

Digging into his neck.

The rope Raven had used to strangle him.

She hadn't even bothered to remove it from around his neck.

The rope wasn't as white as I remembered it. It was grey now, and stained with some fluids I really didn't want to think about. Duke's skin was flaccid and had sagged over the edges of the rope, so I guessed there was no real way to undo it anymore – not without some force, anyway. It had become part of him. And I certainly wasn't going in there, putting my hands into the mass of maggots, to remove it!

I swatted at the flies as they landed on me. The maggots on the floor were branching out, some heading back towards the wardrobe, some making the trek across the floor heading in my direction. The ones I'd stepped on earlier were soggy, wet, flattened pulps of clear nothing now.

I knew the ones heading towards me couldn't see me and probably didn't even know I was there, but that didn't stop me from thinking in those few moments that they were after me.

I turned around and opened the windows above the bed. I had to get rid of the smell, I had to let some fresh air in. But it didn't seem to be working.

I wanted to run to the door, to open it and get out of there, but I didn't want to have to walk over the maggots to do it.

I *know* they're small and harmless compared to me. But, damn it, they're *maggots*! Duke's maggots!

I looked down at them; they were getting closer.

I noticed one halfway up my right leg, almost to the hole in my jeans. I jumped in fright and swatted it away. I must've missed it earlier. It couldn't've got there so fast unless it had been there all that time.

Right?

I looked back into the wardrobe. The maggots swirled across Duke's face. He was, I guess, sitting in the wardrobe, his back and head leaned against one wall, and his feet jammed in hard against the other. It was a cramped area, his legs were bent in the middle and his knees were just a few inches away from his face. Well, what was *once* his face.

That *face* was turned towards the door, looking out at me. I say "looking" but he wasn't doing that anymore. The maggots had taken up residency in his eye sockets and there was very little left of his soft gooey eyeballs. Although, of course, I didn't look too close. I didn't want to get *that* close. So I'm not sure if the white I saw was really eyeball, or whether it was just more of the maggots churning around in there.

His nose looked larger than usual, but I realised that was probably because the maggots were using it as an express freeway to his brain. They'd fall out of his nostrils just as quickly as others would force their way up inside. His mouth was hanging open and wide, and the maggots spilled from there constantly, making it look like he was foaming at the mouth with them. His jaw was hanging lower than you'd expect, but that was because they'd eaten through the sides of his cheeks and, I'm guessing, the muscles and ligaments and stuff that held the jaw tight.

In short, there wasn't much left of Duke to prove it *was* Duke.

But before you go thinking that it *wasn't* Duke and that Raven had killed someone else and done the old *switcherooney*, don't worry, I'm here to set you straight.

It was Duke.

End of story.

Well, end of *his* story anyway.

Actually, the maggots were a vast improvement!

Okay, okay, enough of the sick jokes. Just trying to lighten the mood. I'm sitting here still feeling sick! It was six months ago now, but his face is still burnt into my memory.

At least I've stopped dreaming about him and the maggots now. Those nightmares used to terrify me.

I'd be back in the trailer and Duke was still there. The wardrobe door would be open and I'd walk towards him, wanting to shut the door. But something would happen. I'd trip or I'd slip in the maggots that were under my feet or something, and I'd fall forwards, unable to stop myself, and I'd end up head-first in Duke's lap. My mouth would touch something that felt like oily skin and I'd look down and see his erect cock pointing up at me, its red head throbbing. I'd feel a hand holding down my head, forcing me down further, pushing me closer towards his cock.

"Suck me, I'm going to cum." I'd hear Duke whisper in my ear. "Suck me now."

And then maggots would spurt out of his cock, showering my face, covering me in hot sticky wetness.

I'd wake up screaming.

On other occasions, I'd fall backwards into his lap, and Duke's head would jerk forwards, the maggots spewing from his mouth, all over my face.

Damn it, those dreams *still* scare the shit out of me.

But they were dreams, and something I'd have to deal with much later.

Right now, I'd unleashed chaos in the trailer and I had no idea how to fix it.

The flies were all buzzing around still, although they were the least of my problems. There didn't seem to be that many anymore, and I'm guessing the vast majority had done their job anyway. They'd created the *real* problem.

The maggots.

Some were getting closer. I took another step backwards and the back of my legs hit the bed.

I was cornered.

I was running out of room.

Eighteen

I had to do it.

I *had to!*

"*RAVEN!*" I shouted at the top of my voice.

No answer.

"*Raaaaveeeen! Quickly! Come here!*"

I couldn't hear any noises from outside, the blowflies in the trailer made that impossible. I had no idea if Raven could hear me or not. I climbed onto the bed and knelt by one of the windows.

"Raven, help me! Duke's out of the wardrobe!"

Of course, not technically correct, but good enough. I mean, *parts* of Duke were out of the wardrobe. His maggoty parts...

I looked out the window, trying to see Raven, but the small windows at this end of the trailer didn't really give me a full view outside. I could see the stream across the clearing, and the wildflowers on the hillock, dancing from left to right in the breeze. They looked so beautiful. So free.

But I couldn't see Raven anywhere.

If only I could see the lagoon!

I didn't want to shout again. But I knew I had to.

What if she was underwater when I shouted before? What if she didn't hear me? Or, *oh please no,* what if she's gone for a walk up those stairs again?

I told myself not to panic. Raven hadn't taken any clothes out there with her. She was pretty daring, that's for sure, but there was no way she was about to trek half-way up the rock wall without a stitch of clothing on.

"*Raaaaaveeeeeen!*"

"What the hell happened here?"

I swung my head to the right. She was inside the trailer, standing by the meals table. The buzzing of the blowflies was so loud that I hadn't heard her enter.

She had her hands on her hips and she was staring at the wardrobe, at Duke, then at me and then at the maggots on the floor.

She was wet and glistening. The water dripped from her body and hair. Her curls were longer and straighter, much darker too, and they rested on her shoulders and stuck to her chest, hiding her left breast, but not her right.

She looked great. This is what she must've looked like when she was oiled and dancing against one of those poles on stage at Rawhide.

No wonder the guys loved her.

"Huh?" she asked.

"It's Duke," I said, climbing off the bed to face her.

"I can *see* that," she replied. "Duke and a whole lot of his friends."

I nodded. "We need to get him out of there."

"You *think*?"

Raven's tone was heavily sarcastic. She was pissed at me, I could tell.

"Or we could just shut the wardrobe door," she replied.

"You're not serious?"

"Why not? If *you* hadn't opened the door, we wouldn't have this problem, now would we?"

"Raven, I'm *not* having *him* in this trailer a moment longer!" I jabbed a pointed finger at Duke when I said "him".

She turned her head to look at Duke, or what was left of him.

"It's sick and disgusting and I just can't take it anymore," I replied. "Not to mention, for us, for our health, it can't be good for us to be so close to him like this, breathing in whatever it is we breathe in here every day and night."

Raven kept staring at Duke, and slowly her hands slipped from her hips. She nodded eventually.

"You're right," she said as she sighed. "He's not much use like this anyway."

"Exactly," I replied, although I had no idea what she meant.

"We'll move him."

"Really?" I wanted to make sure she wasn't joking.

She turned to face me and she smiled. "Yes, Amber, we'll move him. We'll do what you want."

Somehow, the smile didn't look right.

"Good," I replied. "Thank you."

"You'll have to help me, though," she added.

I'd figured out that much, but I was still worried about it.

"I know," I muttered.

"It'll take both of us to do this."

I nodded.

"I need the help of a strong, resourceful woman, Amber. Not some scared little school girl, you understand?"

I sure did. That was an insult, but I guess Raven was mad at me for opening the door and having Duke spill out everywhere. So, she'd hit home hard. It hurt. But I took it.

"I'll help," I replied as I climbed from the bed and stood at the opposite end of the trailer, Duke sitting in the wardrobe between us. "I'll do whatever it is you want me to do."

Raven nodded slowly. "Good."

She turned and walked back to the trailer door.

"First of all, grab a spare bed sheet and put it on the floor."

I didn't understand at first, but I wasn't about to question her. I said I'd help and I would. I reached above the bed and opened the cupboard that held our linen and I pulled out a blue sheet.

Raven disappeared outside the trailer for a moment or two. The door didn't close, so I realised she was tying the door open, so it wouldn't shut. That would hopefully help with both the smell and the blowflies.

I held onto the sheet and waited for her to return.

She took longer than I expected, and so while I waited, I glanced over at Duke once more. He hadn't moved much. But there did seem to be more maggots crawling over him now, almost as if opening the wardrobe door had given them new life. They washed over his face in waves, almost as if they were one entity, not just thousands of horrible little scavengers.

Raven returned a short while later, and behind her she was dragging her canvass elephant sack.

"What's that for?" I asked.

"What do you think?" she replied, as she let it crumple to the floor. "It's for Duke."

"Huh?"

"We're going to put him in the sack."

I went to say something, but I stopped myself. I said I'd help her, and that's what I would do. All this mess spilling onto the floor was because of me, and I knew if I asked too many questions she'd leave me to clean it all up myself.

Personally, I thought we were going to put the bed sheet on the floor and wrap him in it to stop the maggots from spilling out and then we'd dump him somewhere. Sure, I know it wasn't much of a plan and I hadn't thought much of it through, but that was all I'd quickly come up with. It wasn't like I'd had time to sit down and work it all out or anything.

But I was wrong.

We were going to use Raven's canvass elephant sack which, up until now, had only been used for her fishing stuff.

Okay, it's called an "elephant sack" for a reason. No, it doesn't have elephants printed on it. In fact, it's deep green in colour and I guessed was used by some army somewhere in the world. All I knew was Raven had bought it at an army disposal store a while back so it would fit her fishing rods easily because those rods were always getting in the way.

Anyway, it's an elephant sack because of its size. You couldn't fit an actual *elephant* in there, but I'm guessing it's the biggest bag of its type, hence its name. I know that whenever I lifted it up by the cord that kept its mouth tied, the bag would stretch out and I'd have to hold it higher than my waist for it to stop touching the ground. So, what are we talking about here? It's maybe three foot or three and a half feet long and big and bulky inside!

Plenty of room.

Plenty of storage space.

Not only for fishing rods and stuff.

But also for Duke.

And that was Raven's plan.

She gave the orders, and I followed them through.

After dropping the bag by her side, she turned and bent down by the kitchen cupboards, opening the long, thin one that housed the broom. She connected the broom's handle and quickly swept the mass of maggots that were writhing on the floor back towards the wardrobe. They rolled and squished and sort of looked like buttered popcorn.

I don't think I'll ever think of buttered popcorn the same way again...

"Spread the sheet out on the floor," she said.

I did as I was told, opening the sheet, bending down and quickly spreading it on the floor, making sure I kept it away from the pile of maggots. But then Raven swept the maggots onto the sheet, their little bodies rolling easily back again, under the guidance of the broom.

Water dripped down and stained the sheet a darker shade of blue and, for a second, I thought that Raven was sweating or crying or something.

I looked up from where I was crouched, by the side of the bed, holding the sheet down, but Raven only had a look of determination on her face.

It was then I noticed the water dripping from her hair. She was still naked, and still wet from her dip in the lagoon. I had a chance then to also see that the bandaid on her right nipple was gone.

She'd taken it off in the water, just as she said she would.

The nipple still looked red and sore, but it was healing nicely, from what I could tell. The barbell sat at a slight angle, and I wondered if Raven had moved it there, or whether it was caught up in the scab and the healing.

She walked a bit closer towards me, still using the broom to sweep all the maggots onto the sheet. I held the sheet firm, but my eyes didn't move from her body.

The bruising was subsiding, which was good, and her other breast looked pretty good as well. I dropped my eyes down further. The water glistened off that small strip of pubic hair, small droplets hanging on the inside of her curls. I watched one drop from a hair and slowly wander down further, towards her vagina, down in between those shaved lips.

She was very close to me then, sweeping up the last of the remaining maggots onto the sheet.

Her vagina was right in front of my eyes. I don't know if I'd ever been so close to her like this. She was above me, towering over me. I could feel her warmth. My eyesight was filled with her most secret and private area of her body. Directly in front of me, those smooth mounds folding into her cleft.

I watched another drop of water slowly make its way downwards, slipping inside her.

But then she turned away from me, threw the broom onto the couch and walked back to the canvass sack.

The moment was gone.

But I still remember it.

"We're going to roll him out onto the sheet," Raven was saying. "Then we'll fold him in half and stick him in the sack."

"How?"

Raven looked at me strangely, her hands going back to her hips and her head tilting to one side. One strand of purple hair glistened in the sunlight streaming through the windows.

"I mean, isn't he still stiff?"

She shook her head. "Nope, not now he isn't. He'll be more than supple, I'm guessing."

It's amazing, when you think about it, how quickly a human can adapt to a situation. Earlier, I'd seen what was left of Duke in the wardrobe and I thought I was going to be sick. The maggots and blowflies disgusted me, and I wanted to get out of that trailer *pronto*.

Now, here I was, having a normal conversation (well, as normal as can be expected under the circumstances) with Raven, about picking Duke up and stuffing him in a huge sack. The blowflies and maggots didn't seem to matter as much now, even though they still unnerved me, and I guess I'd got used to the stench. Of course, having the windows and doors open probably helped get rid of some of the flies and smell as well. Still, we're quick to adapt, no matter what.

And so, we began.

Raven gave me a couple of minutes to prepare myself, and when I was ready (not that I really *was* ready – you never would be for something like this) we both walked over to the wardrobe and stared in at Duke.

"You take his feet," Raven said. "I'll grab his back."

"You don't want to put any clothes on first?" I asked.

She shook her head. "The maggots and stuff would only stain them. At least this way, when we're done I can jump back into the lagoon and wash it all off."

It made sense, I guess.

"You should get undressed too," Raven said.

"I don't think so," I replied quickly. The thought of having maggots and bits of Duke touching me literally made my skin crawl. I wasn't doing that. If I got messy, I was wearing old clothes anyway, so I'd just burn them in the fire if I had to.

"You sure?" Raven asked again.

"*Very* sure."

"Okay," she smiled at me, trying to keep my spirits high. "Let's do it."

We reached inside the wardrobe. I grabbed Duke's feet and Raven placed one hand under his armpit. I'm glad it was her doing that and not me, it would've freaked me out to touch Duke there.

Slowly, we tried to move him. At first, I thought he was still stiff and wasn't going to move, but I guess he must've kinda solidified in that position or something, because it took a few moments of pulling before his arse and back came away from the floor and wall of the wardrobe with a sickening *squelch*. Once he "unstuck" himself though, he was easy to move.

Of course, I had the easy end. There didn't seem to be any maggots down by his feet. At least, not that I could see.

Raven had the rough end of the Duke stick.

As we pried his back from the wardrobe wall, his head fell back further, the sudden movement disturbing the maggots. They broiled up out of his nose and mouth and eyes, out his ears too and the holes in the sides of his cheek. I watched them tumble end over end, cascading down over the rope dug deep in his neck and down onto his chest.

They also tumbled backwards across his forehead, over Raven's arms and onto her chest.

She didn't say anything though. I suppose, at that moment, it wasn't important. We were sliding Duke out onto the edge of the wardrobe and we had to concentrate on doing that.

I was trying real hard.

She looked up at me as I was looking at the maggots falling down onto her. I must've had a disgusted look on my face.

"Concentrate," she said in a stern voice.

My eyes jumped up to hers and I nodded.

"You ready?" she asked. "On the count of three."

I nodded again.

And we counted together.

"One...Two...*Three!*"

We lifted and Duke tumbled. He spun sideways like he was trying to escape from our grip. I tried to hold on, but he slipped free. He hit the floor hard. Within moments he was lying on his side on the sheet, half in the scrunched position he'd been in while in the wardrobe.

The maggot swarm was worse than ever. They were tumbling end over end, scurrying everywhere, his face a mass of live, skittering little white horrors. And they were spreading out too, quickly heading towards the edges of the sheet.

With her foot, Raven kicked Duke in the shoulder, pushing him onto his back. She kicked at his arms and legs too. Straightening and flattening him out and squashing dozens of maggots in the process. Soon he was lying flat on the sheet, exactly where she wanted him. The smell was overpowering.

She then reached over to the couch and grabbed the broom once again. She walked to the wardrobe and brushed out the remaining piles of maggots, making sure they fell onto the sheet as well.

Once she was finished, Duke was sprinkled with maggots all over.

You want salt and pepper with your Duke?

Because that is how he looked.

The maggots were all excited, either burrowing back into him, or heading off for the sides of the sheet, looking for new flesh to prey on.

"Quick, wrap your ends of the sheet around him." Raven ordered as she brushed the maggots from her chest and stomach, making sure they fell back onto the sheet. She was standing on the sheet too, one leg on either side of Duke's head. The maggots fell back into the mass swarming around where Duke's eyes used to be.

If only he could see her now. I'm sure he'd have loved to see Raven naked, standing above him like that. Money can't buy those kind of views! He probably wouldn't have been wild about the maggots though.

I bent down and grabbed both edges of the sheet by his feet. I brought the left side over first, wrapping it around his legs, making sure the maggots fell inside the sheet and didn't spill out over the sides. Then I brought the right side over as well.

I glanced up at Raven. She was still standing there, wiping what remained of the maggots from her. One maggot was twisting and turning in her pubic hair. I wanted to say something, but that would mean I was looking down there, and I didn't want her to know that.

A few seconds later, Raven flicked it out with her finger. She must've felt it down there anyway.

"Done," I said as my eyes met hers.

She nodded.

Then she took a step backwards and crouched down as well. She grabbed her two ends of the sheet. But then she paused. She let the sheet go and leaned forward further, looking closely at Duke's face.

She got way too close to him, if you ask me. We're talking within inches here.

She kneeled and then reached out, her hands digging through the maggot mass.

"What are you *doing*?" I couldn't believe what I was seeing.

"We need it," she replied.

I didn't know what she was talking about until I saw her hands re-emerge holding one end of the rope that was tied around his neck. She held it in her left hand, and then felt around again, through all those maggots, with her right. After a few seconds, she found the other end of the rope. Quickly, she worked in and around the maggots, pushing them aside. The rope came away from around Duke's neck in a quick movement, maggots flying with it. I had a quick second or two to see the deep blue bruise and indentation all around his neck before the maggots fell straight back into the cavity.

Raven wiped the remaining maggots from the rope and threw it onto the couch. Then, she grabbed the ends of the sheet once more and did the same thing I had done. In no time at all, Duke was wrapped up nice and tight, and all the maggots with him.

Just like those Egyptian mummies you see on TV.

We stood there for a few seconds, looking down at Duke. I wanted to say something, but I didn't know what. I was just relieved that we were about to get our trailer back, our wardrobe back. Although I didn't think I would *ever* open that wardrobe door again.

"You want to bend him or hold the sack?" Raven asked.

I must've looked at her strangely.

"He won't *fit* in the sack like this, we'll have to bend him in two. Do you want to do that, or do you want to hold the sack open for me?"

I didn't want to do either, of course. But we'd come this far, and I wasn't going to back out now. She was doing all this for me, so I had to help.

"I'll hold the sack," I said.

"Okay."

I don't think she was surprised by my decision.

So, we swapped ends. I walked up to Duke's head and got the sack ready. I pulled open the mouth of the sack, loosening the cord around the top, ready for Raven's command.

Raven stepped down to Duke's legs, squatted by them and lifted them up.

I thought his whole body would rise like a plank of wood, still stiff. I don't know why I thought that, after all, I'd just seen how flaccid Duke was. The way he fell out of the wardrobe looked just like how any of us would fall out of bed in the middle of the night or something. A dangling arm, then the hip and head hits the ground and the rest follows. The only difference in this case was he was dead...and covered in maggots, of course.

Raven lifted Duke's legs higher. They rose up, pivoting at the hip. She didn't meet any resistance until she had the legs high in the air, straight up. That's when the body would give no more.

So, Raven put her shoulder behind his legs, braced herself and pushed harder. Duke's legs moved a little further, but the rest of his body also slipped along the floor.

This wasn't working. We both knew it.

Raven stopped pushing and looked at me.

"You're going to have to hold him, hon," she said quietly.

I nodded and dropped the sack. I'd figured that much out myself already.

I crawled over to Duke's head.

Even though he was wrapped in that blue sheet, I could still picture what was left of him underneath it. I could see his hollowed out eyes still staring up at me, his mouth open, and all the maggots that swirled within him.

I put one hand on each shoulder.

"Okay," I muttered.

Raven began pushing again. Slowly and painstakingly, Duke began to bend a fraction more, an inch more, almost as if we were stretching whatever muscles were left in his legs.

A bit more. A bit more...

Raven was using all her weight now, pushing down hard and long. His legs arched over the rest of his body, and he looked like a clock whose hands were positioned at five-to-nine.

And then, all of a sudden, it was as if he just gave in.

Not that he was fighting us, but I guess his body was.

With one long push, we heard two sharp cracks. His muscles or bones must've snapped or given way or something, because he just folded easily. Raven continued pushing and he just folded up.

And that's when he vomited.

I heard the noise before I saw anything, and I had no idea where it was coming from. It was a gurgling, bubbly sound, and it got louder and louder. Raven was compressing his legs down further, and that must've put pressure on his stomach, and on the fluids that resided there. Because the next thing I knew, a huge wet stain was spreading out on the sheet, right where his mouth would've been.

Right in front of *me*.

And under the stain, I could see frenzied little wriggles and movement.

The stain spread more and more as Raven brought his legs down onto his chest. It turned the sheet a dark, purple colour, and it spread quickly.

She saw the stain, but she didn't say anything about it. She just worked quicker.

"Grab the rope," she said, still leaning down on Duke's legs.

I reached behind me and grabbed the rope from the couch. It felt wet and oily, a sticky horrible feeling.

"Put it under him," she said.

I leaned forward, my hands fumbling with the rope.

"Lift up the body and place the rope *under* his shoulders," she directed me.

I *knew* what to do. I was just nervous and scared and panicking a little. The deep purple and brown stains on the rope had made it feel all waxy, and it smelled of Duke and maggots and rotting. I was trying as hard as possible to keep away from the darkest of the stains, while also doing what Raven wanted me to do.

I stretched the rope out flat on the floor. Then, I lifted Duke's head, watching as the stain continued to grow. His shoulders lifted with his head, and while my left hand held him up, my right hand quickly pulled the rope down further, under Duke's shoulders and down his back.

I looked up at Raven, who was still resting against the back of Duke's legs, keeping him compact. She nodded and smiled, so I let go.

Duke's head hit the floor hard and we both heard the crack.

Sorry about that, Duke.

"Hand me both ends," Raven said.

I picked up the loose ends of the rope on both sides of the body and handed them to her. She took one in each hand and then criss-crossed the rope over Duke's legs. She started to tie a knot, but there wasn't a lot of rope left to work with.

"Come up here and push down on him with me."

I stood and took hold of Duke's feet. I leaned on the back of his legs, just as Raven was doing, and I pushed hard. His legs moved closer to his face, the gurgling and sucking noises starting again inside the sheet. And with both our weight pushing him down, there was just enough rope for Raven to tie a solid decent knot, keeping his legs pushed hard against his stomach and face.

"There," she said in a whisper. "Done."

We both let go of Duke's legs and stood up. Slowly, we stepped backwards from the body. We watched, waiting for anything, almost as if we expected Duke to spring apart, breaking through the sheet and rope, or explode or something.

He did neither.

He just lay there, gurgling and staining the sheet some more.

It was then I noticed a similar stain spreading from the *other* end of his body.

But I really don't want to talk about that.

There didn't seem to be as many flies around now that we'd covered the body in the sheet. And, in fact, the smell had been cut down too, but that could've been because we had the windows and doors open.

"Now what?" I asked.

"Grab the sack," Raven replied.

"But isn't this *enough*? We've wrapped him up. Won't this do?"

"I want him in the *sack*, Amber," she said, as she turned to look at me. I was pretty sure she was sweating now. The drops of water from the lagoon had long dried and now I could see a heavy sweat on her brow. It must've been hard work getting Duke to fold in half like that.

After all the struggle to get Duke into this position, I really wasn't looking forward to getting him into the sack. But, strangely enough, this was the easiest part yet. It was almost as if he'd given up, bound like he was, and suddenly everything was made nice and easy for us.

Of course, he'd given up long ago, but it sure hadn't felt that way so far.

I walked back to the sack, loosened the cord around its opening some more and then I stood there, holding the sack open.

Raven leaned forward at the other end of Duke. She placed her hands on his ass. Well, where his arse was, under the sheet, and where that new dark stain was spreading.

Don't even think about it!

She pushed him forward.

He slid along the floor with a scratching, slippery wet sound, as a couple of maggots tumbled out from the folds in the sheet.

And then his head was inside the sack. Followed by his shoulders.

I had some trouble manoeuvring the main section of his body, the part where the rope was tied, into the sack. He just wouldn't go. But, with some help from Raven, we soon had his whole doubled-up body inside the sack.

Raven picked up the five or so maggots that had escaped while we were stuffing him inside and studied them as they crawled across her palm.

"You know, when I was a little girl, one day I found a blowfly buzzing around the window in my bedroom," she said in a small voice. "It was trying to get out, to escape the room, and it couldn't work out what invisible force was preventing it from doing so."

Her thumb stroked one of the maggots. I looked on, but didn't say anything.

"I dashed to the laundry and found some fly spray," she continued, still looking at the crawling things. "I ran back to my room and sprayed that fly over and over again, watching it become coated in the white mist and then convulse and fall to the floor. As it lay on its back, struggling to survive, it started to give birth to a pile of little maggots, pushing them out – dozens of them – as quickly as possible, using its last amount of strength to further the species before it died."

She looked up into my eyes.

"Life and death at the same time, Amber," she whispered to me. "There's nothing more primal."

She closed her hand around the maggots and flung them into the sack as well. She also picked up the broom she'd used to sweep them up earlier, and she placed that in the sack too. Like I said, it was a *big* sack!

Raven shut the mouth of the sack tight, pulling the cord hard and making sure nothing could get out. She knotted the cord once, then again.

I sat down on the couch. I was suddenly exhausted. I wanted to run my fingers through my hair and rub my eyes, but I didn't. I knew where my hands had been. Of course, we hadn't yet eaten that morning either. So that was probably another reason I felt rundown.

Raven turned to me and smiled.

"We did it!" she said, almost as if we'd won some special prize.

I nodded. "I'm just glad he's out of here and out of our hair."

"He isn't yet," she added.

"I know, but he almost is. What do we do with him now?"

"We drag him into the lagoon."

You'd probably think that I might object to that, or that I'd tell Raven it was too hard or a crazy plan or something, but I didn't. I was tired and I just wanted him *gone*. And, really, the lagoon was the closest place and the most ideal as well. I guess there were other places we could've thought about leaving him, like digging him a nice comfy little grave somewhere in the forest. But we didn't have the tools for that particular job, and I certainly didn't have the strength to do it. I'm sure Raven couldn't do it all on her own either. My only goal was to get him out of the trailer, out of my *home*.

Vamoosed!

So, even though now I sit here and think that putting him in the lagoon meant spoiling that lovely fresh mountain water, and bringing his rotting decay and disgustingness to that idyllic paradise we then called home, at the time it wasn't even something I considered.

It was simple.

Duke. *Gone.*

That's all that mattered to me.

I'd do anything to be as far away from him as possible. I just wanted my life back. The way it was. The way it had been with Raven before all this started.

"Can we rest for a minute?" I asked.

Raven nodded and sat on the bed. "Good idea. I think we deserve it, don't you?"

I smiled at her.

She leaned back on the bed, her arms behind her, supporting her. Her long thin body draped over the side of the mattress. Even in a situation like this, even with her scratches and bruises, she looked good. She looked strong, determined, in control.

Her legs were apart and I could see all of her. I remembered kneeling before her earlier, while she was sweeping up those maggots onto the sheet. I was so close to her, so closer to her down *there*, I could feel her body heat. I could see everything.

"How about some breakfast?" she asked.

My eyes jumped back up her body to her face. She was looking at me. I think I might've blushed.

"Are you *serious*?"

She nodded.

"I really don't think I can," I replied, pointing to the sack. "Not after doing that."

She smirked. "Don't worry. Just grab some cereal and you'll be fine."

I shook my head. "No thanks. And anyway, I think the milk's probably off. The refrigerator's been without power now for a couple of days."

"That's okay, I'll eat mine dry."

And so that's what she did.

With Duke doubled-over and bound in the sack between us, she washed her hands, rifled through the cupboards and had a feast of dry cereal and stale bread. She ate her Cheerios while I just watched her. It was almost like she was celebrating, toasting her victory over Duke.

"Do you think he's cut?" she asked me after a while.

I didn't quite know what she meant, but I assumed she was asking me if I thought Duke was pissed at us. "I don't think he's able to get angry anymore, Raven."

She laughed out loud and shook her head, her eyes staring down at the sack as she filled her mouth with another handful of Cheerios. "No, no, his *cock*. Do you think he's *cut*? Circumcised?"

"*Huh?*" I sat there with my mouth hanging open.

Her eyes met mine.

"Wanna find out?"

"*No!*" I said as I climbed from the couch. "We just spent all this time getting him *in there*, I'm not about to get him out again."

Raven shrugged. "Okay, no problem. Just asking."

I shook my head, my mind a whirl of thoughts. "Raven, remember, this is the guy who tried to *rape* you!?"

"I know," she said in a quiet voice.

"He was violent and he *hurt* you! He probably would've *killed* you! And you want to fool around with him?"

"It was just an idea."

"Well, it was a *bad* idea!"

She nodded. I think she was regretting mentioning the subject now. "You're right," she replied. "It's just he was poking me with his cock so much when he was attacking me. I could feel it through his jeans. I just wondered what it looked like. Whether it was cut or not, you know?"

No, I didn't know. I didn't *want* to know. It wasn't important to me. What *was* important to me was getting him out of there *now*. Not just for my own sanity, but also to make sure Raven didn't dream up any other "activities" for the day.

Duke's cock? Who the hell cared? That's what got us into this trouble in the first place!

"Come on," I said, walking around to the top of the sack and picking it up by the knotted cord. "Let's get him out of here."

Raven nodded and left her bowl of cereal on the bed. She stood and walked next to me, grabbing hold of some of the cord as well.

We swung the sack around and pulled, both of us walking backwards towards the door, dragging Duke with us.

I was glad to be wearing my Sublime t-shirt, because it only had short sleeves and that meant as Raven and I pulled the sack, our arms rubbed against each other. I could feel her muscles, her strength, her warmth, the friction of our skin rubbing, and that gave me the power to continue.

"Go outside and check everything's okay," Raven asked.

I handed her my end of the cord and turned around, walking down the stairs and outside.

I looked around the lagoon. Everything was just as it always was. Perfect. No one around and nothing suspicious. The sky was cloudless and the breeze blew through the trees and wildflowers.

I smiled and sucked in a huge lungful of fresh mountain air. It was great to be out of the confines of the trailer and not to be looking at Duke. I surveyed the lagoon again. It was a wonderful day.

And with Duke finally out of the way, things would be absolutely perfect.

I turned back around. "Everything's fine," I said.

Raven's back was to me. She was bent down low over the sack, her hands working feverishly.

"Everything okay?" I asked as I stepped back to the trailer.

She turned around and smiled at me, nodding. "Yep, just making sure we've knotted up the sack good and tight. Don't want him getting out of it."

I smiled back. "I don't think that's going to happen."

"I know, hon. Just being extra careful, that's all."

Raven walked backwards down the steps, dragging the sack with her. Once she was just outside the door, standing next to me, she handed half the cord back to me.

Then, we dragged Duke out the door of the trailer. With two heavy bounces, he hit each of the steps as he tumbled downwards onto the ground.

Only in death did he start to use his head.

Sorry. Sick joke.

Raven let go of the sack once we had him outside and she turned around, checking out the whole lagoon as well.

I'd just *done* that. But I guess she was, as she said, being extra careful too.

I let go of the cord and turned to look with her. The sun was high in the sky, and the lagoon looked as peaceful and tranquil as ever.

"All clear?" I asked.

She nodded.

We picked up the cord again and started dragging the sack towards the water's edge. Once we got some pace up, pulling the sack was easy. It slipped and slid across the grass and moss, and we even managed to walk pretty quickly. I started to wonder if this is how the Egyptians built the pyramids all those years ago, but I'm guessing they really didn't have to deal with the disposal of bodies until *after* they'd completed their monuments.

Once we got to the edge of the lagoon, we let go of the sack. I knelt down at the mushy water's edge, breathing hard and sweating. Pulling Duke this far had taken a lot out of me. Raven stood above me, hands on her hips, working on getting her own breathing under control. The sunlight shone on her skin, reflecting in the beads of sweat that had broken out all over her body.

She looked so strong and beautiful standing there.

"Throw him in," I eventually said.

"Huh?"

"Let's throw him in."

Raven shook her head. "Not that simple, sweets."

Now, why didn't *that* surprise me?

"What do you mean?"

"We can't just toss him into the water and hope he goes away. It doesn't work like that. He may not even *sink*! If he does, he could pop up anytime, and I'm sure you don't want to be swimming in the lagoon only to find a bloated and rotting Duke floating towards you."

She was right.

"We need to stay in control. We need to pin him down somewhere, so we know where he is at all times, and can move him if we have to."

I didn't like the sound of the "move him if we have to" part.

I nodded anyway. She was right. And I was too exhausted to argue.

"So?" I asked.

"Let's find some rocks. We'll weigh down the sack. That should help keep him out of sight."

I sighed deeply, climbed to my feet and started searching the clearing for some heavy rocks.

Raven bent down and undid the knot in the cord holding the sack closed. As she did so, I brought back a handful of rocks I'd found.

She shook her head. "No, no, we need bigger ones. Go into the stream and grab some from there."

I did as I was commanded. I dropped the stones I'd already chosen and headed across to the stream. Slowly, I stepped into it, even with my sneakers on. The water felt cool and inviting. I wanted to lie down in the stream right then and there, let the coldness wash over me and make me feel relaxed. My body ached to feel the coolness running all over me, washing away the dirt and sweat and maggots and Duke. I knew then I'd have to go for a swim in the lagoon later. It was just too inviting to say no. And, with maggots and bits of Duke having been on my hands and who-knows-where-else, a swim to wash them out – from my memory as well – would be perfect.

"Found any?" Raven called.

I grabbed the nearest and biggest rocks I could find, and slowly trudged back to Raven.

"Perfect," she replied, smiling up at me. "Another handful or two should do it."

So I returned to the stream and grabbed some more.

He's almost gone, he's almost gone, I kept thinking over and over in my head, pushing myself on, willing myself to take the next step, knowing that soon Duke would no longer be a problem.

As I turned to walk back to Raven this second time, I noticed she was now standing in the lagoon, pulling at the sack on the water's edge. It moved inch by inch in the mud, and eventually it slid into the water as well. The sack started to change colour instantly, the water soaking into the fabric, turning it darker, almost black.

Raven watched me approach. She smiled at me. "Come in, the water's fine!"

I shook my head. "Not now."

"Come on, Amber. Help me! *Please*?"

Her "please" sounded so pitiful, so pleading.

And, anyway, I *did* want to try out the lagoon, so I stepped forward and let the water lap at my feet.

"Further!" Raven prompted.

"Where do you want these rocks?" I asked, holding them up for her to see.

"Place them in the top of the sack," she replied.

I took two more steps into the lagoon and bent down. The big wet gaping mouth of the sack was open, water lapping inside. I tossed the rocks through the opening, not wanting to touch it (or let anything that was in there touch *me*!) and I stood up when I was done. Raven smiled and came closer, handing me the cord with her right hand.

"You can do the honours," she said.

I pulled the cord hard, closing the entrance to the sack, tied it back into a knot, then doubled it.

"Perfect," she said, as I handed the cord to her. "Now, why don't you take off your dirty clothes and have a swim. Relax a little."

"Not now," I said to her.

"You deserve it," she said.

"I'm fine right here, thank you."

She shrugged her shoulders and turned away from me, placing the cord over her right shoulder and pulling the sack out into the lagoon.

"Okay, your loss," she replied as she walked further out, the water lapping at her thighs, then higher at her hips. After a few more steps, when the water was above her waist, she turned around and swam backwards, the sack floating out with her.

For a good while I watched Raven and the sack head out into the middle of the lagoon. The water flowed over Raven's shoulders, her long hair trailing in the wake. Soon, she changed to side-stroke, looking relaxed but with a determined expression on her face.

The sack floated for quite a while, and I found I couldn't take my eyes off it as it floated on the calm surface of the water. I was worried it wasn't going to sink. But slowly, just like an old battered ship, it tilted high and then, as the water took hold, it submerged with a *plunk*.

Raven kept hold of the cord though, and she continued to swim side-stroke, moving further out into the lagoon.

I took a few steps further into the cold, beautiful water.

Drop him. Let him go. Do it now, I thought to myself, almost willing Raven to hear me and do as I said.

But she didn't.

I moved further into the water. It lapped around my knees now. It felt so good. I just wanted to dive straight in.

Take off your clothes and do it.

No! Someone might see.

There's no one around. You want to swim. Do it!

I *can't!*

DO IT!

A few more steps.

The water lapped around my hips.

Sooo good.

I watched Raven, and I'm sure she was watching me. Her progress had slowed since the sack sunk under the water. I guess the water made it heavier, harder to swim with. I could feel my own clothes were heavier on me as I stepped further into the lagoon.

So, take them off, girl!

I waited until the water was above my breasts, and then – *only* then – did I remove my shirt, jeans and shoes. Sure, it was a bit of a struggle, because the water caused the fabric to stick to my skin, but I didn't care. I felt safer this way.

I wadded up my clothes and threw them back to the shore. The shoes tumbled onto dry land, but my jeans and shirt didn't quite make it. But that's okay, they weren't going anywhere just floating at the water's edge.

The water was wonderful. I could feel it across my whole body, caressing me everywhere, flowing across me and around me, engulfing me and keeping me safe, around my breasts, over my erect nipples, and further below, across my stomach and through the folds between my legs. I dived under, the coolness a shock to my face and head for only a second before it became wonderful.

I dived again, longer this time, kicking out with my feet and holding my breath, trying hard to stay under for as long as possible.

It felt great. The water so clear, so perfect. And I knew I'd been really stupid about not coming in for a swim. I should've done it as soon as we arrived.

This lagoon was heavenly, and I never wanted to leave.

I smiled while I was under the water, pushed the air from my lungs and felt the bubbles explode all around me. I came up for air only when my insides started to ache, and I felt the sunlight surround me in its warmth once again.

Perfect.

I ran a hand through my hair, wiping away the water, and I blinked my eyes to clear them as well.

I wanted to tell Raven how great I felt.

But I couldn't see her.

I turned around three-sixty degrees.

But Raven was gone.

Nineteen

I swam around again, my eyes darting everywhere. The wooden stairs, the trailer, the lagoon.

No sign of her.

I didn't want to panic. I tried to keep calm. I swam around in a circle, looking across at the forest, my eyes trained through the trees and bushes.

Nothing.

No one.

Fear crept up my spine. I was in the middle of the lagoon, naked, with nothing to protect myself.

I was alone. Raven was missing.

Suddenly I was almost petrified.

I wanted to swim back to the shore and sprint for the trailer. But I had no clothes on.

Shouldn't've taken them off in the first place!

I wanted to find something to protect myself with.

What? I had nothing! Maybe a stick or rock?

I wanted Raven back.

And so I screamed her name. Didn't even really think about it. It just happened.

"*Rrrraaaaaaavvvvvveeeeennnnn!*"

It started quietly, in the back of my throat, but by the time it ended, it had become a piercing scream.

My voice echoed around the lagoon. A bunch of birds flew off in the distance, having been disturbed by the cry.

I dog-paddled in a small circle, looking around me, around me, around me.

Nothing.

The lagoon was quiet. The water still.

Deathly still.

No Raven. No sack.

So I did it again.

"*Rrrraaaaaaavvvvvveeeeennnnn!*"

The echoes died once more.

I paddled.

Nothing.

I started to think the worst, even though it didn't make any sense. I started to think maybe the water had woken Duke somehow, that he wasn't really dead, just in a coma or something. Maybe the water had shocked him back to reality, he'd got out of the sack and jumped Raven, surprising her and killing her somehow, dragging her body to the bottom of the lagoon. And now, somewhere, he was waiting for me. Just waiting for a chance in the depths of the lagoon. Maybe he was below me right now, or behind me, reaching out for me, so close...

"*Rrrraaaaaaavvvvvveeeeennnnn!*"

The call sounded even more desperate now. Even more panicked. I was just swimming in a tight circle, too scared to head back to shore, and too scared to stay where I was.

I couldn't even drive out of there in Raven's Suburban. I didn't know *how to*!

I was about to call again, when I heard splashing.

Duke! He was swimming towards me! He'd got free somehow!

"*WHAT?*"

It was Raven. She was leaning against the rock wall, just inside the blowhole, one hand reaching out and grabbing a nearby rock, steadying herself.

"There you are!" I called, relieved that it wasn't Duke coming after me. I smiled at her. All my worries and fears evaporated. It was *so* good to see her.

She didn't look too happy though.

I tried to explain.

"I didn't know where you'd gone!"

"Well, I haven't gone *far*, Amber. I'm getting rid of our little problem, remember?"

She used her thumb to point over her shoulder and back into the blowhole.

"You put him back *there*?" I asked.

I think she rolled her eyes, as if it were a dumb question to ask. "Yes," she replied. "I did. Is that an issue for you?"

"No, I just thought – "

"Thought *what,* Amber? That's your problem. Sometimes you just don't think!"

Before I could say anything else, she dived back into the water and started swimming towards the shore. She was side-stroking again, at a much faster rate this time, not being weighed down by the sack. But she wasn't facing me, she kept her back towards me, didn't even look in my direction.

I floated in the same spot, in the middle of the lagoon, watching her swim past me and back to the shore.

Once she got there, she climbed from the water and didn't look at me. She walked quickly across the clearing, water dripping off her hair and back, and she headed to the trailer. She untied the trailer door (because we left it tied open), walked up the steps and closed the door behind her.

I stayed floating in the lagoon.

My eyes darted from the trailer to the blowhole and back again.

I couldn't see inside the blowhole – it was too dark – and I really didn't want to anyway. But I knew Duke was in there somewhere, tucked away out of sight. He was in the water, just like I was. And I wanted to get out again, especially now Raven was back in the trailer.

Suddenly, I felt very cold, very exposed.

And alone.

"Raven!" I called out once more. "Can you bring me my robe? Or some clothes?"

No reply.

"*Please?*"

Just silence from the trailer.

I didn't really know what to do. I paddled in a circle once more, checking out all the trees and bushes, convincing myself no one was around, and then I slowly swam to shore.

I didn't go completely to the shore to begin with. I squatted in the shallows for quite some time, hoping and praying Raven would come out with some clothes for me.

She didn't.

And I couldn't work out why. Did I get her pissed at me just because I panicked when I couldn't see her? Jesus, I was *worried* about her! *That's* why I panicked. Couldn't she see that?

Obviously not.

Or was she mad because *she* was the one who had to drag Duke all the way over to the blowhole and leave him there? She only had to ask and I would've helped her. I just assumed she was fine doing it all herself!

I just couldn't work it out.

I waited a good while longer, but she didn't re-appear.

I swam closer to the shore and reached out for my jeans and shirt. They were still wet, of course, but they were the only clothes I had nearby. So, I climbed back into them. It took a long time and a great deal of effort, especially while still being in the lagoon, but I managed it. Now I could walk out of the lagoon without worrying about being naked.

It was a little victory, of sorts. I'd found a way out without having to rely on Raven. I'd beaten her challenge.

I knew what she was up to. I knew what she was trying to do.

I guess you do as well, dear reader. It probably comes across in what I've written so far. Yes, I *do* rely on Raven for a lot of things. Yes, I'm *not* the strongest individual you'll ever meet. Raven is my support, she's the one who gives me strength. And, I guess, she must get sick of it. Or I annoy her or something, and every now and then, she gives me little tests, little challenges to keep me from becoming totally reliant on her.

So, I'm assuming this was one of them.

This was a way for her to get back at me for panicking when I couldn't see her while she was in the blowhole.

But she *was* gone for a long time. I hit the chicken switch because I was worried about *her*. I hope at least *you* can see that, even though she couldn't!

Still, I'd done it. I'd got out of the lagoon my own way. I didn't need her.

I was proud. So damn proud of myself.

I walked a few steps onto dry land and let the water soak out of my t-shirt and jeans. I scrunched my shirt into little balls, wringing out as much water as possible. It ran in little rivers, down my legs and thighs and arms, and it splashed onto my bare feet. I didn't worry about putting on my sneakers, they could sit there in the sun and dry for later.

When my clothes didn't feel so waterlogged, I walked across the clearing and up to the trailer.

I put my ear near the door, listening for any movement inside, but I really couldn't hear anything. There were a few blowflies still flying around outside, but nothing like the number there had been before.

We beat you, suckers. Fly off and find another piece of rotting meat. This feast has come to an end!

The trailer was quiet.

I took a step back and grabbed the door handle.

I smiled my best smile.

This was going to be fun!

I opened the door fast and stepped inside.

Raven had her back to me. She was bent over the sink.

"Surprise!" I yelled.

And I *did* surprise her.

I *knew* she thought I'd be stuck out in the lagoon until she came to help me. I *knew* she thought I'd be too scared to run across the clearing naked. But I'd fooled her. Outwitted her on this occasion. I'd won!

She swung around to face me, the shock clear on her face.

I beamed at her, my smile huge.

"You can't get me that easy," I said.

She ran a hand through her hair. "Huh?"

"It wasn't that simple, now was it? I knew what you were up to!"

Her eyes darted from me to my clothes and back again.

"Yeah," she said. She tried to smile but it didn't work. "You're right."

She sounded nervous. Like something was wrong.

My smile slipped from my face.

"Are you alright, Raven?" I asked as I stepped closer towards her.

She thrust her hands out towards me, palms up, keeping me at a distance. "Yes, fine, it's all fine."

I was worried maybe she'd got depressed again, having to get rid of the body and everything, and I didn't want her cutting up her arms once more. But at least with her arms out in front of her, I could tell that she was fine. No bleeding. No cuts.

I checked the rest of her body too, just to be sure (she was still naked, of course) but there didn't seem to be any new wounds anywhere.

I was relieved. Maybe I'd just over-reacted. Maybe I just surprised her and frightened her with my sudden appearance back in the trailer.

There was no doubt, she wasn't expecting me.

"What're you doing?" I asked.

"Nothing."

"Doesn't look like nothing to me." I stepped forward further, trying to see over her shoulder, but she blocked me.

I saw the knife though.

"Breakfast?" I asked.

"Yes, that's it," she smiled. "I'm making some breakfast."

"But you had cereal just before," I replied.

She looked at me for a second, like it didn't register. She flicked at a wet curl, hanging across her left eye and her forehead furrowed. "I know, I know. But I'm hungry still. Why don't you go outside and sit and read and dry off in the sun while I prepare something for us. It's almost lunchtime and I'll get something nice for us both."

"I'll help."

"No need."

"But I *want* to help."

"No *need*."

She was being really pig-headed all of a sudden. I must've upset her by actually completing the challenge she set for me. Maybe she thought I'd be out in the lagoon all day.

Why?

"Can I at least get out of these wet clothes first?" I asked.

"No."

"Or grab some dry ones?"

"*No!*"

"Raven, *please*. I'm catching a chill here wearing them. They're *wet*!"

"I'll bring you some." She reached over to me and swung me around, pushing me back towards the door.

"Huh? No, it's okay, I'll get some."

"Just go."

"No!"

"*Do it!*"

She pushed me harder, right in the middle of my back and toward the steps to the outside. But I slipped from her grip, deflecting her push. Her hands were wet and oily and slippery, like she was preparing some fish to eat.

I didn't think we had any left.

I turned sideways, getting away from her for a second, and I looked across to the kitchen.

I saw the knife lying to one side. Saw the dark goo and brown flaky stuff smeared all over it.

She must've caught some fish while she was in the lagoon, I thought to myself. But I knew that wasn't right. I didn't see any. Plus she didn't have the time.

And then my eyes darted across to the other side of the sink.

And I saw it.

I leaned forward and vomited straight on the floor. It was an automatic reaction I had no control over.

I kept vomiting as Raven pushed me violently to one side.

The chunks of sick splattered across her body and down my clothes as I fell backwards out the door, my hands reaching out for anything to grab hold of, but finding nothing.

My eyes locking onto Raven's as I fell.

My head hitting the ground hard.

Darkness swallowing me completely.

Saturday, July 13.

Twenty

So, were my eyes open or closed?
Of course, they were closed. At least, to begin with.
I probably woke up a couple of times that night, but it was dark in the trailer, so I went straight back to sleep. I had some pretty weird dreams too, and they didn't help one bit. But I was in bed, I was warm and safe. And sleep was what I needed.

When I did open my eyes the next morning, Raven's face was smiling down at me from where she sat on the edge of the bed.

"Welcome back," she said as she patted my leg. "How do you feel?"

I ran a hand through my short hair, feeling the bump on the back of my head. It was big and hard.

"Sore," I replied.

"I think that's to be expected," she nodded.

Raven was already dressed. She was sitting there wearing a fishnet shirt with long sleeves that were held in place by hooks that looped around her thumbs. Underneath this, she wore a black vinyl bra along with black vinyl shorts that were very tight and *very* short, thigh-high fishnet stockings and her black riding boots. Sometimes I wondered how her body could breathe in all that tight fitting vinyl. She looked good of course; in fact, she looked *great*. But you'd never get *me* into any of that stuff. Ever.

"You feel up to a busy day?" she asked.

"Busy?" I sat up in bed. My head started to throb as I did so. "How busy?"

"I think it's time we put as much space between us and Duke as possible."

Duke.

I'd almost forgotten about him. I'd woken in the trailer and everything seemed so normal, except for the lump on my head and the headache now pounding away inside. But the mere mention of his name brought it all back.

What we did, where he'd been.

And where he was now.

My hands went to my temples and I slowly massaged in circles, trying to ease away the throbbing pain.

"Headache?" Raven asked.

I nodded.

"I'll get you some aspirin."

She stood and walked over to the kitchen.

My eyes followed her as I continued to rub at my temples.

The kitchen.

It all came rushing back. And once again I didn't feel too well. I felt sick and light headed. I just wanted to go back to sleep and wish all this away, like it was some kind of dream – no, *nightmare.*

My eyes searched the kitchen.

Nothing.

I looked all around the trailer as quickly as possible.

It wasn't there.

What had she done with it?

Even now, I still feel ill thinking about what I saw on the sink. But it was nowhere to be seen.

Sitting there, in its own rotting, stagnant juices, had been Duke's cock and balls. Skin all torn and ragged, covered in blood and ick and goo. No wonder I'd reacted the way I did. It was an automatic reaction that anyone would've had in the same situation.

But right then, I didn't want to think about it, and I certainly didn't want to talk about it.

As it was, Raven was in a hurry that morning. She gave me the aspirin and I got dressed. Neither of us mentioned the events of the day before. It went unspoken between us, almost as if it had never happened. And I could maybe believe I dreamt it all or something, except for the fact I had this huge lump on the back of my head. Every time I felt it, I knew that what had happened was real.

Raven had been out to the lagoon and caught some more fish, so we had an early breakfast. We didn't talk much. We just sat outside, looking across the lagoon. Or "our lagoon" as we began to call it.

It was another beautiful day, the sun clear in the sky, a light breeze dancing through the trees and bushes and wildflowers.

"I'm sick of eating fish," Raven said.

I smiled. "Me too."

"Let's see if we can get some more supplies when we're out today."

"Okay."

The water from the lagoon trickled along the rocks in the stream. The ever-present sounds of tumbling water made me feel so peaceful and relaxed.

"I'm going to miss this place," I said.

Raven turned to face me, the breeze blowing strands of brown and purple across her face. "What do you mean?"

"Here. Leaving here. I don't want to."

"We're not, sweets."

That surprised me.

"You said we were going to put some distance between us and Duke."

She nodded.

"So we're leaving here, right?"

Raven smiled a crooked smile. "No, hon. I like it here too. We're not going anywhere in the short-term. But Duke is."

"Huh?"

She climbed from the deck chair and picked up our dirty plates. "We have to find a...more *permanent* place for Duke to rest."

"But *no one* will find him in the blowhole," I replied.

"It's too risky," Raven said as she walked towards the trailer. "And he's too close to us. Let's head further up the mountain and see if we can find a better spot to get rid of him. There are a couple of places I have in mind."

I turned back to stare out across the lagoon. The trees stood tall and green, the bushes reflected their leaves in the sunlight, the wildflowers danced in the breeze.

So free. So easy.

"Can you unhook the trailer from the Suburban, Amber?" Raven called from inside the trailer. "As soon as I've cleaned these plates, we'll get going."

I did as I was told and soon we were ready to leave.

I sat in the passenger's seat of the car, waiting for Raven.

My mind was spinning. Just when I thought we'd finally seen the last of Duke, Raven still had other plans. In the end, I guess, she was right to want to move him. He was still nearby, in the blowhole, and it's true that the whole lagoon – its beauty and its atmosphere – was corrupted just a little, knowing that Duke's dead body was stuffed down there in that dark little cave, in the same water we were using. So, I'm guessing it made sense to want to move him. Better to remove him from this tranquillity than to remove us.

But I didn't like the idea of dragging him back out of the blowhole, carrying him to the car and then *driving* with him somewhere else, digging a hole or carrying him to a place and *then* leaving him there. It sounded like a lot of work for a guy already well hidden, and I *also* knew I'd have to help out.

I just didn't want to. I wanted to be rid of Duke *now*. This second. But he still kept hanging around, causing problems.

Damn him.

But Raven had plans, and I knew by now that once she had an idea in her head, you couldn't change it.

Raven climbed in behind the steering wheel. She smiled at me.

"Ready?" she asked.

"I guess," I replied.

"Wish I could find my sunglasses," she said as she put the key in the ignition.

Her sunglasses, I remembered, were somewhere at the gas station...

"So, what are we going to do?" I asked as the motor roared.

"Let's just take a nice, easy drive up the mountain, looking for any out-of-the-way place where we could finally get rid of Duke."

"Can't we just leave him where he is?"

"I don't think so."

"But we went to all that trouble of wrapping him and dragging him out to the blowhole."

Raven nodded. "I know, I know. But that served a couple of purposes. Let's just go for a drive and enjoy the day. Don't worry about it, Amber. Don't think too hard. Leave it all to me, okay?"

But I *was* thinking too hard.

"Let's just enjoy the drive and see what we can see. We may leave him at the blowhole yet, you never know. It all depends..."

And with that, Raven pushed her classical music cassette into the car player, and the loud, strong sounds of the orchestra took over.

I looked down at the radio and wished that it worked. We could listen for news reports or updates, we could find out if anyone was missing Duke or if no one cared. If we ever needed the radio to work, it was now.

She should've fixed it long ago.

Raven's words were running alongside the throbbing in my head.

"It all depends..." she'd said.

Depends on what?

I guess I was soon to find out.

Twenty-one

We spent most of the morning driving up to the peak of Lake Mountain and looking around.

"Play the tourist," Raven had said.

But that was hard to do. Most tourists have cameras, baggy pants and Hawaiian shirts. Whereas Raven was dressed in black fishnets and vinyl, and I was tagging along in scruffy jeans, my red Converse sneakers and a Van Helfin t-shirt.

We looked so out of place.

And the blue and white Suburban probably didn't help matters either. We looked like refugees from the set of the Addams Family, I'm sure.

Or maybe I'm being a bit hard on us.

Knowing *why* we were here – to dump a body, not to look at the view – put me on edge. Whenever anyone looked our way, or turned to whisper something to the person next to them, I got suspicious and worried soon the police would be surrounding us from all sides.

But when I think about it now, maybe it wasn't so unusual. Raven *always* got stares and whispers when she was out on the town, partly because of the clothes she wore, and partly because of how she acted. Maybe things were normal after all.

Anyway, one thing was for sure, the top of the mountain was no use to us. It was covered in boardwalks and viewing platforms and wide open spaces and tourists and nothing else. You couldn't hide a body anywhere without being seen, and there were no real good hiding places anyway. That's the trouble with the tops of mountains, they're basically pretty boring unless you're looking at the view.

Luckily, the mountain was pretty big, and there were many roads and paths and tracks we hadn't tried. Just as we'd stumbled across the lagoon on a little-used old backroad, who knew what other terrific hiding places could be found down a short path or disused walking track. But that was one of the problems, with so many tracks and paths, we could be searching for days before we found a good place to hide Duke.

"Let's just leave him where he is," I said as we drove back from the summit.

"We'll see," Raven replied.

"It's easier that way."

"But not necessarily safer."

"At least we know where he is, and we can watch him and know that no one's found him."

"But if the police find us and they search nearby, they'll find him pretty darn quick."

I turned in my seat to look at her. "But the police aren't going to find us, right?"

"I hope not, hon."

"They're not going to link us to this."

"I know, I'm praying that's the case too."

It was then, for the first time, I realised that maybe Raven was as scared and as panicked by this whole thing as I was. She was just better at keeping calm and in control. But I could tell she was worried, and she wanted to be rid of Duke – *properly* rid of him – as soon as possible.

I didn't question the plan from then on. I knew that what Raven wanted to do was the best for both of us. It had to be.

The day got warmer and the sun was high in the sky. We'd wound down the windows in the Suburban and let the air blow through our hair. The music was still playing and the wonderful smell of trees and fresh air permeated the car.

Cars passed us occasionally, heading in both directions, but I realised I wasn't as worried by them anymore. The people who drove past took no interest in us at all. They wanted to see the sights, not the two girls in the car they were passing. I suddenly felt very safe in the old Suburban, with Raven at the wheel. It felt right. It felt like home.

If only we could keep on this road forever. If only we never had to stop driving.

"Finding a place to hide Duke could take days, maybe weeks." Raven said, almost to herself.

I nodded.

"We need help."

"Huh?"

"Someone who knows the area," she replied.

"We can't *tell* anyone what we're doing."

Raven smirked, her eyes still on the road in front of us. "I know what, hon. We're not going to *tell* anyone anything. We just need a bit of local help."

"But from where?"

She pointed through the windshield. On the road up ahead was a road-side stall. It was a dilapidated little shack made of corrugated iron sheeting, with large hand-painted signs nailed haphazardly to the walls. HOTDOGS and FRIES the signs said. BEST ON LK MTN another sign said. They'd obviously run out of room on *that* sign.

"What do you think?" she asked me.

I shrugged my shoulders. I had no real idea *what* to think, or what we were going to say.

"I guess," I replied uncertainly.

"Don't worry," Raven turned to smile at me. "I'll handle the situation. Trust me, okay? Just go along with it."

"Okay," I replied.

"And, anyway, it's lunchtime. And we need a change from fish, right?"

I smiled. She was right about that.

We pulled onto the side of the road, the gravel shoulder churning under our wheels and creating a cloud of dust as we stopped by the stall.

Raven turned off the engine and the classical music shut down with it. We both sat staring out the windshield, looking for any signs of life.

"Do you think it's open?" I asked.

"Don't know," Raven replied. "It's Saturday. I'd think it would be."

The stall was probably no wider than ten feet. I couldn't see how anyone had the room to cook hotdogs and fries in such a confined space. The iron sheeting was rusting and some sheets were blowing in the breeze, hanging on by only a nail here and a nail there. The front of the stall had a little counter, and behind that was just darkness. Underneath the counter was a wooden sign that read FINEST FARE ANYWHERE.

I found that hard to believe.

We kept looking, but we couldn't see anyone. Everything was quiet.

"Hello!"

The voice came from behind and surprised both of us. Our heads whipped around to our right in unison, and I noticed out of the corner of my eye that Raven's hand went for the keys in the ignition.

Just in case.

So she *was* as nervous as me.

The old guy walked towards us from an angle, from behind the car, but I had no idea where he had actually come from. There was certainly no one walking along the shoulder of the road as we approached.

He was wearing an old cream shirt and long baggy cream pants. He looked like those old guys you see in jungle movies. All he needed was a pith helmet and he could've been Professor Livingstone or whoever.

"Sorry about that," he smiled as he walked closer.

His smile was warm, lighting up his haggard old face, and he was balding quite a lot too. What hair he did have left was cut very short and it was white with specks of grey here and there. The sun shone off the shiny skin on the top of his head.

"The call of nature," he continued, pointing over his shoulder at the forest behind. "It's the only place I can do it."

He turned his back on us and walked to the shack.

So he'd been in the trees, taking a moment to relieve himself while no one was around.

Raven turned to face me, a smile breaking across her face, her right eyebrow rising. "Hope he washes his hands," she said.

We climbed from the car and walked over to the shack. I watched as the guy opened a screen door in the side wall and stepped inside. I was suddenly very hungry and even though hotdogs and fries aren't what I'd call a balanced meal, it didn't really matter right then. I wanted to eat something, and as long as it wasn't fish, I'd be happy.

So, I walked straight up to the counter and smiled at the man who was now standing on the other side, waiting for us. It was only then I realised Raven wasn't with me. I turned and found her still by the car, looking left and right, checking out the road and everything around us.

She *was* nervous.

Actually, probably *more* nervous than I was at that moment, as I hadn't bothered to check anything out. That was strange, because I'm usually the cautious one.

"Weird clothes for a road trip," the guy said to me.

I turned around to face him again, and noticed he was staring at Raven. I wanted to say something about her clothes, to defend her, but Raven said to leave the talking to her.

I just smiled nicely back. Part of me was jealous that he didn't think *my* clothes were strange. But, I guess, they weren't really.

I *was* wearing my Janet Leigh Psycho-style bra though, but he wasn't to know that...

I looked down at the badge on his chest. It was a big yellow smiley face and it read HELLO, MY NAME'S VERN.

Vern. Now, there's a name you don't hear everyday anymore.

I also noticed something else right then and there.

Vern only had one arm.

At first I was shocked and I just stared at the space where his arm should've been. The left side of his shirt had been specially altered, so there was no sleeve where it should be, it was just a sewn up hole.

I looked quickly away, back into the shack. I also kicked myself. I was slipping. I hadn't been on the ball enough to notice this guy only had one arm! What else had I missed? I felt better now that Raven had at least checked out everything before charging up to the counter like I had.

Stay sharp, Amber. Get with it. Don't get yourself killed now.

Raven was being careful, and here I was standing next to some strange old guy in the middle of nowhere. *Anything* could've happened to me. Although I'm guessing with only one arm, Vern wasn't going to put up much of a fight.

My eyes danced across the cook plates and refrigerator, packed in against each other in the shack. The building was deeper than it was wide, so there was ample space for one guy to walk around and cook, but you couldn't fit more than one body in there.

I mean, one *person*. We weren't considering storing Duke next to the ice creams and frozen yogurts.

Would you like some Duke with that?

Sorry. Couldn't resist.

Raven was beside me then, leaning on the counter and staring across at Vern. She was leaning *forward*, if you know what I mean. Showing all she had.

Vern was distracted, of course, just as Raven knew he would be.

"Two hotdogs please," Raven said in a small girly voice, twirling a lock of purple hair around her fingers.

I turned to look at her, but she was smiling at Vern and didn't take her eyes off him. She nudged me with her shoulder instead.

I smiled too.

Vern was positively beaming. I think we made his day; compared to the usual herd of tourists he was probably used to seeing day in and day out, we were a treat.

Slowly, he set to work cooking the dogs.

"You two girls on vacation?" he asked, his back now turned to us.

"We're just driving through," Raven replied.

"Picked a nice day for it."

"Don't like the sun," Raven replied. I knew that wasn't really true.

"Oh," Vern replied. "Heading for the summit?"

"Nah. We like more way-out kinda places," Raven continued in her schoolgirl voice. "Quiet, dark places. Spooky places."

"Aaaah," Vern replied nodding, turning around to face us, wiping his one hand on the side of his pants. "I should've guessed."

"All there is on this mountain is tourists and sight-seeing. Boring views and stupid historic commentaries. Nothing dark and scary."

Vern walked to the counter and leaned forward too. He was so close to us, I could feel his breath when he spoke. He smelled of hotdogs. That didn't surprise me.

"No, no," he began. "You're just not looking in the right places. I've lived on his mountain for forty years, and I can tell you you're just going about this all wrong. Don't follow the tourists, they're all just knuckleheads anyway. They read a brochure and head straight for a particular place. They take a roll of film, turn around and head back home. What would they know? They don't stop to savour the whole atmosphere of the mountain. They miss the best parts. You need to take the back roads, need to head out off the normal routes, you'll be surprised what you'll find."

"Like what?" Raven asked, her voice dropping to a whisper. She was hanging on every one of Vern's words – or at least letting him think so.

"Scary stuff, right?"

She nodded. "*Very*. I like scary."

"Dead bodies and stuff?" he asked.

A tremor of fear split me in two when he said that. My mind whirled.

How does he know? How could he tell? What if he tells the cops? How did he know about Duke? What are we going to do?

And, of course, then I realised I'd hit turbo-panic mode. I switched it off, trying hard to stay calm and just let the conversation continue. Just because he said "dead bodies" didn't mean he knew squat about Raven and me.

"*Yeah*, I like dead bodies," Raven replied, playing the heavy Goth. Then she looked over to me. "So does she."

Vern looked at me.

I tried to put on my *I-like-dead-bodies* face, but I didn't know what that consisted of, so I think it failed miserably.

"A-huh, I know what you're after," Vern replied as he turned and walked back to check on the hotdogs.

Raven turned to me and gave me a quick wink. She was enjoying this.

"You're very close to what you want," he said, poking at the dogs with a fork. "It's not far from here."

"Can you tell us how to get there?" she asked.

"Can do. You got a map?"

"I think there's one in the car," Raven replied.

She nodded her head at the Suburban and I took the hint. Quickly, I turned around and walked back to the car. As I did so, I checked out the road, both ways, just to make sure there was nothing suspicious. I couldn't see any cars in either direction, so I guess all was fine.

I walked over to the passenger side of the car and opened the door. Then I reached inside, opened the glove compartment, and rummaged until I found the map of Lake Mountain. We'd taken in the tourist sights last year, in winter while it was snowing, and I knew we still had the map in the glove compartment somewhere.

I pulled the map out and shut the car door. As I started my walk back to the shack, I could see Raven and Vern at the counter. They were both talking to each other in hushed tones. She was leaning even further forward, and they were very close to each other. Vern was smiling, his mouth moving, and Raven's head was nodding.

His eyes slid across and he saw me walking towards them. Quickly, he straightened back up and his smile quivered. Raven's head turned slightly. Her hair was hiding her eyes, but I was pretty sure she was checking to see if it was me.

Suddenly, I felt really uncomfortable.

"Well, you see," Vern then said in a louder voice. "For me, the hardest thing about making hotdogs is putting them in the bags."

The dogs were on the counter now, in their rolls and covered with ketchup and mustard. They looked really good. Vern was using his one hand to slip them deftly into the bags, which Raven was holding open.

Like Duke into the sack...

"There," he said, smiling, once both had been slotted home inside the bags.

"Great teamwork," Raven replied.

I stood next to them and placed the map on the counter, unfolding it quickly.

"Ah, good. Perfect," Vern said, spinning the map around so he could read it. "I'll show you exactly where you want to go."

Before too long, we'd paid for the hotdogs and were on our way again. Vern had circled about half a dozen areas of interest, some of which weren't to be found in any of the tourist literature. He'd picked out a couple of disused houses, Wentworth Dam, the Dam Workers Memorial, a waterfall or two and – more importantly – the old cemetery just off Watercrest Road.

It was the cemetery that really caught Raven's interest.

"What could be better?" she asked as we drove off from the roadside shack, one hand on the steering wheel, the other holding her hotdog. "We could get rid of Duke in a cemetery!"

"You think?" I asked.

"Well, it makes sense, doesn't it? It's old and disused. No one will look there. Another grave would fit in perfectly."

I took another bite of my hotdog. It really was very nice. Vern had done a great job.

"I guess."

"Either way, let's check it out."

I held the map in my hands, looking at the spider's scrawl of Vern's handwriting.

"You don't want to check out any of these other places too?" I asked.

"Nope," Raven replied, eyes on the road. "Let's just do the cemetery. I'm sure it's perfect. If not, we'll try the others."

"Okay."

I gave directions as we drove. The classical music was playing in the car. The day was lovely.

But something was bugging me.

"What did you and Vern talk about while I was getting the map?" I had to ask.

"Huh?"

"Vern? The guy at the shack? When I went to get the map from the car, you and Vern were talking about something. I could tell because you stopped talking about it when I came back."

Raven turned to look at me, her hair blowing in the wind, a smudge of mustard across her top lip.

"Are you serious?" she asked.

I nodded.

"You're having me on, right?"

I shook my head.

"You're getting paranoid, Amber," she replied, smirking.

I sat there and stared back. "Why do you say that?" I asked.

"Because, we weren't talking about *anything*."

"Didn't look that way to me."

Raven nodded. "Which is why I say you're paranoid. We weren't talking about anything."

"I saw Vern's lips move. He was talking."

Raven sighed. "We were *talking* about the hotdogs. That's all. Nothing else. Don't get so fucking paranoid about things."

I didn't think I was.

I simply asked a question and Raven wasn't answering it terribly well.

"We talked about the hotdogs and the weather," she added. "Nothing else. We *certainly* weren't talking about you, hon."

And that hurt.

Deep down inside, even though I didn't say anything or show it, it hurt.

Raven could be so cold, so cutting, on occasion. And it was at those times I wondered why I bothered being her friend. Here I am, by her side, helping her with a *dead body*, for crying out loud, and this is the way I'm treated.

She was my soul mate. But was I hers? Or was I just handy to have around to do the washing and cleaning, and to help dispose of corpses?

The more she denied anything was said or talked about, the more I was sure she and Vern *did* talk about something. And that something was probably me.

I have no idea what they spoke about, but it made me feel uneasy. Was Raven just continuing her school-girl routine? Or was she telling Vern something she didn't want me to hear?

Either way, I knew I'd never find out. There was just no use asking.

And that made me mad…and a little sad.

She wouldn't tell me the truth.

I didn't finish my hotdog. I'd lost my appetite. And, anyway, it was made for me while Raven and Vern were having their little chat, and I really didn't want to eat it now.

I threw it out of the window as we turned the corner into Watercrest Road. The cemetery was only five miles away.

The sooner we got rid of the body and returned to living a normal life, the better.

Twenty-two

I knew cemeteries fascinated Raven, they always had, and I guess she had good reason.

So, when the opportunity arose to visit one, in the hope of it being of use to us, it really shouldn't have surprised me that Raven wanted to go there first.

We sat in the car park of the old abandoned cemetery in Watercrest Road. Well, I say car park, but we actually just sat at the side of the road. The old wooden picket fence had fallen down in some sections, rotted in others, and the tree-lined grove was dotted with old, worn headstones and monuments to those who had left us.

"Wow," Raven said as she turned off the motor. "Cool, huh?"

I, on the other hand, really didn't get excited by cemeteries. In fact, they gave me the creeps. But I think that's probably pretty normal anyway, right?

So, I just sat there and stared out of the windshield.

"You know, over a hundred years ago, people would go to their local cemeteries for picnics. They saw it as a perfect opportunity to sit and chat with their departed loved ones in beautiful landscaped surrounds."

I didn't reply.

Raven turned to face me. "I'm not making this up, you know," she said. "It really used to happen."

"I believe you," I replied. I guess she knew what she was talking about.

"I bet a lot of people did that out here. It looks old enough. Look at those headstones, all rotting and eroding now. Too bad we ate the hotdogs so fast, we could've had a picnic here of our own."

I was more than pleased that we had no food for a picnic. Eating on the graves of some long-decayed locals was not my idea of a party.

"Do you think we can leave him out here?" I asked, changing the subject.

"Hmmm?" Raven was staring out the window of the car.

"Duke? Remember him? Do you think we can dump him out here?"

"Oh, I don't know," Raven said as she climbed from the car and set off towards the rusted old cemetery gates. "One way to find out, I guess."

I followed her across the dry dirt and dying weeds. We stood at the gates of the cemetery and looked around for anything suspicious. All was clear. It was just us. No one else anywhere.

Raven pushed on the cemetery gates and they squeaked loudly as they opened. She marched forwards without stopping.

"Let's do it."

I followed behind her, keeping to the dirt pathway and making sure I didn't get too close to anything that even resembled a grave. Raven walked ahead of me at a faster pace, her hands out wide, like she was welcoming all the dead. She spun around on the spot, her face beaming a large smile.

"Isn't this just *the best* cemetery you've ever seen?"

I nodded and smiled a weak smile back at her.

It didn't look like much of a cemetery to me. Graves lined both sides of the pathway, hidden mostly by brown grass and wilting weeds. No one had taken care of this place for a long time. The path was probably only thirty feet long, and it ended at the cemetery fence, which was partway down a short slope. So, this wasn't a big urban cemetery or anything like that. It was small, it was old, and there was a weird smell in the air. Not of rotting bodies or anything (I'd got used to that smell with Duke), this was more a hot, dusty, dried smell that just sat heavily in the air.

Also, there wasn't a new grave anywhere to be seen. Vern had been right, this place really *was* old and disused. Most of the tombstones had lost their inscriptions, the weather and elements taking their toll, and others had cracked or broken or fallen and decayed, just like the bodies they represented.

I wondered if leaving Duke there was the right thing to do. Sure, it was a cemetery and all, but all the graves were so old, so uncared for, that a new mound of freshly-dug grave soil would really stand out and could call attention to Duke.

Every so often, Raven walked from the path and bent over to try and read an inscription.

I didn't. I kept walking straight.

When Raven reached the end of the path, she turned around and leaned back against the fence. The sun made her hair shine and reflected off her vinyl bra and shorts. The breeze blew, sending her hair flowing across her face, but she made no attempt to straighten it.

I took my time walking down to meet her. I was in no hurry and I didn't want to give Raven the wrong impression that I was actually enjoying our time in this place.

But when I reached her, I realised she was no longer smiling. Her face had fallen, her eyes looked hollow and her arms were crossed over her chest.

"This reminds me of when we buried Paige."

Oh.

I didn't know what to say.

"It was on a day like this. In the corner of a cemetery like this."

Raven was about to hit a low.

A *big* one.

Paige went missing on the day of Raven's twenty-first birthday. She'd walked down to the local mall to buy some last minute extras for the party, but she never returned. When they *did* find her, it was four days later. Her naked body was found laying on its front, face turned to the side, hidden just off a popular walking track a few miles out of town.

Raven had never really told me the whole story from start to finish. It was obviously a horrific moment in her past that she never really wanted to dwell on, but on occasion she would tell me about her sister, about the good times, about how they would laugh and be there for each other.

But that all ended when Paige was sixteen.

Paige was different to Raven and me, so I really didn't ever hang out with her much. I always tried to spend time with Raven when Paige wasn't around. I think it was better that way, and I think Paige felt the same way. Whenever I visited, she would busy herself with other things, or go out and visit her friends. Raven and I never really discussed it; it was just the way things were.

Paige had an athletic body (she was an avid swimmer during summer and looked stunning in a bikini.) She had full breasts, long blonde hair, blue eyes, long legs and firm thighs and was just slightly shorter and thinner than Raven. She was really sweet-looking, almost the girl-next-door, you might say. Wholesome and pretty, she had a smile that could melt hearts.

And she didn't deserve what happened to her.

The autopsy revealed she had been strangled with her own bra and raped in all orifices. Of particular note, at least to the police and media, was that it was obvious that the murderer was anally raping her while strangling her, based on the trauma to her anus and rectum. There were two bite marks on her body; one on the lower left breast and the other just above and to the right of her vagina, and semen was recovered from the back of her throat, vagina, and rectum. It was surmised by the cops that she was abducted and still alive when she arrived at the location where she was eventually found; the murderer performed the rape and murder right there.

The cops were confident that with the DNA sample from the semen, and the imprint of the teeth in her skin, they would soon catch the killer. They tracked down leads, investigated clues, followed up tips from the public...but they never made even one arrest.

It was a horrible end to such a nice person, and it really screwed up Raven for a while. She withdrew into herself and didn't want to see anyone – not even me – for a long long time. And I wonder if that's when she first started to hurt herself. I'd never asked. I tried never to ask about things like that. I never wanted to see her sad or hurting.

I tried not to read the papers or listen to media reports about the murder, because I just didn't want to know. It was all too horrible to contemplate, so I blocked it all from my mind.

But now Raven had brought it up. This cemetery must've resembled the one where they buried Paige. (I didn't go to the funeral – I couldn't. I didn't want to.) After all, I was the same age as Paige when it happened. It could've just as easily been me in that coffin.

"Do you think she was in pain?" Raven asked now, her hair flowing across her eyes and mouth.

I knew this could quickly turn bad.

"Raven, I –"

"When that animal was tightening her own bra around her neck, choking the very life from her, and his cock was pumping away inside her ass. Do you think it hurt? Or do you think she was in shock already and numb to it all?"

"I...I don't know." I leant on the fence next to her and reached out, rubbing her shoulder.

"She would've been so scared."

"Try not to think about it, Raven."

"She would've held her anus so tight, trying so hard to keep him out, but it would've milked his cock as she gasped her last breath. He'd cum as she died. Her face must've filled with fear, knowing she was going to die. Knowing this bastard would get his enjoyment, filling her as life left her. His orgasm would be the last conscious thing she felt."

I put my arm around Raven. She was trying to control her emotions, but I could see them flurry across her face, somewhere between sadness, hate and anger.

"Come on," I said. "Let's get out of here. Being here isn't doing you any good."

She turned to face me. "You weren't at the funeral."

"No," I said softly, looking to the ground.

"You know, even though she lay there, outside in the elements for those four days before they found her, there was hardly any sign of decomposition. We even had an open casket funeral."

"Oh," I replied. "I didn't know that."

"She looked so beautiful, so at peace in the casket. She had a lovely smile on her face, even though her last moments were so violent. And we buried her in a cemetery just like this, on a day just like this."

"She was a vibrant, wonderful girl. I remember," I said.

"Yes," Raven nodded. "She didn't deserve to die that way."

"No one does," I muttered, then realised it probably wasn't the right thing to say, seeing we still had Duke to dispose of.

"I often think about her," Raven continued, almost to herself, one solitary tear escaping her eye and falling down her cheek. "I often wish she was still here, right beside me."

"That's only natural," I replied.

"And then sometimes I lay awake at night, thinking about her. Thinking about how she lay there for all that time, four whole days. Those flies and insects crawling all over her, eager to enter her in the same places her killer did. Her ravaged and filled vagina attracting insects and bugs. Her upturned anus, her tongue protruding from her open mouth, both breeding grounds for flies and wasps. Her lovely full breasts pushed harshly into the cold, dirty ground."

Raven had demanded and fought for permission to see the crime scene photographs. To begin with, the police didn't want her to see them as they were too graphic in nature, but Raven wanted to know exactly what happened to her sister. Exactly what the killer had done to her.

I don't know if it really helped her deal with the tragedy though.

With my arm around her shoulder, I took a step forward, slowly pulling her with me. She stopped leaning on the fence and walked forward also. We headed back up the path towards the cemetery gates.

"I still think of her there," Raven continued. "Exposed in such a horrific way. And I think about the two young boys who discovered her. How they would've first seen her. What they said to each other. Did they touch her and poke at her? Or did they run screaming for help straight away? Or did they just stand there and stare at my sister, exposed and abused, her body discarded by the bastard who had finished with her?"

"I guess we'll never know," I replied. "But you can't dwell on it. It'll eat you up inside."

"And then the cops showed up. What did they think looking at a pretty and sexy body of a sixteen year old? Did they feel any sorrow? Any sympathy? Or were they numb to it all now as well, seeing her as a dead piece of female meat lying exposed in the grass?" Raven shook her head and stared at the ground in front of us as we walked.

"And the medical examiner, probing her body at the scene, taking his damn pictures and measurements and samples from every hole. Then the cops lifting her and watching her breasts dangle and jiggle, her thighs rippling as they put her on the stretcher, covered by only a sheet, a cold white sheet. Her dead nipples showing through, the only sign of a person – a life – ever even existed."

We reached the cemetery gates and I opened them. Raven was still talking, more to herself now than to me.

"She'd be left, stretched out dead on the examining table, fluids still leaking from her, breasts and nipples and vagina being touched and probed by another stranger with his latex hands. She'd be turned and tossed limply, her beautiful body mutilated and abused in the name of forensic science. They're no better than the animal who killed her."

We reached the car and I opened the door for her. She tumbled inside, almost as if she was acting on auto-pilot. I ran around to the passenger side and climbed inside as well.

I turned to look at her, but she was staring out at the cemetery.

"It's not right," she whispered.

"What?"

She turned to look at me. "We can't do it here. We can't dump Duke here. He doesn't deserve such a peaceful end. And those people buried in there don't deserve to rest with such an asshole. It's not right. Duke has to pay, to be made an example of. He doesn't deserve peace."

I wanted to argue that we had to get rid of him somewhere and the further away from us the better. I wanted to remind Raven that dumping him out here was originally *her* idea and that she thought it was an excellent one. But I didn't say anything. Nothing I could say would change her mind right now. She was back with her sister, back when she was twenty-one and Paige was still alive. And I wasn't about to try and step in and separate her from that.

For now, she was with her memories.

And as we drove back to the lagoon, I sat alone in the car.

Alone.

Like I'd always been.

Twenty-three

It was a long, quiet trip back to the trailer, but once we got there, Raven seemed to cheer up.

"It's good to be home," she said as we both climbed from the car.

I smiled. "It sure is."

"I think I could stay here forever," she replied. "It's paradise."

Even though she said that and I agreed, we both turned to look about us, almost instinctively now, to make sure no one was around.

Nothing had changed while we were gone. There was no sign of anyone.

It was late in the afternoon by the time we arrived back, and the sun was already casting long shadows across the water and clearing.

"Looks like fish again tonight," Raven said as she turned and walked towards the trailer.

She was right. We'd both forgotten to pick up any other food. We didn't see any stores on the mountain anyway, and I certainly wasn't going to suggest going back for more hotdogs.

"I think I could learn to really like fish," I replied.

Raven laughed out loud as she unlocked the door to the trailer.

It was good to hear her laugh. I was worried on the way back from the cemetery that she might try to escape further within herself, deep down, and might hurt herself again after thinking about Paige.

The cemetery had been a bad idea. And even though Raven hid behind the gothic chick look, and always acted tough and strong, I know that really, somewhere in side, she was hurting so much. That one tear she cried for Paige symbolised the thousands she wouldn't let herself cry.

I've just never been able to get through to that part of her, never been able to help patch some of those wounds. I'd like to help, I want to, but I have no idea how to get in there, into Raven's most secret places.

"I'm going for a swim," she said as she climbed into the trailer, the door shutting behind her.

"Okay," I called back. "I'll grab the fishing line and see if I can get us some dinner."

There was no reply.

I walked over to the side of the trailer and squatted down, picking up the fishing line from where we'd stored it, behind the left wheel. It was one of those old fishing lines, blue in colour and slightly bent out of shape. I'm sure it was probably an antique of some sort, but I guess it didn't matter as long as it caught the fish.

As I straightened back up, the trailer door opened and Raven walked down the stairs and headed for the lagoon. She was naked. It hadn't taken her long to climb out of her clothes.

I wished she wouldn't walk around like that.

She marched away from me. I could see her back and buttocks. The bruises were almost completely faded now. Her hair danced from side to side, cascading down her bare back as she walked, and before I had a chance to say anything, she'd waded into the water and dived straight in.

Slowly, I walked over to the edge of the water as well, watching her swim strongly into the centre of the lagoon. Once she got there, she turned around to me, a large smile on her face.

"It's wonderful in here, Amber!" she called.

I waved back, setting the fishing line on the ground.

"Come on in!"

"No thanks," I called back. "I'll catch the fish for dinner."

"You won't catch *any* fish the way you're going!" she called.

I don't know what she meant by that.

"Come on," her voice echoed around us. "Live a little! Take off your clothes and swim with me. Let's have some fun!"

I didn't want to. But I had to admit a little part of me felt thrilled by the idea. After the trip back in the car, where I felt so alone and so far removed from Raven and the memories of her sister, suddenly she was inviting me in to the lagoon to swim with her.

Her hair was wet and glistening in the light, plastered down the sides of her face and shoulders, a long purple strand curling around her neck and chest, heading further down.

And the water *did* look nice.

"*Amber*," Raven called. "Time's running out!"

She was right. I *did* need to live a little. I didn't want to end up like Paige, my life cut short all of a sudden, my mind filled with the things I wished I'd done or seen.

If I was out there with Raven, in the middle of the lagoon, our bodies swimming side by side, the water flowing over and around us... What could be better?

So, I ignored my worries and fears. I smiled.

"Here I come!" I yelled to her as I pulled off my sneakers and socks, and climbed out of my jeans and t-shirt. I threw them into a small pile and reached around my back to undo my bra.

Janet Leigh would be so proud of me.

I waited only a second before pulling down my panties.

And then I stood in the clearing, on the edge of the lagoon, naked.

I wanted Raven to see me, to notice me, to have her eyes wander all over me before I dived in.

She was smiling back at me.

"Don't just stand there," she called. "Get out here!"

And that's exactly what I did. I took three large steps into the water and then dived into the lagoon. The shock of the cold water was exhilarating. I dived deep and low, holding my breath and kicking hard, sluicing through the water, letting it touch my lips, my nipples, my stomach and lower down too. Letting it caress me everywhere. And I loved it.

Nothing could be better than this. Nothing could beat this moment. Just Raven and me and the lagoon.

When I broke the surface, I wiped the water from my eyes and saw Raven was no more than ten feet away from me.

"Hello, Amber," Raven smiled.

"Hi," I replied.

"Glad you could make it."

Raven seemed to be her old self again, almost as if the cemetery visit was wiped from her memory. I guess it was locked away now too, deep inside her, where I could never reach.

But I was determined to try.

I swam over to her and we both floated in the middle of the lagoon. I let the water hold me as I floated on my back, arms and legs spread wide, my eyes looking up into the clear blue sky above us. Raven did the same. On a few occasions, our hands or feet touched, but we didn't say anything. We just floated quietly next to each other.

"I'm glad you're here with me, Amber," Raven said after a long while.

I didn't turn to look at her. I just smiled and continued to stare into the blue above us.

"I'm glad I'm here too," I replied.

"Are my eyes open or shut?" she asked.

I thought about it for a second and then I said, "Open."

"Yes," she replied. I had no idea whether she was telling the truth or not, and I didn't want to check.

"Are mine open or shut?" I asked her.

"Shut," she replied.

"Yes," I lied.

We floated a while longer.

"Having you by my side through all this," Raven continued. "It means a lot to me. I'm glad you're here and I want you to know I'm thankful for our friendship."

"Shhh," I replied. "You don't have to say any of this."

But I'm glad she did.

We floated some more.

I watched a couple of white puffy clouds appear from one side of my vision. They blew slowly across the sky, changing form as they did so. They were free to float anywhere. More free than us.

After a while, I could hear splashing, so I turned to look at Raven.

She was swimming towards the blowhole.

"Hey!" I called. "What are you doing?"

She stopped swimming and turned to face me.

"Sorry, didn't want to disturb you," she said.

"That's okay." I started to swim towards her. "Where are you going?"

It was obvious, but I asked anyway.

Raven nodded in the direction of the blowhole. "I'm going to get Duke."

"Get him?"

"Yeah."

"Why?"

"He can't stay there," she replied.

"I'll come and help you." I started swimming again.

"No, no," she replied, her hands out to stop me. "Don't worry about it. You stay where you are and relax. Let me do all this."

I really didn't want to, but I also didn't want to upset Raven after we'd just had some close moments together. What she said about our friendship had meant so much to me, she never usually opens up even that far with me, so I didn't want to harm my chances of her perhaps opening up some more soon. Maybe the visit to the cemetery *had* helped her in some way. Maybe she'd let me in a little closer just given some time.

So, I stopped swimming and dog-paddled in the one spot, watching as Raven swam towards the blowhole.

I wanted to be there with her, but another part of me was glad I wasn't. I didn't want to be in a dark, cold, wet hole with Duke, no matter what!

It was such a perfect day in such a perfect place, but now it had to go and get all spoiled.

Raven reached the blowhole and slowly climbed inside, against the current of the water flowing out into the lagoon. I could see the water splashing against her skin, flowing down her hair and along her back, dripping from her hands and thighs, cascading down her legs and buttocks.

I wished I was there to help her.

But I also realised how thoughtful it was of her that she wanted to keep this from me. She knew I didn't like this kind of thing, and she must've realised how much it had upset me helping her get Duke wrapped up and out there in the first place.

A lot of things you regret in life (like not going to your best friend's sister's funeral) but I knew I wouldn't regret letting Raven handle Duke right now. She was much better at these things than I was anyway.

I paddled and waited. It took a few minutes, but eventually Raven reappeared out of the blackness of the blowhole, walking backwards towards me. She was bent over, and she was pulling the sack with her.

"You need a hand?" I called, hoping she would say no.

She didn't reply.

Slowly, she climbed down into the lagoon, water still cascading across her shoulders and body from the blowhole. She steadied herself for a moment or two against the rock wall and then pushed off with her feet, sending herself backwards and bringing the sack splashing into the lagoon with her.

I didn't feel right being in the same water as Duke, not knowing what he could be leaking or oozing by now. I waited for Raven to swim over towards me, so I could help her with the sack, but she swam in a direct line from the blowhole towards the shore.

I thought about going over there to help her, but part of me didn't want to.

She needed my help, though.

And I knew what I had to do.

Slowly, I began swimming across towards her.

She reached the water's edge first and climbed from the lagoon, tugging at the sack as she did so. By the time I arrived to help, she'd already got it onto dry land and was squatting down by the opening, untying the cord at the top.

I walked out of the lagoon and stood next to her. The light breeze blew across my body, cooling the water and making me shiver just a little. But it felt good to be standing there naked and wet with Raven, both of us so natural and so exposed to the world. My nipples were erect, and it felt good.

I saw hers were too.

The sack was soaked right through, of course, its fabric now a dark colour. I don't know if that was just from the water, or whether Duke had leaked everywhere inside. I really didn't want to find out, but I could tell I was about to.

I tried to smell any weird odours in the air, but I couldn't. I squatted down next to Raven instead. Our wet, bare shoulders touched for a fleeting second.

"Any trouble?" I asked, knowing it was a silly thing to say.

"No, hon. He's dead, remember?"

"I know, I was just –"

Raven smiled and turned towards me. "Don't worry so much, Amber. It was only a joke."

I smiled.

Her eyes were so clear right then. So determined. Droplets of water ran down the bridge of her nose, down her cheeks and across her lips.

My Raven was back.

She turned to the sack. Having finally undone the knot, she opened it and we both stepped back, not knowing what to expect.

I could see the sheet we used to tie Duke up with. I could also see a deep jagged tear in it, where Raven had cut through to remove his cock and balls.

"Let's pull him out," Raven said.

I looked at her. "What for?"

"I need to look at him."

"*Why?*"

"Amber, please. I know what I'm doing, just help me out with him and let's check him. Once we've done that..." But she didn't finish her sentence. Her eyes lost focus and she stared right past me.

"Raven?" I asked, thinking maybe she'd hit a low again, maybe remembering what Duke had done to her, or thinking about Paige once more. I reached out and touched her bare shoulder. "Raven? You okay?"

Her eyes snapped back to me, refocussing on mine. "Tomorrow we might take a drive to Wentworth Dam. We could dump Duke at the memorial up there."

It sounded as good as any other plan we had. The cemetery was out. Raven didn't want to go back there and I understood completely.

And when I thought about it, I didn't want to go back there either.

"Paige would be so proud," she said.

"Huh?" I didn't understand what she meant.

Raven stood up and walked away from me, dragging the top of the sack with her. As she did so, the end of the sack swivelled in front of me.

"Okay," she said. "I'll hold onto Duke and you pull the sack from around him."

I stared at her.

"Amber, concentrate. This *is* important."

I nodded. Reached down. Held the sack.

"You ready?" she asked.

I nodded.

"Okay, I'm ready too."

I stood up in a crouch, my eyes focussed on my hands in front of me. I was holding the end of the sack tight. It felt wet and slimy. As I grasped harder, the blood disappeared from my knuckles, turning the skin pale white.

Deathly white.

"Whenever you're ready," Raven said slowly, an edge to her voice.

I held my breath, took a step back, and pulled.

It wasn't as easy as I thought it would be. I imagined I'd just pull and the sack would come away. But it was waterlogged and I'm guessing so was Duke, so it took probably almost a dozen tugs on the sack before I managed to get it out from around him.

During all that time, Raven was holding onto the sheet (and Duke) inside, giving me advice and ideas. I think I might even have touched the sheet once or twice as I pulled back the top of the sack to manoeuvre it over places where it got stuck. But I really don't want to think about that.

I could see the tear in the sheet and I knew Raven was holding onto Duke's legs or upper thighs. Right near where his *other* bits would've been, if you know what I mean. Not that they were of any use to him now.

With a final pull, the sack slipped off the rest of Duke with a sickening squelching sound. As I pulled it away, lots of maggots tumbled out of the sack and fell to the ground, creating a speckled white trail in the muddy water's edge.

I didn't feel too well once I saw them. I quickly checked my feet and legs, but none of them had fallen onto my skin, thankfully. I expected the maggots to start moving towards us, hungry and eager for new food. But none of them moved.

I walked forward slightly and looked down at them. They were still.

Dead.

"The water should've drowned them," Raven said as she looked over towards me and my pile of maggots.

I turned to face her. Her hands were working feverishly on the rope tied around Duke's body. As she pushed down on his legs, trying to give herself some slack with the rope, the sheet around him squelched and water poured out of its crevices, along with an assortment of bugs and maggots.

I couldn't find a live maggot anywhere. Submerging Duke in the blowhole had drowned each and every one of his hungry little friends.

Serves the fuckers right.

Finally, Raven untied the knot and stepped to one side. Duke unfolded like one of those Japanese fans.

The sheet was stained with a variety of different colours and there was a whole bundle of dead maggots wherever you looked. I could see the stain near his mouth, and remembered how the liquid bubbled up in front of me while I was holding him down.

"You ready?" Raven asked me.

"No," I replied.

She smirked. "Me neither."

Even though she said that, she walked towards me and squatted down next to Duke's head. Slowly, she reached out with one hand and her fingers curled around the wet, stained sheet.

"You don't have to stay here and watch this, you know," she said to me without looking up.

I stared down at her and the sheet, but I didn't want to seem like I was a coward. I was there for her, and I was going to prove it.

"No," I replied. "Go ahead. I want to see."

Raven slowly peeled back the sheet.

What was left of Duke was underneath.

To begin with, I thought his whole face was covered in maggots because all I could see was white puffiness. But I soon realised that was his skin. Sure, there were maggots here and there, a couple hanging onto the corners of his mouth, another half hidden in his left nostril, and a few swimming in the pools where his eyes used to be, but they were all dead as well.

His whole face had swelled up, taking on a sickly white opaque colour. It almost looked like the skin had come away from the rest of him, floating there on top of a layer of water or something. He looked like he'd spent way too much time in a bath and his skin had gone all spongy. In fact, he looked almost like a large dead maggot himself.

Well, he *was*, wasn't he?

Oh, and there was the smell too. That was probably the worst part of it. I didn't think Duke could smell worse than he did in the wardrobe, but the water seemed to have brought out every possible unpleasant bodily odour and magnified it. It didn't hit us until we removed the sheet from his face.

I took a step backwards, my hand covering my mouth, as I fought the need to vomit.

And Raven was pulling the sheet back even further. I don't know how she could stand being so close to him. Maybe she was holding her breath.

She removed the sheet from his shoulders and chest as well.

Maggots fell from the sheet and from Duke's clothes. I watched them fall to the ground, some falling onto Raven's bare toes.

I took another step back and turned away. I'd seen enough by now.

I heard Raven whisper, "*Damn.*"

"He looks even worse," I managed to say.

"I thought his little dip in the water would clean him up, wash away the maggots and make him like new," she said, almost talking to herself. "But not like this. He's no good like this."

I removed my hand from my mouth. I was gulping in lungfuls of fresh air, trying to rid the stink of Duke from my system.

The lagoon was so beautiful, so tranquil.

Except for the rotting corpse on the water's edge.

"Okay," Raven called to me. "Help me wrap him up."

I turned to her. "Huh?"

"Help me wrap him again."

It wasn't as if he was a Christmas present or anything...

"Are you *serious?*"

Raven put her hands on her hips, the rope she'd used to strangle him hanging from her right hand.

"Of course I am. Let's wrap him up and we'll put him in the back of the Suburban. Then we'll dump him at the memorial near the dam tomorrow."

"Can't we just stick him in the sack and leave him in the blowhole?"

She shook her head. "No, sweets. You *know* why. He's no use to us now. We need to get rid of him, and we can't do that here. The memorial is the place for him now."

I ran a hand through my hair. It was still wet.

"I'm just so tired of all this," I said sadly.

"I know," Raven nodded. "And hopefully we can end all this tomorrow. Now, go and grab another sheet from the trailer and we'll wrap him up again."

"Can't we use the one already around him?"

"We *will*, Amber." Raven was starting to sound like she was talking to a stupid child. "I don't want all his mess in my Suburban. Let's wrap his body in another sheet and that'll soak most of it up. *Then* we can empty out the back of the car and put him in there. Then *tomorrow* we'll dump him, okay?"

I nodded. I didn't care. I'd do anything to be rid of the puffy white corpse of Duke now.

Anything.

Raven leaned forward and started replacing the sheet across Duke's face.

Good. I didn't have to look at him anymore.

I turned and headed for the trailer.

I just wanted him gone. I just wanted things back to how they were.

I wanted my Raven back.

Me and Raven.

It shouldn't be that hard.

As I reached the trailer, I opened the door.

I heard it behind me.

A *clatter* and a *clack*.

I spun around to look at Raven.

She was by the body, but she was standing quickly, looking away from Duke, the sheet falling from her hands.

I followed her eyes, across the stream to the other side, over to where the wildflowers were blowing gently in the breeze.

I saw him stand upright.

I watched him walk out from behind the wildflowers.

He was looking at Raven, and she was looking at him.

We'd been caught red handed.

Twenty-four

"Get inside the trailer," Raven called without turning to face me.

I didn't say anything, I just stood and stared.

And then he looked at me too.

I backed up a step, a chill slicing down my spine.

"Get in the *trailer*, Amber, and *shut* the door," Raven said in a low voice.

The guy didn't walk across the stream, he just stood on the water's edge, looking across towards us.

I climbed up the trailer steps, opened the door and stood in the doorway, looking out.

"Close the door."

"No!" I called.

"*Close it!*"

"Not without you in here too," I yelled.

The guy was looking back at Raven now. He stared at her for a long time, and she matched his stare.

Only then did I realise we were *both* naked. I placed one hand between my legs, covering myself.

Not that there was much point. He'd seen everything by now anyway.

Just how long had he been standing there, looking at us? Spying on us! How much had he seen? How much did he know?

The guy was young and well built. He had short-cropped, brown hair, and was probably about six feet tall. He was wearing dark clothing, almost the same colours as the trees in the forest behind him. I guess they were like the camouflage uniforms the recruits in the army would wear. He wore black leather hiking books, green-black trousers and a baggy jacket. The jacket had lots of pockets and was half open, so you could see the black t-shirt underneath.

He didn't say anything.

Raven was backing away from the lagoon now, away from Duke. Neither of us cared about Duke all of a sudden.

"Get out the gun!" Raven called to me.

We didn't have one, but I knew what she was playing at.

"You know where the ammunition is?" she called.

"Yes," I yelled back. "It's here on the table."

The guy turned to face me then, his head tilting slightly, as if he was trying to work out if I was lying.

My hand squeezed tighter between my legs.

Raven was at the trailer steps by then, climbing up and backing inside next to me. She shut the door as she did so, throwing the latch.

"*Fuck!*" she said. "It's all fucked."

We stared at each other for I don't know how long. Staying quiet, we listened but could hear nothing.

"Raven, what are we going to do?" I asked.

She shook her head. "I don't know."

"He saw the body."

"I know."

"He saw *everything*."

"I'm aware of that, Amber," she said as she pushed past me, walking down to the other end of the trailer and climbing onto the bed.

She knelt there on the mattress and I wanted to mention that she was still wet from the lagoon and that she'd get the bed all wet. But at that moment in time, it really didn't seem to matter.

She leaned forward, swept aside the curtain covering the small window by the bed and peered outside.

Taking her lead, I pushed the meals table out of the way and climbed onto the couch. I peered out the window above the couch and out into the lagoon.

He was still there. Standing right where we'd left him, on the other side of the stream, near the wildflowers.

He was looking towards the trailer, his head still tilted to one side. He was hardly moving at all.

"Who *is* he?" I asked, probably to myself.

But Raven answered. "I wish I knew."

"How long has he been there?"

"He's seen everything," Raven whispered. "Probably all of it. And there's nothing we can do."

I turned to look at Raven, but she didn't look at me. She was still staring out the window, but she looked as if she was a long way away, staring at nothing. Her breathing was deep and fast, her chest moving up and down in a steady fashion.

"What can we do?"

She blinked a couple of times and shook her head back and forth. Then she looked over at me. She smiled a sad smile and shrugged her shoulders. "Nothing, hon. I guess it's over. There's nothing we can do now. It's out of our control."

I looked back out the window. He was still just standing there, so still, not moving.

"Why doesn't he *do* something?" I asked.

"Maybe he's waiting for us to do something," Raven replied.

My eyes darted across to the semi-covered body of Duke, lying by the water's edge for all the world to see.

We were so stupid to let our guard down and not consider that anyone could come across our little campsite at any time. I guess we started to think that this lagoon really *was* our world, and only our world, and that no one would dare enter it. Our slice of Heaven that no one else could touch. But it was a public park, and we should've realised that at *any* time, someone could walk right into it and catch us eating, fishing, swimming…or wrapping dead bodies.

It seems so stupid now that we got so complacent about what we were doing. That we thought we were home free. That we thought the rest would be so easy.

You're only immortal for a limited time…

"Do you think -?"

I started to say something, but I quickly stopped as the guy took a step forward. Neither of us said anything, our eyes were glued to his movements.

He took another.

Slowly, like a cat on the prowl, he stepped into the stream. His eyes were still focussed on the trailer and I wondered for a moment if he could see both of us through the windows. But I don't think he could.

He was being very careful, and moving very slowly, almost as if he was ready for anything.

Which is how *we* should've been!

Maybe he thought we had the gun trained on him and could fire it at any time, maybe he thought we were getting ready for a counter-attack with knives and axes and machetes. Who knows what he was thinking, but he was being as cautious as possible.

The water lapped around his boots. Even from where we hid in the trailer, we could hear the trickle of the stream and the splash his boots made as he took another slow step forward.

That lovely lagoon water. So cool and so fresh.

Part of the reason we let our guard down.

With just a few more strides, he stepped out on the other side of the stream. He was standing in the clearing, still staring towards us, still taking each step very carefully and very slowly.

Everything was silent. Like the world had just stopped turning. Nothing existed except us, the lagoon, and this intruder.

He stopped there and stood for a while.

"Come on," Raven whispered. "Show us what you want!'

He was closer to us now and I could make out some of his features. His dark brown hair was being blown about by the breeze. He had a sharp, elongated face, and didn't look as if he'd shaved for a few days. He also didn't look particularly ugly. I guess he looked like any normal average guy you'd see on the street anywhere. It was only his short haircut and army camouflage clothes that made him look scary. That and the fact he'd appeared out of nowhere while we were dealing with a corpse and had scared us half into next century.

He was well built, of that I was sure. I knew it wasn't just what he was wearing. He had a broad chest and even though I couldn't see his arms, I guessed they were muscled too.

The upshot of all this is, he could probably take Raven and me on and win in an instant. We didn't stand a chance against this guy.

Bad news.

Very.

Bad.

News.

He moved so silently, with such stealth, that it wasn't surprising that we hadn't heard him before now. It was only the *clack* and *clatter* that we heard that gave him away. A sound I'm guessing he made by accident. No one in their right mind would blow a cover like that on purpose.

And that's when my brain started processing it all.

How long had he been watching us? How much did he know?

And if he could be so quiet out there, how many *more* of his kind could be hiding along the edge of the lagoon now, still watching us?

I felt sick.

Someone *else* now knew about Duke. Someone else knew what had happened. All our stories and all our plans were shattered. This was the end of the dream.

This was the end of Raven and me.

I knew Raven must be thinking about the same things. She must've realised it was all over, and I turned my head to look at her.

She was still kneeling on the bed, leaning against the window, one strand of purple curl floating across her left eye. I couldn't read her face, but I could see sadness in her eyes, and maybe a look of defeat.

There was nothing I could do to change that. Events were now out of our hands.

I wanted to go over and hug her, to comfort her, but I really didn't know what to say.

I turned back to stare out the window.

Mr. G.I. Joe was standing straight now, his head no longer tilted, his arms out on his hips. He looked as if he was saying, "Well, come on, give me your best shot, if you dare." But, of course, we had no shot to give.

He stared at us, we stared at him.

And I prayed he couldn't see us through the windows and that he would just go away, disappear, leave us here and never come back.

And then he turned.

Yes!

He turned his back on us.

Go on, *shoo!*

He walked straight over to Duke.

"*Fuck*," Raven whispered. "Get the fuck out of it."

He didn't stop. Within seconds he was standing over Duke, his back still to us, almost daring us to do something if we had the guts to.

But we didn't. How could we?

I wanted to look to Raven, to follow her lead, to help carry out her plan. But I knew she didn't have one. Neither of us did.

The guy squatted down, his hand reaching out, removing the sheet from around Duke's head.

I thought he'd pull back in horror, run to the side of the lagoon and lose his lunch or something. But he didn't. Carefully and slowly, he pulled the sheet back some more. His head moving back and forth. So slowly, and with such precision.

He was taking it all in.

I had this sinking feeling in my guts and I knew there was nothing we could do. Our secret was out. There was a witness who could tie us to the body.

"Let's get in the car," I found myself saying.

"Huh?"

"He doesn't know who we are. He doesn't know who the body is. Let's get in the car and get out of here. Just drive and leave the state or something, but let's just get out of here."

I turned to look at Raven, but she was shaking her head. "Won't work, sweets. He's seen the car, he's probably seen the licence plates. He knows we're two girls in a trailer and that we drive a Suburban. Once they identify the body, it's not going to take a brain surgeon to work out that the two girls seen at the lagoon match the two girls who disappeared from the trailer park the day Duke went missing."

She was right.

"There's no point running," Raven continued. "Not any more."

The guy draped the sheet back where he found it, across Duke's face, and slowly stood back up. His head turned slightly, probably checking out the elephant sack and rope on the ground nearby, and then he nodded to himself.

Putting it all together one step at a time.

Bastard.

Then, in one motion, he turned around to face us again, a look of grim determination on his face. He didn't look happy at all.

He put his hands in his pockets and started walking.

Straight towards us.

Both Raven and I instinctively pushed away from the windows, and I think I sucked in a deep lungful of air.

We could still see outside, though, and could see him marching towards us.

Oh please God, no. Don't let this be happening. Please God please!

I looked over at Raven. She was kneeling in the middle of the bed now, facing me. Her body was wet, but I didn't know if it was water from the lagoon or sweat. Her eyes were closed, but her head was held high, almost as if she was defiant to the very end, and the very end was very close indeed.

I turned back to the window, but I couldn't see him now from where I was sitting. Slowly, I leaned forward again, my face getting closer and closer to the glass.

But I still couldn't see him.

One moment he was walking towards us, the next he was gone.

I bent further forward, as far as I dared go, and surveyed the lagoon. He wasn't out there. He wasn't with Duke. He wasn't over by the stream.

Had he really gone?

I couldn't believe it. It was just way too easy.

Then his head was right in front of my eyes, right in front of my window.

I pulled back and stifled a scream, my heart beating so hard I thought it would break through my chest.

Luckily, he hadn't seen me. His head passed from the left of the window to the right. He'd walked past without looking in.

Inches away from me!

But that also meant he'd done something like circle the trailer, or at least walked to the back to have a look around.

Did he look inside one of the other windows?

I sure hoped he didn't!

I leaned forward again, pushing myself up hard against the window so I could look along the side of the trailer. My breath fogged up the glass and I used my hand to wipe it away. He was bent down now, hands cupped around his eyes as he looked into the windows of the Suburban. His head moved from side to side, as he checked out what was in the car.

Then, after a few moments, he dropped his left hand to the driver's door. He opened it and the door swung wide.

I wanted to tell Raven what was happening, but I didn't have the breath to do so. Plus, I didn't want to worry her or make her panic or anything.

By now, he'd climbed inside the car and all I could see were his boots dangling out of the doorway.

Yes, steal it! That's what he'd come for! He wanted to steal the car.

Go on, take it, take it and leave us alone, I screamed in my head.

But it was wishful thinking on my part, a hope that all this could be solved so quickly, if only the guy stole the car and then left us in peace.

He climbed out of the Suburban and closed the driver's door. I checked his hands, but he wasn't carrying anything, he hadn't grabbed anything from the car. He walked back towards us, each step getting him closer to the trailer and to Raven and me.

I pulled back from the window. I didn't want him to see me.

The world outside was still so quiet. Deathly still.

We were trapped.

I turned to look at Raven. She was in the same position, her head high and her eyes closed.

One tear rolling down her cheek.

"It'll be alright, Raven," I whispered. "I won't let anything happen to us."

She didn't respond.

And then he knocked on the door.

Both of us jumped and Raven's eyes sprang open. She stared at the door and I turned to stare at it too.

He knocked again.

It was a light *ratt-a-tatt-tatt*, nothing forceful, nothing demanding. Almost friendly.

Or was he just being wary.

Neither of us moved.

We didn't say anything.

I held my breath.

It was stupid really. I mean, he *knew* we were in there. He *saw* us go in. So, unless we had a secret passageway underground to a safe house or something, then he knew we were still in there.

Ratt-a-tatt-tatt.

Again!

He was persistent, that was for sure. I glanced at Raven. Her eyes darted to me and she shook her head. I had no intention of opening the door, but it was good to know that neither did she.

Ratt-a-tatt-tatt.

I wanted to shout or scream or do something, but there was nothing we could do.

My eyes kept focussed on the door.

And then I saw the door handle move!

Ever so slightly.

But it did.

He was testing to see if it was locked.

My eyes checked the lock. I remembered Raven throwing the latch to lock the door when she came in, but I wanted to check anyway.

It was fine. It held firm.

But the doorhandle moved some more.

Up and down.

All of a sudden I felt too close to him. There was nothing more than a couple of feet between the front door and me. I climbed from the couch as quietly as I could and, without taking my eyes from the door, I backed away towards the bed.

The trailer rocked slightly as I moved, and I knew that he would notice the movement outside, but right at that moment, I didn't care.

Ratt-a-tatt-tatt.

I felt Raven's hands on my back before I felt the side of the bed against my legs. She guided me as I climbed backwards onto the bed and knelt next to her.

She put her arms around me and held me tight. I could feel the warmth of her body against mine as she hugged me.

Ratt-a-tatt-tatt.

She turned and our eyes met. I looked deeply into hers and I'm sure she was looking directly into my most inner being.

"I'm so sorry," she whispered to me. "You shouldn't have been involved in all this."

"Shhh," I said as I ran my fingers through her long, wet hair.

"I never wanted you involved in this," she continued.

I nodded, I understood.

"But I'm glad you're here with me. I need you with me."

I kinda smiled, but it didn't work. Instead, a couple of tears escaped and rolled down my cheeks.

Raven bent forward and softly kissed them. "Don't cry, Amber. I'm not worth it."

She pulled me to her chest and rocked us both slowly back and forth.

I wanted to tell her she *was* worth it. I wanted to tell her how much of a friend she was to me, how much I needed her too. But the words wouldn't come. Just the tears. They rolled down my face as she rocked us more. They fell from my cheeks and onto the tops of her breasts. Slowly, they rolled down to her nipples and across the metal barbells, spreading out over them and making them shiny and reflecting the light.

My tears were soaking into her skin.

I felt scared and safe at the same time.

Ratt-a-tatt-tatt.

Again.

Ratt-a-tatt-tatt.

Twenty-five

I don't know how long we sat there. My crying stopped and the tears dried. Even the water from the lagoon dried from our bodies after a while. Maybe I fell asleep for a short period, or I just let myself escape into the warmth and softness of Raven.

It was a long while before I realised that the knocking on the door had stopped.

When I did, I looked up at Raven. Her eyes were open and they looked puzzled. She was staring at the door, but she wasn't saying anything.

I started to speak, but she shook her head and placed a finger across my lips.

"No," she mouthed to me.

So we stayed there a while longer. Raven's eyes darting across to the windows and to the door. She was listening for the slightest sound, but neither of us could hear a thing.

I turned my head so I could see the door again. The handle was no longer moving and it was still locked shut. So that was good.

But no knocking.

Did he just leave? He couldn't have!

It was weird. Would someone who seemed so interested in what was happening just leave us here?

Then I thought maybe he *had* stolen the car after all and that was all he *really* wanted. But I hadn't heard the car engine. I'm sure if Raven had thought he was stealing the car, *her* Suburban, she would've put up a fight.

So, everything was quiet. It was almost as if the guy had never existed. Maybe he hadn't. Maybe it was all in our minds. Or a dream or something? But he was real, alright, and we both knew it.

Still, would he just *leave* like that? Knowing we're in here?

Raven must've been thinking the same thing.

Slowly, her hands left me and she climbed from the bed. I stayed where I was, watching her back as she walked over to the couch and leaned forward, staring out the window.

Her head moved from left to right, as she surveyed outside.

She didn't say anything, and neither did I. Even though I desperately wanted to know if he was out there. After a minute or so, she turned back to face me and she shrugged her shoulders.

"He's gone," she mouthed, without speaking.

I couldn't believe it, and I guess my face mirrored my thoughts, as Raven walked back to me and climbed onto the bed once more.

"It's true," she whispered as she knelt across from me and held my hands in hers. "He's not out there, I can't see him anywhere."

"And Duke?" I whispered back.

She nodded. "He's still out there. He hasn't moved."

We stared at each other for a long time. I grasped Raven's hands harder.

"Then what do we do?"

"I have no idea," she replied.

"We can't just sit here, not now. We can't stay."

"He's gone, hon."

"He may come back."

"But what if he doesn't?"

I knew what she was saying. I didn't want to leave the lagoon either. But I didn't think we had much choice anymore. He knew about us, he knew where we were, and he knew about Duke.

"What if he's gone to call the cops?"

Raven's forehead furrowed, as if she hadn't considered that scenario.

"Do you think he'd do that?" she asked.

"Wouldn't *you?*"

Raven didn't reply. She sat back on her haunches and let go of my hands. She twirled her curls with her left hand.

"I don't know," she said, almost to herself. "But if he has, he's got enough information for the cops to know exactly who we are." She turned to look into my eyes. "There's no point in running, Amber. They'll find us anyway. Here or somewhere else."

I could feel Raven slipping, losing the fire in her eyes, the spark I needed to keep going.

I had to be strong, I had to keep her focussed.

"We *have* to leave, Raven. Let's put Duke back in the blowhole and get out of here. The quicker we move, the more space we can put between here and us. We can't give up the fight now, we can't let them find us."

Her eyes dropped to her hands and I wondered if she was going to cry again.

"Don't let them beat us, Raven," I said as I put her hands back in mine. "Don't let Duke win."

And I think that's what did it. The thought of Duke beating her, even from the grave, was enough to get her mind working again. Her head lifted and she stared me straight in the eyes.

I could see the fire, the anger, the hope all back in her eyes. I knew Raven was back.

All of a sudden she was back in control.

I'd done it.

"You're right," she said as she climbed off the bed once more and went from window to window, checking all around the trailer. "For all we know, we frightened him off. Two girls, a dead body, and we told him we had a gun too, so maybe he's decided this is one little happy family snap he wants no part of. I mean, he certainly doesn't want any part of a murder investigation, so he's probably fled, tail between his legs, and wants nothing to do with us."

I nodded, even though I thought it was unlikely that the guy would just leave.

But, then again, he *had* just left!

"Nope, he's not out there," Raven said as she looked out the final window, the one over the kitchen sink. "Nowhere to be seen."

Before I had the chance to stop her, before I could say a word, she marched across to the door, unhooked the latch and threw open the door.

"Raven, *don't!*"

But, like I said, it was too late.

She'd opened the door and already walked out onto the top step.

She looked around again and shook her head. "I'm telling you, hon. He's not here. He's gone."

Slowly, I climbed from the bed and walked over to join her at the door. I looked out onto the lagoon and everything seemed as it should. Well, apart from Duke lying there in his splotchy shroud.

The sun was setting and the lagoon was getting darker, as well as colder, and I'm sure I could see steam rising from Duke's body, but I guess I could've imagined it.

There wasn't a whole lot of daylight left for us to do much.

I looked around some more, making sure the guy wasn't hiding somewhere. But really, we had no way of knowing. We didn't know how long he'd been watching us, and in the clothes he wore, he could've been watching us for days. Plus, he could be hiding now and we wouldn't see him anyway.

"I'm going to check," Raven said as she walked out into the clearing.

"Huh?" I said, not sure of what she meant.

She swung around to face me and pointed over her shoulder. "I'm going across the stream to check he's not still in his hiding place."

"Are you *crazy?*" I asked.

"We have to know."

"But he could do *anything!*" I replied.

Raven smiled at me. "He had a chance to do that when we were trapped in the trailer, but he didn't. I'm starting to think he's more scared of us than we are of him."

I didn't think that was right. He just couldn't get into the trailer because it was locked. If it *wasn't* locked, there's no telling what he might've done.

But I knew I couldn't stop her.

"At least put some clothes on," I pleaded.

Raven laughed at that suggestion. "I think he's seen it all, Amber. He's had a real good look already. At *both* of us!"

She turned from me and marched across the clearing, passing by Duke's body without even a second glace and moving on into the stream, like she had a mission to complete and she was going to complete it now.

I stood watching her from the doorway, not sure whether I should stay here or join her.

After all, she'd need protection if he was still in the bushes... but I just couldn't leave the relative safety of the trailer.

Not that I felt safe. Far from it. But I wasn't going over there for anything.

Raven was splashing across the stream, heading straight for the wildflowers, where we'd first seen him. She didn't stop. She charged forward. If she was scared, she didn't show it.

I watched as she reached the other side of the stream and climbed the small hill to where the wildflowers blew gently in the breeze. She stood there for only a second before she stepped through the flowers. They surrounded her, brushing against her thighs. I could tell it would be easy for someone to hide in the flowers, if they were squatting down or kneeling. We'd probably never look that closely to see them hiding there.

Raven peered around and then squatted down. I could see only the top of her head, and that was because she wasn't trying to hide. If she wanted to, I'm sure she could've made herself invisible.

After a short while, she stood up again and turned around to face me. She held her hands out on each side and shrugged her shoulders. I guess that was to tell me she was alone and she didn't know where the guy had fled to.

As she made her way down the slope and back into the water, I slipped away from the door and grabbed my bathrobe. All of a sudden, I wanted to have some clothes on, any clothes, that would protect me from any countless number of eyes that might still be out there.

Raven had finished crossing the stream and was walking back across the clearing as I tied the cloth belt around me.

I felt better then, protected from whoever could see us.

"Find anything?" I asked as she walked up to the trailer.

She shook her head. "Nope. He's not there. But I saw where he's been."

"What do you mean?"

"There's a whole flattened area just behind the slope where I think he's been lying down to watch us. All those flowers are crushed and flattened, like he's been there for hours, maybe days."

"We haven't been here *that* long," I replied.

"I know. But he's been there for a while, maybe almost as long as we have. Or maybe not." Raven shrugged again, running a hand through her curls. "I guess we'll never know."

She turned to look out into the twilight of the lagoon once more.

"Either way," she said. "It gives me the creeps knowing he was watching us."

"I know. He could've seen us fishing and eating. And swimming in the lagoon too."

"And with Duke," she whispered.

"Yeah," I agreed. "He saw us with Duke alright."

And we both turned our heads to look at the half-covered body of Duke, still lying by the water's edge.

I'm sure I could see steam rising from his body. He seemed larger now too, more round. He just lay there like a sack of discarded rubbish. Which, I guess, is what he was.

"We need to fix that," I muttered.

"Yes," Raven agreed. "But not now."

"Huh?"

"In the morning," she turned to face me, a worried expression on her face.

"Are you *serious*?" I asked. "We can't just leave him there."

"He's not going anywhere, Amber. And the guy's already had a real good close-up look at Duke, so there's no point trying to hide the fact."

"But what if someone else comes along and sees him?"

"It's getting dark, sweets. He'll be alright out there. I'm exhausted. The last thing I want to do now is deal with Duke," Raven said as she climbed up the steps and pushed past me into the trailer. "I need time to think. And lots of it. We'll deal with Duke in the morning."

I turned to look back outside again, across to the lagoon and to the wildflowers. As the twilight turned into night, I scanned the water's edge for any sign of movement, any sign of life. I couldn't see any. All I knew for sure was that the darker it got, the less we would see.

"Let's keep it dark in here tonight, Raven?" I asked.

"Good idea," she replied.

All of a sudden, I felt a bit safer. If it was dark out on the lagoon and dark in the trailer, no one would be able to see anything.

Our slice of heaven, the lagoon, was quickly turning sour. What we thought would be our perfect new home, where we could escape from the world, was slowly decaying, just like Duke. And there he was, lying flat on his back at the water's edge, steaming away and slowly polluting our hideaway. Now we had to add the hill of wildflowers, and the knowledge that someone had been there too, encroaching on our world. Souring it. Destroying it.

The darkness felt comforting, like a barrier between us and them. Something that couldn't be defeated by any of us.

I closed the trailer door and made sure it was locked.

Turning, I found Raven lying straight on the bed, her arm across her forehead, her breathing deep and rhythmical. Her eyes were closed and she was deep in thought.

Without saying a word, I crossed to the bed and climbed in next to her. I lay on my side and slipped my arm across her stomach. Her body felt warm and comforting, her skin so smooth and so right.

I closed my eyes and let her think.

And that is how we stayed.

Uninterrupted.

For hours.

Sunday, July 14.

Twenty-six

My eyes were open when Raven woke.

I was staring at her, watching her sleep. The sunlight played across her hair and features, her mouth was upturned in a little smile. She looked so peaceful and so content.

We were both toasty warm and relaxed, our legs entwined and hips pushing against each other. I think we could've stayed like that for ever. I know I certainly wanted to. But as I watched consciousness wash over Raven, I saw the smile slip from her face, and worry etch itself across her forehead.

I hugged her harder, squeezing her against me. I could feel her ribs dig deeper into my stomach and the cold metal barbell from her left nipple touched the top of my right breast. I slowly ran my hand up and down her spine.

She opened her eyes then too.

I smiled at her, but she stared straight back at me.

"Good morning," I whispered.

"Hi," she said.

"Sleep well?"

"Not really."

Which surprised me, because I fell asleep quickly and I'm pretty sure I slept all the night through. But it seemed Raven had been unsettled and troubled, thinking about what had happened and what we had to do.

"You okay?" I asked.

She nodded. "Just a rough night."

"Oh." My hand stopped on her back. I rested it on her hip instead.

"Too many things running around in my mind," she continued and she dug her elbow into the pillow and lifted her head to rest it on her right hand. "I was thinking about what to do, what we *can* do, and how to do it."

I didn't speak, I just looked into her eyes and let her talk. She would know what was best for us. She always did.

"I think I spent half the night trying to factor in possibilities out of our control. What could go wrong, what we'd say and how we'd act. It's all just too hard. Basically, that guy saw us yesterday because I got lazy. It's that simple. I've put us both at risk because I let my guard down and thought everything would be okay. But I was wrong. And I was stupid to let it happen. It puts you in danger and I don't want that."

"Don't worry about me," I whispered.

"But I do."

I smiled. It was nice to hear Raven say that.

"We have to get out of here, and we have to do it soon, before anyone else finds out what happened."

I nodded. "Okay. I think that's for the best too."

"Remember the Wentworth Dam Workers Memorial?"

"Yes," I replied. I remember we visited it last year when we were checking out the tourist sights on the mountain. Raven wanted to stop there specifically. It was a boring old memorial to me, but she spent quite a while there, walking all around and touching it. It was a large, square sarcophagus halfway up the slope where the dam wall was located. It was laid in memory of 63 workers who died when the first dam wall collapsed during construction of the second stage some forty years ago. Maybe Raven had been interested in it because so many people had died there. But I never asked, I just sat in the car and waited until she was ready to leave.

The tourist information had a huge write-up on exactly what the memorial was made of and how it was designed. It was a brick and concrete oblong box, to be truthful, designed back in the days when looks didn't count, only functionality did. So, as far as memorials go, it was pretty ugly. And be damned sure that if one of *my* loved ones was to be remembered by something *that* ugly, I'd kick up a real fuss to get it changed.

"You want to bury Duke's body near the memorial?" I asked.

Raven smiled as she nodded. "Think about it, hon. What could be better? It's a place we could dump him and bury him and no one would ever know! Just you and me. The memorial would be like his tombstone."

"But it's a public place, filled with tourists. How do we get him there without being seen?"

"I know, I know. It's not going to be easy, and some of the details are yet to come to me, but I think it's the best place. For a whole lot of reasons."

I didn't really know how we would be able to do it, but I didn't want to say anything too much. A plan was a plan, after all. The fire was in Raven's eyes and I knew she was working out the details to save us both. I wasn't about to stop that. I'm sure she'd have the answers when they were needed. It was certainly better than leaving him in the blowhole.

"We'll wrap up Duke, get him out of our lagoon and put him in the Suburban. We'll drive to the memorial and sit and wait. Wait for the tourists to leave. Wait for hours if needs be. Wait for darkness. And then we can spend the whole night digging."

It was a Sunday, so there'd be plenty of tourists around. We also didn't have picks or shovels or *anything* to help us dig.

"Are you sure this will work?" is all I asked.

Raven nodded. "It'll work. Trust me, dear."

And so I did.

I trusted Raven.

Like I always did.

We set to work quickly that morning. After resting with each other for only a few minutes more, Raven unlocked herself from my embrace and climbed from the bed.

She dressed in her black PVC bra again, this time wearing a dark long sleeved mesh top that didn't hide much at all. She also slipped into her vinyl drive-in pants. They had two large silver zips for pockets and one even larger zip that went from the front of the pants, down between the legs and right up the other side, all the way to the back. If you opened that zip all the way you'd see *more* than everything. I had an idea why they were called drive-in pants, but I really didn't want to know if I was correct. She didn't put on any shoes or boots, she just kept her feet bare.

She prepared breakfast for us too while I lounged in bed a while longer. I didn't really want to get up. I felt safe and protected in bed with Raven, in her trailer. But without her next to me, that safety evaporated as quickly as Raven's body heat from the sheets.

"Breakfast is ready," she called to me.

It was just dry cereal again, but that was all we had. And I knew we didn't have time to go fishing that morning. Raven had a plan, and she was ready to act it out, right now. Or as soon as possible.

She was eating her breakfast as I climbed from the bed and slowly got dressed. I picked my favourite baggy blue jeans, my blue converse sneakers, a brown Buck 65 t-shirt and my black hooded jacket. I wanted to feel comfortable, so I picked my favourite clothes, and I also knew that they might help me blend in to my surroundings, just in case. Especially with the hood. It would cover my whole head and face if I needed it to.

As I sat down to breakfast, Raven was finishing hers.

I think we were both lost in our own thoughts and worries about what the day would bring, but I also think we were preparing ourselves mentally for what was to come.

Raven was quietly humming some classical tune to herself as she stood and placed her bowl in the sink.

I watched from where I was sitting, my eyes slipping through the curls running down her back, along her spine to the strap of her bra, down through the mesh top to her drive-in pants where that big ugly zip finished up way too high.

If Duke had seen her in *those* pants...

I tried to wipe the thought from my mind.

If Duke had got access to her through *that* zip...

I looked down at what was left of my cereal, trying hard to concentrate on something else, to think about something else. Anything.

It didn't work, so I looked up again at Raven.

Her back was still towards me and she was wiping her bowl with a dishcloth. Once she was finished, she reached up to the cupboard over the sink, but then her hand hesitated for a second before she withdrew it completely.

I dropped my eyes back to the cereal, hoping she hadn't seen me watching her.

So that's where it is...

I waited a few seconds before looking up at her again. This time, she was facing me, leaning back against the sink, the cereal bowl now resting to one side.

She was standing exactly where she was when this whole thing started, when I first walked in to be told about Duke...

Damn him. His name again! He was always there to spoil it for us!

We *had* to be rid of him that day!

"Ready?" Raven smiled a crooked smile.

I nodded.

"Good."

She pushed away from the sink and walked to the door. Unlocking it, she threw it open and breathed in a deep lungful of mountain air.

"I won't let them take all this away from us, Amber," she said as she turned to face me. "You believe me, don't you?"

I nodded, and I think I *did* believe her. If anyone could make our problems go away, it was Raven, I was sure of it.

"Good." She leaned forward and kissed me lightly on the forehead. "Okay, here's the plan. I'm going to go over and wrap up Duke good and proper. While I'm doing that, I want you to clear everything out of the back of the Suburban and bring it all in here and stockpile it on the bed, okay?"

"Okay," I replied. I stood up with my bowl, but Raven intercepted me, taking it from my hands.

"I'll do that," she replied. "You make a start on clearing out the Suburban."

And that's exactly what I did. I left Raven in the trailer and stepped outside slowly, my eyes no longer taking in the beauty of the lagoon. I was now on the lookout, searching for any sign of someone watching us. I looked for any movement, anything suspicious. I focused long and hard on the wildflowers across the stream, but I couldn't see anyone.

Only once I was satisfied no one was there – and how could I *really* be sure? – did I finally look at the lovely morning that surrounded me. But that didn't last long either, as my eyes came to rest on the stained sheet that contained Duke.

This is all *your* fault, you fucker!

I sighed deeply and walked over to the Suburban.

It was a little creepy heading towards the car, knowing the guy had been there, actually climbed *in it*, just a few hours before. I reminded myself to tell Raven that I saw him looking in the car, because I was sure she'd want to know.

First, I opened the driver's door and looked inside. Everything seemed normal. Nothing was out of place that I could tell. I leaned forward and checked out the back seats too, but they were fine as well.

He didn't steal a thing.

Closing the door, I straightened up and looked around me once more, my eyes dancing from the lagoon to the blowhole, to the wildflowers, the trailer, and the wooden steps that lead up the rock wall.

All was quiet.

I tried to tell myself that, but I couldn't get over the feeling someone was watching me. At first, I thought maybe it was the guy from last night. But then, as I walked around the back of the Suburban and opened the back doors, I started to wonder if it was *Raven* who was watching me. After all, she hadn't come out of the trailer yet.

What was she doing in there? I had an idea, but I really didn't want to know.

Duke's cock and balls.

It had remained unspoken between us, and I certainly wasn't going to bring it up now.

I had no idea if she'd got rid of them, or what she'd done with them. But if I had to bet money, I'd say she was storing them in the cupboard above the sink. *That* was something I didn't want to deal with right now, so I tried to busy my mind with other things.

The back of the Suburban still contained most of our clothes. Neither of us had made any effort to relocate them into the wardrobe in the trailer. I don't know if that's because we really didn't want to, because Duke had been in there, or because we just didn't have time. Raven had kept a couple of outfits in the storage area in the trailer, and I'd left my favourites there too, which is how we managed to get dressed without going outside. It was a good idea, in hindsight, as there was *no way* I was venturing out naked into the lagoon this morning.

Or any morning for that matter.

My naked days were over.

Janet Leigh would be so disappointed.

I turned then and surveyed the water's edge. Just to the left of Duke, I could see the small pile of clothes I'd discarded as I went swimming with Raven yesterday.

My old jeans, my sneakers, my bra and panties.

I could feel my face flush.

The guy would've seen them! Last night, he looked at my panties!

I was ready to curl up and die right then and there. I'd forgotten all about that pile of clothes and I realised that when he was looking at Duke and I thought he was looking at the sack we put him in, he could quite easily have been looking down at my bra and panties.

Lying there, for all the world to see. The very centre, the most private, of me.

And what if he came back later, to touch them and sniff them and...?

I turned away, back to the Suburban, and tried to think of other things.

Why are all men so damn *perverted?*

I concentrated on the job at hand, trying hard to push those thoughts from my mind. Trying not to picture the guy slipping back in the dead of night to paw through my underwear, to smell them and lick the very fabric that had touched me so intimately.

I picked up the first pile of clothes (mainly Raven's work gear, including her Lolita and Schoolgirl outfits) and turned to walk back to the trailer.

As I did so, Raven walked down the steps, carrying a clean sheet in her arms. She smiled at me as we passed each other, but we didn't say anything.

I climbed the steps into the trailer and only fleetingly glanced at the small cupboard above the sink. I walked straight down to the bed and placed the clothes there. I wanted to get back outside as quickly as possible, just in case Raven was waiting for me.

As I stepped back out into the clearing, I could see Raven had made it to Duke. She was spreading the new sheet next to him, making it flat on the ground and using some of the rocks I'd left there to pin it down. Slowly, I walked back to the Suburban, watching her as I did so.

She inspected the original blotchy sheet Duke was wrapped in, making sure he was all tucked in and covered, and then she crouched down by his side and dug her hands under him, lifting him inch by inch until he was high enough for her to get her weight behind him and roll him over.

He rolled with a *squelch* and I had no idea if that sound came from Duke, or the marshy water's edge. Either way, I really didn't want to know.

Raven rolled him again. And again.

By then, he was in the middle of the new sheet. Raven wiped her hands on the sheet and stood up, looking down at Duke and nodding to herself.

I picked up the next load of clothes from the back of the car as she started wrapping Duke in his new coverings. I hoped two sheets would be enough to keep his ooze and smell from invading the car. But I didn't like our chances of that.

I turned and walked back into the trailer, heaping the clothes on the bed next to the others.

The sooner Duke was out of here, the sooner we could return to our normal lives. I suddenly felt worn out from the events of the past few days.

I realised how my father must've felt.

How living in the past, and wishing for its return, could be a great deal of comfort. I wanted to be with him then, to hug him and hold him and tell him I knew his pain, his sorrow. But I knew that wasn't possible. I wouldn't be able to see him anytime soon.

He's probably sleeping off a binge anyway.

"Amber!"

I heard Raven's call and fear sliced down my spine. I ran to the door and looked outside, my eyes darting everywhere at once, trying to see what the trouble was, trying to see what had gone wrong.

But Raven was the only one out there.

Well, and Duke, of course.

She waved me forward. "I need your help!" she called.

I stepped out of the trailer and started walking towards her.

"I haven't finished clearing out the back of the car yet," I called to her.

"It's okay," she replied. "Help me carry him closer to the Suburban and then I'll give you a hand with the rest of the clothes."

As I walked towards her, I could see Raven had done a pretty good job wrapping Duke in the new sheet. It was tight around all sides and folded nicely. Still, some of Duke's stains were already discolouring the fabric, and his smell was getting steadily worse. The sooner we dumped him, the better.

"I think we're going to have to keep the windows down," I said as I came to stand next to her.

She nodded. "I know. He's quite the little stinker now."

Raven bent down next to what I guessed was his head. I walked over to the other end and grabbed his feet.

"But don't worry, we'll be soon rid of this particular problem."

We both lifted at the same time. Duke rose between us. He seemed lighter now, but I guess that wouldn't be the case. Maybe I was just used to carrying him. He sure did stink a whole lot more though.

We took a step towards the Suburban, Duke swinging in between us.

"You girls shouldn't be doing that."

I dropped Duke at the sound of the voice. Raven tried to hold on to him. She staggered backwards under the weight, a look of surprise on her face. After a couple of awkward steps, she dropped him too.

He landed with a heavy *thunk*.

I looked around the lagoon and over to the wildflowers, but I couldn't see anyone.

Raven was doing the same.

"No, no," said the voice. "Up here!"

I looked at Raven and our eyes met for a few seconds before we both turned and looked up at the rock wall.

Up to the wooden steps.

Where he was standing, about halfway down.

It was the guy from yesterday.

"Well, hello again!" he smiled, aiming his rifle directly at us.

Twenty-seven

Holy shit.
It was all over.
Any chance we had, any hope of getting away with this was gone. The guy was here to get us, to turn us in, to take the praise and the rewards for bringing two evil killers to justice.

"What the fuck do you want?" Raven called to him.

I dragged my eyes from the guy and looked over at Raven. I wanted to tell her to calm down and not to get the guy angry.

I mean, *Jesus,* he was pointing a *fucking rifle* at us!

But Raven was just staring up at the guy, her arms folded across her chest, her hips thrown to one side and her hair cascading down her back.

I turned to look back up at him. He was halfway down the stairs along the rock wall, and it looked like he was wearing the same clothes he had been yesterday. I don't know anything about guns and stuff, but the rifle he had was long and dark and angry-looking. I don't know what make it was or what kinda rounds it shot, but I knew it could make mincemeat of both of us before we had a chance to turn and flee.

"Hey, that's no way to treat a visitor," the guy replied, smiling back.

"Why don't you just leave us alone?" Raven continued.

The guy shrugged his shoulders. "This is a public place. I'm a member of the public. I have as much right to be here as you do."

"So?"

"*So?* So nothin'! I'm here, you're here, live with it."

He walked down a step and stopped.

I glanced back at Raven for a second, but she hadn't moved, she was holding her ground.

"Do we have any choice?" she asked. "I mean, you *do* have us covered with that rifle."

"Just being safe," the guy replied. "After all, yesterday you two were ready to shoot me, remember?"

I did. Our little ruse of telling him we had a gun had obviously made him think twice. Maybe even scared him, at least for a while. Maybe that's why he left.

"Well, you can see we're not carrying any guns now," Raven replied, holding her hands out to her sides.

I watched her and followed her lead.

He eyed both of us and then nodded.

"Fair enough," he said as he lifted the rifle up, its barrel now pointing skyward.

I felt a bit better then. A little safer.

Just a *little*...

Until he took another two steps closer towards us.

"So, what's two pretty girls like yourselves doing in a place like this?" he asked as he leaned forward on the wooden handrail.

"None of your business," Raven replied.

"Really? Looks like you've got your hands full." He nodded towards Duke who was, of course, still lying between us.

"None of your concern."

"Unfinished business perhaps?"

"I said, it's *none* of your damn concern."

"Okay, okay," he replied, raising his free hand palm-out to show he was backing off. "Sorry I asked. It's just not every day you see two beautiful women trying to dispose of a body."

He was trying to be charming now, but I could see right through him. I glanced at Raven and I hoped she could do the same.

She was smiling. "You just can't get good help these days," she replied.

The guy nodded. "I know what you mean. My name's Tyler, by the way."

"I'm Raven."

He nodded towards me. "And your mute friend?"

"She's Amber."

"I know she can talk. I heard her yesterday."

"Hi," I replied. It came out all croaky and kinda girly and I just felt dumb and embarrassed about saying anything.

Sometimes I can sound so stupid.

"Hi," he replied, smiling back at me.

All charm.

Don't let him fool you, Raven.

"Now, it seems to me," Tyler said as he took two more steps down towards us, "that you girls are in a pretty pickle right about now."

"We're doing fine," Raven replied.

"Oh, I can see that," he nodded. "You two can't even carry a body without dropping him in the mud. Now, tell me, how on earth do you think you can get rid of it without my help?"

"Haven't needed your help so far."

"I can see that."

Two more steps down. Two closer towards us. He was almost at our level now, almost ready to step out onto the clearing.

I wanted to do something, I wanted to grab Raven and pull her to the car, to drive out of there and get away before he could do anything. But that rifle was only seconds away from being pointed at us anytime we did anything wrong. He may have been all nice and sociable right now, but he could turn at any moment, just like most men.

"There are people *looking* for you," he said then, in a sing-song voice.

That made us both freeze. I held my breath. I didn't want to hear what was coming next.

He nodded in the silence, looking back and forth between us both.

"Oh yeah, *lots* of people want to speak to you. It's been all over the news."

We didn't say anything, so he continued.

"Of course, the police are just saying they want to hear from you to, ah, what were the words they used? Oh, that's right, to help them with their enquiries. But we all know what that *really* means, don't we?"

"I think you've got us mixed up with somebody else," Raven replied, but she didn't sound convincing.

"Really?" Tyler said in mock-shock. "Somehow, I doubt it. I know *exactly* who you are, Raven. Your name and description confirms it!"

He looked her up and down the same way I figured her drunken clients would at Rawhide.

Damn...shouldn't've told him our names!

"Look, mister –"

"Tyler."

"Look, Tyler," Raven continued. "I don't know who you are, or where you came from, but why don't you just mind your own business and leave us to ours, okay?"

"Can't do that." He shook his head.

"And why not?"

He thought about his answer carefully. "Let's just say I'm a sucker for damsels in distress."

Damsels? That was sure to irritate Raven to no end.

"We're not *damsels*, and we're not in distress," she replied. "If you wanted to help us, why did you leave last night? Why did you scare us, look around and then run away?"

"Well, to be perfectly honest, you two girls scared *me!*"

Tyler took the final two steps down the stairway and walked out into the clearing.

Raven took a step back, and I held my ground.

"Hey, don't get spooked," Tyler replied, slowly bending down, placing his rifle on the ground next to him. "I'm not here to hurt you girls or turn you in. Don't get the wrong impression, okay? If I was, I could've done both of those things yesterday. But I didn't. So I hope that means you trust me, even just a little bit."

Raven turned to look at me. But I didn't say anything.

"Look, I've put the rifle on the ground, okay?" He walked away from it. "I only brought it to protect myself. After yesterday, I had no idea what kind of weapons you people had."

"'You people?'" Raven mimicked him.

"I *know* you're in trouble, the news reports said that. I know things can get out of control when drugs are involved and – "

"*What?*" Raven asked.

"Huh?" he replied.

"What did you say? *Drugs?*"

Tyler nodded his head and stepped forward further. The gap between us was closing.

"I understand it. I really do. There's been trouble like this in my family too. My brother got hooked and now he's in jail for things he had no control over. That's why I want to help. I want to try and save you both from what he went through."

"Back up, Sherlock," Raven replied. "We're not into drugs. You've got the whole story wrong."

"No, I haven't." He was so sure, so confident.

"Sorry, but you *do*."

"It's all over the news, Raven. There's no use denying it."

All three of us stood in silence for quite some time. Raven's head was tilted to the side, Tyler stood with his hands now pushed into the pockets of his pants, looking at both of us.

"Let me help you," he said.

"Exactly *what* is it that we've done?" Raven asked eventually.

"I told you there's no use denying – "

"Please," Raven said in a soft voice. "We're not denying anything right now, or admitting anything either. Just humour us and tell us what we've done."

Tyler sighed. "If you think it will help."

"It will. Tell us what you know and then I promise we'll answer any questions you have truthfully and honestly."

He nodded. "Okay, I can live with that."

I didn't know if I could, though.

"The news reports are talking about you. The police want to question you about the missing drugs."

"What missing drugs?"

"They said that you're involved with another guy, can't remember his name now..."

"Duke?"

"Yeah, something like that." He pointed to the body between us. "Is this Duke?"

"Yes," Raven replied.

"I see." He nodded. "It's just that we weren't formally introduced."

"Duke's a bit tied up right now. He can't talk."

"I understand. The police say that Duke ripped off some minor drug dealer in town on the weekend, apparently stole a whole shipment of cocaine from the guy and then fled the scene. They traced him to a big party he had at a strip club with some of his friends, where he apparently made contact with you."

He pointed at Raven.

Oh, he made *contact* alright.

But Raven didn't say anything.

"Apparently there was a big fight or disagreement or something between the both of you, he was thrown out of the club, and then he disappeared. You also disappeared around that time and it seems the cops found traces of the drugs in Duke's home."

"Trailer."

"Oh yeah, that's right. He managed the park you were living in, right?"

My God, he knew so much!

Raven nodded.

Tyler smiled a self-satisfied smile. "So, there you have it. The cops think you've fled with Duke and the drugs."

"*With* Duke?" Raven asked.

"Yes, they're looking for both of you and there's this huge multi-state search happening to find you. But I guess you took care of Duke your own way, huh?"

"We sure did," Raven replied. "But not for the reasons you think."

"And to add to that, the cops arrested the guy Duke stole the drugs from. So you've got the friends and family of the drug dealer after you as well."

"Trust me," Raven said. "He's no friend of ours."

"Not anymore," Tyler replied.

"Not *ever*."

"So," he shrugged, "you see, I know it all!"

He looked so proud of himself.

It was almost funny that he was so wrong with the story.

But it wasn't funny at all. If what he said was true, then the police had the wrong idea, the *totally* wrong idea about what had happened between Duke and Raven, and why we fled. We were accused of being involved in trafficking drugs and we had *nothing* whatsoever to do with it! Much worse was the fact that we now had angry drug dealers after us. *Very* angry drug dealers.

I looked down at Duke and wanted to kick him. I hated him so much more then. He'd got us in deeper shit than we'd ever imagined.

Everyone was after us for all the wrong reasons!

And no one really knew the truth.

Would they *ever* believe us if we told them now?

"So, I hope you understand that's why I came with a bit of protection. I didn't know what you girls might try. You both scared the shit out of me yesterday. Plus you *did* say you had a gun."

"We don't," Raven replied.

I darted a look at her. I couldn't believe she admitted that! Now he knew we had no protection against him.

"Your friend looks worried." Tyler nodded towards me.

"She *always* looks worried," Raven replied.

They both smiled at each other.

"So you're here to save us, is this correct?" Raven asked.

"If I can, yes."

"You're going to be our hero?"

He nodded.

Raven laughed. "I don't think so."

His smile fell.

"I think we can do perfectly well without you, thanks."

"Like you have been so far."

"We were doing quite fine until you decided to crash our party yesterday."

His eyes dropped to the ground and he looked uncomfortable. "Ah, yeah, sorry about that."

"Just how long *had* you been watching us?"

"Not long."

"*How* long?"

"A day or two."

"I see."

"I was out hunting and I heard your voices..."

Hunting. The shots we heard!

"...I just skirted the lagoon to make sure you were alright."

"And to maybe spy on us?" Raven asked.

A smile curled the corners of his mouth as his eyes met Raven's. "Just a little. I saw you and I couldn't resist."

"A-huh." Raven nodded.

"I wasn't totally sure who you were at that stage. It wasn't until I saw the body that I put the news reports together with you both. I just assumed you'd killed him to keep the drugs for yourself."

"I see."

"And then I decided to hang around a bit."

"I bet you did."

"You fucked it up, we heard you yesterday," I said. It came out fast and angry and they both turned to look at me.

"My, she *speaks!*" Tyler feigned surprise.

"Occasionally," Raven added.

He nodded. "Yes, you're right, Amber. I had my radio and handgun with me yesterday. I'd watched you both for a good while, and as I got up to leave, my gun slipped from my hand and it fell, hitting the radio and knocking them both over. I tried to stop it, but I couldn't and the noise was damn loud. I didn't know what you'd do or how you'd react. I was out of ammunition too, I was as good as defenceless. So I thought it was time I came out of hiding. I'd been meaning to anyway."

"You were just waiting for us to get out of the lagoon and get dressed, I'm guessing?" Raven asked.

He almost blushed then. "Yeah, kinda."

It sounded lame to me. He only came out of his hole because we heard him and he knew his cover had been blown. He had no intention of coming out before that, as far as I could tell.

"So what do you want from us?" Raven asked.

"Excuse me?"

"What will it take to make you forget you've seen us, to make you turn around and go back to wherever it is you came from?"

He shook his head. "Do you think *that's* what I want?"

"You're a man, you must want something."

Tyler took another step towards us. We were no more than a few feet apart and that worried me.

"Hey, I'm not stupid," he said as he looked down at Duke's body. "I know what happens to guys who get on the wrong side of you two."

"It wasn't like that," Raven said in a small voice. "You've got it all wrong. This wasn't about drugs, we don't *have* any drugs, we had *no idea* Duke was messed up in all that shit."

Tyler glanced at both of us as the breeze ruffled his hair. He put his hands back in his pockets, and pursed his lips.

"You don't believe us?" Raven asked.

"The police said – "

"I don't *care* what the police said," Raven continued. "This has nothing to do with drugs. We got into some trouble with Duke, that's for sure, and we're not denying that. But it was totally removed from drugs, and this is how he ended up."

He nodded. "I see." But I don't know whether he really did.

"It's the truth," Raven whispered.

"Either way," he said. "You have a problem on your hands."

"More like two, now," I added.

Tyler tilted his head towards me. "Is she always so negative?"

"I'm realistic," I replied before Raven could. "We're dealing with one problem and then you come along. You've been spying on us, hiding from us, and if you hadn't *fucked up* yesterday, you'd probably still be hiding behind those wildflowers." I pointed across the stream at them.

Tyler nodded. "Okay, you're right. And for that, I'm sorry. But it's not every day a guy happens across two naked women floating in a lagoon, now is it? What else was I supposed to do?"

Exactly.

Men! Every single one of them would've acted in the same way.

"You could've fucked off and minded your own business," I added.

"Yeah, probably. But listen, I meant what I said. You both look like you're in trouble and I want to help you if I can. I *haven't* turned you into the cops, I *haven't* told anyone about you. If I had, they'd be here by now and the place would be swarming with snipers and sniffer dogs and helicopters and media and crap like that."

Raven rested her arms across her chest.

"What if we don't believe you?"

"Look," Tyler said, sighing deeply. "What if I don't believe *you*? I guess that makes us both even. So, we're level. Let's just try to trust each other for a little while and see what happens. If I don't see any signs of drugs, then I'll start to believe you and not the news reports. If you don't see any sign of the cops, you'll start to believe me and not your paranoia, okay?"

"He could just be playing for time," I countered. "Waiting for them to arrive."

His eyes rolled. "And, yeah, I'd want to be caught right in the middle of this, talking with you girls, when they arrive. I'd have *accomplice* written all over me."

"He could be a cop." I tried again. "He could have hidden weapons."

I was searching for anything to sway the argument.

Tyler raised both arms away from his sides.

"Search me."

I looked at Raven and she smiled.

"Go on," he said. "*Search me!*"

Raven stepped forward slowly. I watched her, then my eyes darted back to Tyler. He was looking straight at me. I couldn't read the expression on his face, somewhere between anger and defiance, as if he was saying, *I'll prove this to you if it's the last thing I do.*

Raven kept walking. I wanted to shout out, to make Raven stop. But she was next to him now, patting down Tyler's chest, and the sides of his body. She ran her hands through his pockets but came up empty.

She kneeled then, right in front of him, as she felt his ankles, patted his knees and up to his thighs, then higher between his legs.

"Careful down there," he smiled, without taking his eyes from me. "I'm rather attached to some of that stuff."

I heard Raven chuckle as she stood upright once more.

"He's clean," she said. "He doesn't have any weapons, Amber." She turned to face me. "We'll just have to trust him."

"Are you *crazy?*" I replied. "We don't even *know* him! Hell, we knew Duke better and look what he wanted to do to us! We've got *no way* to verify his story."

"You missed this," Tyler said as his left hand disappeared behind his back.

I braced myself for anything as his hand swung around and out, holding a small, black something that he pointed towards us. I was ready to run, to duck the bullets, to push Raven to the ground and cover her, protect her with my body.

But nothing happened.

He just handed it to Raven.

It was his wallet.

She opened it up and looked inside. Then she turned it around and held it out for me to see. I was too far away to read it clearly, but I could see she was showing me his driving licence.

"Well, his name is correct at least," Raven said. "Tyler Reynolds."

"At your service, ma'am," he said as he retrieved the wallet and bowed, sweeping his hand forward and bending down low.

I reached across and grabbed Raven's arm. Quickly, I pulled her away, leading her along the water's edge and out of Tyler's earshot.

"*What?*" Raven asked, her forehead furrowing. She looked impatient or upset at me for some reason.

"What if he's a friend of Duke's?"

"Huh?"

"Raven, what if he *isn't* a cop? You heard what he said about the news reports."

"Yes," she nodded. "It's all got fucked up somewhere along the way."

"What if he's a friend of the guy who had his drugs stolen? What if he's here to find the drugs and kill us?"

"He's not."

"How do you know for certain?" I asked.

"Because if he was, he'd have done that yesterday."

"You can't be so sure."

"Well, how did he find us?" Raven replied.

"I don't understand."

"Sweets, if he's tracking us for the drugs, how did he find us when no one else can?"

"I don't know."

"Is he Superman?"

"No." I shook my head.

Raven smirked as she looked over my shoulder and towards Tyler. "I think you're being a touch paranoid, sweets."

"Raven, I *have* to be. You told me this morning you let your guard down and that's how he saw us in the first place. Now you're letting it down again."

"No, I'm not."

"Yes, you *are!* He knows too much already."

"Well, we can't stop him from knowing that now. We might as well use him."

"*Use* him?"

"Amber, listen. He said he hasn't called the police and I believe him. If he had, they'd be here by now. They're not going to wait around for hours on end when they have a chance to grab us without us knowing. They'd be here and we'd be in the back of a patrol car, handcuffed and having our rights read to us. And he sure doesn't look or act like a cop or a drug dealer or a friend of Duke's. I believe he stumbled across us and then hid to enjoy the show for as long as he could. It sounds like the truth to me. If he hadn't given away his hideout yesterday, he'd still be there getting a boner and jacking off while watching us. I think he's harmless."

"Harmless?"

Raven walked to my side, still staring at Tyler. "And I think he could help us out."

"You're not serious?"

"I am. He could come in very handy indeed."

I couldn't believe what I was hearing. A perfect stranger walks into our life, no no, *stumbles* into our life yesterday, finds out all about us, and now she's willing to entrust all our secrets to him in the hope he'll help us!

We didn't need his help.

We *never* needed a man's help.

But here was Raven, about to invite him to do so.

"It's not right," I whispered.

Raven turned to face me, her hands resting on my shoulders, and she looked deep into my eyes.

"Do you trust me?" she whispered.

"Of course I do. It's *him* I don't trust."

"Do you trust me to know and do what's right?"

"Of course! You *know* that. Always have."

"Then trust me when I say I think Tyler can help us out. He's *not* a cop, he's *not* here to turn us in, he's not after the drugs that we don't even *have*!"

"He could be worse," I replied, looking to the ground.

"Huh? What do you mean?"

"He says he's a hunter. But what is he *really* hunting? What if he's just like Duke? What if he thinks he'll get some pussy if he stays around long enough and is charming and helpful? Maybe long enough to get these two girls all to himself. Just him and me and you, all the way out here by ourselves."

"Yeah." She nodded very slowly, her eyes narrowing as she thought over what I was saying.

"No one would ever know. And it's not like we can go to the cops, right?"

I could tell by the look on her face that she hadn't considered that. I could see fear in her eyes all of a sudden.

They slipped from mine and I watched as she focussed on Tyler behind me.

She was thinking it through, making the same connections I had. Wondering about the real reason he suddenly decided to come out of hiding and help us.

And then she smiled. Turned back to me and kissed me on the forehead.

"You worry too much, hon," she said as she let out a small laugh and turned me around to face Tyler.

He was standing in a half-crouch, trying to balance Duke's body between his arms. He was off balance and Duke swung wildly for a second or two before Tyler managed to straighten up and regain control. His face was red, like he'd struggled to pick Duke up in the first place, and I think he was a bit embarrassed to see we were both watching him right then.

"No, no," he called to us. "You girls continue with your little tête-à-tête over there and leave all this to me. I told you I'd help you and that's exactly what I'll do. Where do you want him?"

"In the back of the car," Raven said.

"The Suburban?" he asked.

"Do you see any other car?" she replied.

Tyler laughed. "No, actually I don't. But it would be a shame to put this garbage in such a great car. It will really spoil it."

"He won't be there for long," Raven replied.

"Ah," he nodded as he swung around to face the car, taking a few tentative squelchy steps with Duke swinging from side to side. "You have a plan then?"

"Yep."

"Glad to hear it. Because I'm not carrying this body all day while we come up with one."

He took a few more steps towards the car.

"1970?" he called over his shoulder.

"What?" Raven called back.

"The Suburban. 1970?"

"Nope, '72."

"Oh, okay." I watched his head nod as he walked closer to the car. "They don't make 'em like that anymore."

"They certainly don't," Raven replied in a quiet voice.

I turned to face her, but she was looking across at Tyler. I couldn't read the expression on her face, and I really didn't know if I wanted to.

"Raven," I said. "We have to talk."

"Not right now, hon," she replied. "I have to think."

"We can't do this, we can't let him be part of this."

She looked at me. "A bit late for that now, no matter what we think. He's here, Amber, he's a part of this. What can we do?"

"We need to get out of here and leave him. Escape from him without him knowing where we're going. We need to *leave!*"

"I don't think that will work."

"We have to try."

"We might need him."

"For what?"

Raven shrugged. "I don't know. For something, I guess. He could come in handy."

"We *don't* need him. We've done fine without him. He's only going to cause trouble. *More* trouble that we don't need!"

"I don't think so."

"Well, I *do!*"

Tyler threw Duke's body into the back of the Suburban. There was a loud *thunk* and the car shook slightly, the back lowering under the added weight of the corpse. Then he climbed into the back and pulled the body further in. Duke's legs (or his head, I'm not sure which) disappeared from sight.

"We *don't* need him."

"*Enough*, Amber," Raven whispered, her eyes cutting through my very soul. "*You* may not need him, but *I* might."

Twenty-eight

"Okay, I'm leaving," Tyler said.

That comment surprised both of us.

He placed his plate on the ground, wiped his lips and stood up from where he was sitting on the milk crate.

It was just after lunch and we'd all enjoyed a nice meal of freshly caught fish. Raven had caught them, Tyler had cooked them. It was his idea to have a celebratory lunch after we'd got Duke bundled nicely into the car and had returned all our clothes to the trailer.

Of course, we hadn't let Tyler into the trailer. Well, actually, *I* wouldn't let him inside. He'd destroyed most of our paradise by stumbling into it yesterday, and I was damned if I was going to let him inside our final sanctuary.

"It's okay," he'd said, when I took the remaining clothes from his arms and told him I'd put them in the trailer. "I understand. I'll make myself busy out here."

"Busy" meant standing around talking to Raven while I put the clothes on the bed.

Still not in the wardrobe though.

While Duke's smell had well and truly left the trailer, there were still dried stains and patches of ick in the wardrobe that I just didn't want to deal with. Raven would have to fix them, but I hadn't got around to asking her to do it. Until the wardrobe was cleaned, the clothes stayed on the bed.

We'd sat down for lunch and it was mostly Tyler and Raven who talked. She was sitting in the deck chair as usual and he had pulled up my milk crate to sit on. I was left to lean against the side of the trailer at a distance from them, eating my fish and not participating in the conversation.

Raven told him the story.

The *whole* story.

The *real* one.

LAKE MOUNTAIN

How Duke came to be dead, how she did it, what we did afterwards, the problems with the guy at the gas station and everything.

He sat and nodded and said very little. He just took it all in, only interrupting once or twice to ask a question or clarify a point. His face didn't change much, so he was able to hide his thoughts and feelings and I had no idea what was running across his mind.

He was either not very interested, or he was listening for something very important.

Either way, I don't think she should've told him everything. *Jesus*, he's a *stranger*!

But nothing I could say would stop her. I knew that for sure. She'd do what she considered to be the best thing. She always did.

And when she was finished, it was Tyler's turn.

"Okay, well, you know my name now, so that's no mystery. I'm twenty-three and I'm from the small town of Blackmore, about twenty miles south of here. I only work part-time, do odd-jobs mainly. I'm actually a qualified locksmith by trade, but there isn't a lot of call for them these days. When I can, I come up here to hunt. I love this mountain. I love the scenery, the silence, the smell and the feel. I love waking up every morning to a brand new day, crisp and beautiful, untouched by pollution, people or troubles. I could just walk and walk, never stop, just taking it all in. The rest of the world ceases to exist when you're here on Lake Mountain."

I agreed with him on that point, at least.

"So you have a house up here?" Raven had asked.

"No," he shook his head and looked a bit nervous. "Ah, not quite."

"A shack?"

"No."

"Tent maybe?" Raven was enjoying this.

"No."

"A small cardboard box at the side of the road?"

"I have a valve house," he said in a low voice, looking to the ground.

"A *what*?"

"Up near the dam," he continued, "are a couple of small little round buildings. No one really goes near them anymore, they're just covered in vines and moss and blend into the forest really well. In fact, I don't know if many people know of them at all. In the old days they used to control the valves that opened and shut the dam's outlets. I've never seen anyone near them, and I guess the controls for the dam are managed from a computer somewhere else these days. So, the valve houses are forgotten, or *were* forgotten, until I found them. There's just enough room inside for me and my stuff. That way, I can survive out here without having to go home and make a living for quite a while. I can live virtually free of charge."

"And you can just walk into these valve houses?" Raven asked.

He shook his head. "No, but like I said. I *am* a locksmith by trade."

"I see."

"And the locks on the doors are pretty old. It wasn't too hard to get inside. Anyone could've, I guess."

"Well, certainly someone with your skills." Raven smiled. "And food?"

"Like I said, I hunt and fish and sometimes trek down the mountain to…" He looked nervous all of a sudden. "…to try my hand fishing and hunting down there. In fact, that's how I found you," he smiled, quickly getting the conversation back on track. "I was out hunting and I just stumbled across you both. Lucky, huh?"

I didn't think it was very lucky. Well, it was for him. Not for us.

Didn't sound very likely either.

And now, after we'd both told our stories, he turns to us and says, "Okay, I'm leaving."

Part of me was happy about the news, but another part worried that he was heading straight to the cops now he knew the whole story or – worse still – to his drug dealing buddies.

"Oh, don't worry," he replied as he read the looks on both our faces. "I'll be back. But I think I should go to the valve house and get my stuff. My other guns and my radio. You two need to hear what they're saying about you in the news. And with a radio you may be able to stay one step ahead of them. I gather from the surprise on your faces when I told you what the media were saying that you don't have a radio or TV in the trailer?"

"That's right," Raven replied.

"You can buy newspapers, you know," Tyler added.

"Haven't had the time."

"And I guess there isn't a vendor on every corner out here," he continued, looking around the lagoon.

"Exactly. So, how far is the valve house?"

"About an hour's walk."

"Okay," Raven agreed. "I think that's a good idea."

"You can't just let him go," I said to her.

"Amber, what *else* am I going to do? We can't stop him."

Yes, we could!

"What if he doesn't come back?"

"I will," Tyler replied.

"We can't trust him," I continued.

Raven climbed from the deck chair and ran her hand through her long curls. "Honey, we don't have a lot of choice. If he goes and doesn't come back, we'll move on to somewhere else. If he comes back, he can bring us news from the outside world and some guns to protect ourselves."

"*Guns?* We don't need guns!"

"Couldn't hurt," she shrugged and turned to him. "Do you need a companion for your walk?"

"Oh no," I said as I walked up to them both, grabbing Raven's arm and turning her towards me. "You are *not* leaving with him. You are *not* going with him! You must be crazy. You just can't walk off with him and trust him like that. Remember Duke? Remember the gas station guy? You *can't* trust him!"

"I agree," Tyler was nodding his head.

My mouth was open but nothing came out. I didn't really expect him to agree with me on that point.

Raven turned to face him.

"You two girls should stay here and get ready to leave when I come back, okay? I'll be two hours, maybe three tops, but that's it. If it gets to be four hours and I'm not back, leave without me and get off this mountain and go somewhere where you'll think I'd never look for you. If I get back and you're still here, I'll help you think of a place to get rid of Duke."

"We already have a place picked," Raven said.

Don't tell him!

"The Wentworth Dam Worker's Memorial."

Noooo!

He nodded. "Not bad. Why there?"

Raven smiled. "I think it would be perfect, that's all."

"I'll give that some thought while I'm walking."

"Okay."

And with that, he turned around and marched towards the stream.

"Hey, Tyler!" Raven called, pointing back towards the wooden steps at the rock wall. "You forgot your rifle!"

It was still lying on the ground in front of the steps.

"You girls keep it," he called back over his shoulder. "You look like you both need some protection. And I don't want to carry it all the way there and back. Hang onto it until I return! And be ready to leave when I do!"

He stepped into the stream and crossed it with three large steps. At no stage did he turn around and look at us. We both watched him as he climbed up the embankment and stepped through the wildflowers.

Within a couple of seconds, he was gone.

As if he never even existed.

We stayed there, staring across at the wildflowers for some time.

I didn't know whether to be relieved he'd gone, or whether I should start to panic. What if he was racing through the bushes right now, on his way to the drug gang with the full story? What if he was hiding in the wildflowers, to see how we would react while he was gone? What if he was closer to getting Raven? What if he never came back? Or worse still, what if he *did*?

"You want to go get the rifle?" Raven asked me.

I shook my head. "No way! I'm not going anywhere near it. I'll clean the plates from lunch. You get the rifle."

And for the next hour or so, we busied ourselves with the trailer.

It was weird, neither of us talked about Tyler, and it was almost like it used to be between us. But there was something off kilter, out of whack. Because we didn't *talk*, like we would. We just said enough to get by. We both had our minds on other things, that much was for sure.

We hooked the trailer up to the Suburban again, cleared away our makeshift fire, and I went over to the water's edge to wash the plates and pick up the elephant sack and clothes I had left there the night before (underwear included.)

By the time I got back to the trailer, I noticed that Raven was scrubbing out the wardrobe.

"I'm going to get rid of the last traces of Duke from in here," she said as she dropped the sponge back into the bucket and squeezed. I'd seen her fill the bucket with water from the lagoon some time earlier and wondered what she was going to use it for, but hadn't asked. I don't know what cleaner she was using, but there was a nice pine smell in the trailer now.

My eyes dropped to the rifle resting on the pile of clothes on the bed.

"What are we going to do with that?" I pointed.

Raven shrugged. "Leave it there until Tyler gets back."

If he gets back, I thought. But I didn't say it.

I also noticed that Raven had changed her clothes. Gone was the drive-in pants and mesh top. She was now wearing an old worn out pair of faded blue jeans, complete with holes cut at the knees and thighs, and also a white figure-hugging tank top with the word *FLIRT* emblazoned in large capital letters on the front. Raven's breasts made the word hard to read, as it rolled across them, but I knew the shirt well.

And I also knew she didn't wear it very often.

I guess she was wearing it now because she was scrubbing out the wardrobe and she didn't want to get her work clothes all dirty. It made sense, I suppose.

I didn't like the other alternative though.

"Anything I can do?" I asked.

"Nope," she replied, scrubbing harder at the inside of the wardrobe. "I just need to get this washed out before Tyler gets back."

"Why?"

"In case he comes in."

"He won't. We won't let him."

"Why's that, Amber?"

"Because this is *our* place. It's the only place we have together. He's not *allowed* in."

Raven turned to face me, sweat plastering her hair across her forehead. "That's a bit childish, Amber, don't you think?"

That hurt.

I didn't say anything.

But it hurt bad.

"He's helping us out."

"Is he?"

"Yes, he said he is."

"And you believe him?"

"For now."

"And what if he's lying? What if he *isn't* helping us out?"

"Well," Raven smiled as she nodded over to the rifle. "He's left us some protection from that."

"What if he doesn't come back?"

Raven smirked. "Oh, he'll be back, hon. For me. He can't resist. And that's why we have to move fast to get this place looking normal."

"We *are* normal."

"You know what I mean. I don't want him finding all this stuff, all the clothes and the handcuffs and dildos and everything. Do you know where Duke's sports bag is? I can't find it."

"I put it in the back of the Suburban," I replied.

"Good. I don't want him finding anything like that, especially not my clothes. That's what got us into all this mess in the first place."

She turned back to concentrate on the wardrobe.

"I won't let that happen again," she said, almost to herself.

I just sat on the edge of the bed, next to the rifle and the pile of clothes, watching Raven work. I felt out of place, even in my own trailer, like I was a stranger there.

The way Tyler should feel.

But there was Raven, going out of her way to make him welcome. Going out of her way to exclude me from the only safe haven I had left.

I'd never felt so lonely.

Why was she doing all this? Why was she making such an effort? It just wasn't fair.

Now I was a total stranger again, even in the place I felt so safe. I didn't *want* Tyler in there, I didn't *want* us to change anything just for him.

I wanted it to be just Raven and Amber again.

Was that asking so much?

I guess, maybe it was.

But, of course, I didn't tell Raven any of this. There was no way I could open up and tell her these things, because if I did she'd know what I was thinking and how I was hurting, and I didn't know how she'd react to that.

So I just sat there until she was finished with the wardrobe.

When she was done, it was as clean as it had ever been, I'm sure. It was smelling of pine and there was no sign of Duke, except for the dirty brown sludgy water in the bucket.

Raven leaned back on her haunches and wiped the sweat from her forehead.

"What do you think it would be like?" she asked, without turning to face me.

"Huh?" I didn't understand what she was talking about and was still caught up in my thoughts anyway.

"You know, locked in there," she nodded towards the wardrobe before turning around and kneeling by my legs at the side of the bed. "But not just there, I mean anywhere. Think about it, Amber. What would it be like to be buried alive in a coffin or something?"

Her eyes stared deeply into mine, as if she was searching for the truth, but I really had no clue what being buried alive would be like.

I shrugged. "I have no idea."

"Close your eyes," she said to me as she closed hers.

I did what I was told.

"Think about it. Total darkness. More black and dark than you could ever imagine. Things sound different from inside a coffin, muffled, weird. Your own breathing is loud, so loud. And your heartbeat beats in your ears, getting faster and faster, and you start to wonder if someone is whispering things to you, or whether it's just your own thoughts turning on you, slowly making you crazy."

I opened my eyes. I didn't want to continue with this, she was scaring me.

But Raven's eyes stayed shut and she kept talking.

"Imagine trying to fight off the feeling of being closed in. Trying to push back the darkness and the walls, but knowing you couldn't. Feeling the soft velvet but knowing underneath it was hard, impenetrable wood or steel. Knowing this would be the last place you would be alive. The last few hours or minutes ticking away. The place where you would breathe your last breath, think your last thought. Where your heart would cease to beat. It would be all out of your control, and all you could do is lie back and wait for death to overwhelm you. Or madness first."

She opened her eyes and stared at me. Then she smiled.

"Cool, huh?"

"I don't think so."

She shrugged as she climbed from the floor, taking the bucket and sponge over to the kitchen sink.

"I wonder if that's what Duke was thinking," she said.

"But Duke was dead when you put him in the cupboard," I reminded her.

She nodded. "Still, you wonder what went through his mind in the final moments."

I didn't. I couldn't care less.

She turned around and walked back to me.

"Well, what do you think?" she asked, pointing towards the wardrobe.

"Good job," I replied.

"Yeah, I think so too," she agreed.

Over the next few minutes, I handed the clothes in bunches to her and she hung them back in the wardrobe. We didn't speak. I was trying to get the chill off my spine from her buried alive conversation and didn't feel like talking anyway.

But I knew I had to. I had to say what was on my mind, not just for Raven's sake, but for my own, so I could feel as if I had some control over events again, and to try to convince her that Tyler couldn't be trusted and shouldn't come with us.

"Are you sure we're doing the right thing?" I asked.

She looked puzzled at my question.

"Allowing Tyler to help us," I added.

"I can't see how it will hurt, hon."

"He could turn on us at any time."

"I don't think he'll do that," Raven replied as she placed the last of the clothes (her schoolgirl uniform) into the wardrobe and closed the door. The latch clicked as she leaned against the door and looked across at me on the bed.

"He's a *man*, Raven."

She stifled a laugh. "Amber, honey, despite what you may think, not *all* men are total bastards only interested in one thing. I think he really wants to help. I mean, he left his rifle and everything. Just in case we needed it. I'm sure he realises we could use it on him at any time if he suddenly decided to do something very stupid."

"I just don't trust him," I replied.

"You don't *have* to trust him, hon. Let's just *use* him. He could be exactly what we need."

"And if he isn't?"

She came and sat on the bed next to me. Moving the rifle to the side, she slid onto the bed, crossed her legs in front of her, took my hands in hers and held them tight.

"You know I won't let him hurt either of us, don't you?" she whispered.

I nodded. We were so close, I could feel her breath on my face.

"I'm not going to let anyone come between us, okay? You have my promise on that. You *do* believe me, right?" she asked.

I nodded again, my eyes falling between us, focussing on the *I* in *FLIRT*. I guess I *did* believe her.

"That's a promise I'll keep, Amber," she said, squeezing my hands tighter and drawing me closer to her.

My eyes rose to meet hers and I leaned even closer.

"If he's any problem, we'll kill him," Raven whispered calmly, so softly. "But for now, we just might need him around."

"*Kill* him?" I whispered back.

"Amber, honey," she smiled. "One more dead body is hardly going to matter now."

Twenty-nine

Tyler arrived back at the lagoon three hours and forty-two minutes after he'd left.

"You're cutting it fine," Raven called to him.

He looked at his watch. "I think I have about twenty minutes to spare," he smiled as he walked across the stream and towards the trailer.

We'd both decided to sit outside in the lovely summer sun, waiting for his return. Raven was in the deck chair as usual, and I had reclaimed my milk crate. Raven had just been sitting there, soaking up the sun, while I tried to read a bit more of my book. But I couldn't concentrate on the words printed on the page. I read the same sentence over and over again until I decided to give up and just sit and relax too.

By now the sun was low in the sky and the shadows were starting to grow across the lagoon. I watched two birds fly across the blue sky, and wished it would be that easy to escape the mess we were in. My eyes dropped back to the water and I longed to be swimming naked in there again, with Raven by my side, just the two of us and the water and no one else.

Just the *two* of us.

Tyler stopped in front of us, water dripping from his black boots and sweat dripping from his forehead.

"It's a bit of a hike," he smiled. "Sorry I took so long."

"We were starting to think you weren't coming back," Raven replied.

"Oh don't worry about that, I was coming back, no doubt about it. Just had to make sure everything was okay at my end and also at this end."

"Did you think we'd set up a sniper's nest for your return?"

"You never know," he laughed. "Girls do some crazy things sometimes."

Asshole, I thought. How dare he say that!

"Did you bring the guns?" Raven asked.

He nodded.

We both stared at him. His hands were empty though.

"And they would be...?" Raven prompted.

"I thought you'd never ask," he replied as he squatted in front of us and pulled down the zip on his jacket. He reached inside and pulled out one, then another, and then another.

I have no idea about guns, and I don't want to either. Never needed one and I certainly didn't now. But all of a sudden we were loaded with them. Not only the rifle (which was still on the bed, by the way) but now we had three handguns sitting in front of us on the grass. There were two pistols, one black and one silver, and one revolver that was shorter than the others, black and kinda small.

Just what we don't need!

"How many guns do you have?" Raven asked.

"This is it. I was just worried about leaving them in the valve house while I wasn't there. So I brought them all. Works out well too, one each."

He smiled over at me, but I didn't smile back.

"I don't want a gun," I said.

He shrugged. "That's okay by me," he replied.

Raven turned to look at me. "Honey, if they're here, we might as well each have one. Just for protection."

"Protection? Protection from who?"

"Whoever comes along."

"We were doing fine without guns before *he* came along," I replied.

Tyler sighed deeply and stood up once more. "I don't care what you do with them. You work it out between yourselves. I brought them and I offer them hopefully so you'll realise I'm on your side in this and want to help. What you decide to do with them is up to you. Oh, and there's this," he said as he opened one of the pockets in his jacket and pulled out a small radio. "It's not the best for sound quality, but at least you'll be able to tune in for the news and find out what they're saying about you."

He handed the radio to Raven before he turned around to look over at the lagoon. He put both hands behind his head and scratched at his short hair. Then he took in a deep breath, filling his lungs with the fresh air.

"Mind if I go for a swim?" he asked.

My eyes turned to Raven, but she didn't look at me.

"If you want," she replied. "It's a free country."

"Cool," he started walking towards the water's edge.

"Swimming? What are you *doing*?" I whispered to her.

"Oh, Amber," Raven replied, her eyes dropping down to the guns in front of us. "Don't be such an old maid. He can swim in the lagoon if he wants."

"It's *our* lagoon."

"You know, really, hon, it isn't. It's *not* ours and you know it. Tyler's been kind enough to help us out and bring us these things for our protection and the least you could do is be a bit more civil towards him."

"I see." I nodded my head.

"Do you?" she replied. "Do you really? Sometimes, girl, I understand why you don't have a boyfriend."

I wanted to cry then, but I wouldn't give Raven the satisfaction. I sat back on my milk crate and crossed my arms, looking over towards Tyler who was now bending down by the lagoon, unlacing his boots and taking off his jacket.

The anger I felt towards Raven was so strong, so overwhelming, that I had to force myself to sit still, to stay in one spot, to even stop breathing for a while until I got my thoughts and feelings under control.

Then she handed me the revolver.

"Here," she said. "You don't want a gun, but I think you should have one. You have the revolver and Tyler and I will share the pistols."

Uh-huh.

Second-class gun for a second-class friend.

I leaned forward and looked closer at the revolver. It was cold and heavy in my hands and I had no real idea what to do with it, but I could see through the side of the cylinder that there were no cartridges in there.

Probably a very good thing right then...

My eyes rose to see Tyler's bare back as he took off his black t-shirt and dropped it on the pile of clothes that included his jacket, shoes, pants and socks.

He was wearing only a small pair of blue briefs for underwear. Other than that, he was naked. His legs and back looked tanned and strong as he stretched his arms above his head, and twisted his body from side to side.

Limbering up, or showing off for us? The gall of the guy!

My eyes darted to Raven. She had a smirk across her face. She was in no way trying to hide the fact she was watching (and enjoying) the show.

I looked back at him.

Dive in the damn water and get it over and done with!

He leaned forward.

I thought to get ready to dive.

But then his blue briefs were moving down his legs. My eyes were suddenly fixed on his now naked ass. It was firm, and not as tanned as the rest of his body.

As he stepped out of his briefs, his legs opened wide and I'm sure I caught a fleeting glimpse of his balls, hanging there in the shadows between his legs.

"Now *this* is a show," Raven whispered.

I bet he was enjoying it just as much. Probably hiding a boner from us too. Waiting to jack off as soon as he got into the water.

Then, without a word, he walked to the shallows of the lagoon and waded in.

I'd seen enough. I wasn't waiting around to watch what happened next. I couldn't be bothered. I picked up my gun and, without saying anything to Raven, I walked over to the trailer and climbed inside.

Let them do whatever they wanted together because I didn't give a fuck anymore. I couldn't believe she'd just let this stranger into our world and let him take over like he had without even finding out what he wanted and why he was there. He wasn't there to help us. Of course he said he was but he wasn't. He wanted something else. He wanted

Raven or both of us. He wanted us like every other man on this damn planet and Raven couldn't let him in, she couldn't.

I sat on the edge of the bed and looked down at the revolver, turning it around and around in my hands. It had the words "Smith & Wesson" stamped on the barrel, but other than that, it just looked like any other gun you'd see on the TV or at the movies.

But I still didn't want anything to do with it.

I stood up and shoved the gun under the end of the mattress. No one would know it was under there. I even sat right on top of it, to make sure the mattress didn't feel all bumpy.

It didn't.

That was one of them taken care of.

I didn't like the rifle sitting next to me either, so I pulled that off the bed and slipped it underneath, pushing it right to the back, against the wall. Hopefully no one would find that either.

I knew I was fooling myself, but still I felt safer now. All of a sudden guns outnumbered people in this place and I sure wasn't happy about that.

"You really should come in and join me, you know!"

I heard Tyler's voice through the walls. It was muffled, but I could still hear him.

"No thanks, I'll stay right here," Raven called back.

"It's really nice in here!"

"I know that. I swim in it quite often, as I know you're fully aware."

He laughed then. "Okay, your loss!"

"Oh, I'm sure it is!"

And the conversation ended there.

I was staring at the door of the trailer, leaning forward and listening, wondering what was going on out there, what Raven was doing, what Tyler was doing, but not wanting to go and find out.

I couldn't bring myself to do that. Right about now, all I wanted to do was be away from those two. To be as far away as possible. Take a walk or just pack my things and go, but I knew I couldn't. I couldn't leave Raven and Tyler alone. I certainly didn't trust him and I was worried about what he could do (*would do*) if left alone with Raven.

I mean, let's face it, I *know* what he was thinking. Men are so transparent it's laughable. It's so easy to know exactly what's on their minds. Raven is beautiful, she's stunning, he's *already* seen her naked and he *knows* exactly what she has to offer and the only real reason he's helping us is not because he wants to, but because he wants to get Raven.

He wants to *fuck* her.

There, I said it. But you were thinking it too, right?

He's here, he's being nice and helpful, and now he's naked, swimming in the lagoon trying to turn her on so he can sink his cock into her and screw her brains out.

And that made me mad.

Mad that he thought he had the right to do exactly that.

Mad that he thought he would be able to do it with a bit of charm and manners.

Mad that he assumed the hunt was almost over. He was about to bag his prey.

Well, I had other ideas.

I had ways of stopping him if he went too far.

I knew things he didn't. Things that would make him think twice...

My eyes crossed the trailer and rested on the cupboard door above the sink.

If he goes too far...

"Amber, honey, *quick*!"

It was Raven's voice and I knew she was in trouble. I lunged for the door and swung it open wide in a matter of seconds, ready to attack Tyler.

But he was in the middle of the lagoon, swimming strongly towards the wildflowers, and Raven was still sitting in her deck chair, twisting herself around and gesturing for me to hurry.

I climbed down the stairs and walked towards her.

"Quickly," she said again. "You'll miss it."

And as I got closer, I could see she had the radio in her hand and I could hear a tinny female voice.

> *"...who went missing on Wednesday of last week. The suspect was involved in an operation to steal more than two hundred thousand dollars worth of cocaine from rival drug dealers in the downtown area. The police wish to question a female exotic dancer, also missing, who lived with the suspect at the Pine Hills Trailer Park. The pair are also accused of attempting to murder a gas station owner who was bashed Wednesday afternoon as the suspects stole gas from his gas station on the main road to Lake Mountain. That man is still in hospital, fighting for his life, with massive head injuries. Anyone who believes they have come into contact with these individuals should treat them with caution and contact the police immediately. In other news a large fire is sweeping through Washington State..."*

Raven turned off the radio.

"Did you hear that?" she asked.

I nodded.

"*Living* with him! They said *living* with him!"

"I know, I heard."

"They've got it all wrong. And we had *nothing* to do with stealing any drugs!"

I knew that too, but I guess Raven was just trying to get the story straight in her head and wanted to make sure I heard it too.

"They've got it so completely fucked up, hon. Jesus, I wanted to *pay* the guy at the gas station. He was the one who attacked *me*! We didn't steal any gas."

"I know," I said again. "I guess they're just using all the information they have and they're trying to piece together what happened the best way they can. They don't know the real story, so they're going to get it wrong anyway."

"The guy from the gas station is in hospital."

"I heard."

Raven looked to the ground. "Massive head injuries, they said."

I knelt by Raven and put my arm around her.

"You can't be held responsible for that."

"I didn't mean to hit him that hard," she whispered. "He was attacking me and I just wanted him off me. I didn't mean to hit him so very hard."

I understood and I hugged her.

"Don't worry about him now. I'm sure he'll pull through. You just worry about what we have to do here. The rest can come later, okay?"

She turned to me and smiled. Her hand reached out and she patted my knee. "Thanks, Amber," she said. "You really *are* my best friend."

I smiled then. Everything felt better. Raven and I were one again. With one goal, and one vision.

"And you're mine too," I replied. "Always will be."

She squeezed my knee. Her hair trickled across my arm.

"Er, excuse me!"

Him again. Always *him*.

Always at the wrong time.

"I hate to break up the annual meeting of Women On The Run," he called to us. "But I'd like to get out of the lagoon now."

We both turned to face him. More of Raven's hair moved across my arm, tickling me as it did so.

"We're not stopping you!" Raven called.

"Yeah, I can see that," he replied, standing near the water's edge, the level of the water lapping just above his hips.

He had muscled arms and well-formed pecs, with just a hint of dark chest hair down the middle. His arms made a V across his body, his hands under the water somewhere, probably cupping his privates just in case the water level should drop.

"Come on out," Raven continued. She was enjoying this.

"Ah, well, you see, you risk being blinded by my magnificence if I come out while you're watching me."

Raven laughed loud and strong and the sound echoed around the lagoon.

He was in the water and worried about what two girls might think of him. Far from being magnificent right about then, I thought he might more resemble the Incredible Shrinking Man if we ever got a look at him.

"So it's alright for you to spy on us naked in the lagoon, but not for us to watch you?"

"Ah, well, you see, I didn't think of that before I dived in here."

"Okay, okay," Raven laughed again as she climbed from the deck chair. "We'll go inside."

"Should we?" I asked.

"What, you want to stay for the show?"

"No, no, not really. I just don't think we should leave him out here alone without being watched."

"He's naked and wet, hon. I don't think he wants to do anything other than get dried and dressed. His little plan's gone wrong and he's trying to get out of it somehow."

We smiled at each other and walked towards the trailer.

"Ah, do you have a towel I could borrow? I've left mine at the valve house."

"Hand towel?" Raven called over her shoulder.

"Ah, *noooo*. Something a bit bigger?"

"Yeah, yeah, whatever," Raven replied, opening the trailer door and ushering me inside.

I sat on the couch while Raven grabbed a towel and threw it outside. It landed on the deck chair and then tumbled off.

"He'll want to be quick about this," she said as she closed the trailer door. "We'll give him five minutes before we go back out there."

I nodded.

Raven sat down next to me. I could still smell the pine scent that she'd used to scrub clean the wardrobe, and I wasn't sure it if was coming from her or the wardrobe. Probably from her.

We didn't say anything for a few minutes, instead we listened for sounds outside. First we heard Tyler sloshing around in the water, probably walking out of the shallows, but after that, we couldn't hear anything.

He was being very quiet.

Probably scared half to death we were watching him through the windows.

"What do you think?" Raven then said to me.

"About Tyler? I don't trust him."

She rolled her eyes. "I know that. I meant about what we should do next. The memorial?"

I nodded. "I guess. I mean, what choice do we have? The cops are after us and they all think we're involved in this somehow. If we can dump Duke and get rid of him, maybe we can prove we had nothing to do with the drugs or at least play dumb and say we just took off to see the sights on the mountain."

Raven nodded. "Yeah, I'm thinking that too. If we can get rid of Duke, there's nothing to link us to him. So I guess we really should do that. Then when the cops find us all we've been doing is playing tourist."

"So let's head to the memorial," I said, hoping we could now say goodbye to Tyler, but knowing it wouldn't be that easy.

"Nope," Raven said. "Not today. It's Sunday and there'll still be a whole herd of tourists up there. Better to wait until tomorrow morning to check out the place. There'll be less people around and less chance of us being seen."

"And tonight?"

She shrugged her shoulders. "We sit and wait, I guess."

"And Tyler?"

"He waits with us."

"Are you sure?"

"Sweets, I'm not sure of anything right now. But I know that I'd rather have Tyler where I can see him than have him roaming the mountain somewhere out of our control."

That made a lot of sense. He said he wanted to help us, but we couldn't be sure. So it was a much better idea to have him with us where we could keep an eye on him than to say goodbye and have him run loose to whoever. Anyway, the longer he was with us, the more he became an accessory.

"Well, I guess it's three of us for dinner then," Tyler said as he opened the trailer door and walked inside.

Walked right inside.

Inside *our* trailer.

Uninvited!

"You girls really shouldn't talk so loud." He smirked at us as he stood there. "Anyone listening from outside can hear every word you say."

I hated the way he kept referring to us as "*you girls*."

"Didn't know anyone *was* listening," Raven replied curtly. I think she was a bit pissed at him too right about then.

He was fully dressed again and in one hand he held the towel and in the other the silver pistol.

"You forgot this," he said as he put the pistol on the table between us. "Rule number one of owning a gun, never leave it outside in the clearing when you're running from the cops and need it."

"I'll remember that," Raven replied.

He rubbed at his still-wet hair with the towel one more time before looking around the trailer and throwing the towel on the sink. He took a step back and sat on the other couch, underneath the storage area and across from us.

"So, this is where you two live." It wasn't a question, it was a statement. His eyes darted all around the trailer, checking out everything.

Even the wardrobe.

I had to remind myself that Duke was no longer in there and we didn't have to panic. Duke was tucked nicely away in the Suburban and Tyler knew that already anyway.

"Your kingdom. Your palatial abode."

"Yep, it sure is," Raven replied. "Home sweet home."

"A bit cramped," he added.

"We like it."

"Guess you'd have to. Not much space though."

"It's amazing what you can fit in here," she smirked.

Tyler nodded.

"Oh," he said, his hands digging through the pockets of his jacket. "Something else…"

He dug around and produced three boxes of ammunition that he placed on the table.

"Guns aren't much use without ammunition."

"Is there anything you *don't* have in those jacket pockets?"

He laughed and nodded. "Yes, in fact. There's no kitchen sink. But," he said as he nodded towards our kitchen, "I see you already have one of those anyway."

We sat in silence for a few moments, each of us feeling probably a bit uncomfortable. I know *I did* for sure, and I was glad Raven was sitting between Tyler and me.

"So," he said finally, leaning forward and resting his hands on his knees. His eyes dropped down to Raven's *FLIRT* t-shirt for just a few seconds. I don't know if he was reading it or checking out what was underneath, but he caught himself and looked back at her face. "Did you get a chance to listen to the radio?"

"Yes," Raven replied. "We heard a news bulletin. And they've got it all wrong."

Tyler nodded. "No need to convince me. I know that already. You two don't look like drug thieves to me."

"We're not."

"And I believe you." He smiled. "So, your plan is to get rid of Duke at the memorial. If you do that, then you can try to prove you had nothing to do with him and his drugs. And maybe the cops will blame his disappearance or death on the drug guys who were after him, right?"

"Exactly. And they might leave us alone too. I mean, the news reports make it sound like we were living with him and planning this with him and it's just not true."

Tyler nodded. "So, it's the Dam Worker's Memorial then?"

"Yep."

"Lots of tourists up there on a Sunday."

"Not today. Tomorrow."

"Oh, okay," Tyler relied. "This may be a stupid question, but why not just dig a hole and bury him out in the lagoon somewhere?"

"That's not an option," Raven replied quickly.

"I mean, when you think about it, you could've already had him out of your hair days ago if you'd just stopped and buried him anywhere along the road to Lake Mountain."

"I said, that's *not* an option!" Raven repeated herself, slower this time.

Tyler looked surprised and unsure. His eyes darted across to me, but I said nothing.

"Okay, so not tonight," he continued.

Raven shook her head. "No. I want to stop and plan this properly. Let's go over every possible scenario tonight and work through it all. Let's make sure we each know what we're doing and what has to happen, and let's try to be ready for anything tomorrow. We'll be going to a public place where there could be a lot of people and I want to make sure we get it right."

"That sounds fine to me." Tyler smiled, but the smile was wrong somehow, like he knew something wasn't right. "Or we could just bury him around here someplace."

"I said no," Raven replied. "Not around here. Not here. It *has* to be the memorial, okay?"

"Fine, whatever." Tyler gave up the fight, still looking unsure.

I wasn't so sure either.

In fact, I was worried sick. I was caught up in my own problems and concerns. Tomorrow was the least of my worries right then.

First, there was tonight.

There were three of us. Three of us in the trailer.

And only one bed.

Thirty

I'll never forget that night.
It was long.
It was lonely.

It was the night I felt like crying forever.

I won't go into any great details about what was said and what happened. None of it really matters, I guess, in the end.

But this is a journal to help me remember the events as they happened. The good and the bad. Although I'll never forget the bad. Remember what I said about bad times overshadowing the good?

Well, climb aboard now for Bad Times Central.

I don't know how long it took us, or what we did to pass the time, but that night we sat down and discussed what we were going to do the next day. How we would do it, what we would do if it went wrong.

We would drive to the memorial and check it out, pretending to be tourists and just generally trying to blend in. We'd see whether or not we could bury Duke nearby and what tools we'd need to do it. Tyler said that there was a maintenance shack somewhere near the dam wall, down near the valve houses. It contained a variety of tools he'd "borrowed" in the past, so we could get shovels and stuff from there and use them later that night.

We'd take the trailer with us too, making us look like real tourists. Plus, we didn't want to leave it behind at the lagoon for anyone – cops, drug guys, the public – to happen across it while we were gone. Once Duke was disposed of, we knew we'd have to move on, at least for a while. Until the heat cooled on us.

So, our days at the lagoon were almost over.

The plan could work. It certainly sounded good to Raven.

I still had my doubts though. What if we were caught? What if someone saw us? What if it all went wrong?

But neither Raven nor Tyler were interested in that. They were too busy talking with each other and laughing and planning the events.

They cooked the fish together and cleaned up, while I tried to read my book (although I wasn't really trying at all.)

We kept the radio on as long as we could, even though the batteries were starting to die. We listened to some more news reports, but basically they just said the same things.

On the run. With Duke. Dangerous.

That's all they had. And it was way too much.

The sun set and the night got cold. We lit candles to see in the dark.

Tyler and Raven were still talking late into the night and I was fed up listening and being left out of the conversation.

I wanted to know how this would work. I wanted to know how Raven and I were supposed to sleep in the bed while Tyler was there in the trailer. I didn't want him to know we shared our bed together, but I guess he'd already worked that out once he'd stepped inside and looked around.

You *know* what guys think about things like this.

There was no way I was giving up my bed for some stranger. He could go sleep outside for all I cared.

So while Raven and Tyler talked about their upbringings, their likes and dislikes (notice how they'd stopped planning for tomorrow?), I stood up from the couch and walked over to the bed. I jumped on it loudly, making sure they both heard me and both knew I was in bed.

In bed. Wanting to *sleep*.

But they kept talking.

I lit another candle and kept pretend-reading.

And I got angrier and angrier.

But I wasn't going to say anything because then they would know that they'd got me all mad, so I just sat there and listened to them.

Oh I like that too...

And

Really? I love those as well...

And

I've never told anyone this about myself but...

You get the picture, right?

So I'm not entering any of that in here. It's not worth wasting the space especially as I'm running out of pages in this notebook and I want to finish the story. Can't have you missing out on the final pages or something. You've come this far already.

I guess I must've dozed for a short while. I don't remember doing it, but I was lying back on the bed with my head propped up on the pillows and I guess I shut my eyes just to rest them for a moment and I must've slipped into a snooze.

When I awoke, I could still hear the radio. I didn't open my eyes though. I thought I'd lay there with them shut to hear what Raven and Tyler were saying about me, what they spoke about when I was asleep.

But that was the weird thing...

They *weren't* talking about me.

They weren't talking.

No one was.

I waited for what seemed like ages, but was probably only a couple of minutes. When I heard nothing except the crackling and garbled voices of the radio with its decaying batteries, I opened my right eye a fraction.

The candles were still burning and I could just make out Raven and Tyler through my squint. They were on the couch, both looking at the radio. It seemed like they were listening very intently, but from what I could hear, it was just some night-time talk back jock taking calls from his insomniac listeners.

But they were both looking so serious, so stern. Concentrating so much.

I couldn't work it out.

And then my eye dropped a bit lower, below the table.

It was too dark to see what was happening down there, but I could work it out.

His left hand was on the table, next to the radio, but his right hand was under the table, and between his legs.

Raven's left hand was under the table too, moving up and down in short, jerky movements. No one made a sound.

I couldn't believe what I was seeing, so I opened my left eye a fraction too.

Now his right hand lifted her hand away from his lap, moving it across the table. His arm snaked across her body (I could only see the *FLI* on the *FLIRT* t-shirt, the rest was blocked by his arm) and it slipped under the table, along with her hand, right between her legs.

My eyes rose to Raven's face.

Was she in pain? Was she scared?

Far from it.

She looked as if she was concentrating hard, her eyes blinking slowly, her bottom lip caught between her teeth.

All was quiet except for the static mumblings from the radio.

I closed my eyes and tried to hold back the tears. I wanted to say something, to scream and shout, but I didn't.

I couldn't.

I did the only thing I could think of right then. I rolled over onto my side, my back to them, and tried to sleep.

Of course, I couldn't. There was no way I could sleep now. I just lay there, listening to the radio static, wondering if I heard a deep intake of breath here, a moan of pleasure there. Wanting so much to turn back around and catch them at it, but knowing I didn't have the *fucking guts* to do so.

And who the hell was I anyway? What gave me the right to tell them what to do and what not to do?

It's none of my damn business if Raven wants to fuck up her life. After what she's just been through, if she wants another animal pawing at her cunt then that's her business, not mine.

But it didn't make it any easier.

I'm sure I heard them whispering. Voices fast, talking together, but I couldn't hear what they were saying.

I just lay there, hating him and her and me and Duke and my father and my mother and the world and everything I could think of.

I could take the gun from underneath the mattress and load it with bullets and blow the fucker away.

But I didn't. I just lay there some more, wiping the tears as they ran down my nose and cheek.

Eventually, the radio stopped its noise. I don't know if they turned it off or whether the batteries went dead. Then the candlelight flickered out and after a few more seconds I felt Raven climb over my legs at the end of the bed. She slid down next to me and I was glad it was dark so she couldn't see the tear-streaks down my face.

Her hand came out and touched my shoulder, but I turned away from her, rolled over onto my other side.

I just couldn't touch her right then. Didn't want to. Wouldn't.

I opened my eyes and looked out into the darkness of the trailer.

I couldn't see anything. I couldn't see Tyler. But I guessed he was there somewhere. On the couch or on the fold out bed below the storage area. I didn't hear the door open and close, so I guessed he was inside the trailer somewhere.

Still inside.

With us.

Like he owned the place.

I had trouble falling back to sleep, but I must've done it at some time because later that night, I woke again.

It was still dark.

But I could hear whispers.

At first I thought it was coming from outside the trailer, like someone was out there talking to someone else. But I soon realised the voices were coming from inside.

I turned over onto my back to tell Raven, reaching out to shake her awake. But the bed was cold next to me. Cold and empty.

And then I heard her whisper, "Yes," in a deep primal voice.

My eyes were wide open. They could be because I knew they couldn't see me. But it made no difference, it was so dark I couldn't see them either.

I could feel the trailer gently rocking and could hear her panting breath.

"Touch me," she whispered then.

I could imagine it there in the dark. I didn't need to see it. I could see them without the light.

I closed my eyes and rolled back away from them. I reached out and took Raven's soft pillow in my arms and hugged it tight.

I could smell her on it. Her Black Widow perfume and the smell of her wonderful hair.

Her smell. Her essence.

I wished it was *her* I was holding and not just her pillow.

I wished everything could be as it once was.

I wished Tyler was dead.

I hated him so much right then. But there was nothing I could do. If he could've seen my face then, he would've known exactly what I was thinking.

The whispering continued as I wrapped my pillow around my ears, cutting out the sounds.

He'd keep.

He'd get his.

Soon.

Monday, July 15.

Thirty-one

Monday morning was a late start.
Well, for some of us.
They slept in.

I was awake at the normal time, of course, as I didn't spend half the night rutting like rabbits.

Raven was by my side when I awoke. I could feel the heat of her body along my spine, but my eyes rested firmly on Tyler, who was lying on the fold out bed across the other side of the trailer.

He was asleep, they both were, and I spent quite a few minutes thinking about what happened last night and what had to happen today.

I felt like waking them, getting up and making breakfast and banging plates and cutlery so they'd have to wake up.

"Oh, sorry," I'd say. "Didn't mean to wake you!"

After all, it wasn't my fault if they didn't get any sleep last night.

Because of the way the bed folded out into the centre of the trailer, the only way I could get to the sink was if I climbed over Tyler, and there was no way in hell I was going to do that.

I rolled over and stared at Raven. She was sleeping soundly. Her eyes were shut, half hidden in the mass of hair that fell across her forehead and cheeks, and she had a slight smile on her face.

Naturally.

I felt like slapping her then, just to jar her awake and back to reality.

But guess what? I didn't.

No, I slipped from the bed and, making sure I didn't make a sound, I crept around the meals table and past the couch, alongside Tyler. He was curled on his side, his head burrowed under the blanket so I couldn't see his face.

Hiding it in shame, probably.

Quietly, I undid the latch and snuck out the door.

It was cooler today. Clouds hung low in the sky and the sun was covered. The lagoon was so cold I could see my breath. I hugged myself to keep warm as I looked around what was once our most perfect hideaway.

I looked across at the Suburban and wondered how Duke was feeling.

He'd catch his death of cold in there.

I almost smiled at that thought.

And then I wondered if I could just unhitch the car from the trailer and drive out of here, leaving Tyler and Raven stranded.

It would serve them right if I did.

Instead, I sat in the deck chair and looked out across the lagoon and into the trees. But I wasn't really looking, my eyes stayed unfocussed, looking into nothing but my thoughts.

Today, I thought. Today will be the day we get rid of Duke.

I knew it would be. Something deep down inside told me that we'd finally be rid of him today, no matter what. And I sure hoped I was correct.

I sat in the deck chair for quite a while, just thinking about stuff, life, the events of the last week, my family, Raven.

There was simply nothing else to do.

I sort of wished Tyler and Raven would hurry and wake up so we could get going and get rid of Duke, but they slept longer and longer.

Wore themselves out last night. Doing what they did.

But I didn't want to think about that. So I stood and walked over towards the water's edge, looking into the dark waters of the lagoon and wishing it was warm enough to go for a swim. Also wishing that Tyler wasn't around so I could strip down and swim anyway.

But there was no point. That wasn't going to happen.

The days of us doing what we wanted to do here were gone. He had seen to that.

I turned back and looked at the trailer. It was so small and old and battered. All of a sudden I felt very sad. Sad for Raven, and sad for me. How long had we been living together in that trailer now? It was the first time I really looked at it with an outsider's eye. It was so old and half falling apart. We used to laugh at Duke's trailer, Raven and I, because it was such a wreck, but ours was no better.

I didn't look at the trailer now as a sanctuary or a place to call home, a place to protect me from the outside world. Now I saw it for what it really was, a broken down piece of old junk that should've been sent to the crushers years ago.

And they were *still* inside.

Raven and Tyler.

I walked along the water's edge and towards the rock wall.

If they were going to sleep in and waste our time, there was no way I was sitting around here just waiting for them, lost in my own thoughts and getting more and more depressed.

I wouldn't allow them to treat me that way. So I climbed the stairs along the rock wall.

With no real idea why I was doing it, just that it was something to do, I took each step slowly, staring down at my feet as I did so. The steps were old and rotting, covered in moss, and I didn't want to suddenly take a tumble. They climbed high up the rock wall, and so did I. Within minutes I was standing along the top of the rocks, looking down at the lagoon and the trailer below. Looking down at my world, like some god watching over her creations.

I thought about following the dirt track up the mountain further. Thought about just setting off and walking for hours, days, letting Raven and Tyler worry about where I'd gone, or if someone had got to me. I'd have loved to have done just that, they deserved nothing better, but that wasn't something I was going to do.

Soul mates don't do that to each other. Friends stick together through the good and bad. Plus, maybe that's what Tyler wanted me to do, and there was no way I was going to let that happen.

He could go fuck himself for all I cared.

I didn't trust him. I never had.

I turned around and sat down on the top step, making sure I had a clear view of the trailer in case anyone came out. Of course, I couldn't see the door, it was on the other side, but I had a good view of the back and also the top of the trailer. If someone stepped out and walked a couple of feet, I'd see them anyway.

I leaned my head against the wooden railing and hugged myself to keep warm.

I closed my eyes and wished all this trouble away. I opened them again but the trouble remained.

It was then I saw the caterpillar slowly making its way along the wooden slats of the hand rail. It was fat and hairy and had yellow stripes along its black body. Slowly, it slinked its way along the wood. I smiled and watched it as it moved. It was totally unaware of me, had no idea I was there.

Life was so simple for some.

I watched as it made its way along the wood; over and over again it moved its little body, determined and focussed, it didn't stop. It knew what it had to do to reach its goal. It knew what it took.

And then I saw another one, following the first. And there was another one on the ground below them. I looked around me and I counted probably ten or twelve of them. They were everywhere.

I stood up, making sure my feet were nowhere near the little guys and started counting. Even though I told myself I wouldn't go anywhere until I could count thirty of them, I only ever found twenty-five.

I wanted to pick one up and feel it, touch it and see what it did. But I didn't want to interfere, didn't want to disturb its life pattern. Would *never* interfere like that.

Unlike some people I know.

So I sat back down on the step and overlooked the lagoon once again.

And waited.

And waited.

But still they slept.

"Fuck this," I said after a while.

I stood and turned, walking along the dirt track further up the mountain.

If they wanted to sleep then let them sleep until hell freezes over as far as I was concerned. I wasn't waiting around for them.

The path snaked alongside the mountain. It was mostly dirt and weeds and I could tell that it hadn't been used for a long time. It wasn't as steep as I thought it would be and I actually started to enjoy the walk. I could hear the sounds of water trickling nearby, probably making its way down the mountain to the blowhole, and the trees were tall and beautiful, smelling of that wonderful natural morning smell.

If I didn't know better, I'd think that everything was fine with the world.

I don't know how long I walked, or how far I got. I certainly wasn't in any hurry. I was just enjoying the time to myself, making sure that if Tyler and Raven *were* awake, that they would have ample time to worry about me and consider the ramifications of their actions.

The sun broke through the clouds at one stage and I turned to feel the warmth on my face. It was high in the sky, so I guessed I'd walked for an hour or so, and that it was getting on to about lunchtime.

And I bet they're still sleeping.

Or worse...

I hadn't thought about that. I stopped in my tracks and turned around.

They wouldn't! Would they?

If they woke and found me gone, they were supposed to worry and start searching for me.

But what if they *didn't?*

What if they woke and found me gone and smiled at each other and got into bed together and had sex again, fucked again, fucked again in *my* bed!

Why I didn't think of that before, I had no idea. I'd literally handed them *exactly* what they wanted. I was almost sure that they wouldn't care about me, at least not until they'd fucked once more.

Or twice.

Maybe a dozen times.

And without me around to have to worry about, they could be as loud and as hard and as long as they wanted to be.

"Damn them," I whispered.

I didn't know what to do now. I'd walked so far, it wasn't like I could just turn around and be back at the trailer in a matter of minutes. In fact, I didn't know if I even *wanted* to go back, in case I found them there, naked and cumming, doing exactly what I suspected they were doing.

And could you blame them?

I'd literally handed them the opportunity to do exactly that!

Good one, Amber. Nicely thought through. You earn an extra gold star for missing the obvious, sweety!

I had to get back *pronto.* I had to get them apart.

I had to show Tyler something that would change his mind completely.

That was the way to get rid of him. *That* was the way to change things.

And I had to do it now.

I marched quickly down the track, heading back towards the lagoon.

Thirty-two

"*A*mber!"

It was Raven's voice. I could hear her calling before I even made it back to the lagoon.

"*Aaaammmmmbeeeeerrrr!*"

Tyler was calling too.

Maybe they really *were* worried about me after all.

When I heard their voices, I slowed down my walking. I could afford to take my time.

One thing was for sure, they weren't in the bed having sex right then. The longer they searched, the longer they would be apart from each other.

Seek and ye shall find.

And when I arrived at the top of the wooden stairs, I could see that was exactly what they were doing.

"This is all your fault," Raven was saying to him. She had a bucket by her side and a sponge in her hand. She was washing the hood of the Suburban.

"Mine? How do you figure that? You might want to look closer to home before you sling accusations." Tyler replied, standing out in the middle of the clearing, arms crossed, his eyes searching the lagoon.

"Don't try to blame this on me. She's *my* friend."

"We'll have to take the car and search the whole mountain for her now."

"She can't be far." Raven picked up the bucket and moved it further along the side of the car. Dipping the sponge in the foamy water, she started washing the roof.

"You can't be sure of that."

I smiled.

Maybe I *was* important to them.

"Hi," I called, trying to sound calm and relaxed.

They both swung around to look up at me. Raven dropped the sponge into the bucket and Tyler started to walk towards me.

"Where the *fuck* have you been?" Raven called.

"Went for a walk," I replied as I started down the stairs.

"Without telling us?"

"You were both asleep."

"You could've left a note or something," Raven replied.

I shrugged my shoulders. "Sorry. Couldn't find a pen."

"We were worried about you," Tyler called as he walked to stand next to Raven.

Yeah, like I believed *him*!

"You picked a hell of a day to go for a walk," Raven added.

"You were both sleeping, I wasn't gone long."

I reached the end of the steps, jumped down and walked out onto the clearing. I felt *great*!

"Long enough to have me worried sick," Raven replied.

She walked over to me and the anger etched across her face changed into a smile. She put her wet arms around me and kissed me on the cheek.

I'm sure she smelled different. Maybe even of Tyler.

"Don't do that again, hon. Okay?" she whispered in my ear. "I was really worried."

So worried, she was cleaning her car.

"Okay," I replied as she let go. "Sorry."

I looked over to Tyler. He was leaning on the Suburban now. I couldn't read his face and I wondered what he was thinking about right then.

Maybe he was thinking about where I'd been and what I was doing.

"I'm glad you're okay," he said with a smile.

Yeah, *sure* he was.

Raven was dressed in jeans and sneakers again, the only difference being she was wearing her black tank top with the words *I Fuck on the First Date* printed in little red letters across the front. Below the words was a picture of a white nut and bolt joined together, just in case the subtlety was missed in the wording.

I *hated* that shirt.

You have no idea how much.

In fact, I'd told Raven how much I hated it the last time she wore it. She thought it was a great joke shirt, something that got the guys all hot and flustered and thinking they had a real good chance. That's why she wore it, to lead them on and then turn them down literally just when they're ready to blow their cum all over her.

But I hated it. I didn't like what it said and I didn't like the trouble it could bring her.

And when I told her that, she'd nodded her head and she never wore it again.

But now, here it was once more. She was wearing it to turn Tyler on, I just knew it. It hadn't got too wet while she was washing the car, but maybe I'd arrived back too early. Maybe, given a few more minutes, that tank top could've got real wet. And *real* clingy.

He, of course, was still dressed in the same clothes. Hadn't changed once.

How could she spend time with him? How could she *be* with him?

"Don't you own any other clothes?" I called to him.

He shoved his hands in his pockets and looked to the ground. I think I embarrassed him.

"Ah, yeah, I know what you mean. Didn't think of that yesterday. Don't worry, I'll pick up some others later today when we go past the valve houses."

"What makes you think we're going there?" I asked.

Tyler's head lifted and he exchanged a glance with Raven.

"Well," he said. "Raven and I thought – "

"I thought we were going to the memorial," I said as I turned to face Raven, cutting Tyler off in mid-sentence.

"We are, hon," she replied. "But it's the middle of the day now, and I really thought we'd get a start earlier than this."

"Well," I said as I crossed my arms in front of her. "You should've thought about that last night, shouldn't you?"

It was Raven's turn to be embarrassed now. I saw her face flush and her eyes slipped from me.

I felt bad then, about hurting her in that way, but I didn't apologise. Maybe now she knew that I knew *exactly* what happened last night and that I wasn't too impressed about any of it.

"Come on," I said. "I've wasted enough time today. Let's get out there and get rid of Duke, if that's what we're going to do."

I walked around to the passenger side of the Suburban and climbed in the front. I wanted to make sure I got in first, and that I got the front seat. I didn't want Tyler and Raven up the front, stroking each other as we drove, getting it off while I was in the back.

This way, I could make sure he kept his hands to himself.

I shut my door and waited.

"All secured?" I heard him ask.

"Yep, ready to go. You hitched up the trailer?"

"Yes, locked and ready."

"Perfect."

The smell inside the car was quite strong. Duke was doing his best to unsettle me as well, and I could hear flies buzzing around in the back of the car too. They'd returned for a second course.

I wound down my window.

"Want me to drive?" I heard Tyler ask.

Raven didn't say anything, but I could hear the keys landing in his hands.

Before I knew it, he was climbing in beside me, smiling towards me and putting the keys in the ignition.

Raven never let *anyone* drive her Suburban.

While my plan to keep Tyler and Raven separated had worked, I wasn't at all comfortable having Tyler in the front with me, sitting just a few inches away from me.

What if he tries to grope me?

He wouldn't *dare*!

I closed my legs tight, just in case.

The engine roared in the silence and I heard Raven climb in behind me.

"All set?" Tyler asked as he turned to smile at me.

I didn't reply.

"I think we should keep all the windows down," he added as he wound down his. "Duke's stinking this place up!"

We slowly drove off, Tyler getting used to the car and the pull of the trailer as he turned the steering wheel to the left. We arced past the wooden steps, the blowhole, the lagoon and the stream and headed out of the clearing.

Away from paradise.

Forever.

It was so nice while it lasted.

So nice while we were alone.

Before *he* came.

***

It took us a while to retrace our steps back out onto the main road. Neither Raven nor I really remembered how we drove in to the lagoon, let alone how to reverse the process and drive out.

Still, after a couple of wrong turns, we found ourselves back on the main road to Lake Mountain.

It felt so strange, so alien to be out here, back in civilisation and amongst the population again. Every car that passed us I treated with suspicion. Are they cops? Are they drug dealers? Are they members of the public who read their newspapers properly and who'll think, "That's who the cops are looking for!"

And it didn't help that Tyler was at the wheel. People might mistake him for Duke. If they didn't know what he looked like, two girls and a guy in a distinctive car with an old trailer attached was maybe all they needed to have their memories jogged. He might be the very reason we'd be caught!

All I knew, as we drove up the long and winding road towards Wentworth Dam, was that I wanted to be off this road and out of view from everyone and everything as soon as we could.

No one talked in the car. Each of us was lost in our own thoughts, and I certainly didn't want to talk to either of them right now. I just wanted to be rid of Duke. If we got that far, I'd worry about everything else afterwards.

I turned around to check on the trailer. It was still there, attached and rocking slightly from side to side as it followed on behind us.

Raven was sitting in the middle of the back seats, so she could see out the windshield as well.

I turned back around to face the front.

More cars sped by. It seemed like the road was filled with tourists, even for a Monday. But I'm guessing it was probably a normal day. I was just on edge, knowing that each and every car could spell the end for us. All someone had to do would be pull over and think, then put the pieces together, and call the cops.

Driving out there in the middle of the day was dangerous, but I guess we didn't have much choice.

There was no way I was staying at the lagoon now anyway. It had been ruined first by Duke and then by Tyler, so the sooner we got rid of Duke, the sooner we could be rid of Tyler.

And that was worth risking all.

After we drove on a bit further, we turned a corner and drove past a general store. The signs out the front told us they sold hot food and drinks, and all of a sudden I felt very hungry.

I watched the store as we sped by.

"I'd love to stop and eat," Raven said. She was thinking the same as I was.

"Too risky," Tyler replied. "We can't stay out here in the open for too long."

"I wasn't talking about pulling up out the front and getting out," she replied. "That would be way too obvious. Here, take this next turnoff and pull over."

Tyler applied the brakes and we turned onto a small gravel road, drove down it a short distance and parked the car over on the shoulder.

"Now what?" Tyler turned to face Raven as he switched off the engine.

"I'll go back and get us some food," Raven replied, sliding across the seat and opening the door.

"No you *won't!*" I said. It came out harsh and angry, but I didn't mean it to. They both looked at me. "We can't risk it, Raven."

Tyler nodded in agreement. "She's right. You can't do it."

"But I'm *hungry!*" she added, rolling her eyes. "No one will suspect anything if I go by myself."

"Then I'll go," Tyler said as he opened his door and climbed out.

I didn't know whether that was a good idea or not, but I guess I was relieved knowing he would be leaving us, even if it was for only a short while. I also noticed he left the keys in the ignition. That was another good sign.

If he was away for long enough...

But I knew Raven wouldn't agree to that.

Tyler bent down and leaned in the back window, smiling at Raven.

"What do you want to eat?" he asked.

"I don't know," Raven replied. "Just get something, anything, as long as it's not fish."

He looked over to me and I just nodded.

"Okay," he said. "And a couple of Pepsis?"

"Perfect," Raven replied, wiping a curl away from her eyes.

"Won't be long. You girls keep Duke company until I get back," he said. "Don't do anything you'll regret in the morning."

And with that, he started walking back up the road.

I turned around slightly in my seat and leaned forward, watching him walk past the trailer in the side rear-view mirror. He walked quickly along the road, never looking back once.

He was always so confident. He never looked back.

Once he turned the corner and was out of sight, I let my breath out in a whoosh. I must've been holding it for quite a while.

"You don't like him much, do you?" Raven asked.

I turned to face her.

She was leaning against the back seat, her head thrown back and her arms crossed in front of her. Her eyes were looking straight at me, and she looked puzzled.

"No," I replied.

"Why?"

"You know why."

"Actually," she said. "I really don't."

"I think you have some idea."

She sighed. "Look, hon, about last night. What you think happened…"

"I don't even want to *talk* about last night."

"It wasn't like that."

"Does that make it all *right*? Does that *excuse* what you did last night while I was there with you? Does it?"

She didn't reply. She just closed her eyes.

"I guess not," she whispered after a while.

"I'm disgusted," I continued. "I can't begin to tell you how disgusted and how upset I really am. I can't believe you'd do that and I can't believe you'd let him in to our lives. Not just our *trailer*, but into our *private lives* like you did last night. I'm disappointed and I'm sad and I'm hurt. I don't trust him, I *still* don't trust him and I don't think you should either."

"He's helping us, sweets," she said in a sad, tired voice.

"No, no he's not," I replied. "He's helping himself. He's helping himself to you and treating you like dirt. Just like all the other guys have. He's interested in only one thing, and you're giving it to him. As long as he can get inside your *cunt*, he'll stay around pretending to help us. He doesn't care about you, and he certainly doesn't care about me. He wants your pussy, Raven, and that's it. He can smell it and he wants it and he'll do anything he can and say anything you want to hear to get inside it. That's what they do. They think with their cocks, and they're lead by their cocks."

I guess I went a bit over the top, but I had an opportunity to tell her what I really thought and I took it. It must've struck home, because the next thing I knew Raven was out of the car, slamming the door behind her and walking off down the road.

I hadn't expected that reaction from her, and from what I could tell through the windshield, she must've been crying because I could see her wiping her eyes as she walked.

And so there I sat, in the Suburban with Duke. Tyler had gone in one direction, and now Raven was walking in the other. And she showed no sign of slowing down.

I knew I should go after her and apologise. The thought entered my mind. But so did the idea of sliding over to the driver's seat, turning on the engine and driving the hell out of there. But, of course, I didn't know how to drive, so I didn't like my chances of doing that. I'm sure I wouldn't get far if I tried.

So it was just Duke and me, and all of a sudden I didn't want to be the only person in the car with him. Knowing my luck, it would be now the police would spot the car and arrest me as the ringleader.

I didn't want that.

I leaned forward and looked at the side rear-view mirror once more. No sign of Tyler yet.

Why was he taking so long?

I climbed from the car and shut my door. I looked back along the trailer, but there was no sign of Tyler on the other side of the road either. The sun was shining through the clouds and reflecting its hot rays off the roof of the Suburban. I had to squint as I turned to look in the direction Raven was heading. She was still marching down the road, getting further and further away.

I really should've run after her, but I didn't. I just stood there.

Maybe it was good for her to break away for a few minutes and be alone. To get her thoughts in order and to think about what I said.

I heard it before I saw it, and at first I didn't take much notice. I was watching Raven's back and that's all that mattered.

But the sound got louder and louder and pushed its way into my conscience. It was the sound of a big, heavy motor, and it was coming from directly behind me.

I turned just in time to see the hearse pull out wide and pass me by, heading down the road and towards Raven.

It was black and shiny and empty except for the driver.

It rocked back and forth as it passed by the trailer, then straightened up and drove down the middle of the road. Within seconds it was closing in on Raven.

She didn't turn around to look though. She probably thought it was Tyler and me in the Suburban anyway.

I watched her continue walking. Marching fast and defiantly.

I saw the brake lights illuminate on the hearse.

It was slowing down.

Fuck!

Raven turned towards it, moving further onto the side of the road as the hearse drew alongside her.

I'm sure I saw the driver turn towards her.

The brake lights flashed once, then twice, and then the left indicator began to flash.

No! Oh Jesus, *no*! He's pulling over!

I took a couple of steps down the road. I wanted to call out to Raven, to tell her to run, but there was no point, she wouldn't hear me anyway.

And then the hearse turned the corner.

I couldn't believe my eyes, but suddenly I was very relieved. The guy wasn't stopping to talk to Raven at all, he was just slowing down to turn a corner a few feet in front of her.

The hearse continued along a track that I couldn't see. The trees in the forest had hidden the turnoff.

I smiled and almost laughed. Sometimes, you can panic about the most stupid things.

But then Raven turned and sprinted into the forest.

Following the hearse.

Thirty-three

The sign read:

> Ferguson's Funerals
> Xavier & Todd
> Viewing Tuesday 16th July at 11am
> Funeral 2pm.

I read it as I ran towards it.

I'd left the trailer behind, keys and Duke and all (don't worry, you couldn't see him from outside), and run down the road, following the path Raven had taken. Where the hearse had turned was a paved road, leading up towards a large home with a parking lot to the side.

The house looked old, but well cared for. It had a gabled roof and long veranda, and the wooden walls were painted a modest cream colour. Six windows ran along the veranda, but each of them had their curtains drawn, so I was sure no one could see me as I ran up the driveway.

I looked all around for Raven, but I couldn't see her anywhere.

The hearse was parked at the side of the house, where two large doors stood open, swinging out from the inside. I looked for the driver, but he wasn't in the car. I guessed he'd gone inside the house somewhere.

I had to be quick, before he came back out!

The driveway met the parking lot and I stood there on the edge, my eyes scanning the whole area. There were no cars in the lot and no sign of anyone else. I thought about calling out for Raven, but I knew that might give me away.

Where did she go? Was she inside? Why did she run off like that? Was I too hard on her?

All these thoughts swirled through my mind. But there were no answers.

I looked through the surrounding forest, hoping against hope I would find Raven staring back at me, a large grin on her face. But there was no sign of her anywhere.

I turned to look at the house again. All was quiet.

Damn you, Raven.

I didn't know what to do.

She ran that way, but I couldn't see her. So that meant she'd either gone inside by herself, or talked to the guy driving the hearse and he'd taken her inside.

But why?

Maybe he *did* recognise her from the news reports and was now calling the cops while he held her against her will.

That thought scared the shit out of me.

And I knew I had to act. There was no other option.

I took a deep breath and marched across the parking lot heading directly for the front door of the house.

The lot was larger than I thought and I felt exposed as I walked across it. Everything was so quiet, so eerie. I couldn't hear a sound. Anyone could see me and there was no chance I could hide anywhere quickly if something went wrong. But I couldn't turn back now, no matter what.

I reached the veranda and climbed its steps quickly. If I looked confident and in control, maybe they wouldn't think I was suspicious. My footsteps sounded loud in the silence, even though I was trying to tread lightly. I looked from one side to the other, making sure no one was watching me, checking that there were no faces suddenly appearing in the windows. But the curtains in the windows stayed shut, and there was no sign of the driver anywhere.

I stopped at the front door. It was made of old, heavy wood, but had been lovingly restored and cared for. I rang the doorbell.

The chimes sounded deep inside the house.

What next? I asked myself.

I had no plan, no real idea what I was going to do. I would wait for the door to open and force my way inside to rescue Raven, telling them whatever story that came into my mind at the time.

"What the *fuck* are you doing?"

The voice came from my left. I turned to see Raven's face, poking around the side of the house, looking at me.

"Raven!" I called, relieved she was okay.

"Are you *crazy?*" she asked, her eyes darting between me and the door.

"I thought you were in there," I replied.

"I'm not," she said.

"I can see that *now.*"

I heard footsteps coming from inside. They were getting louder. Closer.

My eyes widened and I'm sure Raven could see I was about to panic. She could probably hear the footsteps too.

"Get out of there!" she called.

My body was frozen. I couldn't move. The footsteps got closer and closer. My head turned and looked down at the doorknob. It was brass, nicely polished, shiny.

Raven was calling to me, but I couldn't really hear her. I was concentrating too much on the brass knob.

And then it turned, ever so slightly.

A hand grabbed my arm, pulled hard.

At first I thought it was someone from the funeral home pulling and tugging at me. But then I realised the door was still shut, the knob still turning. It was Raven who was pulling at me, talking to me in a low whisper.

"Come on, Amber, move it. We've got to get out of here, girl. Come on move it move it moveitmoveitmoveit!"

She was dragging me along the veranda. My eyes stayed fixed on the door for as long as they could. I kept my head turned, wanting to see who was at the door, and as it slowly opened inwards with a loud *creak*, Raven half-lifted and half-pushed me over the side of the veranda and tugged me out into the forest.

Within seconds we were hiding behind bushes, watching as a woman stepped onto the veranda. She was professionally dressed in a dark suit and tie. Her blonde hair was tied up in a ponytail and her makeup was a bit on the heavy side. She had her hands on her hips, and she was looking around for whoever had rung the bell. She shook her head after a few moments and mumbled something I couldn't hear. Then, she turned and walked back into the house, shutting the door firmly behind her.

"That was close," Raven said as she turned back to face me. "Are you *insane*?"

"*Me*? You were the one who ran off like that. I was worried you were in there. I was coming to save you!"

"Save me?" Raven stifled a laugh. "Save me from what?"

"I don't know. I just thought – "

"No, Amber, that's the problem, you *didn't* think. You could've ruined everything."

I didn't like the way she was blaming me for this. I was just trying to *save* her. Protect her. Didn't she see that?

"What if they'd seen you? Or me? Or both of us? What if they worked out who we were? Do you want to be the one responsible for sending us to jail?"

My eyes fell to the ground and I tried to keep control of my emotions. This wasn't my fault, none of this was. I was the good guy here!

After all, *she* was the one who killed Duke. *She* was the one who started all this. It would be *her* fault if we landed in jail. Not mine.

How *dare* she blame me!

But I didn't say any of this, of course. I just sat there and took it.

"I can't believe how reckless you were just then, Amber. You were almost asking for us to be caught! Is that what you want? Do you hate me so much that you actually *want* us to be caught?"

My eyes locked on hers.

"I don't hate you, Raven," I whispered. "You know that."

"You've got a weird way of showing it," she replied.

"I thought you were in there," I said as I nodded towards the house.

"I wasn't in there," she replied. "I was around *there*."

I followed her pointing finger to the side of the house. From where we were in the bushes, I could see more of the house now. This side looked just like the front of the house in design and colour, except that there was a large, sliding metal door cut into the wall about halfway down, with a sign that said *Ring Bell if Unattended*. There was a small ramp that led up to the door and the door handle itself was locked with a large, brass padlock. Something was weird about this side of the house, and it took me a few seconds to realise that there were no windows anywhere along the wall.

"I didn't know you were around here," I replied. "How could I? You shouldn't have run off like that. And why would you want to come *here* anyway?"

Raven shrugged. "It looked like a cool place to check out. Tyler wasn't back and you never know what you could find around a place like this."

"You shouldn't have run off like that," I continued.

"I was in a hurry. I wanted to see what the guy in the hearse would do when he got to the house. I didn't know you would follow me," she replied.

"Of *course* I would. I was worried. You shouldn't've left the car."

"I didn't think you wanted me near you," she replied in a soft voice after a few seconds. "After what you said to me."

"Raven, I was only telling you what I thought, from my heart, because I care so much. That's *why* I said what I said. Not to hurt you, but to make you try to understand."

She nodded.

"We need to get rid of him," I added.

"I know," she said. "We will. That's what we're doing now. Trying to do today."

She was talking about Duke.

I was talking about Tyler.

I was all set to tell her that when the horn blasted the silence.

We both ducked instinctively and looked around, searching for the source of the noise. But there was no one outside the funeral home, no one in a car or hearse or anything.

The horn stopped for a few seconds.

Then it blasted again.

We looked at each other. We knew who it was.

Tyler.

"Quickly," Raven took my hand and led me through the forest.

How she knew where she was going was a mystery to me. But she set off in one direction and didn't deviate. After only a minute or two the forest began to thin and I could see the Suburban just ahead of us, Tyler leaning in through the window, his hand pressed firmly on the horn.

"Over here!" Raven called.

He turned and watched us walk out of the bushes. The look of worry on his face quickly changed to that of relief.

"Do I even want to know?" he asked.

"Huh?" Raven said.

"Look," he continued. "I know it's accepted social behaviour at parties and in restaurants and everything, that when a girl needs to go, she needs to go in pairs, but the least you two could've done was wait until I got back, or written me a note!"

Raven laughed. I almost did too.

"Amber has a weak bladder," she replied as we reached the Suburban. "Don't you, honey?"

I turned to look at her. I was slightly embarrassed, but I didn't care. It saved us explaining the real story of where we'd been. And, more importantly, Raven was actively keeping something from Tyler. A secret just between her and me.

The two of us.

I nodded and smiled. "Sorry," I said.

"Yeah, well," Tyler replied as he opened the driver's door and climbed in. "I was worried about you girls."

"Really?" Raven asked as she let go of my hand and walked around to the other side of the car.

"Of course," he replied. "Plus, for a few moments I thought you'd dumped me out here and left me with the body."

"Don't think that thought hadn't crossed our minds," Raven replied as she climbed into the passenger side.

The *front* passenger side.

Damn it, she'd taken my seat!

I marched around the car, but by the time I got there, the door was shut and she had made herself comfortable.

And I wasn't about to make another scene, not over something like this. I just sighed and opened the back door, climbing in and sliding across to the middle of the seat.

"Ah, so you girls were out there plotting against me?"

"Of course," Raven replied. "Us girls have got to stick together, right?"

Raven turned around to me and smiled.

I didn't smile back. I just nodded.

I didn't like her being in the front seat with him.

Not one bit.

Sitting in the backseat, I had no control over what happened in the front. I was divided from them, closer to Duke and closer to his stench. Although the stench was mixing now with other smells from the food in the front seat.

"You hungry, Amber?" Tyler asked as he handed Raven a small bowl of nachos.

I shook my head. The nachos looked old and burnt, and the cheese on top looked rubbery and stale.

"Sorry," he said as he turned to me. "They didn't have much of a selection. Just nachos really. I got a couple of Twinkies too."

I hated Twinkies.

Raven was shovelling in the nachos like she was starving. I was hungry too, but I wasn't eating that rubbish.

"This is good," Raven said to me, with a mouthful of nachos. "You should have some."

"No," I replied. "It's okay. You have them."

Tyler took a handful of nachos as well.

I sat back in the seat with my arms crossed, watching them eat and knowing we should get moving.

I didn't like sitting there all day.

But I said nothing. I just waited for them to finish. Which they did, eventually. After the nachos, Tyler finally started the engine. He turned to face me. "You ready?" he asked.

That was a stupid question.

"How far is the memorial?" Raven asked him.

"From here, not far at all. Probably a five minute drive."

"I don't think we should drive right up to it with the trailer," she added.

"Don't worry," he replied. "I'm way ahead of you. There's a side road just after the memorial. We'll park there and then walk back to it. It's the safest option."

"Good. We were thinking the same thoughts," Raven replied. "Great minds think alike!"

She smiled and reached over towards him.

I didn't know what she was doing, but I could see her arm reaching out, her hand blocked from my view by the seat. I scooted forward and leaned in between them.

"Let's just get moving and out of here," I said.

It was a quick movement, but I saw her remove her hand from his thigh.

Caught you, Raven.

"Are you after a napkin?" Tyler asked, nervously trying to cover up what just happened.

"Yes, thank you," Raven took one from him.

It didn't work. I'm not that stupid.

She turned to sit straight in her seat as he started to swing the Suburban around.

We drove back onto the main road and onwards towards the memorial.

I'm sure Tyler was watching me. Every-so-often his eyes would glance up into the rear-view mirror. I knew he wasn't looking out the back to check the traffic, because with the trailer there, he couldn't see anything anyway. I'm doubly sure he was checking on me, watching me, making sure I wouldn't do anything that caught him off guard.

That made me feel pretty good, actually. When I think about it now, maybe I should've been weirded out or something. But I wasn't. I had him worried, I had him checking over his shoulder every minute or two.

Perfect.

He wasn't sure about me.

Maybe he was a little scared of me.

And I was more than happy with that.

I even smiled back at him, so he knew I knew.

Thirty-four

Even for a Monday, the memorial was crowded.

I guess there weren't *that* many people there, but there was certainly more than we had expected.

"Jesus, look at them all," Raven whispered as we walked down the path.

All up, there were probably fifteen or sixteen people milling around, looking at the memorial, reading the inscription, and marvelling at the view. That's probably not a huge tourist crowd, but when you want to check out a place to bury a body, even four people is four too many.

We'd parked the Suburban down the side road Tyler had mentioned. The road was old and looked as if no one used it anymore, and we parked along a deep shoulder, literally hiding the trailer from anyone driving past on the main road. From there, we'd walked back along the road to the memorial. It only took us about fifteen minutes to walk, and in that time none of us spoke. We just walked, probably all thinking about what we had to do next.

But the crowd made it hard. Too hard.

"What are we going to do?" I asked.

No one replied.

We walked closer.

Some people turned to stare at us. We probably looked like a weird bunch. Raven in her *I Fuck on the First Date* t-shirt, Tyler in his hunting gear and me, Little Miss Plain. At least *I* was trying to blend in. The others would stand out in everyone's memories for sure. It was only then that I realised Raven probably should've changed her t-shirt. Maybe worn something of mine. My Sublime t-shirt or something a little less...ah...confronting.

But it was too late now. We were standing by the memorial with everyone else, checking it out for a whole lot of reasons they could never imagine.

As far as memorials go, this one was pretty boring. It sat in the middle of a parking lot. I guess that's not actually true. I'm sure the parking lot formed around the memorial to allow people to park and look at it. But from where I stood, the memorial was in the middle of a gravel wasteland, surrounded only by dead trees and mostly-empty parking spaces. Hardly warm and friendly. Hardly a fitting memorial for anyone.

The memorial itself was five feet high and eight feet long, weathered and old. It was made of brick and concrete, although it was finished off in slate. It really did just look like a huge long box. On each corner was planted a small bush, although all four of the bushes had died and only their brittle dry branches remained. On one of the long sides of the memorial was a brass plaque that listed the names of each of the sixty-three workers who lost their lives when the first dam wall collapsed. There they were, names etched in stone (well, brass, I guess), their lives marked only by little one inch letters that people read, but soon forgot.

On the other side was another plaque, this one detailing the events of the tragedy. The date, the time, how it happened, why it collapsed, the inquiry that followed.

I read it all while I was pretending to be an interested tourist.

And, of course, I can hardly remember any of the details now.

As I said, it wasn't a very effective memorial.

Still, none of that really mattered to the three of us. We stood there, walked around, checked out the area, tried hard to fit in and look normal.

It was so out in the open. Not even thinking about the parking lot that surrounded it, the memorial sat in a clearing, open on all sides. There were hardly any trees around it, no private nooks, only the tree-line that surrounded the parking lot. Anyone from further up the mountain could probably see us if they looked, and there'd be nowhere to hide if someone suddenly drove along the road towards us.

The idea was crazy. Why did we need to bury Duke around here?

Trust me on this, the memorial would never feature in the *Top 100 Places To Bury A Body* list, that's for sure.

But still, we stood and we looked. We didn't say anything to each other. Occasionally we would make eye contact, but that was it. After what seemed like an eternity, the crowd thinned and we found ourselves alone at the memorial. Alone, that is, except for one family of four who decided to sit in their car while the guy (the dad?) talked away on his cell phone.

Was he calling the police? Was he ringing to tell them of our whereabouts? Was time running out for us while we stood around the memorial? Just standing here, waiting to be captured?

I tried not to think about those things – he was probably just ringing a friend, a relative or a business associate – but it was hard not to think the worst.

It's amazing how paranoid you can become when you're trying to get rid of a body.

"What do you think?" Tyler asked, leaning up against one of the short sides of the memorial.

"We can't do it," I said as I walked up to them. "There's no way."

"Don't be so negative," Raven replied. "There *has* to be a way."

"There probably *is*," I countered. "But this isn't it. It's too exposed, too out in the open. Even at night, there's no telling who might see."

"She's right," Tyler nodded.

Raven's look of worry turned to anger. "I am *not* carrying that asshole around with us any longer. I've had it with him and all the stress and trouble he's caused. You *both* agreed this was our best option. You both *agreed*! We *have* to do this and do it here. It's our best hope."

"But it's so out in the open," I said again. "There must be thousands of better places to bury Duke on this mountain. This just isn't the right one, Raven. We'll be seen for sure."

"We already agreed we'd do it at night," she replied. "Tonight, when it's dark. And we'll do it here. I'm not waiting any longer. I can't. It's here. We're doing it here."

"With what?" I tried a different tack.

Tyler and I exchanged a glance. He nodded at me to continue. I think he was agreeing with me.

"We don't have any tools!" I added.

She turned to Tyler. "This maintenance shed you talked about," she asked him. "How far is it?"

He shrugged. "Not far from here. A few minutes drive. Or a half-hour walk."

"Would it have what we need?"

"Not sure." Tyler took a step back, turned and surveyed the parking lot and forest that surrounded the memorial. "I know it has shovels and picks and stuff. Burying him isn't the problem, it's picking the right *place* to do it."

I nodded in agreement.

Raven stared at the memorial and seemed lost in thought.

"This is our best chance," she muttered, probably to herself. "We *have* to do this."

"Look, I can go check out the shed. I'll bring back whatever we need."

"Okay, that sounds good," she said as her eyes focussed and she turned to face him.

"But we need to seriously consider if this is the right place to do this, okay?" Tyler said all that very slowly, making sure Raven understood clearly, placing a hand on her shoulder as he did so.

Don't touch her.

She nodded.

"One problem," Tyler added. "This shed is right next to the park manager's office. There's always someone there during the day. I can't risk being seen. So I won't be able to go until tonight."

There was silence between us.

"Is that a problem?" Tyler asked.

"No," Raven said, shaking her head, a smile breaking out on her face. "In fact, that's perfect."

"Oh," Tyler seemed surprised by that. "Really?"

"Yes. You head off to the shed whenever you think it's the best time to go. Amber and I will stay with the body in the trailer and we'll wait for you to return."

Raven was positively beaming. Her smile stretched across her face and there was a sparkle in her eyes that I hadn't seen for a while.

The guy in the car was no longer talking on the mobile phone. He was turned around in his seat. I couldn't work out, though, if he was looking directly at us, or if he was just staring and talking to his kids.

Either way, he was making me nervous.

"I don't think we should hang around here much longer," I said to them both. "The longer we do, the more out of place we look and people might get suspicious."

They both agreed.

So we slowly turned and walked back the way we had come, heading into the forest and away from the memorial, hopefully looking normal and not at all suspicious.

Hopefully.

Thirty-five

Tyler left us just after sunset.

"You can find your way without a flashlight?" Raven had called to him.

He pointed to the sky. "It's a clear night. The moon will be all I need. Anyway, a flashlight could give me away. Don't worry, I know what I'm doing."

I felt uneasy about letting him go out there alone. How did we know he'd do exactly what he said he was going to do?

I probably should've discussed it with Raven, but I knew she wouldn't listen anyway. She'd been totally single-minded and headstrong that afternoon. She knew exactly what she wanted and if I told her about my worries concerning Tyler, or the memorial, I knew she'd just say I was being paranoid and suspicious and that nothing I could say would ruin her chance to get rid of Duke.

With Tyler gone, I could relax in the trailer and reclaim it for Raven and me. I felt at home again now that he wasn't there. But, on the other hand, I worried about what he was doing.

Was he really going to the maintenance shack? Did it really exist? What if he didn't come back? What if he did?

Or, worse still, what if someone happens to spot us on this road and comes to investigate?

I suggested we should move the trailer to a better location, but Raven wasn't interested one little bit.

"We're out in the open here," I said.

"We're hidden enough from the main road," Raven replied. "We don't have the time to move or anywhere else to go. This is close enough. This is close enough to everything we need. We don't need to go anywhere else. We can walk to everything from here. It's perfect."

She was excited and energetic, switched on and sharp. She was preparing for tonight.

When she's like this, there's no stopping her. You can't convince her of anything she doesn't agree with. I knew that, and it seemed so did Tyler. He didn't even try.

So Raven got her way, and I sat down to start reading my book.

A few minutes later, Raven sat down on the couch next to me.

"How are you, Amber?" she asked, a fire in her eyes.

"Good, Raven," I lied, putting the book to one side. I hadn't been able to concentrate on it anyway. "A little worried though."

"What about?"

"Tonight. The memorial. It's so out in the open. I'm worried about that."

She leaned closer. "Don't be."

"But I *am!*"

She reached out with her hand and stroked my cheek. "Don't be. Everything will be okay. If the memorial is no good, we'll find somewhere else to get rid of Duke, okay?"

"Okay," I said.

"I promise. You feel better?"

"Yes," I replied.

We smiled together.

"I'm just happy we're here alone, in the trailer together," she continued.

"I am too," I replied.

"Our time together is special, important, hon. And I know we haven't had much of it the last day or two."

I nodded.

"And I want to make that up to you. I want to show you how sorry I am."

I blushed a little. "You don't have to do that."

Raven took my hand and stood, pulling me up as she did so.

"I do, Amber, I owe you for so much, for standing by me for so long, through everything. The good and the bad. Only you've been there for me and I have to show you how much that means to me."

I couldn't stop smiling. I wanted her to stop but it felt good. I wanted her to continue telling me how she felt. How I made her feel.

We stood hand in hand by the doorway, our eyes locked on each other. I'm sure I could see Raven's very soul, and she could see mine as we stared deeply. I'd waited so long for a moment like this together.

"And I *will* make it all up to you, hon," she continued. "As soon as all this is over. I promise you."

"Oh," I replied, a little let down that I would have to wait.

"But I'm going to ask you to do something for me now, *with* me now, that you may not want to do. But I need you to help me, I need you to be there with me."

"I will be, Raven, you know that. I will always be there for you."

"No matter what?"

"No matter what."

"Only you can help me, sweets. I can only entrust you with this. We have to be quick, we have to do this together, and we have to do this before Tyler gets back."

"Do what?"

"Will you help me?"

"With *what*, Raven?"

"I need to know if you'll do this for me. I need you to say yes."

"Say yes to what?"

"Say yes to *helping* me!"

"Of course, Raven. You know that, anything."

"Anything?"

"Yes, *anything*. Just tell me, yes, anything!"

She let go of my hands and walked to the sink. She hesitated only for a second before reaching up to the top cupboard.

Oh no. Not *that*!

She opened the cupboard door and reached in, grabbing it with both arms.

Don't make me, Raven. *No*!

I stepped backwards, the door pressing hard against my spine. But I didn't say anything as she turned around and walked towards me, holding it out in front of her, holding it out for me to take.

Only this time, it was in a jar.

I stared at it as it came closer.

The jar containing Duke's cock and balls.

Thirty-six

"We've got to be quick," Raven said, pulling on her black sweater with the stencil of a bunny in the woods on it.

I looked down at the jar in my hands. Duke's bloated cock and balls floating in the redish-green liquid. The jar was so cold. My hands were quivering. I didn't want to drop it.

You're probably wondering why she kept them like that. And so did I.

"What are we doing?" I asked.

The eye of Duke's cock swirled in the liquid and bobbed to the top, like it was taking in air and trying to look at me. It was puffy and out of shape. I don't know what kind of liquid Raven had kept them in, but it hadn't done much to retard the decay.

"We're going for a quick walk," Raven replied, opening the trailer door.

I was still looking down at the jar. I couldn't take my eyes of it.

"A walk where? What about Tyler?"

"Don't worry about him. We'll be back before he is. And if we're not," she shrugged her shoulders, "he'll just have to wait."

She grabbed the jar from my hands and wrapped it in one of our bath towels that were still in the storage area. I was relieved to see it gone, hidden.

But I knew it was there. I knew I'd see it again. And that didn't help the feeling subside.

Raven opened a drawer to the side of the sink and rummaged around, finding the flashlight. She checked that it was working (it was) and then threw it to me.

She carried the jar under her right arm and held out her left hand towards me.

"Are you ready?" she asked.

"Ready for what?" I asked as I took her hand in mine.

"You said you'd help me no matter what, right?"

I nodded.

Raven smiled.

"Then help me now," she replied.

We stepped out of the trailer, into the darkness of the woods, and walked through the forest on that cool, clear night, the flashlight rocking from side to side to guide our way. Raven was walking strong, in a determined fashion. She knew where she was going.

But I was wondering why.

And so I asked.

"Why what?" Raven replied, still staring straight ahead.

"Why did you do it? Cut off his cock and balls?"

"I had to."

"Had to?"

"It's a long story, Amber. Do you really want to know?"

I was silent then.

"I didn't think you did," she replied. "Just know that he deserved it. And I wanted to make sure we paid him back, and paid him well. And this way we'll always have a reminder, a souvenir, of what an asshole he really was and what he threatened to do to us. We can also remember how we beat him, overpowered him and took back our control, our lives and our destinies."

"Do we *want* a souvenir?" I whispered.

She shrugged. "It can't hurt. Certainly can't hurt Duke any more."

She laughed, but it came out strangely.

The night was clear and cold, and I could see our breath as we walked. It was becoming a little damp halfway up the mountain, and also slightly slippery underfoot. All the trees and bushes looked the same in this half-light, but Raven kept walking, never stopping once to gain her bearings.

She knew where she was headed.

Our feet crunched on the undergrowth and if you listened carefully, you could hear the *sloshing* of Duke's jar under her arm.

We didn't talk about how she did it or when she did it. But I have a pretty good idea anyway.

Raven carries a switchblade in her purse. You know, to ward off attackers if she gets in trouble late at night. When we'd first "wrapped and sacked" Duke and were taking him from the trailer, Raven asked me to go outside and check if the coast was clear. While I did so, I think she grabbed her switchblade from the purse and slipped it inside the sack while I wasn't watching, probably securing it under the rope or inside the sheet or something.

When we finally carried him out to the edge of the lagoon, she sent me looking for rocks to weigh down the body. As I was there searching for some, she took out the knife and palmed it in her hand, hiding it from me.

I mean, let's face it, I wasn't looking for concealed weapons at the time. I was more intent on getting old Maggoty-britches out of my trailer and into the lagoon so we could be rid of him.

Ha! Rid of him! We were *still* trying to be rid of him!

Remember when Raven went missing after storing Duke's body in the blowhole? I was having a great time in the lagoon, swimming and floating and enjoying myself and when I turned around Raven was gone.

Gone for *so long.*

Well, when she was in the blowhole with Duke, she opened the sack and cut through the sheet and she dug in and cut off his cock and balls from there, in one clean, jagged chomp. She then reknotted the sack and swam back to shore.

Which is why she swam with her back to me all the way and why there was a jagged tear in the sheet that wrapped around Duke.

And why, when I got to the trailer myself, she wanted me out of there *pronto*, so I wouldn't see what she had done.

But I *did*.

At least she finally found out if he was circumcised or not! (He was, by the way.)

And while I was out cold, she'd had the time to slip him into a jar and store him above the sink.

And we hadn't spoken about it again until now. It was as if it was our most darkest secret. So dark even we couldn't talk about it to each other.

I *still* didn't want to. I didn't want to have *anything* to do with it.

But there I was, walking alongside Raven, through the woods, trying to search and locate something.

And that something was dead ahead.

The trees thinned, the flashlight beam stretched further. And there was the house in the middle of the parking lot.

Not just any house.

The funeral home.

Ferguson's Funerals.

I stopped in my tracks, but Raven kept on walking.

I was trying to put it all together, work out why we were here, but it all wouldn't connect.

Raven stopped walking as she reached the parking lot and turned to face me. I could hear Duke still sloshing around in the jar.

"Come on, Amber," she said. "We haven't got much time! We have to be back for Tyler."

She walked over to me and looked deep into my eyes.

"You can do this," she said. But I didn't reply. "We can *both* do this."

I didn't really know if I could.

"Are we going to bury it?" I asked in a small voice.

Raven threw back her head and laughed. It was loud and echoed through the night, like a call of a banshee.

"Just wait and see," she replied, taking my hand and pulling me out of the woods and into the parking lot.

As we walked across the concrete and asphalt, my eyes scanned the house. All the curtains were still drawn and there was no sign of any light or life. It looked larger and taller in the dark, more imposing. It had lost its cute Little House on the Prairie aspect and had turned very dark and all Amityville on me.

The area to the side of the house where the hearse had been parked was empty now. So the guy must've driven it home or something.

As we walked, I thought we were heading straight for the front door. I had no idea what Raven had in mind, but it looked like we were going to just walk right up there and knock or press the doorbell or something. Then I thought maybe we were going to smash one of the windows, but that would be too loud.

As we got closer to the veranda, Raven pulled me to the left, over towards the side of the house. And, within seconds, we were walking down the side where Raven had taken me earlier that day. The side that contained no windows.

At least no one would be able to look out and see us.

We stopped walking when we reached the two metal doors set into the wall. Raven walked up the short ramp and leaned forward, looking down at the shiny silver door handle. There was a brass padlock hooked around it. She reached out and tried the handle, but it wouldn't budge, the padlock made sure of that. It rattled loudly in the night.

"Shit," Raven muttered.

In some ways, I was relieved. We couldn't get in so that meant we'd just turn around and head back to the trailer.

Right?

Wrong!

A simple padlock wasn't about to stop her.

"Quick," she said. "Shine the flashlight along the wall."

Which is exactly what I did. But there were no other entrances or windows on this side of the house.

The longer we stayed there, the colder I got, and the more nervous. My eyes darted around us, into the forest and back along the house, but I couldn't see anyone or any movement. The only sounds came from our breathing... and Duke's sloshing cock.

"There's got to be a way in," Raven said as she stepped off the ramp. "Come on, let's try around here."

We walked around to the back of the house and discovered that a large weatherboard garage connected directly onto the back.

While the house had been kept in perfect condition, the garage was dilapidated and poorly looked after (probably because you couldn't see it from the front.) The walls looked thin and rotten, and the two windows set into the wall were grimy and smeared.

"What do you think?" Raven asked as I ran the flashlight across the garage.

But I wasn't thinking anything.

We both noticed the door at the same time. Halfway along the garage wall, the little wooden door looked old and beaten and easily overcome.

"*Yes!*" Raven said as she marched towards it.

I followed her, still looking from side to side, still trying to shake off the feeling someone was watching us.

At the back of the house, we were closer to the forest than at any other point, as the parking lot didn't extend this far. I was worried someone was out there, close by, watching everything we did.

But who?

Tyler maybe?

You'd have to be pretty weird to be hanging around the back of a funeral home in the middle of the night.

Just like Raven and me.

The old wooden door was tattered and weather-beaten, nothing really much to speak of. It had a small pane of glass at the top and a rusty old doorknob in the middle.

Raven reached out and turned the knob, but it stopped halfway. It was locked.

That didn't stop her. She looked at me and smiled, holding out the towel with the jar inside.

I didn't say anything. There was nothing to say. I just took the jar from her and watched as she took a step backwards, lowered her shoulder and charged.

She hit the door hard, and it rattled some, but it held steady and didn't open. Raven took the flashlight from me and swept the beam around all four sides of the door, looking for a weakness or anything to aim at.

She charged again.

The door held firm.

It was so quiet out there, but every time Raven hit the door, it would rattle loudly and the wood would moan. She would let out a grunt too, as her shoulder made impact, and I was sure this was all loud enough to alert anyone from inside the house.

But no one came.

And on Raven's fifth attempt, the door gave way, swinging wildly inwards, taking Raven with it. There was a huge *clatter* and hollow *bang* as the door hit something metallic inside the garage. I heard a short yelp from Raven as well.

But then everything was quiet again.

She disappeared so quickly into the darkness that I worried she'd fallen and hurt herself, or been grabbed by unseen hands and dragged inside.

I ran through the doorway.

There was no sign of her, no sign of anyone. But I couldn't see much, there was no real illumination inside the garage.

No flashlight beam.

And Raven had been carrying it.

"Raven?" I whispered, knowing it would give me away, but also knowing I had to try to find her.

It was cold and musty in this place, and I could feel dust in the air. I walked forward another step and my foot hit something hard and low. I also think I walked through a cobweb or two, but I really didn't have the time to think about that right then.

"Raven?" I whispered again, louder this time.

The light blinded me, and I raised my arm to shield my eyes.

I panicked only for a second until I realised the beam of light was coming from the floor of the garage, and I could see the shape of Raven behind it.

"We're in," she said.

"Are you okay?" I asked.

"A little the worse for wear, but we made it."

I walked around the spare tire I had kicked when I entered and reached down for Raven. She took my hand and I lifted her up.

"Thanks," she said, brushing the dust and the dirt from her jeans and top. She also swept her hair from her face. "I took a bit of a tumble over that tire."

"I know, I almost did too," I replied.

"Still, it was worth it."

She turned and shone the flashlight around the garage. The place was larger than I first thought, spanning the whole back of the house. Two hearses were parked in there. One had its hood up and the other was covered in one of those car protector sheets. In the far wall were two large doors, shut and probably locked too. I watched as the beam from the flashlight swept across tools hanging on the wall; spanners, screwdrivers and pliers. Service booklets leaned on shelves, grease covered overalls hung from hooks. Then the beam swept across to the door leading to the house.

Everything was quiet. There was no sound from the house. No one was coming to check on us. At least, no one we could hear.

"What do you think?" Raven asked.

But I didn't know how to answer.

"All clear?" she prodded.

"I guess so," I replied.

"Good."

Being careful to point the flashlight at the floor, so we wouldn't fall over anything else, Raven slowly made her way across the garage, and I followed her. We walked between the two hearses and I tried very hard to ignore them.

I didn't want to think about where they'd been or where they'd go. Or even *who* had been carried in them...or how many.

I blotted them from my sight, and thankfully that was made pretty easy by the darkness which surrounded everything except where the flashlight pointed.

We were heading straight for the door.

There were three steps up to the door and a little handrail to help steady yourself. Hanging from the handrail was a little plastic skeleton, an elastic cord tied around its neck in the form of a noose.

We reached the steps and Raven shone the beam at the door. It looked sturdier than the wooden door to the garage, and a part of me hoped and wished that it was locked and Raven wouldn't be able to find another way in.

We didn't say anything. We both knew what was to come next.

Raven took the first step, and then the second.

The door had a silver handle. It looked well used and some of the silver had been worn away.

Then Raven was on the last step, reaching out for the handle, grabbing it and pushing it down in one swift movement.

And the door opened soundlessly.

It swung away from us and we could see inside the house.

We were in.

"That was easier than I thought," Raven whispered.

In the next room we could see an assortment of coffins and caskets, all different colours and sizes, some made of real wood, some fake, some made of other stuff like fake marble and fake stone. They were stacked high, all the way to the ceiling, lids on one side, caskets on the other. Between them stretched a small walkway and another door directly opposite us.

Raven swept the flashlight all around the room before either of us made a move. I certainly wasn't going in there without checking it out first, and, it seems, neither was Raven.

Slowly, she stepped inside.

Duke and I followed her.

"Would you like a coffin?" she asked me over her shoulder.

I shook my head (even though she couldn't see it) and didn't say a thing.

I was in the room with her now, both of us standing in the middle, surrounded by the empty carriages of the dead.

It was eerie and claustrophobic. I worried about knocking one of the piles by accident and sending coffins tumbling down on top of us. I didn't want to be there. But I certainly wasn't about to tell Raven that. I said I'd be there for her and I would be, no matter what.

The next door was in arms reach, and I couldn't help but feel that each door we opened brought us closer to coming face to face with someone holding a gun or someone who was going to end all of this for us, and there was nothing we could do about it.

We couldn't go back.

Raven wouldn't have it any other way, I'm guessing. There was no stopping her now.

She stepped forward, grabbed the knob and turned it. The door opened with a squeak this time, sounding loud in the silence. We walked into a large room and the flashlight beam quickly surveyed the area.

There was a small table to the left, and on it was an assortment of cloths and fabrics, plus a pile of different kinds of crucifixes and handles. There was an empty casket nearby, with only one handle and a small crucifix that was sitting askew, held in place by one single brass screw.

To the right were four caskets and two coffins. Raven told me the difference between the two when we were growing up.

"Coffins have six sides, caskets only four," she'd said, her voice sounding like she was reciting a nursery rhyme.

They were lined up on trolleys with their lids closed, handles and crucifixes properly attached. They looked prepared and ready to roll.

Was there anyone in them?

I really didn't want to know, but the thought did cross my mind.

"A-huh," Raven said, almost to herself as she walked quicker now, right across the room and to a large metallic door in the opposite wall.

There was a sign on the door in big black letters:
Mortuary Staff Only
Beyond This Point.

I stopped on the spot. Literally dead in my tracks and didn't move.

That was the door Raven was heading towards. *That* was where we were going.

I shook my head, but, of course, Raven didn't see it.

She reached out to the door, her hands feeling the cold metal under her palms. She said something, and I guess she said it to me, but I wasn't there. I wasn't next to her to hear it.

Her head swung around and she looked back for me, the flashlight beam coming to rest on my chest.

"You okay?' she asked.

"No," I replied.

She walked to me.

"We can do this," she replied. "I *need* you to help me do this."

I couldn't see her eyes in the darkness, I could only make out her shape. Her face was a deep expansive blackness as the flashlight was pointing away from us.

"You ready?"

She didn't give me much of an option.

She turned and grabbed my hand, leading me to the metal door. Sure, I could've run or told her no I wouldn't do it. But what would that achieve? *Tyler* wasn't there, it was just Raven and *me*. She'd chosen *me* for this because she trusted *me* more than she did Tyler. He'd managed to take her away from me in so many different ways, I wasn't about to let this chance – maybe my *only* chance – slip by. I *would* prove to her I would be there for her in ways Tyler never could. Maybe then she would know who her real soul mate was.

That's why I was there. That's why I was scared shitless but still by her side. I knew Raven wouldn't let anything happen to me. She needed me as much as I needed her.

Raven reached out for the large handle. It was silver and shiny and looked like the kind of handle you'd find on one of those large freezers. She pulled on it and it popped loudly and I could hear the escape of air and the hiss of the seals as they came away from the doorway.

It sounded so loud in such a quiet place.

The cold air washed over us both and I instantly felt much colder, gooseflesh breaking out all over my skin.

"This is it," Raven said as she stepped inside.

I followed.

I stepped into the mortuary.

The beam from the flashlight seemed to be coming from all angles, but I realised it was just shining off the large metal doors and walls, reflecting back at us and making the place glow even more.

There were two large metallic doors to my right, stretching from ceiling to floor, and they had the same kind of freezer handles as the door to the mortuary, so I worked out pretty quickly what they contained.

The flashlight danced around the room, making shadows move and creating things that weren't there.

I heard the suction of the door as it closed behind me and I turned around to find Raven leaning against it, her eyes wide as she took it all in.

And then she turned to her right and reached out for the light switch.

I wanted to stop her, to say no, but I didn't have time.

I heard the click of the switch and the bright fluorescent tubes flickered into life. The blinding light made me squint for a second or two, but eventually my eyes got accustomed to the brightness.

It was so cold in there, I was beginning to shiver. I rubbed my arm with my free hand, but that just made Duke's cock and balls slosh around more.

I stopped moving, and so did he.

Once my eyes were working again, I looked around the rest of the room. Across from the big freezer doors were two trolleys (thankfully empty), with a sink on either side. Along the walls were benches and shelves, filled with medical books, reference works, rubber gloves, masks and tissues and more. You get the idea. Power extension cords and lights hung low from the ceiling over the two trolleys, and they swung slowly in the recirculated air. On the wall directly opposite the freezers were a series of cupboards, but their doors were shut.

And that's where Raven was now. She'd put the flashlight down on one of the trolleys and headed straight towards the cupboards. Without waiting, she'd thrown open the first one and was standing back, looking at all the bottles that were stored there.

The cupboard was full of bottles, all of differing colours and sizes, different hues of pink, green and purple.

Raven reached out for one and grabbed it, turned it around in her hand and read whatever was written on the back.

I stayed in one spot, by the door, trying not to freeze to death.

Should've worn a jacket like Raven did.

"You wouldn't happen to know what *Introfiant* is, do you?" Raven asked as she looked over her shoulder at me.

I shook my head.

She smiled at me. "Me neither," she said, replacing the bottle on the shelf.

She closed the cupboard and walked across to the next one and opened it.

The air in the room was so thin and so clean. I couldn't smell any rotting bodies or anything like that. Nothing smelled like Duke did in the back of the Suburban. *Everything* was so clean. Too clean; weirdly too clean.

I took a step forward, inching my way across to one of the empty trolleys. It was shiny and smooth and had little gutters down both sides. I tried hard not to imagine what it must be like to have a body on there, to have the fluids and blood and stuff leak out and down the drains. But it was hard not to.

I reached out with the jar, my hands still shaking either from fear or coldness. Slowly, I set it down on the trolley, trying not to make any noise at all. I pulled away, glad to be rid of it, and took a step back towards the wall.

"A-huh!" Raven said. "Got it."

She turned around to face me, her hand holding a small white bottle with red printing. The words *ACTION Embalming Powder* were written across it.

"This is what we need," she replied, turning back to the cupboard and pulling out a boxful of the bottles. "We need to take this with us."

There were probably eight bottles of the stuff in the box.

"What for?" I asked.

"For Duke."

"Why?"

She smiled at me as she lifted the box onto the trolley, setting it down with a loud clatter.

"Well, not for *all* of Duke. Maybe just for a special part of him." Her eyes slipped to the jar wrapped in the towel.

"You're not serious," I replied.

"Think of it as a souvenir, hon," she replied. "A keepsake to remind us of this adventure."

She'd already tried that line on me. I didn't want *any* reminders, I wasn't about to forget any of it!

Either way, I didn't care. I just wanted to be out of there. Let her get what she wanted and then we could leave!

"Okay, whatever," I said. "Can we go now?"

"No."

"No? What about Tyler?"

"I'm not finished yet, sweets," she said as she walked around the trolley and towards me.

Her eyes were on the jar and she didn't move them from it. Slowly, she bent forward and lifted it up, unwrapping the towel from around it and letting the towel fall to the floor.

Duke's cock and balls floated in the thick mass of liquid. They swirled around one way and then the next, like some kind of freak show attraction you'd see in those early newsreels.

I watched and didn't say anything.

What *could* I say?

Raven screwed the lid off the jar and slipped her hand inside. She splashed around in there for a second or two, as her hand clasped around the top of Duke's cock, and pulled. But it slipped away from her.

The juice and liquid and blood and stuff must've been slimy in there.

She tried again. This time she grabbed the base of his cock, where the balls were attached, and got a better grip.

Slowly, she pulled it out from the jar.

Liquid spilled onto the floor and also on the trolley and trickled down into the gutters. A smell engulfed us; rotting eggs and sour milk rolled into one. She laid the cock out on the trolley like it was some kind of dead fish and she made sure it was all smoothed out and properly positioned. It sat there, slowly leaking liquid from the jagged tear in the skin and also from the eye in the head.

I didn't want to look, but I did anyway. I may even have taken a step or two forward.

"What are you going to do?" I asked her.

"I'm trying to save it," she replied as she turned from the trolley and squatted by the sink. She said it in such a matter-of-fact way, as if it was a perfectly natural thing to try and do.

There were drawers under each of the sinks and she was going through them now, her hands moving feverishly as she searched though all the stuff stored in them.

There was nothing in the first two drawers that was of value to her. But she found what she needed in the third drawer.

"Gotcha!" she said as she stood up again and returned to Duke's cock.

She was holding some kind of surgical string. Actually, it looked a lot like fishing line, but probably wasn't. Either way, it was thin and strong and hard to handle. But, still, Raven managed.

She leaned forward, bending over the trolley and bringing her face just inches away from Duke's cock. She looked it over, took it in her hands and fondled it in a weird way, almost scientifically, as if she was trying to work out exactly what it was, or how it functioned.

Well, we both knew how it functioned.

The cock was limp and wet and slippery. It rolled in her hands like a slippery dead eel.

And then she flopped it over like a piece of raw steak on a barbeque. It came to rest with a *splat,* the jagged tear now face up for us both to see. His flesh was no longer the bright red I thought it should be. It had faded, replaced with a dull browny-grey. The colour of meat that has just gone on the turn.

I started to feel light-headed and a little queasy.

I was surprised I was still standing anyway.

Raven pulled all the skin together at the base of his cock, trying to seal up the hole that was there. Then she took the surgical cord and wrapped it around and around the base, drawing the skin in tighter and tighter.

She seemed so sure, so in control. Knowing exactly what she needed to do and how to do it. Never once did she pause or look confused or uncertain.

When she was done, she looked over towards me.

"I need you," she said.

"What for?"

"I need you to tie it off."

"*What?*"

"Knot it, Amber. Cut the cord and tie it off at the base."

I moved forward slowly, then stopped. I just stared at the cock.

"Over on the sink, Amber. The scissors are on the sink. Grab them and cut the cord, then tie it off. Hurry!"

And even though I was feeling light-headed and unwell, I did exactly what was asked of me. I reached over to the sink and grabbed the silver scissors. They were small and looked delicate, but I could see they were sharp.

Raven held out the cord and I cut through it easily, my eyes still on the cock, its base tied and held together like the end of a sausage. Holding out the two ends of the cord to me, Raven kept hold of the cock while I tied a knot.

"Double the knot," she said.

I did.

Then I let go of the cord and took a step backwards, bumping into the edge of the sink as I did so. It hurt, but that was the least of my worries.

Raven laid the wet, flaccid cock back onto the trolley and walked down to the cupboards again. She searched through them once more, while my eyes stayed locked on the knot I'd tied. Fluid rolled down the cord and dripped onto the trolley; a small droplet squeezed itself out from the tied stump, slipping to the trolley without a sound.

His balls just lay there, like two old squashed potatoes.

"Here! Catch!" Raven called as she threw a small packet towards me.

It fluttered across the room and I caught it, fumbled, worried about what it was and why she wanted me to have it.

I looked down. It was a syringe inside a sealed plastic satchel. By the time I looked back up, Raven was walking towards me, holding out a long needle.

"Put it together for me, hon," she said, giving me the needle.

In her other hand, she had a bottle of something. I couldn't read the label, but it was some kind of liquid.

She walked back to the trolley and stood there, her back blocking my view of Duke's cock. I didn't complain. I was quite happy not looking at it anymore.

Raven was unscrewing the top of the bottle and removing the silver seal from underneath the lid. Neither of us talked, we just did what we had to do.

And that included me.

It was almost like I was having one of those out of body experiences people talk about when they die (well, I was in the right place for something like that), watching myself open the packet, withdraw the syringe and screw on the needle, even though I knew I couldn't be doing this, and shouldn't be doing this.

But still, I did it. My hands worked fast and skilfully. The only thing that entered my mind was my worry that I might drop the needle on the floor and cause it to be no longer sterile.

Raven turned to me, and I was ready and waiting.

I held out the syringe and gave it to her.

"Thanks," she replied as she turned back around and bent over the trolley.

I couldn't help it. I *had* to watch. Even though I didn't want to.

I took a step forward.

Duke's cock and balls came into view over Raven's shoulder, as did the bottle of liquid.

She dipped the needle in the liquid and pulled up on the plunger of the syringe. The fluid swirled through the needle and into the chamber, bubbling and filling it quickly.

When it was full, she took it out of the bottle and held it up in front of her eyes.

She smiled as she pushed the plunger in slightly, removing the air from the chamber.

"You ready?" she asked me.

I nodded slowly.

We both looked down at Duke's cock.

Raven bent forward, grasping the tip of his cock with the thumb and index finger of her left hand.

I wondered if we should've been wearing those rubber gloves while we were doing this.

Too late by then.

She brought down the syringe with her right hand and slowly slipped the needle in at the base of the cock, right above where I'd tied it off.

She used her thumb to push down on the plunger, and the fluid quickly emptied from the chamber.

We both watched.

The plunger finished its descent.

And Duke's cock began to grow.

Thirty-seven

His cock grew at a steady pace. It became engorged, larger and longer than before.

Raven used her left hand to massage the cock, making sure it kept its proper shape and didn't go all lumpy at one end or the other. She rolled it on the trolley like it was pastry she was preparing to bake.

"That's better," she said to herself. "Hand me the towel."

I bent forward and picked up the bath towel that had fallen onto the floor. I placed it on the trolley, but at no stage did I take my eyes off his cock.

Raven dipped the syringe back into the bottle of liquid and refilled the chamber. She then inserted the needle into both of Duke's balls and injected them too. They reinflated slightly, and Raven remoulded them again, with both hands this time, making sure they stayed round and smooth like three-day-old meatballs.

Once she was finished, she took the towel and wiped down the cock and balls, removing all traces of liquid from the skin and seepage from the holes.

"Empty the jar in the sink," she said.

I looked numbly on.

"Amber," she said again. "Empty the *jar* in the *sink*."

I grabbed the jar full of Duke's old blood and goo and tipped it all down the sink. That heavy, rotting smell engulfed me once more. For a moment or two, I thought I was going to be sick, but I turned away and held my breath just in time. When my stomach settled, I washed out the jar and made sure there was no trace of what had once been in there.

I returned it to the trolley and Raven smiled at me as she continued massaging the now much larger cock.

"What was that stuff?" I asked her.

"Embalming fluid," she replied as she nodded towards the box of bottles at the end of the trolley. "Open a couple of those bottles and pour the stuff in the jar."

I walked down to the end of the trolley and grabbed two of the bottles of *ACTION Embalming Powder*, bringing them back to the jar and opening their lids.

Honestly, I think I was on auto-pilot by then. Maybe I'd turned into one of those zombies you see in the D-Grade movies on late night TV. I didn't say anything, I didn't even think. I just followed her orders.

I Was A Teenage Cock Embalming Zombie, could be the title of the film of my story. I wonder if anyone would ever buy the film rights to this tale? I doubt it. It'd be banned in 31 countries.

Make no mistake, Raven was in control of everything going on here, and I...well, I was probably in shock by then, I guess.

I opened the tops of the two bottles of embalming powder and removed the silver seals. The smell that hit me was weird, it was like a concentrated dose of moth flakes, but also smelled a bit like hospitals do. That so-clean-it-isn't-real smell. I tipped the two bottles into the jar. The powder was flaky; little white crystals shone brightly, reflecting the lights.

The two bottles didn't even fill a third of the jar, but it was enough for now and Raven was happy.

She finished working the cock and balls into shape and then she lifted them up by thumb and forefinger. She dangled Duke's privates over the jar, holding them by the tip of his cock, and then dropped them inside. They hit the white powder with a *thunk* and some of the crystals flew upwards in a small white cloud.

"Almost there," Raven said as she smiled at me.

She reached down for the box of *ACTION* bottles and unscrewed the remaining six lids, pouring the contents into the jar, over the cock and balls, covering them completely with the crystalline white powder.

Within a minute or so, you couldn't see that Duke was in there.

And with that, Raven screwed the lid back on top of the jar and wiped a hand across her forehead. She'd been sweating (in this place? It was so cold!) and I didn't know if that was from fear or determination. Either way, she took a moment to lean against the trolley and rest. She closed her eyes and her smile got bigger.

"That was something," she said.

I didn't say anything, so she opened her eyes to look at me.

"Wasn't it, Amber? That was really something."

"Yeah," I said. "*Something* alright."

"Thank you," she added.

"For what?"

"For being here with me."

"You know I'll always be here for you," I replied. "No matter what."

"You're a good friend, Amber," she said, taking my hands in hers. "The best."

Yes, I *was*. The best!

"This is all quite a rush, huh?" she asked as she turned around to look at the mortuary. I'm guessing it was probably the first real time she'd stopped to take it all in, to see what was surrounding us.

"It was an experience, that's for sure," I replied.

"Did you feel it? *Could* you feel it? The power we had, the *control* we had? The ability to do what *we* wanted, when we wanted?"

I was still feeling pretty numb and cold, really, but I could see it was important to her.

"Yes," I replied.

She swung around to face me again. She leaned forward, her eyes wide. I could see the idea forming as she spoke.

"Let's go further," she whispered, her breath touching my cheek.

"Further?"

She nodded.

I didn't know what she meant.

"Raven, we *gotta* get back for Tyler. He'll be wondering where we are."

"Fuck Tyler! He can wait. He doesn't control us. We control *him*."

"Okay," I replied. "Whatever you say. I'm just worried, that's all."

"Don't be."

"What if he panics and runs off?"

"He won't."

"What if he calls the cops?"

"He won't do that either," she replied as she rushed away from the trolley, still holding my hands, and walked me across the room. "While we're in the trailer together, we control everything that happens. And while we're here, we have that control too. We can do *anything*. It's all ours and we can do whatever we like."

She wasn't making a whole load of sense. I was only trying to keep her happy. To do what she wanted.

"You want that control, right?" she asked.

"Yes."

"You *need* that control, right? The control of your own life and your own decisions?"

"Yes."

"You don't need anyone else to tell you what to do, who to be, or how to act?"

"No."

"Then take your pick," she said as she let go of my hands and turned to face the two large metallic doors.

Before I could say anything, she grabbed the handle of one and pulled. The door made a huge popping sound as the seals parted and even colder air washed over us as she swung the door wide.

Behind the door was a deep, empty space, filled with shelf after shelf of mostly empty trays.

I say *mostly* empty, because at chest level there were two trays that weren't empty. My eyes rested on the sheets that covered them. I couldn't see the bodies, but the sheets silhouetted their figures. I could see the troughs and valleys that were the nose and chin and hips and feet.

As Raven had opened the door, a light inside the freezer had come on (just like the one you have at home!) and I could see all the way to the back wall. The walls were painted a stark white, and the back wall had chips and dints in it, where the trays had scraped and bumped against it time and time again. There was space for about twenty bodies in that freezer alone, not to mention the one standing next to it that we hadn't opened.

I was just glad that it wasn't fully stocked. I was having enough trouble with the two bodies in front of me. I had no idea what I would do if there were a dozen or more stored in there.

But none of this seemed to phase Raven in any way.

"Look!" she said. "*Two* of them. That's one each!"

"Raven," I replied. "We can't."

"We *can*," she turned back to face me. "Take back the control, Amber. We can and we *will*!"

She spun around and grabbed the two sheets, one in each hand, and pulled like some toreador waving a cape towards a bull.

The sheets slipped from the bodies like waves and fell to the floor without making a sound, and I was staring at the top of two heads. One had short brown hair, cropped and set neatly and the other had longer blonde hair, set in a small ponytail to the side.

"Well well well," Raven said as she looked over the bodies. "We have a matching set!"

She grabbed the edge of the tray nearest to her and pulled. The tray slid out towards us with a slight rumble, bringing the body with it.

I looked down. I couldn't *not* look down.

The guy looked young. I mean, not too young, probably not our age, but more like twenty-seven or twenty-eight. His eyes and mouth were shut and he looked pretty peaceful to me, although his head did seem a little misshapen and discoloured. As I looked further down his naked body, I could see a whole lot of incisions and large cuts along his torso and across his stomach, all stitched up with big ugly stitches. His body was a pale bluey-white colour and I realised then that his face wasn't. His face was warm and almost glowing.

He'd been made up, ready for viewing, but they hadn't bothered with the parts that no one would see. He looked so restful and so relaxed, but the rest of his body betrayed the fact that he'd died violently.

LAKE MOUNTAIN

He looked quite attractive. I felt sorry for him then. He didn't deserve to die so young.

Raven was standing down by his hips. She'd pulled the tray out as far as it would go, so his whole body stretched out into the mortuary now.

"Beautiful men without souls are a dime a dozen," she whispered. "But beautiful men without both soul and breath are a treasure."

She was looking down at his cock. It was flaccid and laying to one side, and even I noticed it was quite large.

As Raven was looking at the guy's cock, I walked down the other side of the trolley to his feet. His toes were blue too, and the toenails looked a weird yellow colour. But I wasn't interested in that. I was heading for the toe-tag.

I read it out loud and it confirmed my thoughts.

"Xavier, Jeremy T. He's being viewed tomorrow," I said as I turned to look at Raven. "I saw it on the sign out the front. There's a viewing in the morning and his funeral is in the afternoon."

Raven nodded as she walked towards the other trolley.

"That's why he's made up already," I continued. "Ready for viewing."

"Hello Jeremy," Raven said. "There were two names, right?"

I nodded.

She pulled out the next tray. It extended with a rattle too. And the girl with blonde hair rolled out into the room.

Her hair was lovely and looked wonderful in the ponytail, it shined and looked so healthy. Her face rested to one side, probably to give room for the ponytail and not to mush it, and her closed eyes were turned towards the other body. I could also see some skull and skin flaps at the base of her head. They'd tried to hide them, but couldn't do it all. They'd make sure no one saw them anyway.

She was made-up too, looking relaxed and composed, but I could see the bruising on one side of her face, and her head seemed slightly squished, like she'd had some trauma to it. She had incisions and big ugly stitches down between her breasts and along her bluey-white stomach as well, and a light brown mat of pubic hair covered her more private parts.

I wondered if she had truly loved and was loved in her short life. If as a child she looked cute, and if I saw her alive now, whether she would be considered alluring or even sexy. If the first time she ever had sex was an event shared with a young man who treated her well. And whether she treated him well in return. But I guess there's no real way to ever know for sure.

It was as if the two corpses were just sleeping; lying together, inches apart from each other, but unable to touch. You could almost imagine they were in bed together, back at home in their house or apartment or whatever, just sleeping peacefully.

Except for the deep cuts, blue skin and stitches.

I read her toe-tag. "Todd, Lucy H."

Her name was on the sign out the front too.

A double viewing?

Maybe they died together.

Either way, I'd seen enough.

"Come on," I said. "We have to get going."

Raven turned to face me. "Why?"

"Tyler! He'll be *waiting*."

"Let him wait, this is more important."

Raven reached down and pulled out the foldable legs that rested at the side of the tray the guy was lying on. The legs swung down with a clatter and latched into position just underneath his head, steadying the tray and giving it some support.

"Which do you want?" Raven asked.

"Which do I *want*?"

She nodded as she walked around his trolley and came to stand right in front of me.

"Yes," she said. "You pick."

"I don't want *either*," I replied. "I just want to get out of here."

"This could be your only chance, Amber. This is an offer I can only make once. Don't miss taking it if you want it."

She took my hand in hers and moved it to my right, holding it steady just inches above the stomach of the girl on the trolley.

"Touch her," she whispered.

"No. I can't," I replied.

"Do it," she said as she lowered my hand.

I tried to resist, but she was stronger. And, in a way, I guess I wondered what the girl felt like. And then my warm hand touched her cold skin. The girl felt soft, and cool to the touch. Raven held my hand there on her stomach for a second or two before gliding it up across her rough stitches and over to her right breast. The breast was cool as well, yet still pliable and reasonably soft, as I found out when Raven directed my hand to grasp and squeeze it. Only the nipple felt hard when it pushed against the palm of my hand. After no more than a few seconds, Raven took my hand away. The breast jiggled slightly.

"She's yours," Raven whispered, letting go of my hand and walking back to the trolley in the middle of the room. "You only have to say yes."

I walked away from both trays then, walking fast, leaving the bodies behind. I didn't like them surrounding me, one on each side, and I could still feel the girl's cool tight skin on my hand. I needed space. I needed to breathe real air again. I walked over to Raven, who was busy filling the syringe with liquid again.

"We don't have time for this," I told her.

"I won't be much longer."

"Someone might catch us. The longer we're here, the better chance someone will find us."

"I said, I won't be long."

"We can't ruin this now," I pleaded.

She lifted the syringe and looked at it as she pushed the air bubbles out with the plunger.

"I'm not letting this opportunity slip by," she told me.

And with that, she slipped by me and walked back across to the bodies on the trays. She stopped by the hips of the guy and quickly inserted the needle into his cock.

"Hand me that wire again," she asked.

But I stayed where I was, leaning against the trolley, my arms crossed in front of me.

Raven looked at me and sighed deeply. "Never mind," she said.

She left the needle sticking in the guy's cock and walked back to the trolley. She picked up the cord and shook her head.

"You don't get chances like this every day, Amber. Don't live to regret passing up an opportunity like this."

But how could I convince her *I wasn't interested!*

I didn't want this.

I didn't want to be here.

I didn't want to be doing this.

I wanted to be back at the trailer, back in my bed, with no Duke and no Tyler to worry about. I just wanted to lie there in the dark, Raven in my arms, our warm bodies entwined.

I wanted that so badly.

Was that so difficult? Was I asking too much?

But the last thing I wanted to do right now was to disappoint Raven, to make her feel I was letting her down. And that's how I felt. I just didn't want to do this. She couldn't make me.

Raven wrapped the wire tightly around his cock and tied it off at the end, just like we did with Duke's. Then she injected the fluid, and I could see the guy's cock growing quickly. She massaged it with her free hand as it did so. She kept it smooth and straight and long.

She removed the needle from his cock and then looked at it for a second or two. Shaking her head, she walked back to the trolley – right past me without even looking at me – and took another full syringe of the embalming fluid.

She injected that into his cock too.

By now it was huge. It bobbed there in her hands as she massaged it. It looked like a balloon that had been over-inflated and was ready to burst. It was fat on the sides and I could see the dark stains of his veins underneath the blue skin.

I was no longer shivering. The coldness in the air seemed to be a comfort for me now, keeping me away from everything that was happening before my eyes.

I wanted to run, but at the same time, I couldn't bring myself to do that. I would stay with Raven – as I promised – because I said I would.

Raven placed the empty syringe by his shoulder and massaged his cock with both hands. It was long and fat and looked grotesque, but I'm guessing that was just in my eyes. For Raven, it was more than that. It was what she wanted. Probably what she desired more than anything.

She wanted this more than she wanted me.

And that hurt. Cut me deep. But there was nothing I could do about it.

She continued massaging with one hand, while her other hand undid the top button of her jeans. She pulled them down and let them drop to the floor. Kicking off her sneakers, she stepped out of the legs of her jeans and bent down to remove her socks.

It was then I realised she wasn't wearing any underwear. Her bare arse pointed straight at me and she bent forward taking off one sock at a time.

She only let go of his cock long enough to remove her jacket and t-shirt.

She wasn't wearing a bra either.

Then she stood there naked, just like the other two bodies, only she was standing and was still breathing. Breathing hard.

She turned to me. My eyes dropped to her breasts, and her pierced nipples. The barbells seemed to shine in the light, and her nipples were erect and hard.

"Last chance," Raven whispered.

I shook my head and looked away.

"Okay," she said. "Your loss, not mine."

I tried not to look, but there was no way I could stop myself. I turned back and watched as Raven climbed onto the tray. She lifted herself and threw her right leg up and over, bringing it down between his legs. Then she lifted her other, bringing her whole body up and onto the tray. She was kneeling between his legs, his inflated cock just inches from her face.

She steadied herself, testing the tray would hold and that the legs underneath would take the addition of her weight.

She looked strong and wonderful and so natural, while the body underneath looked more bluey-pale now, more dead, more totally un-alive.

And she opened her mouth.

Leaned forward.

And took him inside her.

I glanced away quickly, looking down at the trolley beside me, but all I could see was the jar full of white flakes, and I knew Duke's cock and balls were in there, and I didn't want to look there either.

I heard the sounds as she sucked on the guy's cock. I heard her moan with pleasure and suck harder.

I couldn't stop myself. I looked again.

Her curls were falling across the lower part of his stomach and hips. Like a dark curtain, it hid what was going on lower down, but I knew *exactly* what was happening. Her head rose and fell, along with her hair, in a rhythmic fashion and I could hear the sucking and the slurping, the popping when he slipped from her mouth, and the wet tonguing sounds that sounded so unnatural here in the mortuary.

I stood. I watched. For what seemed like ages.

I felt sick.

Finally, with one last, long slurp, she lifted her head up and away from his cock, her body arching and her face rising above his chest. There was one long strand of spit or liquid or something hanging from the corner of her mouth and reaching all the way down to the tip of his cock.

She smiled at me.

I didn't smile back.

"You have no idea what you're missing," she said.

I had a pretty good idea, actually.

She sat back on her haunches, kneeling between his legs as she regained her breath, his fat bloated Franken-cock pointing to the ceiling in front of her. And then she pushed herself forward, lifting her legs over his and moving to a new position, kneeling across his hips, one knee on each side. His cock was still pointing to the ceiling, but slowly starting to lean, and her vagina above it, just inches away from his wet glistening tip.

She was staring at me. Her eyes narrowed but she didn't say anything.

And slowly, she descended.

His bluish-white cock got closer, so did her vagina.

Then her eyes dropped to his face and she impaled herself. I heard the air rush from her lungs in a sigh of pleasure. She pushed further down, her hips slamming down on his.

And as she did so, I could feel his fat icy cock push deep inside me too. I could feel him inside, his rotting dead flesh touching my most private areas.

Raven moved into a rhythm, slowly up and down, getting fast and faster as she moaned.

He was still inside me though, his cold dead pole spreading the coldness through my hips and stomach, along my legs and arms. Liquids squirting from within him, his dead diseased skin flaking off inside me.

I felt sick. I felt dirty.

I felt a little bit dead myself.

"All of them have to die," Raven whispered as she moved faster and faster, swinging her hips from side to side now, rotating on his cock. "Sooner or later, they all die."

She worked faster and faster, her eyes closing in pleasure and her breathing getting deeper.

I heard the gurgling before I saw anything. I looked towards her, thinking she was choking or something, but it wasn't coming from Raven. It was the guy. The sound was coming from his mouth.

After a few more seconds, his mouth shot open, blood and bile and liquids of dark horrific colours pumped up through his mouth and nose, over his face and down his chin, in rhythm with Raven's thrusts. The liquids continued, rolling down his chest and sides, flowing down into the drains on the side of the trays.

The smell was overpowering. Much worse than it had been while I was cleaning out Duke's jar. I had to breathe through my mouth, it was the only way I could stop myself from being sick.

She scraped her fingernails down his chest and through the ooze that lay there, making little trails in the blood, and she clawed at the unresponsive skin. Her fingers found his nipples and grabbed them hard, turning them and twisting them, rubbing in the bloody mess that was flowing all around her. She was rising and falling quicker, harder now. Her flesh slapped his. She rubbed her bloodied hands over her own breasts, around her nipples, staining the barbells a dull metallic red. She moaned again. It sounded loud in the small room.

She opened her eyes, looked down at his face, leaned forward and kissed him hard on the lips, her face mashing against his and the purge that still flowed from him. She moaned again, longer and harder this time, as she rose and fell quicker and quicker. She looked up, blood and thick seepage dripping from her chin.

"Is this how *you* treated him?" she asked the girl lying on the trolley next to him. "Were you his girlfriend? Did you treat him properly? Did you give him what he wanted?"

She pumped away faster, faster still, licking at her own lips and pinching her nipples. Her eyes were focussed on the face of the girl.

"Did you give him head when he asked for it? Did you go down on him and make him cum? Did you swallow, gargle or spit?"

She reached over then, reached over and slapped the girl hard across the face. The force of the blow sent the girl's head whipping around, and sounded like the crack of a whip. The blow made her face the other way, away from Raven and the guy.

"Did you have *control*, or did he?" she asked in a soft voice before returning to look down at the guy underneath her.

She pumped away faster still, her hips rising and falling, the guy shaking underneath her like he was having a fit.

And then I heard her cum.

Long, loud and hard. It echoed around the small room.

She sounded like she was in ecstasy.

I worried someone would hear her. And I wished I wasn't there.

I wanted to be anywhere. In the trailer with Duke or at home with my drunk father.

Anywhere but here.

She moaned deeply, it sounded like it came from her very soul, and her thrusts began to slow. She was winding down slowly, enjoying every last second.

She collapsed on top of him, her hair cascading around them, covering them both, seeping into the blood and bile that covered the tray and letting them share a private moment.

I could see her spine running along her back, it poked through her skin at sharp angles, and I could see her ribs as they rose and fell, as she tried to get her breathing back under control.

I could see her hips and knew exactly what was under them.

In them.

Deep *inside* them.

Slowly, she crept backwards, kissing his chest and his nipples, licking at the stitches and the ooze and the deep cuts in his skin. Tasting him and running her tongue along him, moaning again as she lapped up the human spillage.

There was a long slurping sound and then his cock poked out between her breasts as she crawled further backwards. It wasn't the same shape it had been when it went in. It was flatter and squatter, the liquid having moved around inside there I guess, forming to the shape of Raven's insides.

But she didn't care.

She took him in her mouth again anyway. His glistening head slipped right inside her lips and she sucked again. She was tasting him once more, tasting her own juices, mixed with his, mixed with the tastes and smells of death.

And with her mouth and lips, she reshaped his cock. Within seconds it was straight and tall and...well...normal again.

As normal as it could be under these circumstances.

She licked his head, used her hands to rub at the base of his cock, pumping harder and faster. It was almost like she wanted him to have an orgasm too, but I knew that wasn't going to happen.

Still, she didn't let up. She took him deep into her mouth, sucking and licking harder and faster, pumping his shaft and squeezing his balls.

Eventually, she paused, pulling away. He *slurped* from her. She was watching intently, looking at the head of his cock as if waiting, willing something to happen.

And then it did.

A small dollop of thick brownish liquid rose from the eye in his cock. I only saw it for a second, and if it was any other colour I probably wouldn't have seen it. But I saw this, and I saw Raven lean forward and lick it up with the tip of her tongue. The thick mucus-like strand stretched from her tongue to the tip of his cock and it didn't break, it hung there in the air until Raven leaned forward, taking him fully and deeply into her mouth again, sucking and pumping away.

I saw her other hand reach back between her legs and disappear inside her. She was rubbing hard and fast as she sucked. She was going to cum again.

I'd seen enough. I didn't want to watch any more of this. I was here for her, had been, and she knew it. But that didn't mean I had to see *everything*.

I turned away and walked across to one of the benches running along the wall.

Beside some medical texts I found a log book of sorts. It was open to today's date and there was an entry for 10am.

> Xavier and Todd
> Double fatality - car - Binch Street
> Engaged - parents request double funeral.
> Viewing Tuesday @ 11am - Funeral 2pm.
> Xavier cremation - Todd burial

So that made sense. They *were* lovers. Engaged ones.
I wondered when the wedding was scheduled.
They deserved so much better.

Like my mom.

I heard Raven moaning then, but I didn't turn around, I flicked through the book a bit more, looking at past dates and the funerals that had taken place here.

A timetable of death, mourning and misery.

Maybe Raven was right. Maybe she was giving the guy one last moment of joy before he was to be consigned to the earth forever.

No, not *earth*.

I checked the entry for him again.

Cremation.

I didn't like the sound of that either.

But the girl was going to be buried. So even though they loved each other, were going to get married – to spend the rest of their lives together, and I suppose they did – they were going to be torn from each other's arms in death.

So they'd be apart for all eternity anyway.

So sad.

Maybe he *did* deserve one last orgasm.

Maybe he did deserve to be loved by someone one last time.

Maybe Raven could give him something he'd never had.

Something *I'd* never had...

She moaned once more and I could hear her cumming behind me. I stayed focussed on the book, looking at the words but not reading them, concentrating on the long strokes of the handwriting, and wondering about the person who had entered the details in the book. Most of the entries were written in the same hand, so I guessed it was one person's job to enter them.

Was it the woman in the business suit who we saw earlier today when I knocked on the door? Was she the one who wrote down these notes? Or was it someone else, someone who worked on the bodies, busily restoring them, hiding the horrors that death would bring?

I didn't know. I didn't care.

It took my mind off Raven, and when I came back to reality, I couldn't hear her moaning anymore.

So I turned around to find her standing by the trolley.

She had the bath towel in her hands and she was wiping down the body, removing all sight of the blood and goo and purge from his chest and face. Then she did her own face too, continuing lower and wiping her breasts and stomach, all the way down to her vagina. She was still stained – as was the body – but I guess you really wouldn't notice the difference unless you were really looking. She just looked like she had a ruddy complexion. As did the guy lying on the tray.

Someone would have a great deal of fixing and cleaning to do before the viewing tomorrow.

She threw the towel to one side and undid the cord around the guy's cock. Almost immediately, it started to deflate and shrink, flopping to one side like a balloon losing all its air.

As Raven climbed back into her shirt and jacket, I watched as she tucked the cord into the breast pocket of the shirt.

Another souvenir.

She wasn't looking at me, so I don't know if she knew I was watching her. I wasn't about to let her know I was, that's for sure.

She turned and bent over, reaching for her jeans. I could see the inside of her thighs were wet and stained and glistening, and I hoped it was mostly just sweat. I didn't really want to think about exactly *what* it was.

As she climbed into her jeans, I looked back at the bodies on the table. The girl was still turned away from him, as if she was disgusted with him or had just found out he'd been sleeping with someone else.

That'd sure end the marriage plans.

Maybe she'd walked in and found Raven and him cumming together, and she was looking away, her heart and dreams broken.

Don't worry, sister, he's just not worth the trouble.

The guy was lying in the same position on the table, his pudgy wide cock now leaning to one side, losing altitude fast. Even with all the activity of Raven on top of him, he hadn't really moved an inch, except for his left arm, which was hanging off the tray now, palm-up, as if he was reaching for the girl, wanting to let her know it was all right, that it was just sex and that Raven meant nothing to him. But her head was still turned, she wasn't interested.

They're not getting married now.

"You ready?" Raven asked as she turned around to face me.

I'd been ready for ages.

She ran a hand through her long curly locks and I could see her cheeks were all red. She picked up the two sheets that were still on the floor and quickly spread them back over the bodies. I had no idea if what we'd done here tonight would go unnoticed by the families in the morning, but I guess it really didn't matter. The funeral home was not about to tell the world someone had broken in that night and had sex with a corpse in their care.

Not good for business.

They'd hush it up anyway.

Raven then grabbed the syringe from the tray (after first removing the needle carefully) and put it in the pocket of her jeans before squatting down and pulling at the legs of the tray. They folded up to the side once more, and she stood and slid him easily into the freezer, like a pizza sliding into an oven.

"Happy trails!" she called as the tray slid home and hit the back wall.

She slid the girl back as well, but she had nothing to say to her.

Grabbing the big freezer door, Raven closed it gently. There was a hiss of air and then the seals closed.

They were back at rest and the room was silent once more.

She turned around and leaned against the freezer door.

"I've never experienced anything like that," she said to me, a huge smile breaking across her face. "The aura of death, the very smell of him, here in this mortuary and its surroundings. It's all such a turn on, so *very* erotic."

I didn't reply. I just looked dumbly on.

"That's the best date I've ever had."

She walked towards me then, smiling like I'd never seen her smile before.

"I wonder if he was ever that good for her," she said, using her thumb to point over her shoulder as she flicked the needle into a nearby trashcan. "I wonder if she ever came like that when he was inside her. I bet not."

"I don't think we should talk like this."

"I'm sure he was never that huge or that hard in real life either."

I couldn't take any more, I just turned around and walked to the door.

"We've got to go," I said over my shoulder. "Tyler will be waiting for us and I'm sure he's getting worried by now."

"He's never been *that* big," Raven whispered behind me. But I had no idea whether she was talking about the guy in the freezer or Tyler.

Either way, I didn't care.

I wanted to get out of there and back to the safety of the trailer. All of a sudden, it was the only sanctuary I wanted. I didn't even care if Tyler was there or not.

Being around another person, a *live* one, was all that mattered.

Tuesday, July 16.

Thirty-eight

Tyler was waiting for us outside the trailer.

He had his arms folded across his chest and he was leaning against the door. He looked more than a little pissed at us.

"Where the fuck have you been?"

"Out," Raven replied as she walked up to him and unlocked the door. She had Duke's jar under one arm, wrapped once more in the bath towel.

I could see Tyler was looking at the towel, at its weird stains and colours, and I knew he was wondering just what was going on. But he didn't ask.

I just hoped he couldn't smell anything weird.

Raven opened the trailer door and stepped inside, letting the door close behind her.

I'd been walking a few paces behind her since we left the funeral home. We hadn't said much to each other on the walk, we just trudged through the forest, the flashlight leading the way. I needed some time to myself to try to work through exactly what had happened in the morgue, and to figure out how I felt about it all.

So, as the trailer door shut, Tyler rounded in on me.

"What's going on? I've been waiting here for ages!" he said.

"Sorry," I replied. "Raven had something she wanted to do."

"And you couldn't tell me what it was? Or at least say you may not be here when I got back? I walked down to that maintenance shed and lugged these shovels all the way back for you. And for what? This is the thanks I get?"

He was pointing to the ground and I could see three shovels resting against the side of the trailer. They must've been heavy to have to carry through the forest.

"We didn't know we were going out when you left us," I said, and it wasn't really a lie. *I* certainly didn't know we were going to the funeral home until after he had left.

"A-huh," Tyler replied, but he didn't sound like he believed me. "Are you okay?" he asked me.

Like he cared.

"That's none of your concern," I replied.

He turned away from me, leaned over to the tools and picked one up. "So are we going to bury Duke? Or should I just take all this stuff back?"

"Don't do that!" Raven's voice issued from inside the trailer. The door opened and she leaned out, smiling at us. "I'm just about ready to leave."

"We haven't got a lot of time," Tyler replied. "It'll be daylight again soon."

"Not for a few hours," Raven replied as she jumped down the steps. She was full of energy now, almost like she was revitalised. "Plenty of time for us to do what we need to do. You guys ready?"

She looked at both of us and we nodded.

"Cool," she replied. "So let's get rid of Duke once and for all!"

Raven slapped Tyler on the shoulder as she walked past him and headed to the Suburban.

"What are you doing?" Tyler asked.

She pointed to the car. "Getting in the car. To drive to the memorial."

Tyler shook his head. "No way," he replied. "Too noisy and too risky. The last thing we need is to be calling attention to ourselves. We'll walk instead. It's not that far and we can control things much better that way."

"But we've got to get Duke there somehow."

"If we get to the memorial, make sure no one is around, and actually manage to dig a hole for him, *then* I'll come back and get Duke, okay? I just don't want us caught down there along with a dead body. If we dig the hole, fine. I'll come back and carry Duke down. If not, then we've saved ourselves a whole stack of trouble."

"He's gotta go with us now," Raven replied.

"No, he doesn't."

"Leaving him here won't work," she continued.

"And neither will being caught with him while we're digging the grave!" Tyler replied. "Sorry, Raven, this is the only way we're going to work this."

I knew Raven didn't like being talked to like that, especially by a man. So I braced myself for her reply.

But all she did was shrug her shoulders and walk back towards us. "Whatever you say, boss man."

"Now, are you going to tell me where you've been?"

"No," Raven said as she smiled at me.

"Why?"

"It's a secret."

"I see," Tyler nodded and sounded disappointed. "Well, there's no point hanging around then."

He set off quickly into the woods.

"You better bring the rest of those shovels," he called over his shoulder.

Raven and I looked down at the remaining two shovels. Then we looked at each other. Raven shrugged and grabbed them both and handed one to me. It was heavier than I thought.

Quickly, we set off after Tyler. He was the only one who knew how to get to the memorial from here, especially at night. I hadn't taken much notice of the directions to the memorial yesterday, and I'm sure Raven had other things on her mind too.

"Amber, quick," Raven said as we walked. "My back pocket. The flashlight."

I walked behind Raven and saw the flashlight sticking out of the pocket of her jeans. I reached forward and pulled it out, turning it on as I did so. I didn't think we needed it to follow Tyler, but I guess it was good protection anyway.

The darkness fell away in front of us as the beam cut through the night. We were heading in a different direction to the one we took for the funeral home, and I was glad about that. I didn't want Raven to be tempted to go back there again.

Once was enough.

We could see the back of Tyler a few feet in front of us, and could hear the clanking of the shovel he was carrying.

"I think he's pissed at us," Raven whispered to me as we walked.

"I think he has every right to be."

She turned to look at me, a puzzled expression on her face.

"Well, we *did* leave him standing out here waiting for us for a hell of a long time."

"No one was forcing him to wait," Raven replied. "He's lucky we came back at all!"

We marched on, keeping Tyler in sight, his back always in the flashlight beam, but we never tried to gain on him. He took the lead and we stayed a safe distance behind him. No one seemed to mind.

It felt like a long trek, as I was already exhausted from the funeral home visit, and after what seemed like an eternity the trees thinned and we stepped out into a vast open space.

The night was bright and the moon was full. Off in the distance we could see the squat features of the memorial.

I turned off the flashlight, just to make sure there no one was around who could see our approach, but the place was deserted and I realised just how strong the moonlight was. We didn't need the flashlight, we could see alright without it.

We stopped at the edge of the woods and looked all around us.

"All clear?" Raven asked.

"Sure looks that way."

Not that it mattered. Tyler was still marching across the parking lot and towards the memorial, his footsteps sounding loud in the night. He hadn't stopped to check the place out, and if anyone was out there, they'd see him first.

I moved forward, but Raven's hand wrapped around my arm.

"Wait," she whispered. "There's no point us all getting into trouble if there *is* someone out there."

So we hid at the edge of the parking lot and watched as Tyler arrived at the memorial. He walked all the way around it and then quickly walked off into the woods on the other side of the memorial.

There was silence for a few seconds and then we could hear the sound of shovel on gravel, over and over again. He was digging away in the forest.

I turned to Raven. "We have to help him."

She put a finger to my lips. "Shhh."

"We're probably only making him angrier by staying hidden here."

Raven didn't reply. She looked all around us one more time, taking a step forward to glance further up the mountain and back into the forest.

Slowly, she nodded. "Okay."

We made our way across to the memorial.

The parking lot between us and the memorial seemed to stretch on and on. The quicker we walked, the further away the memorial appeared. But that was just a trick of the light or my panicked brain or something.

The digging got louder as we approached. In the darkness and the silence, it sounded so very loud, as did our footsteps on the gravel.

When we arrived at the memorial, we both looked past it and into the tree-line to see Tyler. But I couldn't spot him in the darkness. We didn't say anything, just listened, and Raven circled the memorial, running her hands lightly up and down across the slate.

I took a few steps towards the trees and turned on the flashlight. Within seconds I'd pinpointed Tyler, bending over and digging the hole.

"Nice of you to join me," he said between digs.

He was making slow progress, with only a couple of small piles of dirt and gravel at his feet. The ground around him looked hard and dry.

Tyler shook his head. "We should've thought this through more."

"What do you mean?" Raven asked. She'd crept up to stand right behind me.

He turned to look at her. "It'll take hours to dig a hole big enough, even if you girls help me. This is a bad place to do this, exposed and out in the open to tourists and traffic during the day."

"It has to be here," Raven replied in a slow, deep voice.

"No, no it doesn't."

Raven reached forward and took the flashlight from my hands. Slowly, she walked all the way to Tyler, sweeping the beam from left to right along the ground.

I followed behind her.

She let the beam settle on the hole for a few seconds before she turned off the light.

"Hope no one saw us," I whispered.

Tyler sighed and wiped the sweat from his brow. "I'm sorry Raven."

"Are you?" she asked, as she sighed.

He seemed surprised. "Yes, I am."

"Or are you just saying that because we left you standing alone at the trailer for so long?"

"Look, Raven," he replied, slowly. "I'm saying it because it's the truth. This isn't going to work. This isn't the answer. There must be another way, and we'll find it. We can bury him anywhere on Lake Mountain. Just not here, okay?"

Raven dropped the shovel she was carrying. It hit the ground in an almighty clatter. Quickly, she turned around without speaking and walked away from us. She marched back across the parking lot and climbed the memorial, jumping up at its side and hoisting her way up. Within seconds she was standing on the top of it, towering over us, the full moon just behind her left shoulder.

"Raven, don't!" I called softly as I walked back into the open too, following her.

I could hear Tyler's footsteps behind me. She waited for us, until we were both standing below her.

"I will *not* let Duke beat me," she whispered as she looked down at us. "I have the control. I'm *in* control. No dead asswipe is going to beat me!"

Tyler and I looked at each other. Raven was pacing up and down the memorial now, her features obscured by the shadows.

"Duke will *not* win this. I have control over my life and I now have it over his. *NO ONE IS GOING TO STOP US!*"

She screamed that last part at the top of her lungs, her arms reaching high into the sky as she threw her head back, like she was baying to the moon.

Her voice echoed through the night before trailing off, the scream rolling across the mountain. The three of us were wide out in the open, easily seen, so totally suspicious, and so easily caught.

"Get down!" Tyler yelled at her. "You'll ruin it all if you're not careful."

"Oh really?" Raven replied, hands on her hips now. "And who's going to make me? *You*, lover boy?"

Tyler didn't say anything. He just shook his head.

"Didn't think so. You want to talk about ruining things? You want to know about destruction? How about raping a sixteen year old? Raping her in her arse while you strangle her from behind with her own bra? How about raping her in her cunt and cumming into her dead mouth once you've wrung the life out of her?"

Tyler turned to look at me, a shocked expression on his face. I didn't say anything. He had no idea where this was coming from – or why – but I did.

"How about dumping her and leaving her to be found days later, huh?" Raven continued. "How about the ruined life of that girl's sister and family? How are they supposed to cope with that when the fucker who did it to her is never caught? How are they supposed to survive? How the *fuck* are they supposed to make sense of things, of events like that?"

Tyler was looking at the ground, silent. I guess I should've filled him in about Raven's past...and about Paige.

"He's only trying to help," I said to her, trying to defuse the situation.

"He hasn't done much so far," Raven replied, kicking at the top of the memorial. "Carried some shovels and dug a pissy little hole. Doesn't sound like much help to me."

"I'm only here to help," he said.

"Get what you can, more like it," she replied.

"Raven!" I said.

"Fuck and run, that's your plan," she continued.

"That's not true," he whispered.

"Stop it, Raven," I added.

"Screw the goth chic and then tell all your buddies." She kneeled down on the memorial and leaned forward, her head directly above his now. "That's the plan, right? Fuck her and then leave. Fuck her in the cunt, in the mouth, anywhere. Fuck her in the arse if you can."

"That's *enough!*" he said in a stern voice.

"Tell your friends afterwards. If you've *got* any friends. Sounds mighty weird a guy living at the base of a dam in a valve house. Mighty strange indeed. You sure you're not fucked in the head? As bad as Duke maybe? Or worse? Just what *are* you hiding, Tyler? Why are you here with us? What do you get from this deal, other than my *cunt*?"

"Shut up, Raven." He lifted his head to stare directly into her eyes.

They were just inches apart now.

I reached up and pulled at the legs of her jeans, but she pulled away from me and then stood upright once more.

"Don't fool yourself, you're not anything special, Tyler," she continued. "I wouldn't let you in now, not even if my life depended on it. *I'm* the one in control, I'm the one who calls the shots and I'm not letting you fuck me for anything."

"Raven, *stop it!*"

"So, what are you going to do now, big boy? Now that you know you won't be getting a piece of my ass. You gonna attack me? Tie me up and have your way with me? Fuck me and strangle me and mutilate me on this memorial like that animal did to Paige? Leave me to rot just a few feet from here so some kids can find me in a few days? Cum still leaking from me? What are you going to do, Tyler? Help history repeat itself? Or help me get one back for my sister? Help me kill and bury an asshole right here just like they did to her. What's it going to be, huh?"

The silence engulfed us. Neither Tyler nor I knew what to say.

I knew Paige had been murdered and dumped in the woods, but I had no idea it had happened right here at the memorial. Suddenly it all made sense, and I knew why Raven was so determined to bury Duke here – to avenge Paige. Maybe that's why she also decided to live in the trailer at Pine Hills, because it was so close to Lake Mountain and she could be near her sister.

"Oh, Raven," I whispered. "We didn't know."

She turned to face me. "She would've been so cold out here, so alone, Amber." She shrugged and sighed deeply. Right then she looked so tired. "Oh, what's the use? It's all fucked up now anyway. Only Paige would understand it all."

And with that, she climbed down off the memorial and stood between us.

Tyler was leaning against the side of the memorial, looking up at the moon, his body turned away from us. He didn't look so strong, so self-assured anymore.

"Paige deserved better. We all did. I just wanted to win one back for her," she smiled at me, with tears in her eyes. "I just wanted to take one fucker down, to show her we could do it. To show her we can beat them. To show her we can win."

Poor Raven. And, weirdly, I felt sorry for Tyler then. He didn't deserve any of that. He'd walked into a situation he knew nothing about and had to suffer the onslaught of years of Raven's pent-up stress and anger directed right at him. After all, he *was* helping us. He *did* try to get rid of Duke. In fact, he was the only one truly working on getting rid of Duke. He was out there breaking into the maintenance shed while Raven and I were pumping embalming fluid into dead cocks.

We stood there in silence, all three of us, for a long time. It was dark and cold and just a little bit creepy. Especially now we all knew this was where Paige was raped and killed. She died there, right where we were standing.

"I'm sorry, Raven," Tyler muttered. "I didn't know."

"It's a long story," I said to him.

"I guess." He nodded. "I better get back to digging the hole."

"No," Raven said. "The whole plan was fucked to begin with. It was emotional and stupid. I wasn't thinking straight and you guys were right all along. I was just thinking of Paige. If he's buried here, he'll be found, just like Paige was, I guess. Not tomorrow, or in four days, but he'll be found eventually."

Silence again.

"Everything's so fucking out of control," she whispered after a while.

"There *is* another way," Tyler said.

Raven turned her head around to look in his direction.

"We can get rid of him another way."

"How?" I asked.

"The dam has a spillway," he explained, in a soft, calm voice. I don't know if he was scared or hurt, or whether he just wanted everyone to remain calm. "Every-so-often, when the dam gets too full, they open the floodgates and release some of the water through the spillway. We could take Duke to the dam and wait until the floodgates are opened and then push him into the water. They release millions of gallons at one time; the water will be fast and furious and he'll be carried miles downstream, if he's not bashed and broken into pieces on the rocks below first. He'll be carried out of your lives, and by the time anyone finds him, all traces we've left on him will be long gone. Maybe even all traces of exactly who he was too."

I looked across to Raven, but she was staring intently at Tyler.

"How do you know all this?" she asked.

"I was in a hurry when I went to get the tools from the shed, and I probably wasn't as cautious as I should've been. I should've known when I found the shed unlocked that others might be around, but at that moment in time I just thought it was good luck.

"I got inside easily and looked around. They had plenty of stuff, so I grabbed the shovels. Anyway, I was turning to leave when two guys came into the shed. I had to hide behind an old tractor while they were there and I'm surprised they never saw me. But they were just too busy with that they were doing and what they were saying."

"Two guys?" Raven interrupted. "Not cops?"

"No," he shook his head. "There'd been some trouble at one of the camping sites, campers drinking too much alcohol and somehow it got out of control. I guess these guys were like night security or something, because they'd been called in to break it up."

"You sure?"

"Yep, no doubt about it. They *were* dressed like park rangers though."

Raven nodded. "Okay."

"It was these guys who were talking about the dam and the spillway. Apparently there's a spill due for Wednesday morning and they were talking about the patrols that would be happening later today, making sure no one was in the path of the water by accident. They have to make sure the forest is clear of campers downstream before they open the spillway. That's how I heard. I didn't think of it as a way to dispose of Duke at the time, I was too focussed on this memorial, but maybe the spill is exactly what we need."

He stopped talking and we were all silent for a time, each of us thinking about what he said and what our options were.

"What do you think?" Raven finally said, turning to me.

In the absence of anything better, I thought it was a good idea. At least as good, if not better, than burying the body near the memorial, no matter what the emotional attachment was.

"I think it could work," I replied.

"So do I," Raven added, slowly.

She smiled then, stood and walked up to Tyler and held out her hand. He took it and they shook.

"Thanks," she said as she stepped back and looked into his eyes. "Thanks for... you know... everything. All your help and all your efforts. I think that plan could work."

"I really *do* think it's your best hope," he replied. "Better than struggling to bury him, anyway."

"So what do we do now?" I asked.

Tyler turned to me. "Not much we can do. We might as well head back to the trailer and try to rest up and get some sleep. Then, we can drive down to the valve houses and wait there until Wednesday. They're near the dam wall, but hidden out of sight from the tourists. No one should bother us there. It'll be nice and close and we can make sure we get the body to the spillway in time." He then looked at Raven. "That is if you want to, of course."

Raven nodded as she looked skywards to the full moon. "It's a good idea. I think you're right. There's nothing more we can do here now. I've done all I can for Paige... and myself. It's over." A tear slid down her cheek. "Within minutes of the spillway opening, Duke could be miles from here, floating away from us and taking all our troubles with him."

There was silence again.

"And Paige would understand, I'm sure. Either way, we still win."

And so we all agreed.

We picked up the shovels and walked across the parking lot, heading back into the woods and to the trailer.

I was tired and drained, both emotionally and physically. Bed sounded like the perfect option.

I couldn't wait.

I didn't know if I'd be able to sleep though. I felt guilty for never talking with Raven about the events surrounding her sister's death, and how she felt emotionally about it. But it wasn't the kind of subject that was easy to bring up, if you know what I mean.

All I wanted to do was climb into bed and hug Raven, let her know I was there for her, to help her rest, and to get some rest for myself too.

But I had no idea this would be the last chance for any of us to relax.

Before the end of it all.

Thirty-nine

We slept later than usual, probably because we were all so tired.

I was relieved when we returned home and Raven climbed straight into our bed. There'd be no sex that night. Maybe there would *never* be any more sex between her and Tyler.

We hadn't spoken much on the walk home, although Tyler had asked me if I was okay and I'd nodded my head. Everyone literally just tumbled into their beds and fell fast asleep.

Still, I had enough time to spoon up next to Raven, feeling her body against mine. We weren't naked though. We kept our clothes on while Tyler was in the trailer, although I'm sure he'd seen (and felt) all of Raven anyway.

But that didn't matter any more. She was beside me. We were entwined and Tyler was on the other side of the trailer.

Alone.

It was perfect.

And even though Raven smelled kinda funny, probably because of all those fluids and everything that had been on her body, I didn't care.

I was holding her and that's all that mattered.

It was almost as if everything was back to how it should be.

Almost.

The sun was shining through the windows when I awoke. I rolled over to look at Raven, but her back was turned to me, her long curls reaching out across the gulf between us, stretching across to my left arm. Her hair looked dirty and I could see where some strands had clumped together, stuck by dried fluids.

I guess we all really needed to bathe, but we were a long way from the showers at Pine Hills, or even the lagoon now.

Still, nothing was as bad as the smell of Duke, and I wasn't looking forward to sitting in the car with him again today.

As if she knew I was watching her, Raven rolled over and smiled at me.

"Good morning," she whispered.

"Hi." I smiled back. "Sleep well?"

"Kinda," she replied. "You?"

I nodded. "Yeah, I guess."

Raven lifted her head and stared over my shoulder.

"He's still asleep," she whispered.

I didn't turn around. I really didn't care. Not at that moment anyway. I was just enjoying being with Raven, lying here next to her. Being part of her world.

Our world.

"Busy day ahead," she said.

"I know."

"We have to get rid of him," she continued.

I nodded. "We will, the spillway sounds like the best option."

She shook her head. "No," she replied. "I mean we have to get rid of *Tyler*."

I wasn't sure what she meant, but all of a sudden I had to turn my head around, to make sure Tyler *was* still asleep and couldn't hear us. Most of his body was hidden by the sheet, and he sure looked asleep to me.

"*Tyler?*" I asked.

"Yes. We have to get rid of him."

I was confused. "Why?"

"Because I don't want him to know about what we did last night. About us and the funeral home. He can't find out no matter what."

I was worried about exactly *what* getting rid of him meant. But I couldn't ask. I was too scared to.

"And I don't want him to know about today either."

"But he already does, he planned it with us."

"No," she shook her head. "We'll still do all that, going to the valve houses and everything. But we need to be *alone* this morning. We need to be together, just you and I."

"What for?"

There was a sparkle in her eyes. "We're going back."
"Back where?"
"The funeral home."
I pulled away from her, not sure that I heard her right, but knowing I did. "Are you *serious*?"
"We *have* to."
"What for?" My voice was rising, but I didn't try to stop it. "I'm *not* going back. I can't!"
"Listen – "
"There'll be people there by now. Workers. They'll be preparing the bodies for the funeral. They'll see what we did. They'll find evidence. The funeral is *today*, Raven. There might even be relatives and others there! We can't risk it."

She grabbed my hands and pulled me closer, her eyes cutting through me.

"Listen to me, Amber," she whispered. "We're not going back for anything like what we did last night. The time for that is over. It's gone. We can *never* get that opportunity back now. No, we're going for something completely different. We're going to the viewing."

"Huh?"
"The viewing. Today at 11am, remember?"

I thought she was crazy. And a part of me thought she was trying to fool with me, to see how far I would go. But I realised she was serious.

I just stared back at her. "We can't."
"We have to," she replied. "*I* have to. And I need you there with me."
"We've got to get rid of Duke!"
She nodded. "I know, I know, and we will. But we can't do that until tomorrow when the spillway opens. That leaves us time to do this today. But not with Tyler around."
"Why?"
"Because I don't want him with us, that's all."
"It's crazy! You know how many people will be there?"
"That's the whole point. It's the perfect cover. It's the last chance we have to see them again and it's the very final moments of their existence. We can't *not* do this. We can't miss this opportunity. You were there with me last night and I

want you there with me again. Just you. Not Duke, not Tyler, not anyone else."

My eyes dropped down to the bed between us.

"I don't know if I can," I whispered.

"Try? For me?"

I didn't reply.

"You can stay outside if you want. You don't have to come all the way in. Just be there for me and help me."

What could I do? What could I say?

"After everything went so wrong at the memorial last night, Amber, don't let this go wrong too!"

I closed my eyes, holding back the tears, and nodded.

"Okay," I replied. "I'll do it. But only for you, and only this once."

Raven leaned forward and kissed me full on the lips. Hers met mine and they were warm and full and powerful. They energised me, sending heat through my cheeks and face, down my limbs and into the core of my existence.

Then I remembered what they had been kissing last night, and I pulled away quickly, keeping my eyes closed so I hid my real thoughts, and my shame. I couldn't see the expression on her face either, and I felt better about that.

"You don't have to whisper and plot behind my back," he said from behind us.

We both turned and saw Tyler sitting up on the fold-out bed.

"We weren't talking about you," Raven lied.

It didn't work. He didn't believe her.

"I won't get in the way. I'll stay in the car and wait if I have to. I don't care what you girls have planned, but I want to make sure I can help you get rid of Duke. Just tell me where you want me – or where you don't – and I'll play the game."

I turned to look back at Raven, and I could see the concern etched across her face. She was biting down on her bottom lip and her eyes slid across to me.

"What do you think?"

I waited a few seconds before answering. "I think we can trust him. He knows too much already, and we can easily implicate him in all this too. So I guess he's as worried about what might happen as we are."

"That's right," he replied, throwing the sheet from his body and climbing out of the bed. "I'm as much in this as you two are now. So I'm just as concerned about being rid of that body as soon as possible. I just don't want to be left, not knowing what's happening, like I was last night."

He had a good point there.

If he wanted to turn us both in, he could've done it while we were at the mortuary. But he didn't. He waited.

Waited to help us.

"Okay," Raven nodded. "We'll head down towards the dam wall, and check out your valve house. But first, we make a detour, okay?"

He nodded. "Whatever you want."

He turned around and started to fold up the bed, turning it back into a couch.

I guess that was the sign for all of us to get moving.

It was well past 9am, so we'd have to hurry if Raven wanted to make the viewings on time.

We climbed from our bed too, and I took a moment to straighten the sheets and coverings. I felt as if I wanted to cover myself up too, so Tyler couldn't see me. That's because I was so used to sleeping naked. I guess I felt like I should be naked now. It was weird to have clothes on already, after just getting out of bed.

After a few minutes, we all met in the middle of the trailer. We were ready to go, once again wearing the same clothes as yesterday. Tyler even had his big jacket on already, although it wasn't zipped up at the front.

"What we're about to do only concerns Amber and me," Raven said to him.

He nodded. "That's okay. I understand. I don't want to step on any toes."

He was probably still smarting from the tongue-lashing he received from Raven at the memorial.

"I'll sit in the car and do nothing. I'll even take the radio and scan it for news reports, okay?" he continued.

That sounded feasible.

"Deal."

"So where *exactly* are we headed?" he asked.

"Back along the main road," she replied. "To the place where we stopped for food yesterday."

"The general store?"

Raven laughed and pushed past him, opening the door and stepping out into the daylight. He turned to look at me for an answer but I walked past him, heading for the door as well. His hand shot out and grabbed my arm hard, and he turned me around to face him again.

"I'm here to help," he whispered. "I don't want to see either of you getting in any more trouble."

"I know, I know," I replied. "I feel the same way."

"This could all be over soon and everything will be okay, normal again."

"Yes," I agreed, prying my arm from his grip. "It will be."

With that, I turned once more and opened the door, walking down the steps and out of the trailer.

All of a sudden I was glad to be out of there. It was much better to be out in the sun and the fresh air and the forest. Even though the dusty disused road stretched right by our front door, it was almost as good as being at the lagoon. Although I missed that lovely cool water right then.

A bath in the lagoon would have been heavenly.

I looked around me as I breathed in deep. If only we could stay and relax for a while. But I knew there was no time for that.

These days, there was *never* any time.

Raven was over by the car and climbing into the driver's seat.

"Come on!" she shouted over her shoulder. "Or we'll be late."

I ran to the passenger side and made sure I got the front seat. I climbed inside and slid up next to Raven. She had that fire back in her eyes and we smiled at each other while we waited for Tyler.

Duke smelled worse than ever, and I made sure I wound down my window as quickly as I could. I noticed Raven had already done the same. A loud buzzing came from behind us and that meant the flies had got in again.

Would they ever give up?

The sooner we got rid of him, the better. Although I had no idea if the Suburban would ever smell like a normal car again.

The door behind me opened and Tyler climbed inside.

"Did you lock the trailer door?" Raven asked.

"Yep," he replied. "I pushed in the button. It's locked."

Raven turned the key in the ignition and revved the engine.

Slowly, she turned us around and headed back the way we had come the day before.

"This morning belongs to Amber and me," Raven said, looking into the rear view mirror at Tyler.

He nodded. "I understand."

Maybe he was feeling left out and unwanted. I knew how he felt. I was feeling the exact same way when he first arrived, so maybe it was payback time.

Maybe he deserved it.

As we drove down the old dirt road, heading back to the main road of Lake Mountain, I turned to look at Tyler out of the corner of my eye. I wanted to smile at him to reassure him everything was okay and not to worry.

But he didn't see me. He was rummaging through one of the pockets on the inside of his jacket.

He didn't see my eyes drop down to his waist and notice what was tucked inside the waistband on his pants.

I turned back around quickly, my eyes darting straight out in front, through the windshield and along the road. I sucked in a lungful of air and started to feel light-headed all of a sudden.

I'd seen it, as clear as day.

Tyler's pistol, tucked under his belt.

He was armed and we weren't.

Forty

"Look sad," Raven whispered to me as we walked towards the funeral home.

I let my eyes fall to the ground and I dipped my head forward, hoping I was looking sorrowful, but I was sure that I was just looking suspicious.

There were so many people here that I felt like a rabbit trapped by a pack of wolves. The only difference being that we were walking right into their lair because we wanted to.

Raven had parked the car down the same side road where we stopped for lunch yesterday.

Tyler and Raven had been talking during the drive, but I can't remember what they were talking about. I wasn't really listening anyway. I was just staring straight ahead, trying to work out what to do, what could happen next.

He had the gun, my god, he had the gun!

I couldn't get that thought out of my mind.

Why did he need to bring that with him? Why didn't he tell us he was carrying it?

And worse...

What was he afraid of? What did he think was going to happen? Was he using it for protection? Against who? Against *us*?

And so even though they were talking away, like everything was normal, I knew things were far from it. And that put me on edge even before we got to the funeral home.

"Just where are you girls going?" Tyler asked as we climbed from the car.

"Don't worry about it," Raven said.

"But I *do*," he replied, hanging his head out the window and smiling his best smile. "You *can* tell me."

Don't tell him anything!

"Sorry," Raven smiled as she turned from him and started walking down the dirt track. "Our lips are sealed. Just think of it as some unfinished business."

I looked at Tyler one more time, my eyes slipping down his chest again, trying to see if the gun was still there. But the car door was in the way and I couldn't see down far enough.

"I'm the one stuck here with Duke," he said to me. "Don't forget that!"

I shook my head. "Sorry. Raven doesn't want you to know. All I can tell you is that we won't be far away and we won't be gone for long."

"I could follow you."

"But you won't, right? You'll trust us."

He sighed and sat back against the seat. "Fine, whatever. You know I can link you both to the body if I'm caught. It's Raven's car and trailer, and I can point the cops in the right direction."

I smiled at him. "So don't get caught!"

I turned and raced after Raven. Now that we were out of the car, I felt much safer, more in control knowing that Tyler wasn't there and that his gun was nowhere near us.

I thought about telling Raven about the gun, but after her explosive outburst last night, I didn't quite know how she'd react. She was too focussed now and I didn't want to derail her concentration. You know how she gets when I do that.

We walked on in silence. The day was warm, the sky clear, and it was nice just to walk and watch the scenery go by. We turned down the driveway and walked along it, coming to the parking lot sooner than I would've liked.

When I first saw the number of cars in the parking lot, and the crowd of people milling around outside, I hesitated and took a step backwards, wanting to flee back to the car. But none of that stopped Raven. In fact, it seemed to spur her on.

She marched quicker and more confidently through the cars, head pointing low, a sad expression on her face. Her hair wasn't flowing down her back like it usually did. It sat in clumps and knots and I hoped no one looked close enough to discover what was stuck in there.

I walked after her, trying to catch up to be by her side, but that wasn't easy. I finally drew level with her only as she was slowing down and stopping. She'd walked up to the side of the house, where we saw the parked hearse yesterday. Except now there were two of them, parked there side by side, sitting empty of both coffins and drivers. The two doors leading inside the house were open wide, and a long line of people snaked out from it. Raven was standing at the end of the line, and that's where I joined her.

I felt uncomfortable and out of place on the end of the line, as it slowly inched forward. But I didn't have to worry about that for long, as an old lady dressed in black came to stand behind me. She was crying and had only a small little purple handkerchief to dry her eyes. There was a young boy at her side. He was probably about 10 and I don't really know if he had a clue what was happening. I looked back at them and tried to smile at the boy, but his wide eyes just looked right through me. He wasn't crying though, he just looked kinda stunned.

Soon, there were more people behind them, talking in hushed tones and having conversations I couldn't really hear. There were also the sounds of sobbing and crying, and the occasional blowing of a nose here and there.

The line inched forward and in a short time we were stepping through the double doors and into a long, dark corridor. It smelled stuffy in there, and was more than a little hot. I felt the walls were too close to us, like there wasn't enough space to turn or to even breathe. There were also many more people around us now. They were milling around, talking to each other, hugging one another, sharing the grief. I felt like Raven and I were the only ones not talking to people, the only ones who must've been so obviously out of place.

I lifted my head enough to look around me, while still trying to look sad, as Raven has told me to do. I counted six funeral home employees standing at different sections of the room. Two by the doors we just entered, two further down the hall, and two standing by a small table that we were fast approaching. They all looked the same in their dark, dapper suits, with sad faces. But you could tell by their roaming eyes that they were dispassionate about the events around them. They were cool and calm, and they were going to make sure everything ran smoothly.

They must've known we didn't belong there. Couldn't they see that?

Raven didn't stand a chance!

And then I realised I had no idea why we were here or what we were going to do. Raven was still in the line next to me, her head bowed, her curls hiding most of her face and her expression.

I thought about asking her what we were going to do, but two things stopped me. One, there were too many people near us and someone was bound to overhear the conversation and, two, I was worried about the answer.

I turned and looked behind us. The line of people still snaked back to the double doors and outside. The whole place was getting busier and busier. Everyone had the same sad expression on their face, everyone talked in a low whisper. My eyes dropped back to the small boy behind me. He was crying now too, small rivers of tears staining his face.

I felt sad then. I mean, *really* sad. Not the fake sad Raven wanted me to feel. All these people had lost someone dear to them, whether it be the guy or the girl, and they were hurting so very much. They were here to pay their last respects in a very private and final way, and Raven and I were intruding on that. I felt a little bit disgusted with us both right then. We were interlopers, strangers, and we were here for something totally different. Raven was here to get a buzz, a hit of pleasure from this misery, and it wasn't right.

But there was nothing I could do. To pull out of the line now would look suspicious and talking to Raven about how I felt would be dangerous.

I was stuck where I was, and it was all out of my control. It would be easier to go forwards than backwards.

So I took another step with everyone else, trying to remember to look sad and to keep my head down.

Just act like everyone else.

Soft music was playing around us, and mixed with the fragments of conversations and sounds of sorrow I heard, the whole thing seemed like a dream. A bad one.

We took just a few more steps before the line dissolved in front of us. We came to a low table which held two open books and some flowers. Two employees were guarding them. The female employee was seated at the table, turned slightly to one side. The male employee was standing next to her, his hands clasped in front of him and his eyes stretching along the line.

Raven went first, bending forward and picking up the pen. She spoke to the woman for only a second before writing something in one of the books. Then she moved around the table and continued down the hallway.

I was next.

I walked up to the table and bent down, sure that the two employees were staring at me, knowing that I was not meant to be there, using their training to pinpoint an intruder quickly and setting in motion procedures to get rid of both Raven and myself. I couldn't look at them. I just stared down at the books and tried to concentrate. I picked up the pen and realised my hand was shaking.

Could they see that?

I grasped the pen tighter, but it slipped from my hand, falling onto one of the books.

Fuck!

I reached for it, but it rolled further, down the pages and off the book and along the table.

A hand came from nowhere, picked up the pen and held it out for me. I looked up. It was the male employee. He still had the sad expression on his face, that hadn't changed, but there was something in the way he looked at me that sent shivers down my spine.

He knew. He *had* to know!

He leaned forward, the pen coming closer to me.

"Sorry for your loss," he said in a steady, quiet voice.

I smiled at him –

Don't *smile!*

– and took the pen.

My eyes focussed on the books and looked for Raven's handwriting. Each book had a surname at the top. The one on the left read *Todd* and the one on the right read *Xavier*. Raven had only written in the book for Xavier. She'd ignored the girl altogether.

I read her message:

Knew him only for such a short while. But the memories of

our times together I will cherish forever.

She'd signed it *Rebecca Tyler*.

Concentrate, you *can* do this, I told myself. I felt as if I was taking way too long, holding up the line and making myself look even *more* suspicious.

I thought hard and fast.

Quickly!

I tried again. I put the nib of the pen to the page, but I had no idea what to write.

And then it just came to me:

People leave us all too soon.

But our memories of them will never fade.

I almost signed my real name. I actually wrote an *Am* for Amber, but quickly stopped myself. I paused for a second, my eyes glancing at Raven's signature one more time before I signed myself as *Amanda Duke*.

I smiled at that. I'd done well. Raven would like it too, but I wouldn't tell her what I wrote unless she asked me.

I put the pen down and straightened up. The woman sitting on the chair was looking at me, our eyes met and I made sure my sad expression returned.

"Thank you," she whispered.

I nodded and quickly walked around the table.

Raven was waiting for me further along the hall. She was leaning up against the wall just in front of the doors to the large room beyond.

I smiled at her, but she didn't return it. Her sad expression was still on her face. It looked so real to me. She almost had me believing that she was truly mourning the dead.

When I reached her, she turned around without saying a word and walked into the large viewing room. I followed.

The room was painted a cream colour and was filled with flowers. There were rows of chairs on both sides, split down the middle to allow access to the two caskets that were on a small raised platform at the far wall. While I'd seen a lot of people outside the house and in the hallway, there weren't as many in the viewing room. I guess people don't like to grieve openly in front of the deceased. Instead, they come in, spend a couple of seconds with their loved one and then move outside or into another room or something.

It's their last chance to be with the person they loved, but they let them go so quickly and so easily.

There were only a few people sitting in the first couple of rows of seats. I guessed they were the family members who wanted to stay close by, keeping their own vigil.

The line moved forward slowly, down through the chairs and past the family members before snaking up onto the platform. For those in the line, Jeremy was the first casket to visit, followed by Lucy. Because the caskets were raised on a small platform, I couldn't really see much of Jeremy or Lucy, but I could see their faces, tilted towards us, peeking over the edge of the caskets. (Although, of course, their eyes were shut, so they *weren't* peeking, but you get the idea...)

There were only a couple of employees in this room. One was standing between the caskets, and I was pretty sure there was another one sitting with the families in the front row too.

We inched forward, Raven in front of me.

Don't do anything stupid, I thought to myself, concentrating on the back of Raven's head, almost willing her to hear my thoughts.

We were past the family members by now, and I turned my head slightly to look at them. They didn't see me, they were too lost in their grief to look at me. There were probably eight or nine of them, and I could easily pick out the grandparents, parents and brothers and sisters. They all shared the same look of sadness and loss.

Only the employee who was sitting with them looked my way. When his eyes met mine, I turned quickly away, dropping my head down lower, staring at my shoes and praying that he didn't come over to make a scene.

He didn't.

When I next had the courage to sneak a glance his way, I could see he had returned to talking to the family.

That was close!

And we inched further forward.

A woman in front of us, who was leaning against Jeremy's casket, let out a sad wail, like she couldn't contain her sorrow anymore. I heard hushed voices, calming tones, and I tilted my head slightly to see more.

The employee who'd been standing between the caskets had his arm around the woman. She was crying and shaking her head as he whispered in her ear. Whatever he was saying, it wasn't helping. He turned her around and slowly directed her down the platform, past the chairs and out towards the doors. He still held her, helped her all the way, just in case she fainted or something, I guess.

Raven was watching too. I could see her head move with mine, watching them both leave.

We stepped up onto the platform, just five people away from Jeremy.

Now there was no employee guarding the caskets.

Suddenly I felt worried and scared.

I wish I knew what Raven had in mind.

Inched forward, four people away.

We *shouldn't* have been doing this.

Inched forward, three people away.

It was *sooo* wrong.

Inched forward, two people away.

And then Raven was there, leaning forward into the casket, peering down at Jeremy.

I leaned forward too, peeking over her shoulder.

He looked just as he did last night, except now of course he was lovingly boxed in mahogany and blue satin. His hair was well groomed and his lips were together, forming a pleasant smile. He looked very peaceful, as if he was only asleep. I don't know if it was the softer lights in this room, or something they'd done to his makeup, but

I couldn't see any sign of bruising or trauma like I could last night. He was wearing a very nice dark blue suit and matching tie, and his hands were folded over his stomach, fingers entwined. There didn't seem to be any discolouration to his skin from the fluids that had spilled over him last night, and there was certainly no large bulge down between his legs.

That was a relief, at least!

All looked perfectly normal. Well, apart from the fact he was dead, of course.

Someone had cleaned up the mess we left behind extremely well.

Raven leaned closer.

My eyes darted around the room, but no one was watching us. They were all busy with their own grief and sorrow. No one was looking.

And that was just as well, because what Raven did next would've drawn attention to us no matter what.

She reached out.

Reached out with her fingers.

And touched Jeremy's hand.

It was a quick, darting movement, and her fingers rested on his only for a second before she pulled her hand back and looked around.

I wanted to tell her to stop. I wanted to turn around to make sure the woman and boy behind me weren't watching us, a look of shock and revulsion on their faces. But I couldn't do that. I figured that they'd be yelling and screaming at us if they saw us doing that. So, as long as everyone kept quiet, things were probably okay.

Either way, I wanted to get out of there as soon as possible.

I leaned further forward, my hips and stomach touching Raven's back, trying to give her a hint to move on and leave.

But she didn't. She remained standing there.

And her hand reached out again, this time slipping up his arm and under his shirt sleeve, her fingers snaking higher and higher until they could go no further, her palm and wrist stopped by his cuff.

I heard her moan quietly in front of me, as her hand rubbed up and down his arm. Her head dropped further forward and I had no idea what she was doing, feeling or saying.

Sweat broke out on my forehead and I could feel the panic rising in me.

Raven removed her hand quickly, darting it back to her stomach. She waited for a second or two, as if perfectly timing what she was going to do next. She placed both hands on the side of the casket and I thought she was getting ready to leave. The fear left me, but only for a second.

Then she leaned forward, her whole body pivoting and leaning over Jeremy. Her mouth came down towards him, her lips quickly resting on his and holding there for a second or two, before she pulled away and stood straight again.

His last kiss.

It all happened so quickly I didn't have a chance to stop her. I wanted so badly to turn and look across the room at the pack of funeral home employees who must've been running towards us now, getting ready to pick us up and throw us out or give us over to the cops or something.

But there was no sound of running feet, no raised voices.

Nobody, it seems, noticed.

Raven was still standing there, her head shaking back and forth as she looked down at Jeremy.

I pushed against her again, harder this time.

And this time – *thankfully* – she took my hint.

Slowly, she walked away from the casket and I followed. I know I probably should've stayed and said something to him (isn't that what these viewings are for?) but I had nothing to say and I wanted to make sure Raven headed straight for the exit so we could get out of there.

But, instead, she walked across to Lucy and looked down at her as well. I stayed close by her, right behind her, mirroring her every step and keeping alert, just in case.

The ponytail was gone now. Instead, the girl's hair was spread out around her, resting on the pillow and flowing down over her shoulders. She looked quite different to how she looked last night. There was no sign of the bruising here either, and they'd fixed her hair so there was no way you could see the skull fragments and skin flaps we saw last night. She looked peaceful and relaxed, and she was wearing a lovely white flowing gown, along with a long silver necklace that rested on her chest. The necklace appeared to be very old and fragile, probably some heirloom, and while the stones looked like diamonds, I'm guessing they really weren't. Her hands were crossed in front of her too, and her smile was a bit wider than Jeremy's had been.

Raven stopped, leaned forward.

She reached out.

She clasped Lucy's hands in hers and held them there for a moment, her head shaking back and forth slowly.

I bumped against her once more, but she didn't move, she was staying where she was.

"Come on, Raven," I whispered. "We have to *go.*"

She leaned forward again and for a moment I thought she was going to kiss Lucy as well, but she didn't. She leaned in further, closer to her face, her mouth coming close to the girl's ear, and then I could hear her whispering something to her.

I tried to get closer, but Raven was whispering too softly and too fast. I couldn't work out what she was saying.

A few seconds later she straightened up and let go of Lucy's hands. She went to move away from the casket, but then changed her mind. She turned back to Lucy, took one last look at her, reached in and slapped her hands hard.

The noise was loud in the room, like the crack of a whip.

She *slapped* her!

My head turned to scan around us.

We were fucked. We were going down for sure, they were going to catch us right then!

But that's not what happened.

No one was looking at us.

Everyone was still consumed in their own bundle of grief. And, as Raven walked away from Lucy and stepped down off the platform, I saw the guy who was in charge of minding the caskets quickly walking back down the row of mourners, a grim look on his face. He'd managed to get away from the emotional woman he'd helped outside and he was now heading back to his post.

For a split second I thought he may have seen or heard what Raven had done, but he wasn't looking at us, he was looking at the row of people and the caskets, his mind on the job and not on us.

If he'd walked back into the room only a few seconds earlier, Raven and I would have been in big trouble.

I was still standing by Lucy as he returned to his position between the caskets and his eyes locked on mine. I smiled and he returned a sad smile to me.

He had no idea.

So we were okay.

I turned and looked down at Lucy, pretending to show my last respects.

No, that's not true. I *was* showing my last respects. Sure, I didn't know her in life, but I knew her in death and I felt like I wanted to apologise for what Raven had done to her, both last night and today.

But I didn't know what to say. I just looked down at her and tried to think of some deep and meaningful words.

Good luck wherever you end up, was all I could think of.

I turned and walked slowly away from her and off the platform. Raven wasn't in front of me, and I lifted my head to see where she was.

It took a few seconds to find her, because I was looking for her on her own. I had no idea she'd be talking to someone.

She was talking to an old woman who was standing in the third row of seats from the front. The woman was dressed all in black, including black gloves and a black veil, which was pulled back over her black hat.

Raven was saying something to her, and the woman was nodding, dabbing at the wet spots on her face with a handkerchief.

I quickly walked over to them.

"Thank you," the woman was saying in a quiet voice. "It means a lot to me to hear that."

"They were both so young," Raven added, her voice quiet and full of sorrow. "And just starting out in life."

The woman nodded, lost for words.

"Please pass my condolences on to the whole family. To both families."

"Yes, I will. Thank you."

Raven turned to leave, but the women reached out and grabbed her shoulder.

"Are you going to the cemetery?" she asked, her eyes wide.

Raven shook her head. "I'm sorry. My friend here and I can't make it this afternoon. We have other matters to attend to."

The woman quickly glanced at me and then her eyes brimmed with tears and her head fell forward.

Raven took a step towards her. "Where are they being buried? I can't get there today, but maybe later in the week I can pay them both a visit."

The woman seemed to cheer up then, and quickly she nodded. "Yes, yes. Good idea. But only Lucy is being buried. Jeremy is being cremated."

"Oh, I see," Raven seemed surprised by that. I guess I should've told her what I'd read in the log book last night.

"They'll both be interred at Pine Hills cemetery, so they can be near each other."

"I see," Raven nodded. "At least they'll be together now."

"Yes," the woman agreed. "I can get the address for you?"

"No, no, it's okay," Raven replied. "I think I can find it."

And with that, they said their goodbyes and parted. I smiled at the woman, but she started to cry again and turned away, walking back to the other members of her family.

I followed Raven towards the large doors. As I did so, I ran my eyes along the line of people still waiting to view the bodies.

They all looked the same, all dressed in dark clothes and all with heads bowed.

I turned to look back at the two caskets one last time.

The woman who had been standing behind me was still up on the platform. She was looking down at Lucy and was shaking her head, her hands clasped in front of her, like she was praying over the body.

But the young boy was turned away, facing me, looking straight at me. His head was tilted and his big eyes didn't blink. He just stared right at me.

I tried to smile to reassure him, but his expression didn't change.

Had he seen what we'd done?

It felt strange, all wrong, and I didn't like it one little bit.

I turned and quickly marched to the doors, following Raven and trying to wipe the boy's stare from my mind.

By the time I walked up the crowded hallway and reached her again, she was standing outside, leaning against one of the hearses and waiting for me. She twirled a business card in the fingers of her left hand.

She smiled and held it out to me.

I read it. It had the words *Ferguson's Funerals* in swirly writing, with the address and contact details printed underneath.

"Another souvenir," she whispered to me.

"Are you crazy?" I asked as I grabbed her by the shoulder and walked her around the hearse and away from the crowd of people still milling near the doorway and within earshot.

She smiled and chuckled to herself.

"You stress out too easily, hon," she said as we walked away from the house and back down through the cars in the parking lot.

"Do you have *any* idea how close you came to being caught?" I asked her as we walked.

"But we *didn't* get caught, did we?" She turned to me. "And it was so worth every second!"

"It was a stupid risk," I replied.

"Life is full of risks, Amber. And the only people who are stupid are those who don't take those risks."

I just shook my head and walked through the cars, a few steps behind her.

"So much grief," Raven continued. "And no one saw us. It's almost like we were invisible to them all. As if the sorrow blinded them to what we were doing."

"*I* saw what we were doing."

"Of course you did," she said as she stopped in her tracks and turned to face me. "You were part of this with me. You always *have* been. You and me. We're in this *together*."

"Are we?"

A puzzled expression crossed her face. "Of course we are."

"Then why don't my concerns, my feelings, ever matter to you?"

"They do, hon."

"Really?"

"Yes, of course."

"Sometimes I think you care more about those dead bodies than you do for me."

"That's not true and you know it," she replied as she turned from me and walked into the forest. "I thought *you* of all people would understand."

"Well, I don't," I replied, following her. "I can't."

She lifted her palm to her nose and sniffed at it.

"He smelled only faintly of decay," she whispered. "But the girl, she smelled different again. Probably because of her wounds. They couldn't hide them all and she smelled more of death. It was all over her, rising from her as she lay there."

"Raven, stop it."

"He was so soft to touch," she continued. "Almost lifelike. But she was hard, rubbery and dry. They were so different, even in death. It was such a turn on."

"*Please,* Raven? I really just don't want to know."

She licked her palm then.

I can still see her doing it if I shut my eyes, even after all this time.

Her tongue sliding from her wrist all the way to her fingertips.

"Stop it!" I called to her.

She turned around and held out her palm to me.

"Lick it," she said. "Join me and lick it."

"No."

"Do it."

"No!"

"You want to."

"*No*, Raven, I *don't*! Just stop it, okay?"

She shook her head and turned away.

"Honestly, Amber, I give you a home and a place to live, I give you *everything* of mine, but you're so cold, so lacking passion. You're just as dead as those two back there in the caskets."

That hurt real bad. Cut right through me. She'd never said anything like that to me before and it hurt like you wouldn't believe.

I dropped back behind her as we walked on in silence, through the woods and back towards the trailer. The further we put between the funeral home and ourselves, the better. I wanted the safety of the trailer and the car, even if Duke and Tyler *were* still there. I needed Raven distracted by other things, so she wouldn't spend time talking to me and hurting me with her putdowns.

"No one saw a thing," Raven said then, laughing to herself. "We could've done anything there."

"Well, I'm glad we didn't."

"*I* did."

"I *know!* I saw exactly what you did!"

"Did you?"

"Yes, of course!"

She turned to face me. "Everything?"

"*Everything!*"

"So, what's in my left pocket right now?" she asked, her smile stretching even further.

"Huh?"

"Tell me what's in my left pocket. If you saw everything, you'd know."

"Stop fooling," I replied.

"I'm not fooling."

"You *are*. You haven't got anything in there."

"Really?"

"Really!"

"So what are these then?" she asked, pulling first a watch from her pocket and then one small earring.

She held them out to me and I looked at them.

The watch was a man's watch. It had a pretty gray face with a chunky silver and gold band. It looked heavy and pretty new. The earring was old and very ornate, about an inch and a half long, and had a small purple amethyst in the centre, surrounded by intricate metalwork.

"You *didn't*?" I asked.

She nodded. "I sure did! One from him and one from her!"

I shook my head in disgust. "That's a low thing to do," I said.

"Why?"

"It just is."

"They won't be needing them where they're going," she replied, stuffing the watch and earring back into her pocket.

"What if someone back there notices they're gone?"

"What are they going to do? Strip search the relatives? They'll just assume some grief-stricken aunty couldn't part without taking something to remember them by. No harm done. They'll mean more to me than to anyone else there. Anyway, I gave him the best gift of all. I gave him the final gift. You've gotta understand that, sweets. It's not burying the body with the wedding ring or with grandma's old necklace that makes the difference, it's leaving your love inside forever. Cum or juice, it should be the last liquid to pass through their lips. That's the *best* gift, the *true* gift."

"I don't like it," I added.

"Like what?"

"I don't like what we're doing, what we've become. I want things to be as they were."

Raven grabbed my arms. I could feel her wet palm, slippery on my forearm.

"Listen to me, Amber," she said, angrier now, her eyes narrow and sharp. "Things will *never* be the same again. We've come too far, *gone* too far. We can only try to escape, and this is the best way to do it. This is what we have to do to finally be rid of Duke and Tyler and them all. To be truly free we have to take back the control and make sure we're the ones who come out on top. It's only up to us now, and we *have* to be stronger and harder and tougher than ever before."

"I just want to be with you."

"And you will be, you *always* will be, but we have to stand together in this, we have to make sure we win. And to do that, I need a girl by my side just as tough and just as strong and as gutsy and daring as I am. I need you to be like me, with me, as *one* with me."

I nodded.

"That's all I ask. That's *all* I want. Can you do that? Can you promise me you can do that?"

I nodded once more. I had to. In a strange way, I guess she was right. The only way things could ever get back to normal now was if I were able to help her through the mess we were in, to get through safely what was to come. Then, maybe, just maybe, things could be like they once were.

"Good," she replied. "You with me?"

"Yes."

"Just you and me?"

"Just you and me, Raven."

"Perfect. Now, lick my palm and feel his power. Take it inside you and make it yours."

And that's exactly what I did.

I leaned forward and stuck out my tongue, licking her palm and tasting her skin and her spit and what remained there from the two bodies Raven had touched. It tasted sweet and tangy, like her sweat was mixed with some sort of chemical.

"That's it," Raven replied. "You'll feel stronger, more powerful. Soon, we can take them all. They won't beat us now."

I grabbed her hand and licked longer, lapping up the taste and enjoying the feel of her skin on my tongue, knowing that she had touched them both and felt their cold dead skin in the very final moments of their existence, made contact with them in a way I never would.

I licked my lips, taking it all in, every last taste.

Suddenly, I *did* feel more powerful.
Raven was right.
We could do *anything*.

Forty-one

Tyler was asleep when we got back to the car.
He was lying sideways along the back seat, his feet hanging out the window.

"Good to see he's making sure we're not discovered," Raven said as she walked up to the car. "God knows who could've come past and seen this while he's been asleep."

She pushed hard at his shoes, sending his feet flying back inside the car. Tyler woke with a start.

"*Whoa!*" he said, fumbling around for grip as he sat up and rubbed at his eyes.

"Hey, sleeping beauty," Raven said, bending down and sticking her head through the window. "Thanks for a terrific job, Mr Guard Duty Man."

"Sorry," he mumbled as he looked around him. "Must've fallen asleep."

"You think?"

He nodded. "I was tired."

"That much is obvious."

"Maybe I was overcome by Duke's fumes," he added.

That was certainly possible.

I walked around to the other side of the car and climbed in, taking the opportunity to peek through the window at the waistband of Tyler's pants. I got a good look while he was still rubbing his eyes, but I couldn't see the stock of the pistol. It just wasn't there.

Did he move it? Think twice about carrying it? If he did, where was it now?

The flies were still buzzing and Duke smelled as bad as ever. I just hoped and prayed that we would be rid of him tomorrow, that the plan to throw him into the spillway would work and we could try to live normal lives again.

I licked my lips and could still feel the salty taste of Raven's palm.

There's no need to hope. We *would* make it happen!

Raven jumped into the driver's seat.

"You girls have a fun time?" Tyler asked.

Raven looked over to me and smiled. "You could say that."

"Lots of cars heading down this road," he continued.

"Really?'

"Lots of people dressed in black."

He was letting us know that he had an idea about what was happening. He hadn't been asleep that long then, if he'd been asleep at all.

"I guess there's no point asking exactly where you've been or what you've been up to?"

"Nope, none at all."

"Didn't think so," he replied. "But I think I can work it out."

"Can you?" Raven asked.

"Yep. All figured," he nodded as he yawned and stretched.

"Okay, sleepy head," she continued. "Where do we go from here?"

"The valve houses, I guess," Tyler replied as he sat up straight, shaking himself alert.

"I *know* that, but you're the only one who knows how to get there."

"It's not hard." He ran a hand through his hair. "Get back on the main road and follow the signs to Wentworth Dam. I'll direct you from there."

And that's exactly what we did.

***

In the six months since all this has happened, I've been struggling with a whole variety of dreams. No, not dreams. Nightmares. Night terrors. Whatever you want to call them.

Bad Juju.

Karma.

Whatever.

I've already told you about the ones with Duke in the wardrobe (they were the scariest for sure) but there were others too. A whole variety of different horrors and terrors from the depths of my subconscious that had me screaming and bolting from the bed in the middle of the night.

Probably just as bad as the Duke ones is the one where I'm sitting in a small rowboat on a huge river. To begin with, it looks like I'm floating back on the calm waters of the lagoon. I can see the blowhole and a whole mass of wildflowers, and if I turn my head around I can see Raven's trailer behind me. I smile and think to myself, "I'm almost home," and I try to row towards the trailer and the shore, but no matter how hard or fast I try, I stay in the same place.

Then as I look around again, I can't see anything that looks familiar. The lagoon has gone and all I can see is water and desolation, like I'm in the middle of a flood or something. I sit there in the boat and I start to shiver, even though it's a nice day and the sun is out. I call out for Raven, but there's no reply. My voice echoes around me before it fades into the silence. So I turn around in the boat and call out again. Still nothing.

Then, all of a sudden I hear a *popping* noise and the waters around me start to bubble. A casket breaks the water's surface and bobs back and forth, floating towards me. It's an ornate, dark mahogany casket and it looks brand new. The water spills from its seams and it comes to rest right against the side of the boat, knocking against it like it's trying to get my attention. I look over at the casket and bend forward, reading the serial number on the side.

Yes, coffins come with serial numbers now. Raven told me that once. It's used to help identify the corpse if, in a case like this, the casket is unearthed or moved or dislodged from its home in the ground by floods or other natural disasters.

So, I'm looking at the serial number, but it doesn't make too much sense to me. *629w* is what's stamped on the brass plaque screwed to the side of the casket. I have no idea what that means or even if it's a proper serial number, but it's there nonetheless.

I reach out and touch the casket, feel the smoothness of the wood under my palm, and then I reach down to lift the lid. It's heavy and slippery and won't budge. I can't quite get my fingers to grip where they should. But I keep trying nonetheless.

As I do so, I hear more popping sounds, and then another three caskets float to the surface around me. These are different though. These caskets are all rotting and falling apart. I can smell the horrible stench almost straight away as the caskets surround the boat.

I look at each of them, at the disintegrating old wood, at the thick mucus-like black liquid that is pouring out of them and doesn't look like stopping.

I scream for Raven once more, calling out her name at the top of my voice. It echoes and echoes and echoes. And then, as if my scream was their cue, each of the lids of these old caskets spring open, and the rotting carcases bolt upwards into a sitting position, their necks twisting and turning to look at me.

You can't tell who they are from looking at them, because they're all rotting and being eaten by a blanket of broiling maggots. But I *know* who they were, even without being able to identify them.

Dreams are weird that way.

I'm surrounded by the corpses of Duke, Jeremy and Lucy. The girl's corpse is the easiest to identify, as she's wearing that old-fashioned necklace still and the golden threads of her hair flow down her maggot-ridden face and shoulders.

I try to row quickly, as fast as I possibly can, trying with all my might to get away for them, but they float towards me and continue to surround me, their arms out, clawing at me as I fight to keep them away.

My only hope of escape is to open the new casket, the mahogany one that is floating right beside me. As the corpses pull at my hair and my clothes and my arms, their miasmic smell invades the very air I breathe, choking me. I manage to get my hands under the lid of the new casket and begin to lift it up.

For some strange reason I always think the new casket will be empty. Even after I had the dream countless times, every time I lifted the lid and looked down inside, I expected the casket to be empty. But I would always be totally scared and totally shocked to see another corpse in the casket. This one not touched by maggots or any type of decay.

I scream.

And I wake up sweating and shivering and in total terror.

I still get those dreams occasionally, even after all this time.

***

"Park over here," Tyler said, pointing through the windshield.

He was sitting forward in the back seat, his face almost level with ours.

"We can hide both the car and the trailer behind those bushes, no one will see them over there."

"You sure?" Raven asked, as she turned the steering wheel and pointed the car in that direction.

"Yep," he replied. "No one really comes down here anyway, but just to be safe, those trees should hide us well. Plus, we're only about a five minute walk from the dam wall and the valve houses."

"Okay," she nodded.

We were driving towards a small hill that had, just in front of it, a row of tall pines and smaller bushes. They certainly hid the lower part of the hill well, and I was sure you *could* hide both the Suburban and trailer there without anyone noticing them. I mean, if they went around there and looked, then yeah, they'd find us, but if they were just driving past on this small gravel road, then they probably wouldn't even look twice.

We'd entered the official Wentworth Dam National Park only a few minutes earlier. There was a big sign at the gateway that said *Welcome to Wentworth Dam* in weird writing, like it hadn't been updated since the 60s. The main road lead down to a parking lot with signs and information about where tourists should seek out their next great photo opportunity.

There were some cars parked in the lot, and we passed a few families having picnics or barbeques. In one direction was a large cleared area which held a variety of tents and trailers.

Who knows, if we liked it there, maybe we could stay at this trailer park once all this was over.

As we drove, Raven said, "This place looks busy. Are you sure we'll be okay here?"

I was thinking the same thing.

But Tyler had nodded confidently. "Don't worry, we won't go anywhere near where the tourists go. We're heading somewhere else."

And he gave us the directions that took us well away from the tourist areas. Soon the information kiosks and picnic tables gave way to more trees and more bushes. And finally we drove down a small lonely service road which, in turn, led to where we were now. But still, the whole drive had only taken a few minutes from the front gate to here.

Raven drove the car in behind the row of trees and bushes.

We all turned our heads to make sure the trailer would fit, and it did, but only just. The tight squeeze meant it would be hard to get in and out of the trailer without being scraped by branches and leaves from the trees, but I guess that was a small price to pay if it meant we could finally be rid of Duke for good.

Raven turned off the engine and let out a deep sigh.

"Finally," she said.

I climbed from the car, pushed away at some branches from a nearby tree, and looked around. The trees gave shelter from the outside world and also from the sun above. It was starting to set in the sky now that it was mid-afternoon, and the shadows were thrown across the car and trailer, keeping us all in a cool semi-light. The small hill rose steeply behind us, so at least that meant no one would sneak up on us from behind. We really only had to worry about being seen from both ends of the track we had just driven along. And, if what Tyler said was true, that no one came along here anyway, we were probably just as safe here as we had been at the lagoon.

Or, maybe, safer.

"What do you think?" Tyler asked as he climbed out too. "Is this perfect or what?"

Raven closed her door and looked around too. "I like it," she replied. "This just could work!"

"*Could work?*" Tyler replied. "It *will* work!"

"Time will tell," Raven said, as she walked past him and over to the trailer, pushing back the tree branches as she did so. She even snapped some branches too, right near the trailer door, as she unlocked it and stepped inside.

Tyler looked over the roof of the Suburban to me. "You're impressed, right?"

I nodded. "It's pretty cool."

"Told you it would be." He smiled, like he'd scored bonus points in the Get-Amber-To-Like-Me contest.

"How far are the valve houses?" I asked.

"Why?" was his reply.

"I'm just curious. I'd like to see them."

"*Really?*" He sounded surprised.

"Yes, maybe once we settle in here you can take me to them?"

"Yeah, sure," he said, sounding happy and worried at the same time. "I guess I'd need to tidy the place up a bit first."

"Why?"

"Well, you know, I wasn't expecting anyone to drop by or anything. And I *am* a guy."

We both laughed.

Why wouldn't he want me to see the valve house? Why would he be uneasy about that? I was sure it would be fine if Raven wanted to see where he lived.

"Back in a few minutes," Raven called as she stepped down from the trailer.

She was carrying a towel and her toiletries bag.

Tyler turned to look at her, his eyes narrowing. "Where are you going?" he asked.

She pointed over her shoulder. "We drove past a trailer park. They must have showers and other amenities there."

Tyler nodded. "Yeah, they do. I've used them myself."

"Good," she replied as she turned away from us. "I need a shower like you wouldn't believe."

And with that, she walked past the trailer and along the dirt track, heading back the way we had come.

Tyler turned back to face me.

"I better get going too."

"Really? Where?" I asked.

"I'll go clean up the valve house a bit and then you're welcome to come over later, okay? Sound like fun? I'll even come back to get you and escort you there myself."

"You'll have to," I replied. "I don't know where it is."

He laughed, like he hadn't thought of that. "Good point. But it's not that hard to find. If you can find the dam wall – and it's so big you couldn't miss it – and search off to the left, you'll see them."

"Okay," I replied.

"But don't pay me a surprise visit, okay? I want everything to be just right for you."

Yes, so he kept saying.

"Okay," I smiled. "I'll stay here and wait for Raven to return."

"Alright then, I'll head off."

"You do that."

"You'll be fine here by yourself?"

"I'll manage."

"You don't need anything?"

"Like what?"

"I don't know. Anything?"

"I'll survive, I'm sure."

"Okay. See you soon."

"Yep."

"I won't be long."

He was taking his sweet time at that moment!

"Fine. Hurry back!"

And with that I turned and walked around the car, smiling at him as I did so. He smiled back. But neither of us looked away. We both kept our eyes on each other until I arrived at the trailer and opened the door. I climbed the steps and broke eye contact with him as I stepped inside.

The door closed behind me and I stood perfectly still for a couple of seconds. Then, I quickly squatted on the fold-out couch and peered out the small window underneath the storage area.

From there, I could see the back of the Suburban and everything nearby.

Including Tyler.

He was still standing there, hands on his hips, looking at the trailer. But I was pretty sure he couldn't see me.

I hoped so, anyway.

After what was probably a minute or two, when he was sure I wasn't going to step back out of the trailer, he slowly opened the passenger door of the Suburban and bent down inside.

I couldn't see what he was doing in there, but when he climbed back out and straightened up, I saw what he had in his hand.

The pistol.

He slipped it down his pants again, turning quickly so his back was towards the trailer. But it was already too late. I'd seen it in his hand as he climbed out. He must've hidden it in the back of the car or under the seat or something.

Once he was sure the pistol was safely tucked away, he turned back to look at the trailer once more, before zipping up his jacket and walking off through the bushes.

When he was gone, I actually felt relieved. I sat on the couch and stared across the trailer to the bed. After the events of the last few days, I just wanted to curl up and sleep for a week. But I knew I couldn't.

Hang in there, I told myself. By this time tomorrow, Duke will be out of our lives, for good.

I nodded. I was looking forward to that.

And then, there was just Tyler to deal with.

Forty-two

I needed a shower too, but I didn't want to leave Duke alone in case someone came along and stumbled over him.

Not that I particularly cared for his well-being, but I was damn sure I wasn't going to be the one who let the side down now. We'd come this far, I didn't want to leave my post and have something happen to ruin everything. I wasn't going to take the blame for that, no way.

So, I sat in the trailer and played the events of the past week over in my mind and tried hard to get it all in order and to have it make sense. And then I tried to decide about tonight and tomorrow, what would happen and what could go wrong.

We were so close to being rid of Duke now, that it almost felt like I was dreaming.

This time tomorrow, I kept thinking over and over again. He'll be gone by this time tomorrow.

After a while, I heard footsteps on the gravel, and they were getting closer. I jumped onto the bed and looked out the window at the back of the trailer. Raven was walking slowly towards me, her hair up in a towel. She was wearing the same clothes, but she was carrying her sneakers and walking barefoot. I could hear her whistling to *Camptown Races*.

The door to the trailer opened and she walked inside, smiling at me.

"Jeez, do I feel like a million bucks," she said as she threw her toiletry bag onto the table.

"You look it," I replied.

"Sorry I took so long, I had a lot of scrubbing to do, and the showers here are a thousand times better than anything Pine Hills had to offer."

"That's okay," I replied. "You didn't miss much."

"Where's Tyler?"

"He went back to the valve house."

"Oh," she nodded her head, but didn't seem concerned. "Good. We can do without him for a while."

She unravelled the towel from her head and let her wet, dark curls cascade down her face and shoulders.

"It'll be good to just chill out and relax until tomorrow."

"Yes," I agreed, sitting on the bed. "I've been thinking that too. By this time tomorrow, this should all be over."

Raven smiled and walked down towards me. Grabbing my hands in hers, she squatted in front of me so our eyes were level.

"*Exactly*. By this time tomorrow we'll be free from them all," she whispered. Then, she leaned forward and kissed me on the forehead as she stood.

"And hopefully our lives will return to normal," I added.

She stood in the middle of the trailer and removed her t-shirt. My eyes scanned her chest and stomach. Her ribs showed through her skin and both her nipple barbells were shining in the light once more, no longer covered by the red murky liquid splashed there in the mortuary. The scab that had formed on her nipple seemed to have almost gone by now.

Once she'd healed completely, there'd be no memory left of what happened to her. No evidence, no proof.

Then she undid her jeans and bent down, climbing out of them.

She wasn't wearing any underwear, and I could see where she'd had to scrub hard to remove the remaining stains from her body. Parts of her thighs and stomach looked red raw.

"It's great to finally get out of these clothes," she said as she walked towards me, naked.

My eyes dropped further down, making sure she was clean all over. Which she was. Her cleft looked clean and soft and smooth and wonderful.

She climbed onto the bed, crawled to her side and lay down on her back, spreading her arms and legs wide.

"I think I could lie here for days," she said.

And I knew I could lie there next to her for days on end as well.

I was about to do just that when she turned and looked at me.

"You should go and have a shower too," she said.

"Oh," I replied.

She smiled. "Don't take it the wrong way, hon. You don't smell, if that's what you're thinking. You certainly don't smell as bad as I did. It's just that the showers here are really nice and I think you'd enjoy one. Go and have one and come back soon. Then maybe we can both have a rest before dinner."

I liked the sound of that. We could both lie there, clean and naked and together.

Just like it used to be.

Just like it *should* be.

"Okay," I replied. "That sounds like a great idea."

"Be quick."

"I will."

"I don't want to be left here alone for too long," she replied as she closed her eyes.

I grabbed the things I needed, including a change of clothes, and headed for the door.

"Amber!" Raven called to me.

I turned to face her. She was sitting up on her right elbow, her breasts falling slightly at an angle.

"There's a pay phone by the showers," she said. "Take some money and call your father. It's been a while."

I nodded slowly. It was a good idea. I felt wonderful that she'd taken the time to suggest it. She was thinking about me and about my situation, my emotions. And she was worried about me and my father.

That showed she cared.

Really cared.

About me.

About *us*.

"Okay," I said. "I will. Thanks."

"All part of the service, ma'am," she replied as she flopped back onto the bed. "Just don't be too long."

"I won't be."

And with that, I left the trailer and headed for the showers.

***

I won't bore you with the details of my shower or phone call to my dad. For one thing, hearing about how I wash myself is not that interesting (unless you're one of those weird kinky types with a shower fetish), and I'm sure as hell not about to write about it here. But, more importantly, I'm seriously close to running out of pages in this notebook, and I want to make sure I get the story out before I run out of lines to write it in.

So, I had a shower. It was nice. I felt better.

Okay?

I rang my father. He answered. He was drunk and demanded to know where I'd been for the past week, telling me I didn't care and that he was out of food (alcohol) and needed chores to be done (the buying of alcohol). So, it's fair to say that the phone call took a bit of the gloss off my shower, and that I walked back towards the trailer in a grumpy mood.

Of course, the closer I got to the trailer, the better I felt, as I could imagine crawling into bed, right next to Raven as she slept, my skin touching hers, our warm bodies combining and protecting us in a cocoon of relaxation and pleasure.

I tried to keep the conversation with my father out of my mind, but it kept coming back, like all bad memories. They stain you for life, and no matter how hard you scrub, they'll always be there.

Anyway, it wasn't much of a conversation. I said hello and then he just went for it, tearing me to pieces for not being there, not loving him, not caring.

He should've thought of that before he drove his wife into a tree. Asshole.

But, like I said, I was trying to forget all that. It sure wasn't easy though.

Seeing the trailer come into view made me feel a lot better.

Nearly there.

Seeing Raven fully dressed and sitting out the front of the trailer in her deck chair, reading a book, made me feel not so good.

I mean, don't get me wrong, seeing Raven was great, but I'd had my heart set on climbing into bed with her, relaxing and holding her, sleeping with her.

But she had other plans, it seemed.

She'd placed the deck-chair hard up against the side of the trailer, and it looked like she'd trampled on a few of the bushes to give her some room to sit down and read.

As I walked closer, she turned to me and waved.

"How was it?" she called.

"Great," I replied. "They're terrific showers."

She laughed. "I meant the call with your dad."

"Oh, not so hot. About medium," I replied, using the sliding scale we implemented for Amber/Father visits.

"I see," she nodded, returning to the book. "Still, at least you called."

"Yeah, and got an earful from him."

"I guess it's to be expected. He hasn't heard from you since Monday of last week. You just disappeared without a word."

"True," I replied. I guess I couldn't blame him. He was probably worried I'd left him or something.

Not that he didn't deserve that anyway.

Maybe I should've tried to get in contact with him earlier, just to let him know I was okay. But things had been so busy, so hectic, I just hadn't had the time or the opportunity.

He'd never understand any of it anyway.

Raven was wearing a short black vinyl skirt that showed way too much leg (and more) as well as a tight purple corset that covered just enough of her breasts in dark frilly fabric. Between the skirt and corset was pure flesh.

I loved seeing her dressed that way, but I didn't like the idea that Tyler would be back soon to drool over her for sure.

Of course, he wouldn't be drooling over me. I was wearing my best blue jeans and blue Converse sneakers, and I was wearing my black Van Helfin t-shirt once again. Compared to Raven, I looked as drab as could be.

But that was okay, I didn't want Tyler drooling over me anyway.

I returned my dirty clothes and towel to the trailer before I pulled out the milk crate and sat down next to her.

She was reading (the book I had been reading, as it turned out) and I just sat by her, my back resting against the trailer, watching the sun through the trees, getting lower in the sky.

Raven finished a chapter and then put the book aside.

"Do you ever wonder what it would feel like to be dead?" she asked me.

"Huh?"

"Dead. What would it be like?"

"I don't know," I replied. "I've never given it much thought."

Which was kinda half-true. After we buried my mom, I gave it a lot of thought, in fact. But I didn't want to think about it now.

"It would be something, don't you think?" Raven continued. "Spread out on that table in the mortuary. Naked and so alone. At the mercy of anyone."

"I don't know," I replied. "I guess you wouldn't be there to know anyway. You'd be somewhere else."

"Where?"

"I don't know. Heaven? Hell? Somewhere in between? No one knows."

"But that's just it," she said as she turned to face me. "No one knows. So you *could* still be there, trapped inside your body, still conscious of what's going on."

"I guess."

"Just think about it for a moment. What if that guy was still aware of what I was doing to him last night? What if he knew I was on top of him, giving him pleasure as he gave it to me? What if the last thing he remembers before being consigned to the fires of the crematorium today is the image of me naked above him?"

"We'll never know for sure," I concluded.

"If only we could," she turned back around and stared into the trees. "I could be lying there, dead and unable to move, and anyone could do anything they wanted to me. A guy could work there. He could climb on top of me and slide his warm cock deep inside my cold pussy, thrusting in and out, almost as if he was trying to revive me with his love."

"Who?"

"It doesn't matter who. It's a guy, he works there or something. Or maybe he broke in like we did and found me lying out on the trolley, waiting for him."

"I don't think it's very likely," I replied.

"I *know* that, hon. What we did last night wasn't very likely either, but we still did it! Imagine if it happened, though. He'd pump away and soon he'd cum inside me, shooting his warm life-force inside. Life inside a dead vessel. His sperm wiggling and travelling inside me, even though I was dead, seeking out my womb, the female's source of all life."

I didn't say anything. I didn't even want to think of things like this.

"He'd kiss me then as he slips from me, and he'd close my legs, trapping his gift inside me. And while I cooled even more, his warmth would be inside me. I'd go to oblivion with his love flowing through my veins where the blood used to travel. His soul blending with mine, bonding with me, in a way that will never leave my body, never be expelled. It would be the final gift of love…"

She fell silent then for a moment or two.

"…and the best gift of all."

I looked at her. Her eyes were closed and her head was resting on the back of the deck chair. She had a large smile on her face.

"Would you *really* want that?" I asked her.

She nodded. "Of course, who wouldn't?"

"You'd want a man to rape you after you were dead?"

"It's not rape, sweets," she replied, opening her eyes and turning to face me once more. "He's just doing what comes naturally."

"Like Duke, huh?"

"No."

"Or the guy at the gas station?"

"No, Amber, not like that at all."

"Sounds the same to me. Except if you're dead you can't fight back."

"Sweets, you've got it all wrong. It's the purest form of victimless procreation. No one is harmed, abused or emotionally scarred. It's not like rape or any other kind of forced lovemaking. No one is hurt or left with horrific memories. No one. The dead are dead, and the living enjoy every moment. Whether it be a guy or girl fucking me, I'd give my body freely to their love. You don't think that I harmed Jeremy last night, do you?"

"No," I said. But I didn't mention Lucy.

"If he was still there in some way, then I'm sure he enjoyed every moment. No one will ever have bad memories of that night."

Except maybe *me*.

Forty-three

As the sun got lower in the sky, Raven and I continued to sit and relax by the trailer. Because Raven was reading my book, I didn't have a whole lot to do, so I went inside for a while and tidied up, just trying to keep myself busy.

It was clear to me that Raven was settling in for the night, and was quite happy to continue what she was doing. However, I was more than a little restless. I couldn't sit still and I wanted to be doing something.

Maybe I was excited about tomorrow, maybe I was nervous, or maybe I was both. Whichever way, I had to do something to make the time go faster.

Tyler had been gone an awful long while, and that worried me as well.

The restlessness and the worry grew and grew until I really couldn't take it anymore.

"I'm going to find Tyler," I said as I walked out of the trailer.

"Really?" Raven seemed surprised by that.

"Yep."

"Okay," she said, turning a page of the book. "Have fun."

"Somehow I doubt it."

And I set off through the bushes the same way Tyler had gone.

Even though the sun was setting, it didn't take long for me to find the dam wall. You really couldn't miss it. It was huge and quite ugly, and it towered above everything else.

The grey concrete wall, curving through a small valley, looked out of place amongst the trees and the flowers and the bushes. The wall was cracked in countless places, and you could see where it had been patched in dozens more. It was easy to make out where each huge concrete block had been placed on top of the others, the wall building up, piece by piece, and on an angle, curving until the very top where the blocks straightened out and reached for the sky in a vertical finale.

The wall was thick too. Almost as wide as two car lanes on a highway, and I noticed you could walk right along the top of the wall, right across it to the other side, if you wanted. The entrances to the top of the wall were hidden in trees and bushes on both sides, but I could see the pathway leading to the one nearest to me. So I guessed anyone could walk along there if they wanted.

On one side, millions of gallons of water, and on the other, a sheer drop of a couple hundred feet. In between, a few dozen feet of concrete at the most.

A modern wonder.

As I walked down the sloping hill, towards the base of the dam, I could feel the temperature dropping with each step. I guess with all that cold concrete and also with the water on the other side of the wall, the moisture or pressure or something changes the balance on the other side.

There'd be a scientific explanation for it somewhere.

The concrete wall was scarred from years of weathering and the closer to the bottom I walked, the more moss and algae I started to see. Even the grass underfoot started to feel slippery and slimy, and the ground went from being solid to a little spongy and muddy.

I slowed my pace, but continued onwards.

Finally, I made it to the bottom. I stopped and turned my head, looking up at the wall towering above me.

It better not burst right now, I thought to myself. Then I laughed. I bet everyone thinks things like that when they stand at the base of a dam, knowing the only thing stopping millions of gallons of water washing you away was concrete and steel.

I turned my head and looked off to the left, my eyes searching the trees and bushes for the valve houses. Tyler said they were in that direction. Of course, I had no real idea what they looked like, as he had never described them to me, but I soon found both of them.

They didn't look as I imagined they would, but they were the only buildings at the base of the dam, so I knew it must be them.

The valve houses were squat little concrete bunker-like buildings, perfectly round and covered in moss and ivy. If you looked really quickly, you probably wouldn't see them, or would think they were some weird type of tree, as the ivy growing all over camouflaged well with the trees and bushes around them.

They were no more than twenty feet apart from each other and looked exactly the same, completely round and with a dome top, almost like the top of a lighthouse, just without the body.

I walked up to the valve house closest to the base of the dam. Stopping for only a second to inspect it more closely and to make sure no one was watching me, I then walked around it, trying to be as quiet as possible. The roof was slightly larger than the base, so there was a small overhanging veranda all the way around that allowed the ivy to spill downwards, blowing in the breeze.

There was a window high up in the wall, too high for me to see in, and it was covered by a rusting metal grill. The grill looked old and weathered, and I could tell by the number of huge bolts attaching it to the wall that it was there to stay. You couldn't budge it for anything. I thought about trying to climb up and see in, but I really didn't see the point. It was probably so dark in there I wouldn't see anything anyway.

Around the other side of the house was an iron door, set down low, three small steps leading down to it. The door looked just as rusted as the grill on the window, and there was a sign riveted to it telling people to keep out.

But that didn't stop me. I walked down the steps and grabbed hold of the rusting handle.

I pulled. But the door was locked.

Damn.

I tried again, but there was no use. It was locked and wasn't budging.

I thought about knocking. Tyler might be inside. He said he was a locksmith, so there's no reason why he couldn't have duplicated a key and made his home secure.

But I didn't want to announce my presence yet. Just in case. So, I decided I'd check the other valve house first before trying to make myself known to anyone who might be there.

I climbed up the steps and kept walking around the building, until I returned to where I started. It was larger than I thought, probably thirty feet around, but I was still certain it wouldn't hold much inside. Probably no more than three or four people at the most.

I quickly walked across to the other valve house and marched around it, checking it out as well.

They both looked identical to me, even down to the metal grill, warning signs, moss and ivy.

But there was one difference.

I could hear voices coming from inside this one.

Yes!

I walked to the window and tried to listen. I hoped the voices would be clearer there, but I still couldn't hear what was being said. The window was too high to look through, just like the other one, so I couldn't peek in and see what was happening either. I really had no choice. I had to just walk straight in there and find out what was going on.

And that's what I did.

I found the door (just like the other one) and walked down the steps (same again) but the difference this time was that when I pulled on the handle of *this* door, it opened.

I expected a huge clatter or a loud squeak from the rusty hinges, but it wasn't like that at all. The door opened soundlessly and there were five steps descending in front of me. The floor of the valve house was much further down than I expected. The floor was actually lower than ground level outside. I stepped inside slowly, closing the door behind me before walking down the stairs to the concrete floor.

The inside of the valve house looked almost the same as outside, curved concrete walls and little else. Although the ivy wasn't growing in such abundance inside, it could still be seen in patches here and there.

As I entered, I could see Tyler sitting on the left side of the small room. His back was to me; he was sitting on an old stool and he was busy looking at something on a small workman's table in front of him. He was wearing sneakers now, a black t-shirt and a pair of jeans.

My eyes scanned the room quickly.

He was alone.

The voices I could hear were coming from the radio that was sitting on the table next to him. The volume was low and I still couldn't work out what they were saying.

In the middle of the room was a large yellow pipe, probably a full twenty inches in diameter, rising up from the concrete floor and stopping at hip level. The lid of the pipe was sealed tight, with at least a dozen bolts securing it down. On top of the lid was a large red circular handle. The pipe and handle looked very old to me. The paint was peeling and covered in a white crystalline substance that looked like salt but probably wasn't. There was a ceramic plate on top of the handle, a half-eaten apple resting in it, and the remains of other food I couldn't identify. Nearer to the floor, two smaller pipes ran off from the main pipe in different directions, heading towards the walls of the valve house before turning at right angles and burrowing through the floor.

To the right, by the other wall, was a small makeshift bunk. It was low to the ground and made of wood, and looked like it had been hastily put together. The blankets and sheets were all tossed in a pile at the end of the bed and they looked pretty dirty.

Did he really sleep there?

The small window was above the bed and the rays of the setting sun provided just enough light, even through the ivy growing across the grill.

Now that I was inside, I felt a bit out of place, like I was invading his own private world.

I turned quickly to go back outside, thinking maybe I could shut the door and knock and pretend I only just arrived.

I started up the steps.

"You found the place okay then?" Tyler asked.

I turned to look back at him as he shifted around to smile at me.

"Ah, yeah," I replied, a little flustered. "It was easy."

"I told you it would be. By the way, a piece of advice?"

"What?"

"You'd never make a good burglar. You're too noisy."

"Oh, yeah, sorry." I was feeling just a little embarrassed right then.

"So what brings you here to my humble abode?"

"We were worried about you," I answered quickly. "Came to see if everything was okay."

"A-huh." He didn't believe me.

"You were gone so long."

"Wanted to give you girls some space," he replied. "I didn't want to outstay my welcome."

"You could never do that," I lied.

"Really?" His right eyebrow rose in surprise. Now he *definitely* knew I was lying.

I didn't reply.

"Sorry," he said, as he stood and offered me his stool. "There really isn't a lot of space in here for entertaining."

I looked around. "No, it's pretty cramped. But it's okay, I'll stand."

"Suit yourself. I can't even offer you much to eat. I've only got some fruit."

"Don't worry, I'm not hungry."

We stood there staring at each other, the low-pitched blabber of the radio the only noise in the room.

There was no way around this. I had to do it now.

I opened my mouth to speak, but so did he.

"I'm glad you came…" he said.

"You have to know…" I said.

We talked over each other for a few fumbling seconds, then stopped.

"Ladies first," he said.

I took a deep breath and began.

"This can't work, you know."

He looked puzzled. "Sorry? I don't quite know what you mean."

"You and Raven, it can't work. It *won't* work."

"Her and me?"

Was he really *that* dumb, or was he just playing with me?

"Look, I know Raven better than you. I've known her all my life. I've seen things and done things with Raven you just wouldn't believe, and I know that there's no chance she'll fall for you or want to be with you, okay?"

There, I'd said it.

"Back up a little," he replied, holding his palms up as if I was about to physically attack him. "We hardly know each other. We're just friends."

"I *know* what you want."

"Huh? Do you?"

"You want Raven."

"No, Amber. I want – "

"It's clear and plain and easy to see. And I'm here to tell you it *won't* work. You want the same things every man wants and you need to know she's not interested. She knows *exactly* what you're about and what you want. She's *not* stupid and neither am I. She'll never love you, she'll never want you like you want her."

"I see." He nodded. "I understand."

"I don't think you do. She wants something totally different to what you can give her, she wants things you could never imagine."

He crossed his arms in front of his chest and sighed. "You've got it all wrong, so very wrong."

But he couldn't stop me now. "You *fuck* her and you think you own her."

"Fuck her?"

"Yes, I saw it all. I heard it too. Don't you dare try to deny it. You screw her and think you control her, but you're wrong. She's controlling you."

"No one's controlling *anyone*," he replied, leaning up again the workbench and rolling his eyes. "But I think you'd *like* to control the situation more than you can. You'd like to control *both* of us."

"That's not true."

"It is."

"You're lying."

He took a step towards me. "No, I'm not. Amber, please, calm down for a moment. You've got it all wrong. But I think it's time you woke up. It's time to get a dose of reality. No matter how much you love Raven, she's *not* in love with *you*."

I stood there and couldn't think of anything to say. My whole body was frozen and I couldn't move, couldn't think or talk.

"Did you hear me, Amber?" he continued, walking closer to me, his face worried, concerned. "I've been around you both long enough now to know what's going on. She doesn't love you."

I turned around and climbed the stairs, stumbled and lost balance, flung my hands out to grab the steps and half-crawled up them. I had to get out of there quickly, before the tears started to flow, before he saw me lose control and break down.

"Amber!" he called. "*Please!*"

I kept going.

I was on the final stair and was reaching for the door, about to step outside, when I heard him behind me, his arm grabbing my shoulder and turning me around. I tried to struggle, tried to fight back, but he was too strong.

I started to cry.

He hugged me, held me tight for a few seconds.

I'd lost control. He'd taken it from me.

He walked me back down the steps and over to the stool. I didn't fight, I didn't even try. There was no point. I just let the tears roll down my cheeks as I sat down. He squatted down in front of me.

"I'm sorry," he whispered, a sad smile on his face. "I didn't want to hurt you like that. I probably said too much."

He looked deeply into my eyes, our faces just inches apart.

I shook my head and closed my eyes. The tears continued.

How could he be so hurtful? How could he be so *wrong* about things?

Suddenly I didn't have the strength to go on and fight, I didn't care anymore. I was tired and stressed and I just didn't care.

"Here." He gave me a handkerchief to blow my nose.

After a few minutes, I calmed down. He was standing now, resting against the pipe in the middle of the room.

"Sorry," he said again.

"It's all right," I replied in a crackling small voice.

But it wasn't.

Why are all men so hurtful? If they're not scarring you physically with their strength, they're scarring you emotionally with words.

He just didn't understand the real story.

"I really *am* here to help you, okay? You do believe me, right?"

I nodded again.

Here to help himself to Raven.

"And I can prove it," he continued. "I'll show you. Look at this."

He reached over to the workbench and handed me a crumpled newspaper. It had weird coffee stains and food stains all over it, and it smelled bad too.

"I was reading this when you came in. You should read it too."

I scanned the newspaper. It had today's date, and it also had our story as front page news.

POLICE CLOSE IN ON DRUG RUNNERS was the headline.

"The reason I was so long," Tyler continued as I read, "was because I wanted to see if I could find today's newspaper. It took me a few searches in some trash cans around here before I found it. Plus, I wanted to have a shower, so I did that as well. I haven't been back here long myself."

I finished reading the article.

Most of the information in the article we'd already heard from the radio reports, but there was one bit of news I didn't know, and it wasn't good.

The guy from the gas station had died yesterday from his head injuries.

Fuck!

So we had two murders stacked against us now.

As if one wasn't enough.

Still, at least the media and cops didn't know we'd killed Duke. From what I read, the police still thought Duke was the leader of our little gang and that he was responsible for the bashing (now killing) of the gas station guy. Maybe we *could* get away with this after all, if Duke could take the blame somehow!

"There's more," Tyler said as I lifted my head from reading the article. "I just heard it on the radio. They found the rope."

"Huh?"

"You know, the one you girls were using to keep Duke all nicely tied up?"

"We took it with us when we left the lagoon," I replied.

He shook his head. "Nope. It was just part of a newsflash on the radio. They're at the lagoon now, the cops I mean, and they've found a long piece of rope with what appears to be bodily fluids on it, along with quite a few dead maggots. They say they're not sure what this means right now, but they're combing the area for more clues."

At the lagoon!

They were *that* close?

"Are you sure that's what they said?"

"Positive."

"But we took the rope with us!"

"Do you remember *actually* packing it? Or have you seen it since?"

I shook my head to both questions.

Somehow, we'd left it behind.

Double Fuck!

Just how could *that* happen?

"Time's running out," I whispered, my eyes dropping to the floor.

"It sure is. Let's hope they don't reach here until after tomorrow. As soon as the spillway opens, we can dump the body and get out of here."

I nodded.

"Where's Raven?"

"I left her at the trailer, she was reading." I was talking, but I wasn't really listening. My mind was spinning with the news that the cops were so close to us. Tomorrow *had* to work. Tomorrow was the last chance to make it all work out.

"I was just heading back to tell you both about what I heard on the radio," Tyler said.

One last chance.

"I'll tell her," I replied as I stood up from the stool.

"We can both go together."

"No," I added. "Raven asked me to come down here and tell you she thinks it would be better if you stayed here at the valve house tonight. And we'll stay in the trailer."

"Really?"

I hoped he would believe me.

"Yes." I nodded.

"Then why didn't she come down here and tell me herself?"

I rolled my eyes. "Because she's not *interested* in you and doesn't care about the valve houses. We were talking about it while you were gone and we both agreed it would be better for you to stay here, because you're crowding us in the trailer and I said I'd come and tell you because I wanted to see the valve houses anyway. That's why I'm here."

He nodded and turned away.

"Okay, sure. Whatever."

"Then, in the morning, I'll come and get you and then we'll get Duke and we'll prepare for the spillway opening. Okay?"

"Sounds fine to me," Tyler said as he flopped down onto his bed. "Whatever Raven wants is fine by me."

He picked up an old tattered Batman comic and started reading it, totally ignoring me. It didn't take a brain surgeon to realise this conversation was at an end.

I turned and walked back up the stairs, heading out of there before he could say anything else.

I braced myself for some cutting final remark, but it never came. I walked from the valve house, closing the door behind me, and out into the clearing in front of the dam wall.

He didn't say a thing, or even come after me.

I smiled as I walked away.

I'd put him in his place, and I was back in control.

I walked up the slope beside the dam wall and back towards the trailer.

The sun had set now, the twilight was giving way to darkness, and I didn't want to be left out here alone at night. While I was confident of finding my way back with some light, I wasn't too sure how I would manage in the dark. Even in this murky twilight, things looked different to me.

But it wasn't long until I was walking up the track towards the trailer. I only looked back a couple of times, while the valve houses where in sight, to make sure Tyler wasn't following me.

But he was probably still on his bed, reading his Batman comic and sulking.

I walked quicker up the dirt track. The trailer was dark.

Raven must've been asleep already.

I crept closer and tried to be as quiet as possible.

He'd said I'd never make a burglar. The fucking nerve of the guy!

The deckchair was folded and resting against the side of the trailer. My book was sitting on the milk crate.

I reached down and picked it up. The night air was getting chilly and damp.

I hoped Duke didn't mind a touch of frost.

I turned to look at the Suburban.

It was gone.

I blinked and looked harder, as if maybe the twilight was somehow masking the car from me.

It wasn't there.

The trailer had been unhooked and the car was gone.

"Raven," I called softly.

No answer.

"Raven!"

I fumbled for the trailer door – my hands wouldn't work like they should – and the cold metal was wet with dew. But finally I got it open. I climbed inside and stared into the dark interior.

"Raven?"

I felt my way across to the kitchen, my fingers digging around in the top drawer for a box of matches. I found them, opened the box quickly and struck one along the side. The flame flickered into life.

The trailer was empty.

The bed unslept.

Raven was gone.

Forty-four

Sit tight.

-- Raven

That's all the note said. I'd found it on my pillow and read it over and over.

I sat on the bed and didn't know what to do. My mind was working overtime, but even so, I had no idea what I should be doing.

Did someone come along? Did Raven flee with the body to save Tyler and me?

Was it the cops?

No, if it was the cops, they would've left someone behind to catch us.

What if it was worse?

That's what scared me the most. What if it was the drug guys after Duke?

What if it was worse than *that*?

What *if...*

I needed to tell someone, I needed to talk it all through, but Tyler was the only one I could turn to right now, and that was the last thing I wanted to do. I couldn't do that. Going back to the valve house now, like this, with this news, would hand control back to him and I didn't want that.

I was a big girl. I could work through this on my own and make sure everything was okay.

But I really didn't have a plan, other than fleeing.

Yes, *fleeing...*

After all, there was nothing here to link me to Duke or Raven, no body and no evidence. Only me sitting there right then was enough to implicate me.

Pack your things, girl, and *vamoose*!

And I *did* seriously consider it for a time.

Although I wouldn't do that, I *couldn't* leave Raven like that.

But she did that to me!

No, no. She wouldn't leave without a valid reason.

I stopped myself each time I got ready to make the trek back to the valve house. It was dark now, pitch black outside, and there was no hope of finding my way in the night anyway.

I could've used the flashlight, but I didn't want to go. It would look like I was weak, like I needed his help and I wasn't crawling back to him.

No, I'd have to work this one out myself.

So, I hit on a plan and told myself to stick to it.

I'd sit there, in the dark, and wait.

Wait to see what happened.

And that's exactly what I did.

***

I guess my exhaustion took over from the worry at some stage and I must've fallen asleep on the bed.

But I woke to the sound of an idling engine.

At first, I panicked, sat up and froze, trying not to breathe or move an inch, just in case they would discover I was in there.

Who "they" were, I had no idea. But I wanted to make sure, no matter what, that they wouldn't hear me.

But then the engine cut out and I could hear the car door open and shut, followed by footsteps on the gravel.

My eyes moved across to the trailer door. Even though I couldn't really see it in the darkness, I knew where it was located and I held my breath, ready for anything.

It swung open silently, and I could make out a murky shape in the darkness, but little more. I heard footsteps on the stairs and I felt the trailer rock gently back and forth as the figure's weight was transferred onto the floor.

My hand reached out beside the bed, feeling for the box of matches. I didn't really want to use them, but I knew I had to see who was there. I'd have control if I could surprise them by striking a match.

I needed that control back, and so that's what I did.

I fumbled with the box, the matches sliding around inside and sounding loud in the silence. I grabbed one and struck it fast.

The match flared, and Raven sure got a surprise when the trailer filled with light.

So much of a surprise that she almost dropped the small urn she was carrying in her hands.

"*Fuck*, Amber!" she called, as her eyes squinted and she fumbled with the small brown object. "Tell me when you're going to do that!"

I was so relieved I didn't know how to show it. I let out a whoosh of breath and smiled at her. I lit a candle near the bed and then blew out the match before jumping up and walking towards her.

"You're back!"

She nodded as she placed the urn very carefully on the meals table. "Of course I'm back. Where else would I *go*?"

"I don't know. Your note didn't say."

"Yeah," she said as she turned to face me. "Sorry about that. I had an idea and I just had to go through with it. Plus, I didn't think I'd be gone this long. It took longer than I thought."

By then I was standing next to her, looking at her clothes. She'd changed out of her black vinyl skirt and skimpy chest corset, and she was wearing another pair of jeans, sneakers and a brown tank top with the words *Orgasm Donor* written across it in large lettering.

Not that you could read the words too easily, as the t-shirt and jeans were covered in a thick layer of dust and dirt. Raven's hair was all tattered and dirty too.

She looked down at herself, following my glances.

"Yeah, sorry about that," she said, brushing some of the dirt to the floor. "Looks like I'm a candidate for another shower."

"Where have you been?" I asked.

"Where's Tyler?"

"He's at his valve house."

"Oh," she replied. "*Still?*"

"Yes, he decided he wanted to stay the night down there, by himself, in his own place."

"Really?"

Oh, yes, really!

"I asked him to come and join us, but he seemed more at home reading his huge pile of Batman comics."

"He reads *comics?*" Raven looked astounded.

I nodded.

She laughed and turned around in a circle. "Well, the things you learn about people!"

I laughed with her too. "He said he'd meet us in the morning and we'd get rid of Duke then."

"Okay."

"You *do* still have Duke, right?" I asked, just making sure.

She nodded. "Yep, I took him for a spin, but I didn't get rid of him, even though he's stinking up the place worse than ever. I still think tomorrow's plan is the best."

"Me too."

We went silent then as Raven slipped behind the meals table and sat down on the couch. Her eyes rested on the urn and her hands reached out to grasp it.

"Where did you find that?" I asked.

"Pine Hills cemetery," she replied in a whisper, her eyes coming up to meet mine.

I didn't have to ask anything more.

I knew exactly what it was.

And *who* was inside.

Forty-five

Slowly, she unscrewed the lid.
"Raven, don't," I replied.
But she didn't stop.

Turn after turn after turn, the lid scraped around and around, and then eventually it came away.

She leaned forward and looked inside.

I couldn't help myself, I wanted to look too. So I walked forward, my eyes falling deeper and deeper into the urn.

Inside was a fine light-brown-grey powder. It was heaped in there, filling no more than two thirds of the urn.

And that was it.

Nothing more and nothing less.

"Oh," I muttered, almost sounding disappointed.

Raven's eyes met mine. "What did you expect?"

"I have no idea. Just...I guess...*more*."

She nodded. "I know what you mean."

She rested the lid on the table and then reached into the urn with a finger.

Don't!

But she did.

Her finger swirled around in the ashes for a few seconds, sinking in deep and coming back out with the dust sticking to her skin.

She brought it closer to her face and sniffed at it guardedly.

"Smells of burnt stuff," she replied.

Then she opened her mouth and touched her finger to her tongue, tasting the ashes.

Tasting Jeremy Xavier all over again.

"How did you get this?" I asked, slipping in beside her at the meals table and trying to take her mind off tasting the guy one final time.

"When I was sitting outside by myself, and playing all the events of last night and today over and over in my mind, I realised I was missing something, one last thing, and that was to say goodbye to him properly. If I had the opportunity to be with him one last time, I should take it. But I didn't see how I could, knowing that he'd been cremated and everything. There's just nothing left, right? And then I remembered that old woman telling me where they were to be buried and I knew I had to give it a shot."

She dipped her finger back into the urn, swirling it round and round.

"I knew *exactly* where the Pine Hills cemetery was, and we still had the shovels. So, I thought the opportunity was just too good to miss. I unhooked the trailer, took a shovel and drove down, probably a few minutes after you left. I'm sorry I didn't leave a longer, more detailed note, but there just wasn't time."

"I was really worried when I came back and saw you weren't here."

"Yeah," she smiled at me, but she was concentrating on rubbing the ashes between her fingers, feeling its consistency as she did so. "Sorry. I didn't know I would be that long. It took…ah…a little while *longer* to get into the cemetery than I thought. I just figured I could use the shovel to somehow break open the gates, but they're all steel and very modern and I just couldn't get in that way. I had to walk around the cemetery, looking for a tree large enough, with branches that overhung the main fence. It took me a while to find one in the dark. Then I climbed it and jumped across."

"Weren't you scared of being caught?"

"Of course! But that's all part of the excitement, right?"

"I guess."

"Then I had trouble finding the place where they keep the urns. But once I did, it was easy." She lifted the urn in her hands again and rotated it around slowly. "He was housed in such a small, cramped little hole. I was really just there to pay my last respects, to say a few words and to let him know he was the best fuck of my life. But it seemed such a *waste*, just bricking him up in that small place forever. It just didn't seem right to leave him there. So I used the shovel to pry off the metal plaque. It was so easy, I don't think the glue had dried yet anyway, and he was sitting there, just waiting for me. So I took him. Saved him."

"I can't believe you did that!"

"Try some," she said, dipping her finger back into the urn and scooping some of the ash out for me.

I shook my head.

"Go on," she said again. "He won't bite."

I have to admit I was a bit curious.

So I leaned forward and opened my mouth, taking inside Raven's finger and the small pile of ashes heaped there. I sucked hard.

The ash was gritty, and tasted slightly bitter. It smelled of burnt wood and something else I just can't describe.

"And no one saw you?" I asked, as I worked the ash around in my mouth.

"Nope. At least, I don't think so. They would've kicked up a hell of a fuss if they did."

I'd worked most of the ash away with my tongue by now, swallowing some while the rest just seemed to dissolve.

"What are we going to do with him?" I asked. "Another souvenir?"

She nodded. "I guess so. We've amassed quite a collection, haven't we?"

"We need a little display cabinet for them all," I said as I smiled.

Raven laughed loud. It was so good to see her smile and have her laugh like that.

"Yeah," she replied. "But where would we put it?"

We both laughed then and it felt good and healthy. Once the laughter had faded, we both sat there for a few seconds longer, so close to each other on the couch, our eyes locked, our legs touching.

"Thank you for being such a great friend, Amber."

I smiled and had to look away. "It's my pleasure," I whispered.

Raven's hand touched my knee, gently stroked and squeezed for a second. And then she was gone, standing up quickly and walking across to the bed, opening the cupboard doors above it and shifting through our bathroom stuff.

"I've got an idea," she said as she did so. "It'll be so cool."
"What are you looking for?"
"The Vaseline."
"The next cupboard," I told her.

She found it and her smile widened. She turned to me, pulled the lid off the jar and stared inside. "Almost a full bottle!"

"Yeah, we bought some just a week or two ago."

A week or two ago, when life was so normal. No Duke, no Tyler, no cops...

The *cops*!

"Come over here, Amber," she said in a deep slow voice.

I'd forgotten to tell her what I'd learned from the newspapers and reports in the valve house.

"Raven, I have to tell you something." I said as I stood and walked over to her.

"Take off your clothes," she commanded.

"But this is real important."

"No, sweets. It can wait. *This* is more important right now. Take off your clothes."

I did what I was told. I didn't hesitate. The fire was back in Raven's eyes. My Raven was in control again.

Quickly, I took off my t-shirt and unbuttoned my jeans, stepping out of them after kicking off my sneakers. I stood in front of her once I was finished.

"Bra and panties too."

I unhooked the bra then bent over to remove my panties.

And then I was naked, standing there in front of Raven, and her eyes took in every part of me.

Her smile got wider.

"Lie on the bed."

I walked past her and climbed onto the bed, moving slowly so she could see every inch of me. Every curve, every muscle, every crevice.

And I lay down on my back, spreading my arms and legs wide.

She put the Vaseline on the bed and then removed her *Orgasm Donor* t-shirt (she wasn't wearing a bra); her shoes and jeans were next, and I noticed she wasn't wearing any underwear either.

She stood over me. Her breasts swung down, close to my face. I could see the barbells so clearly, so shiny, and what was left of her scar.

"Lie back, relax and close your eyes," she whispered.

Which is exactly what I did.

After a few seconds, I could feel her kneeling on the bed next to me. I wanted to look, so desperately to peek, but she said to keep my eyes shut, and that's what I was going to do. I didn't want this to stop for anything.

I was holding my breath, and I listened for any sound, anything that would tell me what was to come next.

And then her hands were on me. They were sticky and slick with Vaseline, rubbing all over my chest, arms and breasts, kneading and massaging, slowly heading lower to my stomach and hips.

She stopped only long enough to get more Vaseline out of the jar and onto her fingers. Then she continued her work, rubbing and massaging slowly lower.

When her hands touched my vagina, I moaned loudly. I didn't mean to, it just slipped from me as I felt her fingertips roll across my lips and pry them slightly open, her fingers sinking further in, deeper, then finding my clitoris and rubbing slowly, rhythmically.

She stopped after a short while, removing her fingers gently, before moving on further down to my thighs.

I wanted her to go back, to move higher once again. I wanted to feel her probing me, discovering me.

Entering me.

But when she had rubbed the Vaseline into my thighs, her hands left me and I felt the bed rock as she stood up. I could hear the sound of her bare feet slapping on the floor and I turned my head to sneak a quick peek at what she was doing.

She was standing in the middle of the trailer, rubbing Vaseline all over her body too.

I couldn't stop looking. I wanted to watch.

Needed to.

Her eyes were closed now, so I was safe to watch a bit longer.

One hand was rubbing the Vaseline over her breasts and chest, the other was working lower, rubbing her stomach and slipping through the thin line of pubic hair, darting lower before curling and sliding inside.

I watched as she used the last of the Vaseline on herself, scooping out the final globs and running them down both arms, returning for one final rub of her clitoris before opening her eyes and turning her back to me.

All this was done in silence.

Complete silence.

And then she walked over to the table, picked up the urn, and tipped it sideways, pouring a small pile of ashes into her other hand.

She looked at me and smiled.

I quickly shut my eyes again, hoping she hadn't seen me. But she had. We both knew it, but neither of us cared.

The trailer rocked as she walked back to the bed. I felt the springs take her weight and I knew she was above me again.

"Feel his power," she whispered. "Take his life-force."

And then the ashes were showering over me. It was weird at first, a funny tickling feeling, but then I quickly got used to it. It felt just like I was out walking in the snow, the flakes pattering down all over me.

I felt so energised.

So *alive*.

The ashes fell across my chest and breasts in waves, back and forth, and then lower, lower still, across my hips and then down my thighs.

Raven kept the best until last.

She paused for a second or two, and I almost thought she wasn't going to go through with it, but I guess she was teasing me, making me want it more. Finally, I felt the ash float onto my vagina, softly touching it, gently landing and sticking and holding and joining.

Becoming me.

I was so horny I thought I was going to cum right there and then. So horny and wet and turned on.

My eyes shot open. I couldn't keep them shut any longer. I *had* to watch and take everything in.

Raven was leaning on the bed, her face only inches from my vagina, her eyes concentrating hard as she scattered the ashes across my pussy. She looked so shiny and so right, so perfect in every way.

She turned her head and smiled at me.

"How do you feel?"

"Wonderful."

She nodded. "I thought so."

She changed positions, leaning forward, crawling back up my body towards me. Within seconds she was kneeling over me, our bodies just inches apart, her face above mine, her breasts above me, her pussy just inches from mine, her cleft wet and glistening.

Inviting.

She smiled as she looked down at me. She bit her bottom lip.

"You look so hot," she whispered.

I opened my mouth to answer, but I didn't get the chance. Raven's lips slapped mine hard and I could feel her tongue deep inside my mouth, prodding and playing, probing and searching.

Her body lowered too. I felt the cold steel of her barbells touching and dancing across my nipples, her ribs digging deep into my stomach and, further down, her pussy grinding hard and fast against mine. Our bodies rubbed against each other, the friction caused by the ash was painful to begin with, but then became sensual, a good hurt, something that made this moment even more special.

We kissed and hugged and made sure our bodies didn't part.

At one stage, Raven grabbed me in a tight embrace and we flipped over on the bed. Suddenly I was on top, I was the one pushing hard against her, feeling her breasts flush with mine, feeling her strip of pubic hair slippery and wet and warm against my clit.

I have no idea how long we were like that. Kissing and hugging and grinding. Hands and lips and skin and breasts and more.

It was just perfect. I never wanted to leave Raven's embrace.

Ever.

We were there together, for each other.

We were one. We had control.

And we could thank Jeremy Xavier for that.

Wednesday, July 17.

Forty-six

I don't know when it happened, but we must've fallen asleep in each others arms at some point in time.

I can remember waking up on top of Raven, her warm body spread out underneath me, our skin still glued together with the Vaseline and ash and sweat and more.

She looked so peaceful, so at rest, I didn't want to disturb her. So I placed a soft kiss on her lips before I slowly began to lift myself away.

I thought the sound of our skin sliding apart might wake her, but there was still enough Vaseline left on our bodies to allow me to lift myself up without making too much noise.

Slowly, I climbed from the bed.

It was late, I was sure. The candles had burned low, but it had been the perfect night.

I could still taste some ash in my mouth, so I walked over to the kitchen and grabbed a warm can of Pepsi from the refrigerator. I drank it down and it spread through me.

Putting the can down, I turned to the meals table and picked up the urn. There wasn't much ash left. It looked like we'd used most of it.

Thanks for making this night so special, I thought as I looked at the ashes. I didn't say anything though. I didn't want to wake Raven.

I put the urn back on the table and looked across at her. She was lying on her back, her hair messed above her on the pillow, framing her beauty. She was covered in brown ash, just like I was, although it wasn't so much ash now as a dusty grey-brown smear. It looked like we'd painted each other's bodies with weird paint.

But she looked great nonetheless.

I peered down at my own body, at the smears and lines and swirls of ash and passion.

Yes!

I started to pace up and down the room. I felt energetic and strong and I needed to be doing something.

I paced up and back, up and back.

The ash still stuck to my body and, in a short time, my personality shifted gears in a sense. I was fully conscious of what I was doing, but it was like I had received a kind of emotional injection, a psychological rush that was not only sexual but also opening my mind to a new sense of strength and gratification.

And only Raven and I would feel it. It was a feeling that only those who have touched or worn dead human remains could fully feel, let alone appreciate. It was an overpowering feeling of control of my own destiny, of wanting and *obtaining* what I most dearly desired.

I felt invincible.

I felt the urge to stroll naked out of the trailer, down to the valve house and show Tyler exactly what Raven wanted and needed. What we *both* needed. To tell him to fuck off because he certainly wasn't needed here anymore. I'd do all this with a smile on my face, massaging the ash into my pores, around my nipples, inside my pussy and across my clit. He wouldn't know what to do. He might just drop dead on the spot.

Or flee.

Even better!

But I didn't do that. I wouldn't leave Raven's side. But I knew I *could* go down there and do exactly what I imagined, and that was all that mattered.

"It feels good, don't you think?"

I turned around. It was Raven. She was lying on her side now, her head propped up on her arm. She was smiling and looking at me.

I'd been so caught up in how I was feeling, I hadn't noticed she had woken and was looking at me. I have no idea exactly how long I was pacing in the trailer, or how long she was watching me either.

Still, her skin shined in the overhead light and the brown swirls that our bodies had painted stretched across her wonderful skin.

"It does," I replied. "I feel so *alive*."

She nodded. "This is the best yet. The *ultimate* rush."

I agreed.

She swung her legs over the side of the bed and sat there on the edge, looking me up and down.

"Do I look okay?" I asked.

"You look terrific," she replied. She held out her arms to me and I walked across to the bed, falling into them and hugging her tight.

I sat down next to her and we looked deep into each other's eyes.

"We've seen so much, been through so much together," I whispered. "Let's never part, okay? Let's never let anyone get in the way of what we have."

She smiled a sad smile. "Sshh," she replied, touching my lips lightly with a finger. "Don't speak. We have a lot to do soon and we have to make sure it all goes to plan."

I knew that, but I didn't want to think about it now. It was still early morning and I just wanted to enjoy these moments I was spending with her.

"I know," I whispered.

I reached out and hugged her again, bringing her closer and feeling her warmth, feeling her curls across my forehead and cheeks.

We held the embrace for a while.

"You feeling itchy?" Raven asked as she pulled away from me.

In fact, I was a little. The Vaseline was drying and the ash was starting to irritate in places, mostly in crevices and under my arms and between my thighs. Although my vagina wasn't itchy. I put that down to the fact that there was more than enough moisture in there for now.

"A little," I said.

Raven stood up and moved to the kitchen sink, grabbing a hand towel as she walked. She brought it back to the bed.

"Lay down," she whispered.

I did exactly that, spreading my arms and legs wide. Raven spent the next couple of minutes wiping the Vaseline and ash from my arms and legs. She climbed onto the bed and straddled my thighs. A couple of times, the towel touched my vagina, and I'm sure at least once her hand touched there again too.

I willed her to let it stay there, but she pulled away and continued cleaning me up. Just like I did when I cleaned her after our problems at the gas station.

The gas station... The guy. They said he'd died.

"Raven, I –"

"Don't speak," she whispered. "Not yet."

When she had finished, only a small amount of ash and Vaseline remained, and it stretched from my chest, down between my breasts and ended just below my bellybutton.

"Another souvenir," she told me as she climbed off me and lay down next to me. "My turn."

And I did the same to her. Paying very close attention to her vagina and breasts, making sure the ash didn't interfere with her barbells or her scar.

I wiped away the ash from her arms and legs, and the insides of her thighs, leaving enough on her chest and between her breasts, just like she had done for me.

I was kneeling down, wiping her pussy when she let out a little giggle.

For a moment, I thought the towel was tickling her, so I pulled it away, but she was still giggling.

"What is it?" I asked.

She shook her head. "Nothing."

"Go on," I continued. "Tell me."

She folded both arms behind her head and looked down along her body at me.

"I was just thinking, that's all. If Tyler was here watching us now, he'd be so turned on. He'd have cum so much his balls would've fallen off."

"*Tyler?*"

"Yeah," she looked at me strangely. "You remember him? Big guy? Been here with us for the past few days."

I sat back on my haunches. "*Yes*, Raven. I remember him. I just can't believe you were thinking about him."

"Why not?"

"Not right *now*, while we're here together like this."

"But that's *exactly* why I was thinking about him. Because we *are* here like this and he'd be so turned on his cock would probably explode."

I didn't want to be talking about Tyler.

"You can't do all this with him, you know," I said.

"I know that, hon. I can do this *only* with you."

"Exactly!"

"Still...I wonder what he's doing."

I rolled my eyes and threw the towel to the floor. "After everything we've done together? After all this? You wonder what *he's* doing?"

She nodded. "Yes, it's strange he didn't want to stay here tonight, that's all."

"Maybe he doesn't like us."

"Oh, I think he *does*, hon. Very much indeed."

I climbed off both Raven and the bed. I stood in the middle of the trailer with my arms folded in front of me. All this talk of Tyler made me feel lonely, sad and angry. And very exposed.

"What is it?" Raven asked.

Was she serious? Did she really *not* know? Not understand?

I turned to face her.

"You don't know him," I replied. "You don't know *anything* about him."

"So? What's that got to do with it?"

"A whole lot, he could be *anyone*!"

"Well, he doesn't know a whole lot about us either, hon. We could be *anyone* too."

"He knows enough. Way too much."

Raven lifted herself into a sitting position on the bed, resting her back against the wall of the trailer.

"Honey, you're not making much sense."

"You can't trust him, Raven. You just *can't*! You can't let him in between us."

"He's *not* getting in between us."

"Yes, he *is*!"

"He's not here now, is he? If he wanted to be here with us, he would be. But he's not!"

I sighed deeply. "He's not here because I *told* him you didn't want him here!"

There was silence between us and a look of confusion spread over Raven's face.

"Say that again," she said slowly.

"He's not here because when I went down to the valve house to see him I told him you didn't want him anywhere near us tonight or any more."

"You did *what?*"

"Don't worry," I replied. "I don't think he believed me anyway."

"Why would you do a thing like that?"

"*Why?* Why do you think? Because he's coming between us. He already has!"

"He hasn't, hon."

"This is how it should be, tonight, *this* is what it should be like every night. Just you and me, Raven, and no one else!"

She folded her arms across her breasts. "So you *lied* to him and told him *I* didn't want him around?"

"It's for your own good."

"*I'll* decide what's good for me, Amber. Do you understand?"

This was all going so wrong. After such a great night together, after being so close, this conversation was dragging us apart so fast.

"You just don't understand," I mumbled.

"I think you're jealous," she said. It came out sounding like she was disgusted with me.

"*Jealous?*"

"Yes, I think you want Tyler for yourself and I think you're jealous that he wants me instead of you!"

How could she get the facts so wrong?

"I think you need to take a moment and have a real good look at yourself, Amber. You can't stay here forever. I can't protect you forever. Someday soon you're going to have to go out into that big, bad scary world and survive by yourself. I won't always be here to help you and maybe I shouldn't have helped you in the first place. Especially when you plot and scheme and lie behind my back."

"I *don't* lie!"

"Don't you?"

What did she mean by that?

"No, I don't. *I'm* not the one who lies. You're the one who plays a game every night you're at work and with every man you meet. *You're* the one who needs to control them. *You're* the one who lies, dancing up there on stage, showing them how you'll put out for them, cum for them, but never actually doing it. *You're* the one who's fake."

She laughed then. "Hon, I lie for entertainment. But *you* lie to believe yourself! Your whole life is a lie, you've even begun believing your own stories."

"My own stories?" I couldn't believe she'd said that, so I hit back hard. "*You're* the one who changes stories to suit who you're talking to. You're the one who can play all innocent when I know you're not. It wouldn't surprise me if you led on the guy at the gas station and enjoyed every minute of the encounter until it got out of control."

I didn't really believe that, but judging by Raven's shocked look and the silence between us, I realised I may have been correct.

So, I continued. "You don't know me. You think you do, but you don't."

"I can see that now."

"I'm not just another pawn in your big game, to be moved around at will, Raven. I'm sorry, but –"

"I don't know if I can trust you anymore," she said.

How did such a wonderful night get so twisted and destroyed so fast?

"I had no idea you felt this way," she continued.

"It's hard for me," I replied. "I didn't know how to say things sometimes."

"But I'm your friend. Why couldn't you just tell me?"

I looked to the ground, at my feet. Some of the ash had spilled down there too.

"*Why*, Amber?"

"Because I didn't know if I could trust you either."

There, I'd said it.

There was silence between us.

Long. Heavy.

"Couldn't trust *me*?" she whispered.

"That's right."

"Why?"

I turned on her then, swung around and rushed towards the bed, my hands raised, fingers pointing like daggers. "Because you were *fucking* him in our trailer. *Fucking* him while I was here! *Fucking him instead of fucking me!*"

She braced herself, like she was ready to ward off my attack. But I stopped at the side of the bed and looked down at her.

Her mouth was open wide. So were her eyes.

"All I ever wanted was for *you* to fuck *me*..." I whispered. "To love *me* the way I loved *you*. Is that too much to ask?"

No reply. Raven was still.

I turned away and fumbled for my jeans and t-shirt that were still piled on the floor.

Raven didn't say anything. She just watched me as I dressed. I didn't worry about underwear, I didn't even worry about my shoes. I headed for the door slowly, waiting for her to call me back. To take me in her arms and apologise and tell me everything would be okay.

But she didn't.

I stepped out of the trailer and into the darkness of the night, my tears blinding me as I ran through the forest.

Forty-seven

I just walked and walked, with no real design or plan. It was dark and I couldn't see much anyway, but I just knew I wanted to be as far away from the trailer as possible right now.

I'd said what I had to say. It was up to Raven to think it all through, and to decide what she really wanted and who she really loved.

I walked, I cried.

And I eventually found myself standing on the top of the dam wall. I stopped and looked over the side, out across the millions of gallons of water below. The wind blew stronger up here and I was shivering, the concrete cold on my bare feet.

Everything looked so peaceful.

I didn't really care about anything much right then.

Raven had said some really horrible things to me back at the trailer. I didn't want to be friends with somebody who could be like that towards me.

It was all becoming clear to me now. She wanted my respect and that got me so mad. Because she couldn't have it. Respect is *earned*, not just given, and that's what she didn't understand.

I think she wanted me to treat her like everyone else did, to hold her in great admiration, up on a pedestal and to bow down before her.

Just like Tyler did.

But he wasn't a friend. Not a true one. He was an admirer. A lover. He's there for one thing, and she's giving it to him so easily.

I was being her *true* friend, her soul mate, and was treating her like I wished she would treat me. As an equal. As a partner. And I was being realistic, totally honest with her.

As I stood on the dam wall, looking out over the water and to the full moon above, I didn't really know if I wanted to be friends with her right now. It would make me feel like I had failed myself... short-changed myself, if I backed down.

She's mad at me when she should really be mad at Tyler.

Why couldn't she understand what I was trying to tell her?

Why?

Why, all of a sudden, did *I* seem to be the horrible person?

I didn't want to go back to the trailer, even though I knew I had to.

Raven could make it hell for me because she has that kind of power over everyone. She could humiliate me and laugh at me and just hate me.

She and Tyler both. They could turn on me.

And the tears started to flow again. Long and hard.

"Hey, you okay?"

The voice frightened me. It was the last thing I was expecting, and I swung around, wiping the tears from my eyes and blinking quickly.

It was Tyler.

Him.

Bastard.

The reason everything was going wrong.

"What are you doing here?" I asked.

He walked towards me.

"I often come up here to think. To clear my mind. It's such a wonderful view that I find it really puts your troubles in perspective. I couldn't sleep. When I can't sleep, I walk and think."

"A-huh." I didn't believe him. "Were you following me?"

"Excuse me?" His head cocked slightly.

"Were you *following* me?"

"No, I didn't expect to find you up here. In fact, I wasn't sure who you were to begin with. I would've left you alone except I realised it was you and I thought I could hear you crying."

"I wasn't," I replied, wiping away the last of the tears.

"I think you were." He stepped closer to me now – too close – and I could see a little sad smile on his face. "Want to talk about it?"

"No."

"You girls have a fight?"

You girls, you girls.

"No."

"I guess she didn't like hearing that the police found the rope at the blowhole."

Jesus!

I'd tried to tell her, more than once. But I never actually did.

"I didn't tell her," I muttered, hoping the breeze would hide my reply.

"*What?*"

It didn't.

He was beside me then, turning me around, his hands on my shoulders, his fingers touching my skin.

Don't *touch* me!

"Are you serious?" he asked.

I nodded. "It slipped my mind. Other things happened and –"

"Other things? *Nothing* is more important than this!" he said.

I could think of a couple of things that *were*.

"Amber, I *told* you that information because I wanted you to tell Raven. It's *vital* she knows it and knows it as soon as possible."

I guess it must've been the official Heap-Shit-On-Amber Day, and everyone just forgot to tell me.

"If you thought it was so important, you should've told her yourself."

"I *would've*, but you said she didn't want to see me."

"Yeah, well, big deal. I *lied*!"

I didn't want to say it but I did. I was angry at her and at him and at everyone and it felt good once it was out there.

I thought he'd yell and scream, call me all sorts of names and everything, but he didn't. His hands dropped from my shoulders and he didn't say a thing. Maybe he wasn't surprised. Maybe he knew I'd been lying all along.

He sighed, placed his hands into his pockets, turned and looked over the dam wall and out to the horizon.

Silence. Only the wind in the trees, rippling across the water and around us.

"Then I guess one of us should tell her," he said after a short while, his voice quiet and calm.

I stayed silent.

He turned to face me. "Me or you, Amber?"

And that's what it came down to, didn't it?

Me or him.

"I don't want to talk with her right now," I replied, folding my arms across my chest.

He nodded. "Okay, I'll go tell her," he said as he turned from me and walked away.

He sounded sad, but I didn't know if that was because he was disappointed in me, or because he was disappointed that he'd have to tell her.

I guessed he'd be more than happy to go down there and see Raven, to talk with her and be with her, so they could both discuss me behind my back and plot and backstab and scheme and probably have more sex and laugh at me before having even more sex.

I watched him go.

Fucker.

He was the cause of all this.

He was the one who ruined everything.

I hoped he'd *fucking die*!

He walked slowly along the dam wall, right against the concrete railings, looking over across the water.

With one quick push…

I turned and followed him.

…if he didn't know I was coming…

Matched his speed and then walked faster.

…no one need ever know…

Gained on him.

…he just disappeared…

Right behind him.

Lake Mountain

...just like Duke. And it was such a clear and pleasant night...

I had to be in control.

...for murder.

I reached out, my arms in front of me, ready to push him square in the back, to feel him buckle under my force and to stumble and hit the side of the wall so I could lift and tilt and throw him into the water. He'd fall and scream but no one would hear and he would drown and die and disappear and no one would care.

I lunged.

He turned.

Grabbed both my wrists hard and twirled me around before I could do anything to stop him. I was the one stumbling and falling into his arms, my back hard up against his chest as his arms locked around me, his fingernails digging into my wrists.

I struggled and fought, tried to break free, but he was holding me in a grip I couldn't break, my arms held across my own chest. The more I fought, the more his strength crushed me, the more it hurt.

"Steady," he whispered in my ear. "Calm down, Amber."

I fought for only a few seconds longer. I soon realised there wasn't really any point.

He'd won.

I couldn't beat him at this.

"I told you," he said. "You'd *never* make a burglar."

"Why are you doing this?"

"To stop you pushing me over into the dam."

"No." I struggled one last time. "Why are you with us? Why are you here trying to help us? Why do you *care*?"

He let go of me then and turned me around to face him. The breeze ruffled his hair and the moonlight reflected in his eyes.

"Because I *do* care," he replied.

"I see," I said, making it clear I thought it was a lame answer.

"Listen, Amber." His voice got stronger, direct and to the point. "I don't know why you feel the way you do towards me, but I have *always* been here to help you in any way I can. I said that right from the very beginning and I don't know whether you believe that or not – "

"I don't."

" – but it's the truth. I've *never* lied about my reasons for being here. I've never *lied* to either of you."

"You just want to fuck her!"

"No, I don't."

"Fuck her *again!*"

"I've never had sex with her, Amber."

"That's bullshit." I turned away from him.

"No, it isn't. It's the truth. Raven and I have never had sex."

"That's not true." I leaned against the wall of the dam, looking across it and wishing I was a million miles from here. As far as the full moon, the stars...further. "I heard you, I saw you both!"

"I don't know what you think you saw or heard that night, but we didn't have sex." Tyler stepped closer behind me. "Oh, I'll admit Raven *tried* to get me to have sex with her, but I made it clear to her that I wasn't interested. She's a very forceful girl, and I had to physically stop her, but she eventually got the message."

I sighed. "I just bet you did."

"It's the truth, Amber. I've *never* been interested in Raven. She's not the reason I've stayed around so long. From the moment I saw you, I've only ever been interested in you."

Now he was trying to be Prince Charming, and I wasn't having any of that. "You mean from when you were spying on us, perving on us naked in the lagoon."

"No, before that," he replied. "At the gas station."

I turned to face him. "More lies to try and win me over?"

"No, it's the truth. Ask Raven, she saw me there."

"She did not," I scoffed. "I was there too, remember? I would've seen you."

"No, you were too busy getting the first aid kit from the trailer. Raven saw me as I checked out Al, the owner, the guy she killed. I saw her watching me from the Suburban."

It didn't make sense. I couldn't work out how he knew such detail about what happened at the gas station. The news reports were sketchy at best, and while Raven had told him our story, she only gave him generalities, not specifics.

"We saw each other only for a few seconds, until you climbed from the trailer and dashed back to her. I was there, Amber, and from the moment I saw you, I wanted to help. I wanted to be near you."

I was shaking my head. It was too much to take in. I didn't know what to say or ask. Eventually I whispered, "How?"

He sighed deeply and leaned against the railing, looking across the water, his eyes far away.

"I saw you when you were in the office. You were searching around looking for something, you grabbed Raven's purse and her skirt, plus the bottles of water. You looked worried and upset. I didn't see anything that went on before that, I didn't see Raven with Al or anything, but I snuck a look when you were cleaning up the mess."

"Where? I didn't see you." I was trying to fit all the pieces together.

"I was out the back when it all happened. I knew Al, the guy at the gas station. I bought most of my supplies and bait from him, as he was the only guy selling that stuff on the mountain. We got to know each other pretty well, to the extent that Al told me to just help myself out the back to whatever I needed and then bring the stuff to the counter to pay. He kept most of his bait and fishing gear out in the back room.

"So, that day, I entered through the back door as usual, and was out there getting some bait when I started to hear some pretty weird stuff. Now, Al was no angel, he used to creep me out too, so I just guessed he was listening to the radio or watching porn or something. But then I heard screaming and yelling and I thought I better check it out.

"I crept up the hallway to the front of the store and that's when I saw you. You were only there for a few seconds, and then you were gone. At first, I thought you'd done the screaming, but I soon realised that was wrong. I waited a bit longer to make sure you'd left the office before I ventured further.

"It's not like Al to leave the place unattended, so I walked into the store and looked around. That's when I saw all the broken glass and Al on the ground. I didn't really know what had happened, so I rushed outside to him. *That's* when I saw Raven for the first time – she was looking at me through the window of the Suburban. I couldn't see you, though, not until you climbed from the trailer. I dashed back inside then, ready to call the cops, but there was something in the way you moved, and something in Raven's eyes that told me not to. Instead, I hid in the hall again, just in case you came back."

"And I did," I replied quietly. "To clean up."

"Yes."

"You watched me?"

"Yes, I saw all of it. I watched you drag Al back into the office and leave him behind the counter. I saw you cover all the blood with the mulch."

I closed my eyes. He'd known it all, even from the very beginning.

"I didn't know what to do when you left. I wanted to follow you, to make myself known to you, but I didn't know how. I'm not very good at these kinda things."

"Who is?" I smiled.

"I watched as you both drove off and saw that you were heading *up* the mountain, so I hoped and prayed you were going up there to stay. I even kept to the main road for the rest of the day, just in case I saw you both driving back down."

"You didn't help your friend?"

"Al? Yeah, I called an ambulance for him, but that's all. I figured he'd brought the attack on himself. He had some pretty weird ideas, so it didn't surprise me he ended up like that."

I looked at him again. "What do you mean?"

"Well, we weren't friends or anything. It was just a client and customer relationship. I spent some time in the store and the more I was there the more he'd talk about the girls who would stop for gas, or the models on the covers of the magazines he sold. He'd say things like, 'Pal, some nice prime arse would do me just about now,' and, 'Those young things today, I'd love to slide right into 'em like a knife through butter,' and, 'Women today, a good rape would put them all in their place.'"

"Lovely."

"Yeah, and he'd always finish with, 'And I'm just the man to rape 'em.'"

"I can't believe you'd spend time with him," I replied.

"Only enough time to get the supplies I needed. Never any more than necessary. He made me feel uneasy too, like if I didn't agree with him then I wasn't a real man."

"Go on," I prompted.

"Well, from what I knew about Al, I initially thought *you* had been attacked. I mean, the signs are there, his pants and underwear are off, his cock was out, and there was blood everywhere. I got real angry when I thought he'd attacked you. But you were in control, Amber, you knew what you were doing. It was then I realised it must've been Raven who was attacked and you were attending to her injuries. So, I figured Al had finally gone too far, and got what was coming to him.

"I hid and watched you, waited for you to leave, and then I called for an ambulance and left to head back up the mountain. After all, I didn't want to be found there either! It was only later that I heard the news reports and realised they were talking about Raven by the description of the Suburban and the trailer."

"You should've said something earlier."

"What could I say? I knew you wouldn't believe me, and I didn't want to risk having Raven tell me to fuck off. If anything, I think she wanted me around to try and work out what I wanted, or what I'd do. While I was hunting, I searched all the trailer parks, and then some of the more out-of-the-way places I knew. I was so happy when I happened across you both at the lagoon.

"I was worried about you, but I was relieved to find you both okay. I was going to leave you alone then, but I just couldn't. You didn't know I was there, and I couldn't just leave, so I stayed in my hiding place until I blew it. I'm sorry about the story about my brother being mixed up in drugs, but I didn't know what else to say once my cover had been blown. It was the only thing that came to my mind."

"Yeah, it *was* lame," I replied.

"I didn't know whether to flee or introduce myself that first night, but you both hid in the trailer and wouldn't come out. So I guess you made that decision for me. I left, determined to come back and try again the next morning. I'm surprised you let me stay like you did. But I know Raven recognised me from the gas station anyway."

"It was her decision, not mine."

"Yeah, I guessed that," he said in a soft voice. "And look where we all are now. I'm sorry I wrecked everything for you, Amber. So sorry."

There was silence for a while. I didn't want to look in his direction, didn't want to give him the satisfaction. I stared and looked into the night sky, counting stars and watching the clouds.

I wished that time would freeze right now and I could stand here *forever*.

Maybe the wind would become colder, freeze me to the spot and snuff out my existence as easily as I stepped on those maggots falling from Duke's body.

I thought back to the gas station. Raven had been staring out of the car window when I came back with the first aid kit. I thought she was looking at the guy who attacked her. But maybe, for those split seconds, she'd been looking at Tyler. Then I remembered the day he stumbled out of the wildflowers. She'd ordered me back inside, but didn't flee or panic herself. She just stood there for a while, staring Tyler down. I thought about that night when Raven and Tyler had sex. Thought about what I'd seen and what I'd heard. And all of a sudden I realised that maybe they *hadn't* been having sex. I mean, I didn't *see* them doing it. I didn't see anything. I just saw glimpses and heard things that maybe made me jump to the wrong conclusions. Maybe Tyler *was* telling me the truth after all. About *everything*.

And then I felt bad for the way I'd treated him. Maybe he was right. Maybe they were *both* right and I'd gone a little psycho on them.

What would Janet Leigh think about *that*?

I smiled then, and felt a little better.

Things would turn out okay in the morning. I just had a feeling that they would.

I turned to look at him, to apologise and try to explain why I felt and acted the way I did, to try and make him understand what I'd been feeling.

He was gone.

I was alone on the dam wall.

Alone *again*.

The smile slipped from my face once more.

Forty-eight

I waited for the sun to rise before I started to walk back to the trailer.

Part of me didn't want to go back there. I kept telling myself I could walk out of here and let Raven and Tyler deal with Duke. But that would mean they'd win, they'd have beaten me and I'd have retreated in defeat.

I wouldn't allow that.

I also thought about jumping from the dam wall, ending it all and living in an everlasting peacefulness.

Maybe Raven would love me *more* if I were dead.

But that was all just crazy.

Still, to make sure I didn't do anything stupid, I left the dam behind me, walking endlessly and aimlessly until the sun rose.

It was a cool morning, and I could feel the dew under my feet. I was cold and wet and miserable, but I really didn't care.

All I could think about was Tyler and Raven in the trailer, talking about me, laughing, *fucking*.

Fucking? I wasn't really sure about that now. There was no reason for Tyler to lie about that. Admitting he'd had sex with Raven would, if anything, destroy me even more, so why not do it?

I stopped by the phone at the camping grounds and dialled my father's number. I knew it was early and he was probably asleep, but I needed to hear the sound of his voice. The phone rang and rang, but no one picked up on the other end.

No one at all.

When I hung up the receiver, I waited for the phone to return my quarter to me. It didn't.

Even the phone was against me.

I didn't need it anyway. I had no one left to call.

I stared at the number pad on the phone. It shined in the clear morning light, dew glistening on the edges of the numbers.

I ran my fingers across the numbers one last time; they felt cold to the touch.

As cold as the nipples on a corpse in a mortuary...

***

I entered the trailer with my head held high and a proud look on my face. I wasn't about to let them both bring me down. I would hold my dignity throughout all this, no matter what.

I was surprised to find Raven sitting on the bed, wrapped in her robe, almost as if she were waiting for me. The robe was slightly open at the front, and I could still see the brown stain of ash across her chest and lower down.

"I was starting to wonder if you'd deserted us," she said as she smiled.

I looked around, but Tyler wasn't there.

"I'd never do that," I replied, testing to see where this was conversation was heading.

"I was worried about you last night," she said. There didn't seem to be any trace of anger in her voice. Or of hate.

"I needed to walk," I replied. "To think."

She nodded. "I understand. Still, it was a cold and lonely morning without you."

"Did Tyler come by?" I asked.

Her eyes dropped and she nodded.

"Where is he now?"

"He's gone up to the spillway to check everything out, just in case. He thought it was better if he went first to look around, less suspicious that way. He shouldn't be much longer. If all's okay up there, then we'll get ready to dump Duke."

I nodded.

"You look a mess," Raven added.

Just what I needed to hear.

"It's pretty damp out there," I replied.

Raven leaned over and grabbed a bath towel. "Here, dry yourself off."

I reached over and took the towel from her and did just that.

I climbed out of my damp clothes and dried myself as quickly as I could. I was surprised to see that while a good deal of the ash had rubbed off, some of it still remained, mostly between my breasts and down around my stomach.

So we were both still marked with the events of last night.

I didn't want to be naked then, not anymore, not here. So I grabbed my underwear and put it back on, stepped into another pair of jeans, my Converse sneakers and my *Buck 65* t-shirt. I felt better once I was in warm clothes again. They felt right. Comfortable. Mine.

The only things left that were truly mine.

Raven was standing at the meals table by then, eating a bowl of cereal.

"You hungry?"

I shook my head.

She shrugged. "Suit yourself."

I didn't quite know how to say it, so I just came out with it.

"Did Tyler tell you about the rope?"

Raven nodded. "And the stories in the newspaper, about the gas station guy."

"They're getting close, Raven."

"I know. But we'll make it. Today we'll finally escape all of this. We won't have to worry about Duke anymore."

She smiled, but the worry was still etched across her face.

"I'm sorry," I whispered. "I was going to tell you but – "

"Don't worry about it now," she replied, untying her robe and letting it slip to the floor. "I didn't give you much of a chance to tell me anyway. We know about it, that's the main thing, and we need to make sure today goes to plan."

She walked towards me. I could see the brown ash stretch between her breasts and down over her stomach. I could see her vagina, where I'd cleaned so carefully just a few hours ago.

Raven opened the wardrobe door and rummaged around inside.

"Today should be special," she said. "Today should be the start of something new. Our new lives, our new existence. We'll look back on today and see it as a turning point, Amber, I just know we will."

"I hope so."

She smiled at me and leaned forward, kissing me on the forehead for only a second before turning back to the wardrobe and pulling out some clothes.

She picked her favourite black leather pants and leather boots, and then she selected her blue metal corset.

The corset was her favourite and she wore it only on special occasions. She'd said in the past that it was uncomfortable to wear, because it really *was* made out of some kind of metal or aluminium or something. You couldn't really bend too far in it, and there was no way you could dance at the Rawhide wearing it.

So, she only brought it out to wear on special occasions, birthdays or parties or whatever.

"You sure you want to wear that?" I asked, thinking about what we had to do in the next hour or so.

"I'll manage," she replied. "I want to feel invincible today, and this will help me."

She sat down next to me on the bed and slid into her pants and laced her boots. Then I helped her into the metal corset. It was painted a deep blue and was made up of four separate vertical sections (two for the back and two for the front) that were held together with strong leather straps that slipped in and out of the rivets along each of the sides. They were designed the same way a shoelace threads between the holes in a shoe and they did a great job keeping the four panels together, while also allowing for a bit of movement and for a peek of flesh all the way down the front, sides and back as well.

The corset cupped her breasts perfectly, the metal rising to meet them and then tapering off to two rounded points near her shoulders. I tied the straps nice and tight on her back and made sure she was comfortable.

"How's that?"

"Perfect," she smiled. "What would I do without you?"

I smiled a sad smile back. "How long has Tyler been gone?" I asked.

We both sat back down on the bed.

"A while," she replied. "Should be back soon."

We sat next to each other and didn't speak. Both lost in our thoughts and worries, I guess. It was just nice to sit there with her for a while. Sit and wait. Do nothing. We didn't have to say anything, we'd known each other too long, been there for each other so often. We could sit and say nothing and it wouldn't bother either of us.

Even the argument from last night seemed to have been forgotten. That was a good thing, I think. We both knew we'd said the wrong things. There was no reason to discuss it any further.

My eyes wandered around the trailer, taking everything in.

It was so peaceful and so quiet.

Home.

"Here," she said, breaking the silence after a long time. "I've got something for you."

She walked to the kitchen and opened a cupboard. Reaching inside, she pulled out a small tray. Sitting on the tray was the urn from last night, along with a small straw and a mirror. As she walked towards me, I could see the two lines of ash neatly heaped on the mirror.

I looked at her strangely. I didn't understand.

"It's the last of him," she said as she sat back down next to me on the bed. "I saved him for you."

"You want me to *sniff* this?" I asked.

She nodded. "I've already had mine."

I looked down at the ash. I didn't want to do it. I didn't do things like that. Drugs or ash, it didn't matter, I don't do it.

"Go on," she whispered as she raised the tray closer to me, her eyes so open and aware. "It's what you need. If we internalise him, he'll live on within us, making us stronger too."

It sounded crazy.

But maybe she was right.

"Live," she whispered.

I bent forward and picked up the straw. I'd seen enough films and TV shows to know exactly what to do. I slipped the straw into my nose and quickly sniffed up the first line of ash.

The smell of burning wood and flesh and whatever was overpowering, as was the stinging sensation deep inside my nostril. I sat back and shook my head, my hand rubbing at my nose, trying to make the stinging stop.

Eventually it did.

And then I sniffed the other line up my other nostril.

Raven looked on, smiling.

When I was finished, she put the tray aside and hugged me tight.

I closed my eyes to stop them from watering and I rubbed both nostrils until the sensation went away. When I finished, I opened my eyes again and stared across the trailer.

I *did* feel more aware.

More *alive*.

"We can do this," she said.

I turned to face her, but she was staring off into space. Maybe she was trying to convince herself too. I really didn't know.

Slowly, her eyes refocussed and she turned to face me.

I leaned forward towards her.

I had to tell her. Tell her now.

"Raven?" I asked.

She smiled at me. "Yes?"

"I – "

But I didn't get to finish the sentence.

Because all hell broke loose.

Forty-nine

The thumping on the trailer door scared both of us. We jumped in fright as the loud *bang bang bangbangbang* shattered the silence.

Raven leapt from the bed and dashed to the door.

"Who is it?" she called.

"Me. *Tyler*. Quick!"

She opened the door and he stood there looking up at her. He didn't come in. He was out of breath and sweating, and was still wearing the same clothes I saw him in last night.

"What is it?"

"They're here."

"Who? The *cops*?"

He shook his head. "No. Worse. Come on, we gotta move."

I was standing too then, rushing to Raven's side.

She turned to me. "Get into the car," she ordered.

I nodded.

"No, no!" Tyler was holding up his hands. "Too noisy. They'll hear. We have to carry Duke. Carry him to the spillway."

"Are you serious?" Raven asked.

"Yes."

"It can't be *that* bad."

He reached up towards us, his hands beckoning. "Come *on!* We're running out of time! We can't take the car. They're nearby."

"*Who* is?" I asked.

"I don't know. But they're not cops, I'm sure of it. They're dressed in dark suits and they've got a big Ford and even bigger guns. I stumbled onto them when I was walking back from the spillway. We *have* to be quiet and we *have* to get out of here *now!*"

"It can't happen like this," Raven said softly.

"Well, it *is* happening like this," Tyler replied. "So let's move it! I'll get Duke out of the car. Raven, you get the guns. We may need them after all."

Things were happening too fast, way too fast. People and events were moving around me and I felt stuck to the floor.

It can't happen now. Not like this.

My breath was short and my heart was pumping hard through my chest.

I didn't want things to move so swiftly. I couldn't control them like this.

Tyler had disappeared. Raven was saying something to me as she grabbed the pistols from the storage area.

"Quickly!" she added.

I hadn't heard what she said, but I found I could move again, and I was running down the stairs of the trailer.

I looked around.

Everything seemed so quiet. So peaceful.

Tyler was at the back of the Suburban, the doors open wide. He was pulling at Duke, gripping the sheet hard, dragging him towards the ground.

I looked around again. Slower this time, really trying to focus on the details between the trees and bushes. But I couldn't see anyone or anything out of the ordinary.

Raven was by my side, locking the trailer door, turning and rushing to help Tyler.

I walked down towards them, still looking all around me.

I couldn't see them. Where were they?

Was Tyler telling the truth?

Raven was by his side, they were carrying Duke away from the car, dropping him quickly. He thudded into the ground with a *squelch* and I could see that his sheets were all wet, as if he'd been left out in the rain. But that hadn't happened, so the dampness must've come from within. He was smelling really badly too, and he looked much bigger than before, like he'd put on weight or something. On the ground and on the sheet, I could see a few new maggots crawling along, trying to find food after being dislodged by the movement.

"...too slow and too difficult to manoeuvre," Tyler was saying as he slammed the Suburban doors shut.

"You *can't* carry him yourself," Raven replied.

"I'm stronger and I'm quicker. And you certainly can't carry him dressed like that! We need to get him to the spillway and ready to dispose of as soon as possible. He's light. *Trust me*, I can carry him."

"Okay," Raven shrugged. She handed him the black pistol and kept the silver one in her hands.

He stuck his pistol down the back of his pants before bending to lift Duke. He hauled him like he was a sack of mouldy potatoes, and slung him over his shoulder.

I heard a grunt, and for a moment I thought it was Duke, but then I realised it must've come from Tyler.

He staggered, one hand grabbing onto the side of the Suburban for balance, a whole new crop of maggots shaking lose from the bottom of the sheet. He steadied himself and started half-walking, half-falling down the dirt track.

"You okay?" Raven was by his side.

"I can manage. I *can* do this."

Within seconds, he'd turned to the left and disappeared through the bushes.

Raven followed.

And so did I.

We rushed through the trees and up a slight hill. In the full light of day, everything around us looked more than beautiful, except for the maggot trail Duke was leaving. They were falling out from the creases in the sheets while he was bouncing back and forth on Tyler's back. I hoped no one saw them and used them as a trail to find us.

Like little moving, wiggling breadcrumbs.

Raven was out in front, turning from side to side as she crept along the trail, ever aware and vigilant for anything suspicious.

As if *we* weren't suspicious enough.

Tyler was in the middle, and I was bringing up the rear.

"What am I looking for?" Raven asked.

"Just keep walking," Tyler replied, huffing. "If you see two guys in suits and packing guns, let me know. But for now, keep walking straight. We have to get to the spillway as soon as possible."

All the trees and bushes were a blur, one after the other after the other. The greenness, the smells of life, all of it captivated me. I kept my senses sharp, I stayed focussed, but I couldn't see anyone out there.

But they wouldn't make it *easy* for us to see them.

Unless they didn't know we were coming.

Maybe we could get the jump on *them*. Surprise them before they surprised us.

Perhaps we'd already passed them, and they hadn't even heard us or seen us. We could even be heading in opposite directions.

Us towards the dam wall.

And them towards...

Fuck!

"Which way were they heading when you saw them?" I asked.

"Towards the trailer," Tyler replied without looking around at me.

"What if they find the trailer first?" I asked.

Tyler turned then, Duke swinging around with him. "Don't worry about that now. It's okay if they find the trailer. There's nothing there to link you both to the body now. All the evidence is here, on my shoulders."

Raven stopped walking and we looked at each other. Our eyes locked and our expressions must've given us away.

"*Is there?*" Tyler asked slowly, suspicion sweeping his face.

"Quick, Amber," Raven said to me. "You got your keys?"

I shook my head. "No. I left them there!"

Raven's hand dived into her tight pants and she pulled out the key, throwing it to me over Tyler's (and Duke's) head.

"Hurry back there. You know what to get, right?"

I nodded. "Yes. Where is it?"

"I hid it at the back of the wardrobe."

"Okay," I replied, turning around.

"You know how to get to the dam wall?" she asked.

I nodded as I set off, running back down the hill and towards the trailer.

I had to get there before anyone else did.

"We'll meet you up there! And hurry!" Raven called after me.

I waved back at them.

"Exactly *what* is she going back to get?" I heard Tyler ask.

But I didn't hear Raven's reply.

Fifty

I opened the trailer door and stepped inside.
No one there.
Just like outside. There was no sign of anyone.

Dashing straight over to the wardrobe, I opened the door.

I fumbled through the clothes, pulling them off their hangers and off the rod, pushing them out of the way, throwing them to the floor and burrowing into the back of the wardrobe.

And there it was.

The bloodied bath towel.

And inside it, Duke's cock and balls.

I reached in and grabbed it, pulling it to my chest. The towel felt warm and the stains on it were dried and flaky.

I'm sure that under usual circumstances I'd probably be a bit freaked out having to hold this jar in my hands again, but right then there wasn't any time to do anything except stand up, turn around and head back out the door.

Which is what I did.

Well, *almost*.

I ran to the door, but then stopped myself. I turned around and looked at the trailer again, making sure everything else was in order.

It sure seemed fine.

Except for the urn still sitting on the tray.

I walked over to the bed and picked up the urn as well. I didn't want them finding that either.

I turned to leave. Stopped again.

I put the urn and jar down on the meals table and quickly kneeled by the bed. I knew time was important, I knew it was running out, but I felt calm and level-headed, if a bit breathless from my run back to the trailer.

I was in control. I could do this.

Lifting up the mattress, I removed the revolver from where I'd stored it. It felt heavy and cold in my hands, but I felt better for carrying it.

If the others were armed, then I should be armed too.

I walked the length of the trailer and hunted around in the storage area, pushing clothes and bags and magazines to one side, until I found the boxes I needed. I opened them and my fingers fumbled around inside nervously. Pulling out the ammunition, I slipped the bullets into the chambers. When they were full, I pushed the cylinder closed with my palm and it clicked home.

Done.

I shoved the revolver down the front of my jeans and turned back to the meals table, collecting the urn and the jar as I left.

My eyes scanned the trees and bushes outside. I could see no one. Everything looked peaceful and serene.

Just another ordinary day.

I locked the trailer door behind me and set off back along the track. Duke's cock and balls were heavier than before, and the urn was slippery and difficult to hold, but I managed.

I had to.

***

Even though I was running through the forest, trying to catch up with Raven and Tyler (and Duke), I was still being very careful about how I ran, how noisy I was, and where I was going.

My eyes darted all around me, and I tried to keep my breathing under control, just in case.

The last thing I wanted to do now was ruin the whole thing by getting myself caught. Raven would *never* forgive me if I let something like that happen.

But that's nearly what *did* happen.

I was probably about halfway between the trailer and the dam wall, running along the path, looking from side to side, peering through the blur of bushes and trees and trying to see if anything looked out of place.

I was so concerned about what was around me, to my sides, that I didn't pay full attention to the path ahead.

And as I ran over a slight rise, I saw them.

Walking down the path. *My* path.

Right in front of me!

I slowed as quickly as I could, jumping from sight and diving behind a couple of bushes.

That was so close!

I was sweating and my heart was pumping hard. Seeing them had given me quite a fright. I placed the jar and urn on the ground next to me and I wiped my palms on my pants, then I flicked the sweat from my eyes. I waited until my breathing was under control again before I dared to stick my head out to look down the path once more.

I watched as they continued down the path, walking away from me and towards the dam.

At least they hadn't seen me!

They were two guys dressed in very nice dark suits, and they were carrying guns. One in each hand.

Subtlety wasn't their strong point.

Maybe they just didn't expect to be seen.

But there they were. They stopped for a second as one of them fumbled in his pocket for something. He pulled it out, holding it up for the other guy. They both turned as the guy lit a cigarette from the lighter.

And then I recognised them.

Mr Moustache and Mr Sunglasses from Pine Hills Trailer Park!

The guys who had tried to stop us when we were fleeing the scene of the crime.

What were they doing here?

The guns told me what they wanted to do, and who they were after.

Fuck.

And they were between me and Raven and Tyler.

Double fuck!

Now I *really* had to move quickly to warn the others.

The two guys were talking to each other now. I was too far away to hear what they were saying, but Mr Sunglasses laughed at something the other said.

They weren't in any hurry, at least. Or so it seemed.

I sat back on my haunches and leaned against the trunk of a tree, wiping the sweat beading on my forehead. I had to think clearly and work out what I was going to do before I did it.

I really had no choice. I'd have to leave the path, circle around the suits and get in front of them, then get back on the path and head for the spillway.

Pronto.

Fifty-one

The dam wall was in sight and, to the side of it, I could see the spillway.

Yes!

I'd made it in good time and I'd made it safely.

My eyes scanned the area for Tyler and Raven, but I couldn't see them. It didn't really concern me, though. There were too many places to be seen out there, and I just guessed they'd be hiding in the woods nearby.

The spillway was a huge concrete lip, probably more than forty feet wide, built to the side of the dam wall. Shaped like a question mark, it stretched from a small inlet inside the wall of the dam, then curved alongside the wall, before dipping lower and forming a huge chute which ran down the hill and out into the forest below, ending at the jagged rocks where the old riverbed once flowed.

It'd certainly be a hell of a ride for Duke. And there was no doubt that once he was thrown in there, his body would join a raging current and probably be smashed to bits when he met the rocks below.

I don't know how strong dead rotting bodies are, but I was pretty sure Duke would be spread into thousands of pieces pretty soon.

Good. He deserved it.

There was a short walkway built across the spillway that allowed access onto the dam wall, but I couldn't see anyone up there either. The whole place looked deserted.

I looked back the way I had come, but Mr Moustache and Mr Sunglasses were nowhere to be seen.

I'd run as fast as I could as I circled around them, giving them the widest berth I could possibly afford and hoping and praying they wouldn't see me or hear me.

And they didn't.

I'd returned to the path just a few minutes before reaching the dam wall, and I couldn't see them anywhere.

Success.

I still carried Duke's bits and the urn. I had to make sure Raven got them safely and in one piece, but it was a struggle as the urn was just slightly too big to carry in one hand, and the jar was an odd size and hard to hold. So, I held them both under my arms, one on each side.

I marched quickly along the track, my eyes darting, looking for Raven and Tyler in the woods and also making sure no one was on the dam. On the other side of the dam wall was a small office that looked like a mini airport control tower. But the dam wall blocked the view of the spillway from the tower, which was good news for us. We wouldn't have to worry about anyone seeing us from there at least.

I walked closer to the spillway.

Still no sign of anyone.

I could hear the sounds of engines or motors, some kind of heavy equipment turning and groaning. It was coming from near the wall.

And as I walked, I could also hear water. Lots of it. Pouring and running and cascading.

They must've been getting ready. They must've started letting the water into the spillway inlet on the other side of the dam.

I started to run.

I desperately wanted to call out to Raven and Tyler, but I couldn't risk it.

The sun shone brightly, the sky was cloudless. Sweat trickled down my face.

I ran on. Almost to the spillway now.

Where the fuck were they?

I began to panic.

Were they even there? Had they left me? Set me up?

Was sending me back to the trailer a ruse to divert my attention from what was really going on?

Had Tyler turned Raven against me that much?

"Amber!"

I heard her voice and swung around to see her waving at me from some bushes near the spillway.

I smiled and turned, so glad to see her.

Changed direction in mid-step.

Tripped on something.

A rock or a branch or my own feet or something.

And I fell forward, the jar and urn spilling from my grasp.

I reached out even as I was falling, watching the towel unravel in front of me, seeing the lid fly from the jar as it spun from my reach, the white crystals spilling and arcing as the jar tumbled and spun, hitting the ground, glass shattering.

I fell hard. The gravel burned into my hands as I reached out in front of me, my head jerking forward, forehead ploughing into the dust and glass shards. The stones and glass cutting and digging and tearing.

Good going girl.

My lungs breathed in dust and grit, and I coughed and spluttered, trying to clear them from my airways.

I looked up, sweat and blood dripping. Raven was running towards me, a look of anger or fear on her face, her flowing hair and metal corset making her look so powerful, so in control.

Spread between us was Duke's cock and balls, resting on a mat of crystal flakes and surrounded by shards of glass, flecked with blood. It looked like it had been thrown there like some discarded Catch Of The Day. His cock was still tied, still bloated and fat, like a deformed sausage, and the flesh had taken on a sickly pale white colour, probably from the crystals it had been sitting in.

The jar was broken into thousands of bits.

Fuck it.

Raven was by my side, helping me stand.

"You okay?" she asked.

"I guess," I replied.

I brushed the dirt and dust from my jeans, but that only left long streaks of red from my bloody palms. I looked down at them. The fall had really cut them up bad. Glass and gravel dug in deep under the skin. They were starting to sting as well.

"Quickly," she said. "Follow me."

She turned and picked up the urn, which was nearby (it was intact, of course) and then she bent down and grabbed Duke's cock and balls, picking them up by the head of his cock and carrying it like you would a dead rat.

She dashed towards the bushes and I followed her, Duke's cock and balls swinging by her side, the urn held in her other hand.

I held my palms together, trying to stop the bleeding, but they were cut deep and looked nasty.

Tyler was waiting for us just inside the forest. He was squatting down by a small bush, his hair looked matted by sweat and his forehead was creased with worry. Duke was standing on one end, sagging against a nearby tree.

Tyler looked at me. He must've seen the whole thing too. I felt really embarrassed right then. Of all the times to fall, I had to pick when they were both watching.

"Sorry," I said to him.

"Don't worry about it, Amber," he replied, in a soft voice. "You're here, that's all that matters."

Raven walked past Tyler and over towards Duke. She started unwrapping a small piece of sheet from around him.

As she passed, Tyler's eyes dropped down to the cock and balls in her hands, but he didn't say anything. She must've already told him what to expect. Maybe he'd seen so much in the past couple of days that a girl carrying a severed groin didn't really phase him. Or maybe he was just concentrating on what was to come.

"You okay?" he asked me, inspecting my forehead and hands.

"Yes," I lied.

He looked at his watch. "Any moment now the spillway will open."

"I can hear it," I said as I squatted down next to him, making sure I didn't drop any blood on him.

"Yeah, they're letting the water and pressure build up on the other side of the dam. When they're ready, they'll open the second set of gates and the water will flow right past us."

"How will we get Duke into the spillway?"

"The walkway above it. We'll lift him up over the railing and drop him from there."

"It's pretty exposed up there. You can see it from all around."

He looked at me and smiled. "It's a chance we have to take. We have no other options."

"I saw the two guys in suits," I said to him.

He just nodded.

"We've seen them before, and they're getting closer."

Raven was by our sides again.

"The two guys Tyler saw," I said as I turned to face her. "They're the two guys who tried to stop us at the trailer park."

A puzzled look swept her face. "Really?"

I nodded, but Raven didn't say anything more. She stared out at the spillway and nodded slowly, like she was making all the connections in her head.

She didn't have the cock and balls in her hands now. I looked over towards Duke. The sheet she had unwrapped was back in place now, and a slight bulge protruded halfway down.

"Don't worry," she added. "Duke is complete again now."

I nodded.

"It would never have worked properly anyway," she added, her eyes turning to focus on mine. "Not like Jeremy did."

I smiled at her but felt incredibly uncomfortable right then.

Raven continued. "And I don't think we need this anymore either." She held up the urn and looked at it one last time.

She bent down and pawed at the dirt with her fingers. I watched her for a moment and then I started digging too. Quickly we created a small hole. I turned to look at Tyler, but he wasn't watching us, his eyes were still on the spillway.

In a few moments we had a hole deep enough to bury the urn.

"Your final resting place," Raven said as she put the urn in the hole. "Thanks for the ride."

Then we both covered the urn with the dirt, burying it quickly, patting the dirt down hard and throwing leaves and sticks on top to hide it from view.

Finally Jeremy Xavier could rest.

Or what was left of him.

I turned back and looked across to the path where I'd tripped, where the broken glass jar and towel and flakes still laid strewn for anyone to see, like a huge arrow pointing towards us.

"What about them?"

"We'll worry about that later, hon," Raven replied as she touched my shoulder lightly. "They're the least of our troubles right now."

The sound of broiling water was intensifying, and the ground beneath us was starting to vibrate.

"Here," Raven said, handing me a handkerchief. "Mop your brow and palms with this."

I took it from her. Her blue metal corset was dusty and smeared with dirt, but I could still see some remains of the ash on her chest too. I remembered the ash on my chest too, and I smiled then as I lightly patted my forehead. The handkerchief came away wet and bloody. I must've looked horrible, really beaten up. I placed it then between my palms, picking out the larger shards of glass before pressing hard, trying to stop the bleeding, trying to stop the pain.

"It's almost time," Tyler said. His eyes darted from his watch to the spillway and back again.

From where we were hiding, we had a good view right along the wall of the dam, with the spillway and walkway directly in front of us.

All we had to do was run out onto the walkway with Duke, lift him high, drop him into the torrent of water in the spillway underneath and run back.

To freedom.

Finally.

"Come on," Raven said. "Why's it taking them so long?"

Tyler stood up and walked across to Duke. I watched him go, pressing my palms together harder, willing the bleeding to stop.

He bent down and picked up Duke, throwing him across his shoulder once more. As he did so, he stumbled, one hand reaching for the tree and one knee buckling under him. Duke slid off, hitting the ground hard, like a felled log.

"I better go help him," Raven said.

"Me too." I stood to follow.

She turned and shook her head. "No, not with those wounds. We'll manage."

She walked over to Tyler as he was trying to pick up Duke again. Suddenly Tyler looked a little exhausted and unsteady on his feet. She said something to him and he shook his head.

The sound of the water was getting louder, and I couldn't hear what they were saying, but I guessed he was trying to tell her he could carry Duke himself, but she insisted she'd help.

They both bent down, took one end of Duke each, and carried him towards me.

"Can I help?" I asked.

"No," Tyler replied. "You've done enough already."

I didn't really know what he meant by that.

He looked at his watch. "They're running late."

"Open the fucking gates," Raven muttered, letting her half of Duke slip to the ground. "They should be open by now."

And almost as if she commanded it, a high-pitched siren began to wail, getting louder and louder and repeating over and over. That was followed by the sounds of hydraulic pumps and concrete on concrete and flowing splashing cascading water.

The vibration in the ground intensified and a split second later we could see the white foam and blue wonder of the water pouring down the spillway.

"This is it!" Raven yelled as she hugged us both, her arm on my shoulder, her hair touching my cheek. "It all comes down to this. Let's do it!"

She picked up Duke and looked to Tyler. He nodded and then turned to me. It looked like he was going to say something, but then changed his mind. He just smiled and I smiled back.

Then they were on their way, out of the woods and along the path.

I followed. I felt totally useless, my hands all cut up like they were. I felt as if I was letting them down by not helping carry Duke, but the blood just wouldn't stop. Even so, there was no way I was going to hide in the bushes like some scared little girl.

I'd be there for them.

I'd be by their side.

No matter what.

Duke swung back and forth between them as they carried him along the path and across the walkway. It only took a few seconds to get out above the spillway, right to the centre of the churning water below us.

A fine mist enveloped us, the spray from the water below reaching us easily. Within seconds we were damp, the mist clinging to our clothes and skin and hair. After the initial deluge of water, the mist thinned slightly as the torrent below flowed more evenly, the first few seconds of churning chaos gone. But still it was hard to see further than a few feet away. The mist was thick enough to cut down some of the daylight and surroundings.

"Lift him up!" Tyler yelled over the noise of the water.

"What?" Raven called.

Tyler pointed to Duke and then pointed upwards to the spillway's concrete handrail.

She nodded.

I was standing right there, but they both ignored me, too intent on the task at hand. They hauled Duke higher, up to hip level, getting ready to lay him on the handrail.

The noise of the water below became louder, deafening, and the wind swept all around us, buffeting us with great force. I leaned against the handrail for support, staggering against the wind. I couldn't believe the strength of the wind.

Tyler's eyes slipped upward, looking above us.

His mouth fell open and I saw him mouth the word, *Fuck*.

And Duke slipped from his fingers.

Raven looked at him, probably to ask why he'd dropped Duke, but then she looked skywards as well.

And so did I.

The police helicopter was above us, hovering above the dam, a uniformed cop leaning out the door with a megaphone at his lips.

He was saying something, yelling at us about something, but over the noise of the water and the rotor blades and the pumps and whatever, we couldn't hear.

I turned to Raven.

Her hair was blowing all around her, the dark curls flowing with the wind, lifting and swaying and swirling, dancing with the wind and noise and mist.

She wasn't looking at the helicopter now. She'd turned to face Tyler.

She had hate in her eyes, and she had her pistol pointed at him.

"You fucker!" she yelled.

"What?" he took a step backwards.

"How *could* you?"

He stared at her in disbelief for a moment. "I didn't do this!"

"I should *never* have trusted you."

I stepped up beside Raven, pulling my revolver from my pants. "He must've called them this morning!" I yelled into her ear. "When he said he was coming up here to check the spillway, he must've gone and called the cops on us instead. Or met with them and told them where we'd be."

Tyler turned to face me, his head cocking slightly and his eyes narrowing. For a moment all was still, there was just him and me and the rest of the world had vanished in the white mist that surrounded us all.

"Raven!" He stepped backwards further. "I told you they were close, but I didn't lead them here. Why would I? Why? I don't want to be arrested for this any more than you do!"

Then he reached around and pulled out his pistol from the back of his jeans. He did it so quickly neither of us had a chance to try to stop him.

His gun was pointing at me. At my chest.

His finger on the trigger.

"Don't you *dare!*" Raven called to him, stepping in front of me.

"Don't you see, Raven?" he said. "Can't you see what's happening here?"

"He's betrayed us." I said to her. "Both of us. He's turned us in!"

"That's bullshit, Amber! And you know it!" Tyler was shaking his head, walking back further, faster.

The wind buffeted all of us, making it hard to stand and hold the guns straight. I splayed my legs more, hoping not to lose balance. The noise from the helicopter and spillway was deafening, and over it all I could hear the sounds of sirens.

I looked past Tyler, further along the dam wall, and I could just make out the shapes of three cop cars charging towards us from the other side. They were moving fast. They'd be here any second.

"Raven," I said as I pointed towards the cars. "Quickly, *do something!*"

"I trusted you!" she called to him. "*Fucking* trusted you with everything!"

"I never betrayed you!" he called back, his gun still trained right on me. "It wasn't me, Raven! I swear to you, it *wasn't*. I wouldn't do that to you! I wouldn't do that to Amber!" He paused, then continued. "Why don't you ask Amber why I'm here? Why don't you ask her why we're really all here today? She knows the real story. I've already told her!"

I couldn't believe he'd said that.

She paused for a second, then turned her head slightly to look at me over her shoulder.

I stepped forward next to her, shoulder to shoulder, and I looked her in the eyes. "You know me, Raven," I said. "We've known each other all our lives. Think of everything we've done together. Would I do anything to hurt you? Do anything to tear us apart?"

She stared back at me.

Our eyes locked. Our souls combined.

And then she nodded, only slightly. Only so I could see. The fire burned bright in her eyes.

"Amber, please!" he called to me. "Listen to me, I –"

She pulled the trigger.

The gunshot was loud, even with the noise of the spillway and helicopter around us, the *bang bang* hurt my ears.

I turned.

Tyler buckled and hit the ground, a look of surprise on his face and blood on his shirt.

Just above the heart.

She turned to me and dropped her gun, staggering slightly as she did so, grabbing for the handrail.

"Run, Amber," she yelled. "Quickly, get out of here."

I looked around. Through the mist I could see the cop cars were halfway along the dam wall. They were slowing down, their lights flashing and their sirens adding to the noise. They were blocking off any chance of escape across the far side of the dam wall.

"*I won't leave you!*" I screamed at the top of my voice.

She turned and hugged me. Hugged me tight and hard and stronger than she ever had. She felt warm and so right. So perfect.

I hugged back.

"It's time to fly," she whispered in my ear.

Our hug ended and we let go of each other. She stepped back from me and as she did so, I noticed the deep red stain on my Buck 65 t-shirt. It was down low and for a second I thought I must've wiped my bleeding palms on it.

But here was too much blood.

Way too much.

My eyes darted across to Raven, to the small bullet hole that had punctured her corset just to the left of her bellybutton, to the blood I could see flowing underneath.

"Oh God! Raven!" I screamed. "*No!*"

I bent towards her, my hands out to help but she pushed me away. She fell to her knees and looked up at me. "Go!" she yelled. "Get the fuck out while you still can!"

The fire was still in her eyes, but it was fading.

"*Please!*" she begged. A solitary tear slipped down her face. "Use the mist for cover and get out of here!"

"I can't!"

"You have to!" Her hands were holding the corset, trying to stop the blood that was spilling out between her fingers. "There's nothing more to do here. It's over. Do this for me, *please!*"

I didn't want to.

"*Please!*"

But I did what she asked.

I bent down and kissed her one last time on the lips. I could feel her breathing was short and fast, weakening by the second, but her lips were still warm, still full and luscious and beautiful.

"*Go!*" she said, her blood-soaked hand caressing my cheek. "*Leave!*"

I straightened up and looked across the dam. The cops were climbing from the vehicles now, getting ready to cover the area with their guns.

There was no time. No time for anything now.

I turned around, ducked down low and dashed back the way we had come, along the walkway and towards the forest.

I wanted to stop, retrace my steps, go back. Every part of me needed to help Raven to the safety of the trailer. But I knew what Raven said was right. I had to do as she wished.

I have no idea if the cops even saw me through the mist. I kept low and dashed towards the forest, where we had been hiding only a few minutes earlier. And then I was stopped in my tracks.

Fuck!

I could see the faces of Mr Moustache and Mr Sunglasses staring out at me from between the bushes, their smiles wide.

I couldn't head back there, back towards them. I couldn't risk being caught or seen by them.

I paused only for a second or two before running to the left, hoping they wouldn't follow me or chase after me. I made it to the forest without any trouble, my breathing hard, my arms and legs shaking.

I couldn't keep running though. I couldn't leave her like this. I couldn't turn my back on her and never look back. I couldn't leave without knowing.

So I stopped and turned around, watched from the bushes.

Raven was standing now, trying desperately to lift Duke up from the ground and onto the handrail of the walkway.

The helicopter hovered above her, as close as it dared get to the mist and swirl created by the charging water. The cop screamed through the megaphone at her, but she didn't stop. She lifted one end up onto the railing.

The cops on the dam wall were all squatting low by their cars. From what I could see through the mist, they had their guns and rifles trained directly on her.

She pinned Duke to the side of the wall with her shoulder while she struggled to lift his other end. She coughed, doubled over in pain and dropped him, tried again.

But it wasn't working. She couldn't do it that way.

Then she bent down, got her hands underneath him and lifted, strained and screamed as she lifted him higher and higher. The sheet became smeared with red.

Her blood. Her life force.

Her hair madly danced around her drawn and gaunt face, every muscle in her body straining tight. She lifted him, her eyes staring straight ahead, over the spillway and across the valley.

And then Duke was on the handrail. On the ledge.

Raven collapsed over the top of him, coughing hard, blood spilling from her mouth and raining over Duke's sheet.

I wanted to go and help her. I *needed* to. But I couldn't risk it.

"*Push him and run, Raven!*" I yelled. But she couldn't hear me over the deafening noise.

The cops, with their guns raised, were moving nearer and nearer to her in a slow, rhythmic march.

Raven turned her head to the side, saw them coming. She stood and turned towards them. She raised her gun and pointed it at them and they froze on the spot.

Seconds passed. No one moved.

It lasted for ever.

Everything froze except for the sound of the spilling water and the *chopchopchop* of the rotors.

And then with her other hand, she shoved Duke.

He balanced on the edge for a second, and then she pushed him once more.

He tipped and fell, his body falling end over end into the spillway. Within seconds he was swallowed by the foaming waters below.

Gone.

Destroyed.

At last.

The cops were yelling at her, advancing on her again. And she was yelling back.

The noise was deafening. I wanted to hear what she was saying. I wanted to help.

She staggered forward a few steps.

The helicopter pulled away, like it knew something was going to happen, and the cops took another step forward in unison.

Then she turned to look around, her eyes scanning the bushes, looking in my direction. Maybe she even saw me. I don't really know. But she turned and looked anyway. Only for a few seconds though.

"I'm sorry, Raven," I whispered.

She turned to face the handrail.

The helicopter circled around her. The cops lowered their guns.

Her hair danced, the purple strands vibrant in the sunlight, her blue vest strong and powerful, her smile large and victorious.

She charged to the side of the ledge.

Jumped high.

And as the cops shouted and sprinted towards her, she tumbled through the air, her body falling and twisting

and turning into the churning waters of the spillway below.
   I screamed.
   Fell to my knees.
   Screamed more.
   But no one heard me.

Today.

Fifty-two

And, I guess, there you have my little story. My tale of intrigue.

It ends right here.

These events took place almost six months ago now, but it still feels like it was just yesterday. And now here I sit on Christmas Eve and I've finally finished telling you the whole tale.

It's actually quite a relief to get this off my chest. I feel much better about it, being able to put my version of events across.

Life's certainly a whole lot different now, much different than the life I knew with Raven, that's for sure.

But change is good, they say.

Although things were tough for a while.

Real tough.

But I made it.

The police searched the whole area once Raven had dived off the spillway. But I knew they wouldn't find me. As long as I got through their search lines (which I did) I knew I could trek back to the lagoon and hide in the blowhole.

It was cold and dark and horrible, but I stayed hidden in there, way up the back, in the dark and the slime and the cold for I don't know how long. Probably almost a week, I figure.

It felt like forever.

But the cops did stumble across Mr Sunglasses and Mr Moustache; caught them red-handed as they tried to escape back down Lake Mountain. Seems the police were on the lookout for them as well, as they were mixed up in the drug gang that was trying to hunt down Duke. I think they'll be sent away for a long long time, once they go to trial.

But they never found me.

The cops moved on soon enough. Other crimes to solve. Other people to hunt.

And so, six months on, I'm still living out here, on Lake Mountain.

But, don't worry, I'm not still hiding in the blowhole. You can't live there. No way.

I live in the valve house. Tyler's valve house.

It's small and it's cramped. But no one comes by. No one disturbs me.

Anyway, I've still got his gun for protection, not that I've needed to use it yet. But it keeps me feeling safe, and that's the main thing.

I can forage for food and steal stuff from other campers when I need to. That's how I got this notebook and pen to write my story. It's also how I got a brand new fishing rod to help me catch fish, and the cd player that I can listen to the radio with. Although I don't have any cds to play in it, not yet anyway.

The cops got it wrong, of course. I mean, they didn't have all the details, so they could never know the *true* story.

Unless they get hold of this notebook! But I'll make sure that doesn't happen.

Raven and Tyler were both blamed for the death of the old guy at the gas station, as there were no witnesses to what really happened (except me of course, but they *never* found me!) Her DNA was found on the old guy, and Tyler's fingerprints were all over the phone, so the cops worked out the rest from there.

They thought Tyler was Raven's boyfriend or something, and that he'd helped her kill Duke, or he'd killed Duke as they fought over Duke's stolen drugs, or had killed him in a jealous rage or a lovers' tiff or whatever.

Honestly, the amount of speculation in the media was horrendous. Especially when it was so wrong.

And no one mentioned me.

Like I didn't exist.

Wasn't alive.

And, when I think about it, maybe I wasn't.

Not then anyway.

Not really.

It was only when I was forced to face the world myself, to find some way to survive, maybe only then I came alive.

Really alive.

It didn't take the cops too long to find the trailer and the Suburban. They towed them both away a day or two later, probably for evidence and whatever it is courts need. I never saw them again.

I lost everything when they took them away. My home, my security and the few possessions I called mine.

Including the photo of my mother.

I'm pretty sure the police never checked the valve houses. I mean, I can't *prove* that, because I was hiding in the blowhole at the time all this happened, but when I got up enough courage to come down here and break in, everything seemed to be exactly as Tyler had left it. Nothing was touched. Nothing was missing.

So anyway, this is where I live now.

My valve house.

I'm quite proud of it, actually. I've tidied it up and really made it my home. Too bad I can't have visitors though.

They fished the bodies out of the river a couple of miles further down, probably two days later. Duke was a wreck, in pieces mostly, but Raven wasn't too beaten up. Tyler had died at the scene. Even though they tried to revive him, he never regained consciousness. He died where he fell.

In the end, it's probably good he died that way, because the real story died with him.

In fact, the media even told me where Tyler and Raven were being buried. Two totally different cemeteries, miles apart from each other. I was glad about that.

It took me a while to get up the courage and strength. I mean, I was pretty emotionally fucked after the events at the dam, and it took me a while to pull myself together properly. But I did manage to get down there and see her. To pay my last respects at her gravesite.

It was hard, you know, to visit her like that.

I wanted to tell her how sorry I was.

How very sorry that we hadn't talked, *really* talked, just before Tyler had hammered on the trailer door.

I'd lived with Raven a long time, and I've learned a lot from her. She taught me everything I know and I owe her greatly.

I'll keep her memory alive forever. I'll always be her soul mate, no matter what.

So, "Merry Christmas, everyone!" Remember to take the time to be with the ones you love, and let them know how much you love them, because you never know when they could be taken from you.

It could happen in a matter of seconds... but true love never dies, no matter what.

Me? Well, I'm about to climb into bed and go to sleep.

Curl up next to her soft skin, spoon her and hug her tight all night.

Kiss her cool, gorgeous lips and run my fingers through her shiny, luscious hair.

Tomorrow we'll open our presents. I've got a nice new box of *ACTION Embalming Powder* for her. Eight bottles in all. Should keep her going for quite some time.

It's easy to break into that funeral home when you know how, especially when you've done it before and know exactly what you need. And Tyler said I'd *never* make a burglar. He was wrong about that!

She deserves only the best, does my Raven. And she'll always get exactly that.

Her eyes may be closed now, but mine are forever open.

THE END.

Steve Gerlach is one of Australia's few thriller writers. Born and bred in Australia, Gerlach's fast-paced, cut-to-the-bone style is a refreshing voice in the dry, barren Australian literary scene.

Steve's background includes many varied roles. He has worked as an editor for a book publisher; as the editor-in-chief of an Australian motorcycle magazine; editor and publisher of an international crime magazine, Probable Cause; a researcher and columnist for a major Australian daily newspaper; a Technical Publications Officer in the security industry; marketing executive for an international telecommunications software company; a writer for Australian Defence training and software producers; and currently works as a freelance writer.

He was also the Historical Advisor on the Australian film, Let's Get Skase.

Steve Gerlach lives in Melbourne, where he is currently working on a new novel or two.

The next Steve Gerlach release
by Probable Cause Publishing

THE NOCTURNE

Coming 2017

37.6419° S, 145.5514° E

Printed in the USA
CPSIA information can be obtained
at www.ICGtesting.com
LVHW041459040224
770895LV00033B/316

9 780957 864122